lucky boy

lucky boy

. . . .

SHANTHI SEKARAN

G. P. Putnam's Sons
New York

G. P. PUTNAM'S SONS
Publishers Since 1838
An imprint of Penguin Random House LLC
375 Hudson Street
New York, New York 10014

Library of Congress Cataloging-in-Publication Data
Names: Sekaran, Shanthi.
Title: Lucky boy / Shanthi Sekaran.
Description: New York : G. P. Putnam's Sons, [2016].
Identifiers: LCCN 2016008418 | ISBN 9781101982242 (hardcover) |
ISBN 9781101982259 (ePub)
Subjects: LCSH: Single mothers—Fiction. | Motherhood—Fiction. |
Illegal aliens—Fiction. | Mexicans—United States—Fiction. |
Married women—Fiction. | Domestic fiction. |
BISAC: FICTION / Contemporary Women. | FICTION / Literary. |
FICTION / Family Life. Classification: LCC PS3619.E45 L83 2016 |
DDC 813/.6—dc23
LC record available at http://lccn.loc.gov/2016008418
p.   cm.

First G. P. Putnam's Sons international edition published January 2017
G. P. Putnam's Sons international edition ISBN 9780735212275

Printed in the United States of America
1   3   5   7   9   10   8   6   4   2

Book design by Meighan Cavanaugh

For Avi and Ashwin

But leave me a little love,
A voice to speak to me in the day end,
A hand to touch me in the dark room
Breaking the long loneliness.
In the dusk of day-shapes
Blurring the sunset,
One little wandering, western star
Thrust out from the changing shores of shadow.
Let me go to the window,
Watch there the day-shapes of dusk
And wait and know the coming
Of a little love.

—CARL SANDBURG, "AT A WINDOW"

PART I

soli

prologue

CLARA, PATRON SAINT OF TELEVISION AND EYE DISEASE, stood three feet tall in the church at the end of the road. The road was known generally as la calle, for it was the only one in the village. Scattered along it were one church, one store, and a one-room schoolhouse, recently closed. The road sprouted caminos and footpaths as it went, and ended in a small square, where the town hall stood, and a cantina with the town's only television, which sat atop a folding table. When the men weren't hunched around it watching fútbol, it spun lazy afternoon offerings of love and betrayal, murder and long-lost sons.

Clara, beauty of Assisi, nobleman's daughter, ran away one night to a friar at the roadside, was brought to Saint Francis, and shorn. Her hair fell like corn silk to the ground and she traded her dress for a rough brown habit. She walked barefoot and lived in silence and begged for her daily bread. But she didn't mind. She'd fallen in love with something larger than her world.

Clara was ill one day, Papi said, and couldn't go to Mass. She lay faded in her bed, and what flickered on her wall but a vision of the daily service, from processional to homily to Eucharist? And so they made her the patron of eye disease, because what could have visited her but a dance of glaucomic flashes? And then television came along and needed a patron, and the pope said Clara. And how about the time, Papi once said, when she faced down an invading army, alone at the convent window with nothing but the sacrament in hand? Now Clara spent her days tucked into a dim chapel. Day in, day out, alone in the shadows, and if anyone did visit, it was only because they wanted something.

But that night was La Noche del Maíz. The village priest brought her down from her perch and wiped tenderly her web of whisper-fine cracks. He wrapped her in finery, silk robes and nylon flowers, and loaded her on her platform. Four strong men raised her high and she wobbled down the road but didn't fall—not once had she fallen—and so it began: a line of altar boys, a trumpet's cry, the swing of a cloud-belching censer.

Fine for a saint, thought Solimar, to wait all year for a single tromp through the village. Fine for a saint to spend all of eternity with her mouth shut, her feet still. Solimar Castro Valdez was no saint. She was breaking out. She'd come out that evening to meet a man, not a friar. His name was Manuel. He owned a car and a passport—the right kind—and he'd be taking her away from this place. And he was there. Right there in Santa Clara Popocalco.

For months, the idea of leaving had lain dormant. But it was stirring now, snuffling to life. Every cell in her body strained against its casing. It was time to leave. It was time.

Manuel would meet her at the entrance to the town hall. Slowly, slowly, the procession moved on. She walked hand in hand in hand with her mother and father. She squeezed their papery old fingers and pulled harder with each step. When they turned a corner, she spotted the clock tower by the church. Seven minutes late already. She flung off her parents' hands. "See you there!" she cried, and ran.

At the town hall doors: no Manuel. No one who looked like he owned an American passport. A man like that would have to be handsome—not that handsome mattered, not when all she wanted was the land beyond the border, except that she was eighteen and helpless against the nether-murmur of romance.

At the town hall doors, breathless still, she waited. Papi found her and brought her a plate of tamales, which she was too jumbled inside to eat. Mama would be milling through the village plaza and finding old friends from nearby towns, stretching spools of gossip that had begun a month, a year, a decade before.

As the sky dimmed, drums and horns throbbed through the square. Drink had been drunk and around her the village swarmed with new faces: Where had they come from? A pair of teenagers leaned and kissed against a tree, a flutter of children linked arms in a circle, running themselves off their feet, a perilous carousel of arms and legs and fevered teeth. Still, no Manuel. She felt she should smoke a cigarette, though she'd never tried one before. She believed a cigarette would make her feel like less of a fool.

Never had she seen so many people here in her little village. Most days, it seemed the world had forgotten Santa Clara Popocalco. It was the sort of place that existed only because no larger town had cared to claim it. It lay dry and hollow, anchored to this earth by the Sierra Norte to the east, Oaxaca City to the west. Every morning a cold front rolled in from a distant shore. It collided with the hillside and smothered the valley in fog that smelled faintly, sweetly of corn. Every afternoon, the sun burned through the fog and houses regained their low and addled forms.

Popocalco offered no work, only the growing and eating of a few stalks of corn. When the money left, the people followed, except for the very poor and very old, who still grew crops to feed themselves and sell in local markets, who gurgled through the village square every morning and in the evenings, visiting the church, nodding to the faces, always the same faces, and napping and cooking and eating and washing, sweeping their front steps each day, not exactly waiting to die, Soli believed, but not quite living, either.

For too long, she'd pushed away the thought of leaving. Papi! She was his only one. And Mama. Mama would crawl into bed and never crawl out. But decay had spread like the valley fog, until it found its way to Soli. She'd breathed so much of it in that she couldn't breathe it out again. She was filling up with silence and heavy bones. She was eighteen. And then, the letter from Silvia. Inside, somewhere between her chest and chin, a seed split open to the sun and she began to wonder: Could she? And how? And eventually: When? And why not? And how soon? Her life lay elsewhere. If she stayed in Popocalco, she'd be staying for them, the gentle old souls, her mother and father and the sullen corn, watching all those lives wind down to their modest end.

The fireworks family entered the square, pushing the castillo de luces, a tower of scaffolding rigged with rockets and sparklers.

In the big picture, Popocalco was nowhere. In the big picture, it was a thin and spiny stretch of the past.

She waited for an hour at the church door, until all her readiness had been sighed away. Papi wandered off. She stood deflated and alone, certain she'd missed Manuel by seven minutes. A brass band began to play, the somber nasal tune Soli had heard every year, for as long as she could remember, at La Noche del Maíz. She closed her eyes. Applause. She didn't need to open them to know that a teenage boy was climbing the castillo, lifting a fiery pole to the highest joints of the tower. In a moment, the first sparks would pinwheel through the night. And they would begin, one small explosion followed by the next, a rapturous storm.

Punctuality. Seven minutes. Time was religion in America, Papi had warned. If she'd missed her chance by seven minutes, it was her own wretched fault.

But then, a layer beneath the noise, a rustle. "Solimar." She opened her eyes. At first, all she saw were the bushy jut of his chin and the gleam of hair slicked back. He could have been the Devil in the firelight, for all she could see. He stepped forward. Papi, all at once, beside her. He shook Papi's hand.

Now this, now here, was a man with a passport. Manuel would visit the next day to go over their plan. He'd get Soli to California, he said, no matter what it took. She was leaving! The promise of it stoked a flame that blazed through her. Already, Popocalco, this house of smoke, was shrinking away. Already, this existence was nothing but a distant prick of light. Electrified by the promise of forward motion, Soli stretched up to kiss the sky, growing and growing, until she too was a flaming tower, a castle of light, sparking from the eyes, spitting streaks of joy.

1.

Preeti Patel was getting married. Kavya was wearing black.

The decision wasn't a symbolic one. She'd bought a black Mysore silk sari on University Avenue on a whim one day. Also on a whim, she'd had the sari blouse stitched in the provocative new cut, held together by nothing more than a thin ribbon tied across her back. She wanted to surprise her husband, so she tied the blouse herself, guided by the bony hills of her scapulae. Eight yards of silk, woven with silver thread. At the end hung a swathe embroidered with banyan trees and antlered deer. She straightened the pleats that cascaded from her hips to her ankles, climbed tidily over her chest and down her back. She clipped on a pair of heavy silver earrings that spilled down to her shoulders and matched her silver choker. Her feet she slipped into silver stiletto heels.

Rishi looked up when she emerged from the bedroom. He was striking in a blue silk kurta. "You're wearing black," he said.

"It's classy," she answered.

He crossed his arms, then walked over and kissed the junction of her neck and shoulder.

The sun beat down as they drove. Coastal waters gave way to outlet malls and farmland. It was warm, even for July. Kavya was getting over-warm, but when she turned the AC dial, nothing happened. "What's going on?"

"Push it in."

"I did."

Rishi shrugged. "Open a window, then. It's better for you." It's what they did in Berkeley, where the air was crisp enough most days. But Kavya knew well this strain of windshield glare. An open window would bring nothing more than a blast of sick heat. She spun the knob, jiggled it, pounded at it. She was sweating now, itching, moisture beading above her lip. She grunted at Rishi, who seemed to have no intention of helping.

"Sorry?" He sent her a sidelong glance, a wan smile. He glowed in the heat, the way a woman should, his face a collection of plains and fine ridges. He placed a hand on her knee as he drove, which he seemed to think would disarm her. In the old days, Rishi would have pulled over and inspected the air-conditioning himself. He would have pulled out the manufacturer's manual or even reset their route to take them through more temperate territory. Those were the days when they'd first met, undergrads at UC Berkeley, when Rishi would make his daily appearance in the student café where Kavya was a barista. He'd spend too long at the counter, ignoring the line behind him, asking her about the coffee beans (about which she knew nothing) or the pastries (delivered weekly by a supplier). He'd do anything, those days, to get their brief transactions to last longer than they should have; he'd show up on campus where he knew she'd be, find reasons to bump into her, leave behind his desi posse to linger on Sproul Plaza, where she recruited for activist groups and ran teach-ins and sit-ins. She was his object of fascination, though she'd been plain without makeup, and he a sculpted ideal. Back then, she wondered why he would be interested in her, aside from the fact that she was tall and reasonably fit. She concluded that a person as immaculately beautiful as Rishi might stop looking for beauty in others. He'd search instead for the non-physical: intelligence, humor, all-around chutzpah. Kavya reasoned that she must have possessed some combination of these—or was it simply the fact that she seemed, for a while, to want nothing to do with him? In a world that admired handsome men, obeyed them, promoted them, Kavya became the unattainable, the object of Rishi's devotion.

But this: This wasn't devotion. The hand on her knee was a gentle plea to please be quiet, to let him drive and think in peace of whatever it was he was thinking. She jerked her knee, and the hand slid off.

What Rishi was thinking about was the wedding; specifically, the wedding invitation, and more specifically, the groom's name, Vikram Sen, etched in crimson. Vikram Sen was CFO of Weebies, the Silicon Valley megapolis where Rishi worked. The Internet supersite had cornered the market on baby and children's gear, social networking for parents, and a steady feed of articles designed to affirm a reader's existing parenting style while simultaneously triggering worries—the smallest and most niggling—that trying one notch harder might make the difference between decency and brilliance for their wee ones.

Sen was rumored to have a stuffed Bengal tiger in his office and a liquor cabinet that took up an entire wall. At Weebies, they called him the Don. Rishi read in a *Forbes* profile that he'd graduated from Harvard Business School, moved into a two-bedroom apartment in San Francisco with five other software engineers, and helped build the walls of the empire over which he now presided. Yes, there had to have been closed doors and failures along the way, but no one spoke of those now. All anyone talked about now were share prices and visits from Brangelina and the boom-boom-boom of unmitigated industry success. Vikram Sen was indisputably an Internet wonder boy, a divinity of the Silicon Valley pantheon, walking proof of the pulsing, breathing

American dream. And Rishi was going to his wedding. His gut twisted at the thought of possibly, very probably, meeting Vikram Sen, face-to-face, palm to palm.

Rishi himself worked in a remote corner of the Weebies campus. He had a desk in the PR office, where he managed ventilation, an engineering oddity in a building full of well-groomed image slingers. Only once had he stood outside Vikram Sen's office, sent to test-run an air-quality monitor. He'd lingered, hoping to meet the man himself, but the Don hadn't emerged.

Kavya let out the sort of deep, tremulous sigh that begged for commentary. "Hey," Rishi said. "You'll be fine. We'll have fun. I promise." Though he knew where the sigh came from, he knew asking about it would invite an outpouring that would throw the afternoon so far off course that they'd end up ditching the wedding and turning the car back to Berkeley. If Kavya wasn't going to start, he most definitely wouldn't.

When they arrived, he waved his way past the valets and parked more than a block away, along the neighborhood sidewalk. He turned to Kavya. "Ready?" She frowned and touched her hair. The wind from the open windows had plucked ringlets from her updo, and they sprang off her head like confetti. He opened his door and paused. "Hey, beautiful." He tucked a ringlet behind her ear. "We'll have fun. I promise." He kissed her cheek, then her hand.

"Okay." She took a deep breath and opened the door with a thrust of her toe.

A mandap was set up at the far end of the Patels' backyard, three acres on the outskirts of Sacramento, land that used to be gold territory but now lay fallow. It belonged to Hitesh and Suma Patel, her parents' oldest friends. Hitesh Patel moved among his guests, his belly shaking with every back he slapped. Above the land floated gold, pounds and pounds of it, on earlobes and chests and wrists of ladies wrapped in silk, their brows arched and perfectly threaded, scanning the land like aging lionesses.

In the beginning, Kavya's parents had befriended the Patels because they had little choice. The scarcity of Indians in the 1970s had propelled this North-South friendship. Preeti grew up three blocks from Kavya in a modest, tree-lined neighborhood. Three blocks in India might have kept them from ever meeting, but among the Caucasian tundra of sub-urban Sacramento, it had felt essential that the girls be friends. Soon enough, their parents realized that they got along, as well, that they shared more than nationality, and that the neutralizing effects of American soil would allow their friendship to flourish.

Kavya hitched up the folds of her sari to walk over the wet grass. After the girls grew up and left home, the Patels moved here, to a gated community on the outskirts of town, at the foot of the Sierra Nevadas. Houses here had bathrooms the size of Berkeley bungalows and lawns that stretched without purpose, unfettered by other plant life, disrupted only by swimming pools and the occasional gazebo. Calling it a com-munity was a stretch. Houses—mansions, really—were spread so thinly across the grassy hills that neighbors went mostly undetected.

She wouldn't have gone, except that not to go would have made a stronger statement than she was willing to make. Preeti Patel was get-ting married and sealing forever her victory over Kavya. Over the years, the girls had grown from playmates to rivals and begrudging friends. To be fair, it was Kavya who begrudged; Preeti was endlessly gracious, completely unimpeachable in her maintenance of friendship. Preeti was infallibly interested and interesting, and if she felt superior to Kavya, she never spoke of it, never mentioned her own achievements. That was left to the mothers.

And also to be fair, there wasn't much rivalry to speak of. Rivalry suggested equality, and Preeti beat Kavya at every step, in a flurry of accomplishment, beautifully and without comment: The day Kavya smoked her first spliff, Preeti won the state spelling bee. The night Kavya first let a boy's hand crawl up her blouse, Preeti won the national spelling bee. The day Kavya gave away the drum set she had failed to master, Preeti became first-chair violinist of the Central Valley Youth Symphony. The week Kavya got into Berkeley, Preeti got into Berkeley. A week later, Preeti received fat envelopes from Stanford, Brown, Yale, UPenn, and Princeton. Harvard had said no, most likely a typographical error that the Patels didn't bother to pursue. When Kavya spent her weekday afternoons trying to free Tibet and bring back affirmative action, Preeti ensconced herself in the Stanford library, resting only to call her mother. When Kavya spent her weekends cocooned in Rishi's unwashed sheets, Preeti returned home to eat her mother's food. When Kavya graduated from Berkeley and became a barista, Preeti won a Fulbright and spent a year studying diabetic blindness in rural Gujarat. The year Kavya started culinary school, Preeti moved back to California with a degree in epidemiology from Johns Hopkins. The week Kavya got audited for misfiling her taxes, Preeti bought her first house, a three-story Victorian in San Francisco's Noe Valley. They were the Goofus and Gallant of the Central Valley Indians, and most people knew it.

For seven years, as the girls slipped from their twenties to their thirties, Kavya had this over Preeti: She was married. Matrimonial completion had always been her trump card. Today, it would be swept from her grasp.

If there had been a belly to stroke, a smooth hill of skin rising bare and brown from the front folds of her sari, she would have had something that Preeti didn't have, and even when Preeti did have sweet-faced and well-behaved children, it wouldn't have mattered, because Kavya would have had her own. Even if she'd been mid-cycle, still trying that month, she might at least have declined to drink and felt the murmur of a harbored secret when asked, one hundred times or more, when she and Rishi were having children. But she'd lost again that month. She had tried and failed. She would try and fail and try again.

Kavya's mother was the first to see them. She broke from a group of ladies to stalk across the lawn. Still yards away, she cried out, "Where is your mangala sutra?" Kavya only wore her wedding necklace, a thick gold rope with a cluster of pendants, when she knew her mother would be checking. She'd forgotten.

"Why you're wearing black?" her mother asked.

"Hi, Amma."

("Hi, Mom," Rishi eeked from behind.)

"Why you didn't wear the green sari?"

"I like this one."

"Come, maybe Suma Aunty has something you can change. I'll ask."

"No, thank you. I'm wearing this." Kavya kissed her mother's cold cheek and caught there the scent of white wine.

"Are you drinking? Is that alcoholic punch?"

"Why you couldn't dress like Preeti? See how lovely she looks!"

"She's the bride."

Preeti Patel stood at the head of a receiving line, revealing herself, unconventionally, before the ceremony began. She wore a red sari, her hands laced with henna, her neck, face, and hair meshed in gold.

"Preeti has her head on the right way," Uma said, her gaze flickering like a moth wing over her own daughter. "Did you eat? Go eat. They have pakoras and some samosas. The samosas are too oily. All this fried food. And go get something to drink." In the distance was what looked like a fully stocked bar. Rishi spotted an appetizer table and was gone.

Uma Mahendra clicked her tongue. "See who all is wearing black?" She swung her nose to the group at the far corner of the lawn: Maya Gulati, divorced. Sapna Kumari, lesbian. Aparna Dutta, some sort of filmmaker. Neha Murthy, single. Rakhi Viswant, single. Geetha Nalla-sivan, Sheela Chatterjee, Veena Jain, all belligerently single. They glided to the bar in black saris and stilettos, a coven of the shameless. They seemed to be having an excellent time. Kavya patted her mother's shoulder, stuck her purse under her arm, and stalked off to join them.

"Drink juice," her mother called. "No boozing!"

Kavya hadn't done any boozing for approximately nine months, the length of a pregnancy, but in her case, a steady parade of losses. That evening, her ovulation yet to start, faced with hours of this place, these people, boozing was precisely what Kavya planned to do. A great deal of booze would be required to outlast the mingling, the questions, the ceremony, the post-ceremony mingling, the reception, the speeches, the tearful send-off of bride and groom. Her mission was to reach the bar without interruption, but the odds of making it across the grass without being grabbed for embraces and interrogations were slim. The grass sucked at her heels and halted her step. She was a slow-moving target, easily detected.

"Kav-YAH!"

A fierce clamp on her forearm spun her around to face a woman with buttery arms and an enormous and complex, somewhat frightening, bindi. "Hi, Aunty," Kavya said and fell into the warm cushion of an embrace. The woman pulled Kavya into the waiting gully of aunties, where arms circled her waist, fingered her hair, pinched the skin of her abdomen.

"Is this Kavya?" came the cry. "Looking just the same, darling! Still working at the pizza parlor, Kavya? Hello, beta, looking sooo lovely, why so skinny, Kavya, where is the belly fat, hah?"

Like gulls thrown a crust of bread, they frenzied around her, their voices rising to shrieks.

"Remember, ladies, we got married and fat and that was the way it was, isn't it, and now these girls are staying so slim, it is good, it is good I think, no, to stay healthy, my knees! My knees are paining me day and night and I think if only I had stayed slim like this, it is good, Kavya, good to stay healthy, but what is this flat belly, hah, when will we see some you-know-what in there Kavya, if no fat then how about a baby, no? How handsome that Rishi is, nothing stopping you, isn't it? Your poor mother is probably wanting a little one, isn't it, something to keep her young, nobody's getting younger, Kavya, we need some grand-children, isn't it, that's what I told my Raju, Raju, go do hanky-panky and bring me the baby, Raju! Go eat, Kavya, you're looking so tired, these girls work too hard now, isn't it, remember, ladies, we got married and sat down and that was it, we had to watch the servants, to make sure they didn't steal, isn't it, but then we could relax, these young girls stress themselves too much, and then they cannot conceive, isn't it, no, no, Kavya beta, not saying anything, you will have no trouble noooo trouble having a baby, you will have a hundred babies!"

Kavya broke from the group and ran, her heels sinking into the lawn, threatening to topple her. As she neared the group in black, they turned to receive her. Maya Gulati plucked a fresh glass of prosecco from the bar. Turning back to Kavya, she lobbed her a small smile, nodded, and raised her glass.

2.

ARNO, THE BOY NEXT DOOR, WAS THE FIRST SOLI HAD EVER kissed. She was fourteen at the time, and he was an altar boy, noble and broad-shouldered in his white robes. They would meet in the dark and humid side chapel, beneath the saint's gaze. Soli had thought for twenty-six days that she loved Arno, that they would marry and live together in the village, but then Arno left. Set your heart free, Solimar, Doña Alberta would say. My boy's doing so well up there, he's never coming back. Never! Arno went North to work, and Soli, heart-weary, had moved on to the altar boy who replaced him, falling again with gusto, only to lose this second love to the temptations of the North. She wound her heart around the next altar boy, and the two, three, four that followed, resigning herself to the knowledge that she would have to unwind it again, lest it break. When Arno did return, no longer a boy, married now to a woman from Veracruz, he came back with creases around his eyes and dollars tumbling from his pockets and built his mother a home. Soli didn't want Arno anymore. She wanted a life that moved.

"She's the proudest woman in town, that Alberta," Mama said. "She's friendly enough, yes, to your face. But I can tell there's something devil-ish in there, some devilish kind of pride." Arno was building a solid

American brick house, a dollar house, and from her crumbling adobe cube, Soli watched it every day, rising from the ground, one proud wall and then another. Four brick walls and a tidy flat roof, and then, when they thought it was finished, metal spindles sprang from the roof, the anchors of a second floor. Arno's mother would have the tallest house in the village. Arno, who had left school at fifteen, who worked like a donkey up North, who had borne humiliation and solitude, had made it all worthwhile.

"It's time for me to leave," Soli had said that spring, for maybe the hundredth time. It had been weeks since Silvia's letter. This time, her mother turned to her. Her father put down his mug.

"And what would you do?"

The conversation, at last, had begun. Soli felt her future, like a winter-shriveled bloom, begin to soften to the sun.

She watched the dollar house grow, and so did Mama and Papi. They didn't gawk like Soli did—Mama couldn't look at it when they walked by. She would lift her eyes to the sky. Soli knew her mother wanted a dollar house. She knew she needed to give her one. She wanted to buy her parents a new roof, so they wouldn't have to patch the tin that warped and leaked every spring. She wanted to buy them their own telephone line, so they could call her and she them, like the laughing families in the commercials. Papi had raised her to be as focused as a man; Mama had raised her not to depend on one. If she was as independent as they'd raised her to be, then she had no choice but to leave. She could have gone to the city, but who knew what waited there? If she was going to leave, she would leave like a man.

There were certain risks, of course, to leaving as a woman.

"*¡Violación!*" Mama hissed the word, a spark of spittle flying from her lips. It was a word never to be said aloud, lest it caught and flared. "If they rape the ugly ones, think what they'll do to you."

Soli hadn't known what to say to this. She didn't know where to begin.

"Manuel seems to be a good man," Mama comforted herself.

"How do you know?" Soli asked, and regretted it immediately.

"Señora Ruiz. Juanita's mother? You know the old one with the mole? You know she was born with that thing? The doctors said it would grow into her eye socket and blind her, but her parents said no, no—"

"Mama."

"Okay, so. Señora Ruiz has another daughter. This is her daughter's nephew, this Manuel."

"And?"

"And so we know him, don't we?"

Soli knew there was only one answer.

"I will be fine."

"Yes. You will."

No one's nephew, she wanted to say, could be anything but a saint. Surely the mere fact of having an aunt would fill a man with virtue. But she kept her mouth shut. It seemed like a good time to start.

MANUEL CAME TO THE HOUSE the day after the festival. When he pulled up in front of their home, the neighbors seeped out of their doorways and gathered on the drive. They stood with their arms crossed, examining the man—still handsome in the daylight—who'd come for their Soli. A few gazed solemnly at the Cadillac.

He wore a tie and shiny black shoes. He had a neat black mustache and a small patch of hair on his chin. He spoke respectfully to her parents and showed them what he'd be driving. It was a lion of a car, long and black, with a red-and-gold crest on its hood. Papi ran his hand over its roof and nodded. Manuel's eyes rested on the fingerprints left behind.

She remembers this: The prospect of riding in such a car with such a man made her feel like she could lift off the ground, soaring.

"Look here," Manuel said. He had a radio in there and a cell phone. He had cases of bottled water in the trunk. And he whipped from his pocket a navy blue passport with a crisp picture of him on one page, stamped with symbols that winked in the light. Soli would ride with him to the border, and then she would hide. Manuel, with his blue-and-gold passport, would be welcomed home to America. He showed them how the backseat lifted up to reveal a small compartment, big enough for a girl like Soli to fold herself into. She'd stay hidden until they crossed safely, cleared the guards and vigilantes, and then she'd emerge, an American butterfly.

The compartment looked as small as Popocalco felt.

Papi took one look at it and shook his head. "No," he said. "No, no, no. Thank you, señor, for your time, but no way will my daughter be climbing into a trap like that."

"Papi! I can do it. I'll be okay." And with Papi, Manuel, and all of Popocalco watching, Soli climbed in to prove it. "See," she called, her lips smashed against her knees. "No problem!"

Manuel said, "Señor, you have my word. She will be safe in there. She will spend thirty minutes. Forty. And see? Breathing vents. Cut into the fabric." He grinned at Papi. "Pretty smart, right?"

Soli climbed out. "Please, Papi."

"She's lucky she's small, señor. A man could never do this." Papi walked away. He would help her go, she knew, but he would never say yes.

PAPI WAS A CORN FARMER. His father and his grandfather were corn farmers. It was what the family did, until the corn became too expensive to farm, and then impossible to sell. The strain of corn from Soli's valley was eleven thousand years old, an age beyond her understanding.

But now the stalks bent to the ground, or lay heaped like dead grass-hoppers.

The day before Soli left Popocalco, her father took her on a walk through town. They walked to the church and lit a candle at Clara's altar. The saint gazed down. She knew things of Soli that no one else did. Soli believed in saints, mostly because she'd been told to, but as she grew from a child to a woman, she'd started to question the parameters of the arrangement. Could this supposed patron be two places at once? Was she confined to the village? Would she follow Soli down the highway and across the border, or hang hovering above the cantina television, keeping the picture from fizzling to static in the crucial seconds before Granados broke from the defensive line to strike?

They walked past the cantina and ignored the buzzing television and the voices that called out to them. They walked past the village's only billboard, hand-painted: *Señora Garza makes the freshest tortillas! 57 La Calle! Señora Garza's for the best and the freshest!* Her father held her hand. "Listen, m'ija," he said. "The place you're going? Not everyone makes it there. It isn't easy. People die from the heat, they die from hunger. They get shot. You take care of yourself. Make sure you get fed. Call the cantina from every phone you can find or borrow. They'll come get me. Stick with Manuel. He is a good man, a trustworthy man, and we're giving him all the money we could find. You hear that? We're paying him. You don't need to pay him. You don't pay him in any way."

MANUEL CAME FOR HER on a Wednesday morning before dawn. It was strange, thinking back, that the day was nothing but a Wednesday, that it had no more momentous name than that. There were people who woke that day and did nothing to change their lives. And then there was Soli. Manuel waited with the engine running. She had a coat and one rucksack. Inside the house, Papi said goodbye. He pressed a folded

American bill—five dollars—into his daughter's palm. Then he hugged her. Papi held her for a very long time, until her ear ached from the press of his sternum. Instead of wrapping her arms around him, Soli lifted the bill and studied it. She'd never held American money before and couldn't pull her gaze from the ashen green.

Mama wouldn't say goodbye. She locked herself in the bedroom. "Mama," Soli called. She banged on the door. "Mama, come and say goodbye to me. Mama?" She said it twice, and then she shouted it. She commanded that her mother come out. She scraped at the door, as she used to when she was small and her parents would shut themselves in there some afternoons.

"Mama," she said. "Don't be angry."

From inside, she heard her mother sob. "M'ija, get out of here."

"Mama! This is your last chance."

But she didn't come out. Later, Soli would realize that if her mother had come out, if she had wrapped herself around her girl the way Papi had, she would never have let her go.

SOLI SPENT TWO DAYS in a car with Manuel, and the one good thing she could say about him was that he didn't lay a finger on her. He didn't talk much, either. When she asked him questions, he answered them and fell silent again. Mostly he hummed to the radio, American music she recognized from youth nights at the church, which she'd stopped going to because eventually she and not-all-there Torta were the only youths left. They drove first from Popocalco to a place near Oaxaca City. Soli had been to the city before, but never beyond it. After a night in Morelia with her mother's aunt, they were meant to head up through Mazatlán, then Obregón, as Manuel had shown Papi, tracing his map with his highlighter pen. Soli was no genius, but she could read a map. And so, when Manuel veered right and sped off on a junction marked for Monterrey, she sat up fast. All this time, they'd been heading west. Without warning, Manuel had turned east.

"What do you think you're doing?" she asked.

"What do you mean?"

"You're going the wrong way. You're going east."

"You mind your business."

"This is my business. Where are we going?"

"I've got business to take care of this way, okay?"

"With who?"

He waited before answering. "With a contact." His eyes slid from Soli to the road.

"That's not what you told my family," she said. "You need to get me to California. You gave your word!"

He said nothing.

"Get me out of here! Let me out!" She pulled at the door handle. She beat on the window.

"Who's the driver?" His roar filled the car. *"Who is the driver?"*

Soli cowered in her seat, certain he would strike her. The doors were the high-tech kind that locked while the car was moving. A good thing, too, because if she'd opened the door and jumped from that car, her story would have ended there.

Later, it would make sense that this handsome man who was supposed to be her companion, her easy ticket in, had veered east when Papi had given everything for a promised west. She'd had a lot of time in the car to think—sixteen hours, precisely—enough time to come to a few conclusions.

First. A man like Manuel doesn't do things to be kind. Soli had heard how other people crossed, in the backs of trucks, stacked like tortillas, one atop the other. Sitting in the cool cushion of that car, she realized that her parents could not have begged, borrowed, or stolen enough money to pay for a chauffeured, air-conditioned ride through the border. It was a conclusion that could come to light only when she'd broken from her parents, when the speed and sky and solitude of her journey opened new vistas of logical thought. When they took the eastern route to Monterrey, she knew for sure that polite Manuel, handsome Manuel, Manuel with the gleaming, purring lion of a car, had told her father a big sweaty lie.

Second. Never trust a man who plucks his chin. Manuel plucked his chin every time he thought she was asleep. Sometimes he'd do it at high speeds, one hand on the steering wheel, the other plying his devil-beard with a pair of gold tweezers.

Third. With the ship sinking, she'd have to rescue what she could. When Manuel walked off for a piss in the bushes that day, she opened the trunk and crammed as many bottles as she could into her backpack. Later that afternoon, he stopped the car and said he had to make a call. When he was out of sight, she opened his glove compartment and found three things: a tape cassette from someone named Prince, a tube of hand cream, and a blade, nine inches long and sharp enough to make her fingers tingle through its sheath. She took all three.

Soon they came to an encampment with red trucks and large tents, dusty men and a few women sitting in groups, waiting in lines. Like her, they were heading for the border, and the camp was a place to stop, sleep, and, if they were lucky, eat.

"This is where you stay tonight," Manuel said.

"And then what?"

Manuel sighed through his nose, turned to Soli, and said, "Okay. I'll show you." He pulled over at the outer edge of the camp, hopped from the driver's seat to the back.

"The compartment?" he asked. "Remember that?"

He yanked at the backseat and the cushion lifted. The compartment into which Soli had folded herself, all those days ago, was packed now with cloudy green plastic, wrapped around blocks of white. Even through the green, she could see how pure the white was.

"You want me to do something with that?"

"Good girl. Fast learner." Soli listened with equal parts denial and fascination as Manuel explained his plans for her, speaking with a buoyancy she'd never seen in him. In Manuel's mind, Soli would get to the United States, all right, but she wouldn't be going through the border, not in his Cadillac, and certainly not in the secret compartment. He held his sides, laughing high and wheezy, when she reminded him that she'd planned to hide in there. "I can't believe you fit in that thing," he said, and giggled. "I couldn't believe it when you got in! I was like, *Oh, shit, she's getting in!*" He broke into full-gale laughter, and then paused. "Soli." He took her hand in his. "We've spent many days together, and I feel like maybe we're friends." He searched for her gaze. "Are we friends? Yes?"

She nodded slowly.

"Then I feel like I can trust you. I feel like you can do this, like you're smart enough. Take a walk with me." As they walked toward the camp, Manuel explained to Soli that he would drive her to Piedras Negras, on the Texas border.

"Texas? You said California. Is California close to Texas?"

He looked into her eyes then, and she caught a shimmer of irritation. "Yes, Soli, Texas is very close to California."

She waited for more.

"I'll take you to a market run by my friends, very nice people. Good people, Soli. And from there, you'll pass into America. With a few small packages."

"The ones from the car?"

He closed his eyes, smiled, and nodded. "That's it! Easy, don't you think?"

"But what about the border? And what about the car? Can't I just come with you?"

"The border, Soli, is up here." With his foot he drew a line in the dirt. "And the passage you'll be taking?" He pointed at the ground. "The passage you'll be taking is way down there. Under the ground." He took a step closer to her, his lips at her ear. The base of her spine caught a warm shiver. He murmured low. He murmured like a lover. "You'll be crawling under the feet of the pinche idiota border guards, Soli, and they won't have a clue. I urge you to give them the finger as you pass. They'll never know. From Mexico to the States, just like that." He began to laugh, quietly, through his teeth. "Good, right? Right, Soli?"

"I'll be crawling? Through a tunnel?"

"You're small. You fit in that compartment? You'll have no problem with a tunnel." He gripped her elbow, leaned in until she hardly had space to breathe. "It's *good*, right, Soli?"

Soli searched for words, for her voice, for a gust of air. "Yes," she whispered. "It's good."

"Good! Now go get yourself some food, chula. Beans are hot!" He gave a small hop and spun around. "The beans are hot and good, Soli," he called, as she walked away. She turned to watch him lean back, open his arms, and roar to the sky: "THE BEANS ARE HOT AND GOOD!"

3.

THE WEDDING CEREMONY BEGAN. IT HAD BEEN NINE MONTHS since Kavya had stopped drinking. Two glasses of prosecco, and she began to rock and keel like a storm-weary ship.

"You're leaning on me," Rishi muttered.

"You're comfortable."

He sighed and put his arm around her. Kavya closed her eyes. She could feel the light wind in her nostrils, the fading sun on her eyelids. Soon she felt nothing. She was asleep.

Rishi squeezed her arm. "Wake up."

The ceremony had begun. The guests around her had been watching her and smiling, but turned back to the mandap when she woke.

"Jesus."

"Sorry," she whispered.

Uma sat several rows away, and hadn't noticed. She'd grown used to the small embarrassments her daughter chose to inflict—her undesirable hairstyles, the torn jeans she'd worn for the duration of the nineties, the time she was interviewed on camera at some sort of protest, surrounded by a gang—and what if they really were a gang!—of young men, their angry mouths, their arms around her shoulders. Later, she bore with dignity Kavya's failure to dive straight from college into a professional degree, the jobs she took making coffee and pizzas. Her own husband rarely emerged from his study, and she was forced to save face alone. She brought her woes to her lady friends, in a Munchausen by proxy of maternal strife. Her friends played their roles. No need to worry, Uma. The world is getting smaller. If this Rishi doesn't marry her, somebody else will. She is a good girl, she will know what to do. She is a smart girl, no?

This was little comfort to Uma, who had watched the smartest girls, the goodest girls, fall victim to caprice, some marrying Europeans and running off across the world, others marrying Americans and quickly divorcing, one caught cheating on her husband. Another—and this bored into Uma's deepest fears—married an African. And moved to Kenya. Or maybe it was Uganda. I think of it and want to faint, Uma told Kavya. Even the arranged marriages seemed to falter—one girl marrying a caste-compliant engineer who turned out to be a homosexual. Uma had assumed her own daughter was more vulnerable than these other good-smart girls, and that she too would end badly. The world was getting smaller, and the smaller it got, the more intensely Uma sensed its darkest corners.

KAVYA AMBLED THROUGH THE REST of the evening without overtly embarrassing her family. After the ceremony, a summary of Hindu ritual during which the priest translated his Sanskrit prayers to English and the guests actually listened, Rishi took Kavya by the arm. "Let's go say hi," he said. "Come on."

As they approached the head table, Preeti stood and took off her marigold garland. She reached out and clasped both of Kavya's hands in her own. "Kavya! You always look so elegant." She turned then to Rishi. "Rishi, you must know Vikram already."

Kavya was still digesting the fact that Preeti remembered Rishi's name. That their husbands would know each other hadn't occurred to her. Vikram spoke first. "I hear you're at Weebies, Rishi-bhai." His accent was thick with education, and like some Indian-Indians, his English was so fluent it was nearly incomprehensible.

"It's a big place," Rishi said to Preeti. "Huge." Kavya searched for some flaw in Vikram Sen, but could find none. His jaw was strong, his teeth perfect, but not disturbingly so. His eyes were piercing and black, and his hair was cropped close to the scalp, salt-and-pepper, perfectly suited to the angles of his face. He was neither haughty nor sniveling. He held Kavya's hand after shaking it and spoke to her with gravity that conveyed respect, grace, class. He patted Rishi on the back and called him "brother," as if they'd one day be old friends.

Rishi cleared his throat and leaned in toward Vikram. "If I can do anything for you at Weebies," he offered, "don't hesitate to call."

"Thank you for coming," Preeti said. Then she leaned farther over the table and hugged her friend around the neck, for longer than Kavya expected, the scent of marigolds hypnotic and deep.

"Stupid," Rishi muttered, as they walked away.

"What's stupid?"

"If I can do anything for you," his voice a hokey mockery. "Like he'd need anything from me."

"What does he do there?"

"He runs it. More or less."

She halted. "He *runs* Weebies?"

Rishi nodded. Kavya fell silent.

THERE WERE RULES around portion sizes at these things: Just enough was not enough. Excess was adequate. Inadequacy unthinkable. Kavya ate until the drawstring of her underskirt cut into her belly. She let the others leave the table to dance, ignored the calls to the dance floor. The DJ played nothing but bhangra, and there was a limit to how long she was willing to shrug and hop on one foot. So she sat by herself and went on eating, because when she ate with a particular brand of intense focus, most people left her alone. That was when Anuja Jain pulled up a chair and fell into it, her knees ramming into Kavya's. Kavya barely recognized her. As girls they had gone to school together, and to each other's birthday parties. Anuja Jain didn't seem to notice she was eating. She leaned in.

"I hear you're trying to have a kid."

The food in Kavya's mouth went dry.

"Listen. I'm giving you fair warning. I love my kids, okay?"

Kavya sighed.

"And you'll love your kids, too, but they will suck you dry, Kavya. They will suck away your time, your body, your mind, your sleep, your plans—everything you wanted to do. Gone. You will be a dry husk of your former self. You will be an angry drone. You, as you know it? Over."

Anuja Jain sat back and waited for her words to take effect. Kavya shoved another wedge of naan into her mouth.

"You won't recognize yourself in ten years, my friend. You will be a tumbleweed. And you'll never have sex again. With Rishi or anyone else."

"Okay."

"It's over. It's over for all of us, but no one tells us, do they? I'm telling you, though. This is your warning."

Kavya said nothing. A long silence followed.

"I mean, I love my kids. I do. I love being a mom. You'll see what I mean when it happens."

Kavya swallowed her food. "Fair warning," she said.

The childhood friends, women now, looked each other over. "Let me ask you something," Kavya said. "Did my mom tell you I wanted to get pregnant?"

"Oh. You know." Anuja gazed across the yard. "These things, weddings. It's all talk talk talk."

Kavya rose and stepped away from the table. She abandoned her plate and Anuja Jain, the dried and angry husk of Anuja Jain, and went off to find a dark and quiet corner.

Tucked into a distant nook of the yard, she found what seemed to be a surplus gazebo. But because there were no dark or quiet corners when her mother was around, it wasn't long before she heard a familiar shuffle and the high tinkle of Uma's bangles. The prosecco had made Kavya happy first, then sleepy. Now she sat in its depressive exhaust. A moment later, Uma stood before her, her bun of hair haloed by a nearby floodlight.

"Kavya?" Uma sounded angry. "Kavya? Why you're sitting here?"

Kavya didn't answer. When she was a child, she'd pretend to have stomachaches when her mother was angry, and Uma would melt with guilt and worry.

She waited for her mother to sit. "Why did you tell people?"

Uma crossed her arms.

"Why did you tell people I couldn't get pregnant?"

"Pah! I didn't say anything."

"Then how do people know? Why did Anuja Jain come over and warn me not to have kids?"

"She's a bad mother. She has no patience."

"That's not what I mean."

"Chih! Don't insult me."

"Who did you tell?"

"Kavya, kanna, listen to me." She tilted her head, honey-voiced, conciliatory. "I only said you are wanting to have a child. Nothing more. Why so much fuss?"

"But you told people. I told you not to tell."

"And so? When they ask me about you, they say why this Kavya isn't having any babies, and what do I say then? Of course you want a baby, isn't it? You are trying. This is what I tell them."

"And then they spin it into this huge thing, Mom!"

"Don't call me that."

The floodlight timed out, and they sat in the fresh black of the garden. In the distance, she could hear the galloping beat of bhangra, the shouts of people who could let go and enjoy themselves. She wondered where Rishi was.

"So?" Uma asked quietly. "What now? What's the plan?"

Kavya sat back and crossed her arms. "I'd rather not say."

Uma blinked. "And if no baby comes? What then?"

"I guess we'll adopt."

Uma threw her head back and laughed. It was not an amused laugh. It was more a shout to the heavens, a final renunciation. And with that she stood, sighed, and exited the gazebo. In the moist grass, her footsteps faded to silence.

Kavya let her mother go. From beyond the foothills, a breeze blew across the property, heavy with magnolia, sweet with camphor. It was time to go home.

4.

IF SOLI FOUND A PHONE AND CALLED THE CANTINA, PAPI would find her here and take her home, away from Manuel and his tunnel. They would ride a dusty bus, side by side, for hours.

But she did not want to go home. She did not want to go back to that life. She wanted California, and she wanted it badly enough that anyone who threatened to take it away, even someone she loved very much, would have to be ignored.

She spent that night lying on a plastic mat, courtesy of Grupo Beta. She didn't sleep, of course. Her backpack, bulky with bottles that she'd stolen from Manuel, lay next to her. She cradled it like a boyfriend. Exhaustion was everywhere. The others were too tired to care about the hard ground or the heat. She watched the stars and thought about Popocalco. When summer days baked their house and made sleep impossible, they'd lie outside and let the mountain breezes cool them to a stupor. There, like here, she could see the languid moon. But here, she couldn't hear the whisper of the valley or the shlack-shlack of corn stalks in the wind. Here, the air was dense. Into its silence seeped the whine of power lines above, the snores of coyotes, the anonymous trumpets of gas and passing motorcars. An airplane droned overhead. She heard an animal howl, loud and close. She sat up. What a feast they would make for a hungry beast, she and these weary pilgrims.

And then she saw someone else sit up but couldn't see his face, just the lean arch of his torso. He had hair that rose in a mad crown around his head, and across that rustling meadow of bodies, they watched each other.

He lay down again, and so did she.

WITH THE MORNING, the sun sliced through her, blinding at first. She had to squint until the glare softened. It was this light that brought her Checo, wild-haired and warm, as certain as a ray of sun.

An orange truck pulled into the camp. Already a line of people waited for the men to set up tables. At a separate table, they had set up a medical station, bandaging feet and checking for head lice. Why Grupo Beta bothered helping them, a bunch of hopefuls heading for the exits, she could only imagine.

She spotted Manuel in the distance, leaning on his car and talking on his phone. He plucked at his chin with his fingernails.

When she reached the front of the food line, the Beta man dripped a half-ladle of beans onto her plate, where they sat in a sheepish pool. The men before her had been given full servings. Soli knew this food was free, that she should have shut up and taken what she was given. But the thing is, she was hungry, and she wanted as much as everyone else.

"I want more," she said.

"That's enough for you."

"The men before me got more."

"Move down the line, please."

She stayed put.

"You're small. That's all you need. Now move down."

The men behind her began to make noise. Move on, señorita! Keep it moving, chica.

There was much grumbling and shouting. Soli didn't budge. Behind her, she felt the rising cloud of irritation. Whistles and more shouts. Someone yelled, *"We're all hungry, so move your pretty pompas!"*

And then, from the swelling hubbub of the food line, a single voice: "Give her mine," it said. It flared again: "Give her mine!" A voice of wood and air, it blew like a mountain flute.

The Beta man looked down the line, locked eyes with the voice, and cursed. He slopped more food on her plate.

Soli made a decision. This was the voice for her. She would stick with this voice.

It belonged to a young man, thin and capable. From his head rose a hurricane of hair, pushed back with a headband. She'd never seen anyone like him. He couldn't have been much older than her. Twenty, maybe. He sat in a cluster of men and boys. He squinted into the sun, shook his head, threw his hands in the air as he spoke. Thin ropes circled his wrists. His name was Checo.

She could tell this much from where she sat: Checo wasn't scared. And she was. He seemed to know what he was doing. And she hadn't a clue. She looked back at Manuel, who was scanning the crowd now, looking for her. For all her ignorance, she knew she'd have to make her own move. The key, she sensed, was to pretend she didn't care. Take him or leave him, whoever he was, this man who radiated promise. He stood at the edge of the camp now, staring down the train tracks, when she walked to his side.

He saw her. Nodded. "Get enough to eat?"

"Sure." She peered down the tracks herself and saw nothing but quavers of heat. "You headed to the States?" she asked, at last.

He smirked. "I sure am, señorita. And you? Japan?"

She had no reply to this, so she mustered her courage and said, "I think I'll come along with you."

This earned an outright yelp of glee. The man doubled over, hands on knees, laughing. Soli stared. She'd never made a person laugh like this before. Other travelers turned to watch them. A few of his friends gathered round, looking from Soli to the man and back. Soli turned to leave.

"Wait!" He held up a hand, waved a finger at her. "Don't go," he said. "Okay."

"Okay what?"

"If that's what you want? You can come with us." He smiled for real then.

A small boy stepped forward from his group of friends, looked Soli up and down. "Can you ride trains?" He whacked her on the arm. "You ever ride a train before?"

Soli gazed at the boy, rubbed her arm.

"I can ride a train," she said. Anyone could ride a train, she thought.

Soli found Manuel by the latrines.

"Keep your tunnel," she told him. "And keep my Papi's money. I'm going on my own from here."

He peered at her, shook his head. "You don't know what you're saying, fresa. There's no thank-you-and-goodbye for us. You're part of this now. You know that, right?"

Soli's heart pounded through her temples. She fought the urge to cry out. If she ran, Manuel would surely catch her.

"Okay," she said. "Okay, Manuel. I'm going to the bathroom now, okay? Wait here."

He shrugged, grinned. "I can wait all day."

The bathroom was packed with women: women washing their faces, women hunched over sinks and splashing water under their arms, women waiting for the three toilets. Where had they all come from? She grabbed one. "Trade clothes with me," she said. "Please!"

The woman scoffed at Soli, looked her up and down. "I don't think so."

She tried another and another, until finally one shrugged and said, "Okay."

"*Thank* you," Soli said.

"What's wrong with your clothes?"

"Nothing! They're fine."

And with that, she traded her pink T-shirt and blue jeans for a pair of old brown trousers that cut off at her knees, and a T-shirt that read *Soccer Players Do It for 90 Minutes.* When she took out Manuel's knife and stood at the sink, hacking at her hair, no one seemed to notice. Desperation was strength, and Soli's enabled her to saw through her ponytail and shred away the locks that hung loose around her forehead, until she looked like a bona fide, wholly unnoticeable fourteen-year-old boy. Luckily, her breasts were negligible. She ambled from the bathroom with a masculine limp, spat on the ground, and marched past Manuel, still stationed by the bathroom entrance, who barely turned her way.

"Idiota," she muttered, as her heart petered down to a workable beat.

LATER, CHECO LAUGHED AT HER. "You're becoming an American already," he said. "Give me my food! It's mine, it's mine!"

"I wasn't being American. I was hungry. And if this were the States, they would have called the police."

Checo hadn't gone hungry, either. "I knew they were bullshitting," he said. "They had enough for everyone. They just like to be in charge." He paused. "You look like a boy now. What happened?"

He had no sense, that first morning, of what would grow between them, those days on the trains. But Soli knew, from the second he shouted down the food line, that Checo was right all over. With his hands, his hair, his heat, he was the wind that would carry her North.

When the small boy had punched her and asked if she could ride a train, Soli had envisioned boarding a passenger train. She'd worried that they'd be boarding without tickets, without money, that they'd have to hide when the collector showed up. She was more wrong than she could have imagined. Later that morning, a freight train pulled onto the tracks near the camp. It hissed its arrival, a great metal snake. There it stopped, waiting to be loaded and unloaded.

The Beta man was firm: "No one is to ride this train," he said. "It is illegal to ride on top of a freight train. It is against the law. You will be arrested," he said, "and sent back home." Then he paused. "Please watch out for tunnels. If you see a tunnel coming, lie down flat. Hitting the top of a tunnel will kill you."

Here's the thing: The police weren't going to stop them. There were too many travelers to arrest them all, and no one, not even the police, had any interest in stopping a horde of penniless kids from getting out of Mexico.

Soli began to understand that getting on a freight train when you haven't been invited wasn't a wise thing to do. Checco explained it to her beforehand. "You wait for the train to start moving, you run like hell and you climb on," he said. "If you fall, you're carne molida."

"Why can't you get on before it starts?"

"You'll get caught," he said. "Now, listen. You run alongside it and catch up to one of those ladders on the side. See those? You run, you climb, and you get onto the train. You go first, and I'll come up behind you."

"Okay."

"I won't be able to pull you up," he said. "You'll have to do that yourself. You got strong arms?"

"I don't."

He clasped her arm where the muscle should have been.

"Well. You're light. You'll be fine. Give me your backpack," he said. "I'll carry it."

She hugged the bag more tightly.

"There you go again. I'm not going to take it. I'm going to carry it so you can run."

She took it off and gave it to him. He had to loosen the straps to get it on. "What's in here?" he asked.

"Water."

He took the pack off, opened it, and cursed quietly. "You brought these all the way from Oaxaca?"

"I took them from that man. And there's a knife in there, too. And a Prince tape."

He shook his head. He was wondering about her, she could tell. What passed across his face was a cool, fast cloud of doubt. She wanted to tell Checo that on a journey like this, you kept the things you owned, because you never knew what might be stolen by rough hands or sorry circumstance. But because she was a girl with hummingbirds in her heart, she kept this wisdom to herself. She let Checo do the knowing.

And then he put the backpack down and looked straight into Soli's eyes. "You'll have to keep up, okay?" He cupped her elbow. "Don't get left behind."

Running for a train was easy enough because she had a goal in mind, and that goal made her forget the raw skin between her thighs, the pounding in her feet and knees. It was a race she had a chance of winning. Pulling herself onto a moving train was something else. It was then that she began to doubt herself, when she realized just how weak her arms were, how fickle the elbows. The train gnashed its wheels at her, sent the sound of metal on metal right up through her bones and into the marrow.

Soli's hand grasped a railing. She faltered. Her elbow flailed and the momentum of the train was harder and stronger than she was. She felt her grip slipping. She felt the ravenous suck of the tracks below.

And then she felt Checo, his arm around her waist, pushing her up and shouting as the train picked up speed. "Hold on to it!" he yelled. "Pull yourself up. Pull! Grab on!"

She pulled up, she grabbed. Her foot found a rung and she was on. Checo was behind her, his chest pressed to her back. "Climb up," he breathed. She climbed, crying without shame, her arms shaking uncontrollably at each rung. When she reached the top, he hoisted both of them to the roof of the train. They lay there for a long while, catching their breath.

"Thank you," she said at last. "You saved me."

"You fall, I fall." Either he was making a promise or stating a fact. He unzipped her backpack and opened a bottle.

"Salud," he said, took a sip, and passed the water to her. "We'll get stronger stuff than this tonight." Soli turned and watched the shrinking past, the faraway camp, and let her nose, her throat, her mind fill with the pleasures of a promising wind.

As they rode that day, she began to understand the boy-man who'd opened an escape route from Manuel. Checo's barbaric crown of hair was born of the ceaseless wind. His voice, loudest in the day and with no apparent volume control, came shouting over the rumbling tracks. Everything he said was certain, a pronouncement, because on this train, running beside it, lying flat atop it, you needed to know exactly what you were doing. And if you didn't know exactly what you were doing, you acted like you did and hoped for the best.

Soli searched for something to look at. The world rushed past, and her eyes yearned to focus. "Just don't look so much," Checo said. "Stop looking. Soften your eyes and try not to see."

Clustered around Checo at all times were the collection of young men and boys who had found one another on this journey. They were Mario and Flaco, both fourteen. There was Pepe, whose face still carried a soft, fatty cushion of infancy. "How old are you?" Soli asked. The boy raised his fist and up sprang his middle finger.

"We're pretty sure he's eight," Checo answered.

There was one they called Nutsack. Nutsack was older than the rest and spoke good English. He'd made the mistake of translating the word for them, and the name had stuck for good.

In the afternoon, the group grew quiet. They couldn't sleep, because sleeping meant falling. But the late afternoon was a time to pretend they were somewhere else, to think of home and slip feathers into the cushions of their futures. When Soli started to doze off, she felt a pinch. "How are you?" Checo asked. She opened her eyes and found herself unable to speak with his face just inches from hers. He cleared a strand of hair from her mouth. If they had been alone, he would have kissed her.

As DUSK SHOOED AWAY THE DAY, the train came to a stop. In the distance, not far from the tracks, they spotted the hanging lanterns of restaurants, people out for the evening, music. After the endless rush of wind in their ears, the music was like dew on a leaf.

"Come with me," Checo said. They headed into the busy part of whatever town it was. "Tomorrow we ride La Bestia," he said. "Tonight, we celebrate. What're you wearing under that coat?"

"Why, we're going dancing?"

He took her hand and led her into a store. "Wait," he said, and slipped a slick hand—she gasped—around Soli's neck. Then he unzipped her backpack and pulled out her rosary.

"Put this on," he ordered.

"What? Why?"

"Just put it on." He strung the beads around her neck, straightened the cross and set it on her chest, on full display.

"Better. Let's go."

Because Checo told her to, and Checo hadn't been wrong yet, Soli walked in, pretending to peruse the back wall of the store. Those boys, they always had plans.

The only store in Popocalco stocked its liquor at the front so hoodlums like them couldn't steal it. Checo picked up a jug of wine—not a bottle, but a jug, the kind with a handle.

"That won't fit in my bag," she said.

"It's not going in your bag." He stepped close and hugged her, and as he held her, he pulled up the hem of her T-shirt and shoved the jug inside.

"Ai!" she cried. The glass was cold on the skin of her belly.

"Va dar a luz!" he shouted across the store. "My wife is in labor!" She watched him button her jacket up. He frowned at her.

"Ai!" she gasped. "Ayudame!" She pressed her palm to her back the way pregnant women did and shuffled down the aisle, bending her knees as if the weight of childbirth were driving her into the ground. She wheezed, she whimpered. She made the suffering sounds that she'd seen and heard from others. "Ai, Dios mio!"

Checo dragged her out the door, leaving the clerk wide-eyed. "We're having a baby, señor," Checo shouted as she shuffled out. "Congratulate me!"

They ran down the road holding hands, her arm supporting her belly. They ran through busy streets and into the dark. Back at the train, the other boys shouted their welcome.

Pepe's eyes went wide. "How'd you get that?" he asked her. "You got money or something?"

"No, Pepe," Checo said. "She's got something else you'll never have."

The boys clapped Soli on the back, congratulated her. "You're one of us now," Nutsack said.

"Fuck off. She's not like you." Checo screwed the cap off the wine.

When Pepe reached for it, he pulled the jug away. "No, no, no, Pepito." He pointed to the restaurants. "You know what you've got to do. Get my wife a bite to eat. She's just given birth, right?"

Pepe came back with a bagful of food—a packet of french fries, half a sandwich, two apples, and a tin of biscuits.

"Where'd you get all this?" Soli asked. "Did you steal it?" She turned to Checo. "Did he steal it?" There was something wrong with making a little boy steal.

"You think we'd send him? He couldn't steal daylight from a blind man."

It was later that she realized that Pepe had begged. For a little boy with watery eyes, it was easy.

With the wine that night, they turned their throats to sandpaper, their teeth to gray pebbles. There was no shelter for them there, no red Beta truck or mats to sleep on. Checo made sure Pepe found a decent place to lie. He was short and thin enough to stretch out on a roadside bench. "Yell if anyone bugs you," he said to Pepe. "You got your knife?" Pepe nodded.

Checo's shout died down at night.

They lay side by side and away from the others, their shelter a humid cloud bank, their blanket the dark. The stars had hidden themselves. Even with the faraway restaurant lights, she could barely see her own hand. Checo laid his jacket on the ground for her. From somewhere else, he brought a sweater. It was shapeless and smelled male. It was big enough to cover her. Checo slept facing Soli, one hand on her shoulder. Through the thick weave, she could feel every inch of his palm, his solid knuckles, each finger a separate promise.

"Are you warm enough?"

"Yes."

She didn't believe she could sleep with Checo lying so close, but she hadn't slept for two days. She thought of how he'd called her his wife, how he'd held her in the store and trusted her to know what to do, how they ran holding hands. And in the middle of all the thinking, she drifted off. Her brain shut down, even as her body buzzed with the nearness of a man.

When you sleep outside, it feels all right to wake at dawn, no matter how tired you were the night before. She woke to Checo's open eyes.

"La Bestia," he whispered.

"It's here?" She sat up and looked around.

"Lie down, it isn't ready yet." He grinned. "Are you warm?"

"I'm fine," she said, though the clouds had scattered and made way for the morning's violet chill.

Checo propped his head on his palm. "Everyone's asleep." He reached for her cross, poked the pads of his fingers into its corners. "You take this everywhere?" he asked.

"Everywhere."

His gaze settled on her. She flooded with joy and terror and wanted to vanish. She couldn't look up. He was too bright. He would blind her. He lifted her chin and kissed her. They both tasted bitterly of wine and sleep. He kissed her again. His hands, ice-cold, found their way to her waist. Her skin leapt to his touch. His fingers rode the seam of her jeans and she let out a small cry. If anyone had woken and watched, if Pepe had spied on them from his distant perch, he would have seen a peculiar double person, its arms wrapped around itself, its two heads meeting and parting, meeting and parting, a beast in the half-light, quietly surging.

After sunrise, La Bestia, the death train, growled to life. It was larger than the last train, or any train she'd ever seen. People had fallen from it and died. People had lost limbs. La Bestia was nothing to be excited about.

. . .

THE TRAIN CRAWLED TIRELESSLY up the country, stopping occasionally, sometimes all night, to refuel and take on cargo. From the soles of her feet, through her knees and the base of her spine she could feel the churning of its wheels, the steel blades that would eat her for dinner. When her fear spiked, she fingered the rosary that still hung from her neck. She hadn't taken it off, even though only the Virgin wore the rosary and to wear it herself was improper and vain, even if she'd been a virgin of the everyday order. It was uppercase blasphemy, but Checo had put the beads there. The cross sat cradled between her breasts, and there it would stay.

On that train, she didn't watch the horizon. She focused on Checo. She stared at him. Even with his hair whipping in the wind, he was the most stable thing there.

"Stop staring like that," he said.

She couldn't. When it was warm enough, he took off his shirt and lay down on it. Only Checo could lie down on La Bestia. Soli didn't dare.

"Checo," she said. "I'm lucky I ran into you."

He shushed her, his eyes still closed, and said nothing, seemed only to care for the sunlight that slathered itself across his lids. Just when Soli grew jealous of the sun, he reached for her hand and held it.

Checo was something between a man and a boy. She didn't know what to call him. With his friends, he acted like a boy, told dirty jokes and wrestled and laughed at nothing. With Soli at night, in the trackside nests they built of coats and backpacks, he was a man, rough-skinned, sure with his hands, redolent of fuel and bark.

Eventually, Soli told Checo about Manuel and the tunnel to America. Checo shook his head. "It's good you got away from him, Soli."

Perhaps it was La Bestia's death roar, or maybe the promise of the North coming ever closer, and with it, the knowledge that they would all be going their separate ways: Soli wanted to tell Checo something memorable. But instead she acted like herself and spouted nonsense and couldn't stop, even when the wind swallowed her words, even when Checo frowned and pressed an arm over his eyes. She told him where she'd come from, what she thought the North would be like, what she dreamed and feared. She told him about Mama and Papi and the old corn ways. She wanted to tell him everything that she would have told him if their time together hadn't been ticking down with each passing field. And so she did. It's a wonder, after four days together, that she still had things to talk about, and it's a wonder he didn't push her off the train, and only sat up, looked her in the eye, and said, "Soli, talking time is over."

He lay back down and closed his eyes.

But she wanted to say one more thing. Just one more meaningful and memorable thing, something he could carry with him, should this journey throw her off its back.

"Checo," she said. "You are so high-tech."

He opened one eye. "I like that," he said. Soli tucked her hand in his, and lost herself to the dizzying rush.

5.

Kavya cycled to work every day, one of the perks of living in Berkeley. She knew the streets like the hush of her own breath. She could navigate them blindfolded, could tell where she was just by the smell of roses or baking bread or Thai food or urine. She knew where earthquakes and tree roots had split the sidewalks, which hills were best for biking in the morning sun, and which cafés caught the evening light. Her otherwise terrible sense of direction was centered here and framed by the hills to the east and the ocean to the west.

On a cool August morning, with only the whistle of wind through her helmet to keep her company, Kavya pushed up the north campus hill. She took the long way around, turning from Cedar onto Oxford, ducking under low-hanging oaks, skimming the short concrete wall that bordered the street. She'd started taking this route, ostensibly to avoid the steep slope of Euclid, but really, she could admit now, to avoid the playground. Looking at children drove a jagged blade through her, left her riven and weak. She'd stopped speaking with friends who were pregnant, had stopped attending showers. She vaguely and irrationally worried that the infant supply would be tapped out by other lucky women—that in the great heavenly handout, no babies would be left for her. One month since Preeti's wedding, and the urgency of her desire was expanding daily. If she were ready to tell the truth about herself, she'd admit to a fear that Preeti would get pregnant before she did. It was childish, petty, and true.

She and Rishi used to bike together in the mornings, heading south along Shattuck Avenue, Berkeley's main thoroughfare, until they split off downtown—Kavya heading uphill to the sorority and Rishi to the BART station, where he would be yelled at and pelted with fruit for riding the Weebus, working in the Valley, and driving up housing prices in the once affordable boroughs of the East Bay. "I'm not going to bike to the bus anymore," he had announced one morning five months earlier. It wasn't the fruit or the abuse that was making him stop. It was his conviction that his bike seat was killing his sperm. The doctors hadn't found anything wrong with either of them. Rishi's sperm count was healthy. Kavya's ovaries were diligent and her uterus hospitable.

"There's no way a bike seat could kill your sperm," Kavya had said.

"You don't know that. Why do you think Europe has a declining birth rate?"

"Because their women are educated and contraception's free."

Rishi had started wearing sweatpants, even to work. "It's all very sensitive down there," he'd concluded. Having renounced his bike, he drove his Prius to the Weebus instead, which riled up the protesters even more. Without having to ask, Kavya knew that this filled her husband with contentious, barely hidden glee.

KAVYA PUMPED HER WAY to the top of the hill and stopped on the corner to catch her breath. Here, she dismounted, took off her helmet, wiped the sweat from her hairline. Before her rose a broad flight of stairs, crowned by the white columns of Gamma Gamma Pi. As she drew near, she heard her assistant, Miguel, grinding rice for fresh horchata.

She'd been working at the sorority for nearly a year. Financially, it was a step up from her head chef position at Green Pizza, but she was still getting used to the idea of it. For four years, she'd allowed her position at Green to define large segments of who she was: her political beliefs, her esthetic tendencies, her respect for the Earth and the food that sprang from it. They all wove nicely into her role at Green. In her world, being head chef at a trendy pizza restaurant was the sort of informational tidbit that dropped harmoniously into conversation.

Oh! people used to say. I love that place! Wait—you're head chef?

But soon came the onset of what people were calling *this economy*. The lines that once trailed out the door and around the corner grew shorter with the passing months, until there came a time when customers could actually arrive and be seated. Prospects were darkening. Kavya began to look for something new. She found Gamma Gamma Pi, with its nine-thousand-dollar salary bump. It wasn't her dream job, but as far as she knew, sororities were economy-proof. She would be starting a family soon. She took the job.

The conversations had changed, of course.

I'm head chef at a sorority, she'd say.

Oh.

And then the questions: Are you *in* the sorority?

Were you in a sorority?

What's it like?

Did they initiate you?

Are they total bitches?

"Total bitch," Miguel muttered. The kitchen door swung closed. Miguel was Kavya's assistant chef and designated wok-reacher. He was six feet tall. In Peru, he'd once told her, I'm a Godzilla! The total bitch in question was Gamma Gamma Pi's house mother, Martina McAfee. Kavya didn't see her as a bitch so much as an authority figure uncomfortable with her authority. She'd never formally introduced herself to the two kitchen employees, but appeared on Kavya's first day, in blond bob and nautical stripes, and began reciting the weekend menu. Given that this was Berkeley, she could really have been anyone—a Realtor off her lithium, a truant professor, a well-preserved homeless woman. It was only later that Kavya noticed her picture on the WELCOME!!!! board at the sorority's entrance. When Martina McAfee spoke to Kavya, it was to relay instructions, ask questions about ingredients, and check off weekly menus. She didn't seem able or willing to say hello, to ask Kavya about her weekend or take up the threads of chitchat Kavya proferred. Kavya hadn't been used to being a mere employee. She was used to being an integral cog of a professional family, the creator and preserver of her culinary universe. But for the extra nine thousand, she could live with being staff.

In the end, Green Pizza survived. The economy returned, and so did the clusters of pizza eaters that sat on the grassy traffic median. Often, Kavya wondered if she should have given up on Green, if the family she'd left it for would ever come into being.

It was the third Monday of the month, Roast Day, so Kavya was rubbing a trio of chickens with lemon and rosemary when Martina entered. She stood in the corner of the kitchen, silent, until Kavya sensed a glint of yellow hair and turned.

"The girls are complaining about the garlic," Martina said, crossing her arms over her chest, arranging long fingers over her elbows.

Kavya put down the lemon wedge and wiped her hands on her apron. "Is there a problem with the garlic?"

"There was too much of it in the arrabiata sauce. It wasn't good."

Kavya happened to know that her arrabiata was, without fail, good.

"Thanks, Martina. I'll take that on board."

It was a phrase Kavya resorted to when she sensed an outsider fingering the confines of her kitchen. It was a phrase that allowed her to reclaim some authority in her professional space. When orders were flung at her, Kavya took them on board. She became their captain. And the complaints and demands little more than compliant stowaways.

Martina McAfee breathed deeply, turned on her heel, and left.

"I'll take her on board," Miguel muttered.

Kavya couldn't help smiling. She had recoiled from her workplace at first, despite the oak-paneled peace of the house, its crystal chandeliers, its lush rugs and fainting couches. The sorority was just— It was just so. She couldn't think of a single word to encapsulate how she felt about the Gamma Pis, mincing around their lavish home, caked in makeup at breakfast, singing their mortifying predinner song, fawning over the campus a cappella groups and crew teams who visited for dinner. But in the end, what really mattered was that the Gamma Pis smiled and thanked her when she carried out chafing dishes piled high with rice or vegetables or meat. When she brought out something they liked especially—like moussaka or macaroni and cheese—they clapped their hands and squealed in that very girly way. For the most part, sorority girls were just girls. She might one day have her own sorority girl, as unlikely as it was starting to seem—a daughter like one of these, born with her own free will and a closet full of cocktail dresses.

KAVYA HAD MOVED TO BERKELEY eighteen years earlier for college. She had graduated, traveled, become a chef, and married Rishi, in that order. They found a bungalow with Craftsman moldings and light fixtures. It sat wood-shingled at the end of a short drive just off Shattuck Avenue, within wafting distance of bakeries and storied restaurants. After they bought their house—a small miracle, possible with their parents' help—they'd walked hand in hand through a horticultural nursery to pick out plants, wandering among aisles of miniature fruit trees and exotic blooms. On Sunday mornings, they lay naked in bed. They often slept clothed against the cool Berkeley nights, then stripped down for the pleasure of a lazy morning. They spent hours individually wrapped, Rishi in the bedsheet and Kavya in the quilt, dozing and staring at each other and checking their e-mail, until the prospect of skin on skin and plunging one into the other grew too electric to resist. When they remembered to, they went for head massages at the Sunday farmers' market. With Rishi, Kavya took bike rides through the low hills. She walked to the movie theater. She walked to the shops. She walked and walked. She cycled. She flipped off cars that got too close to her on narrow and overparked roads. She glared at SUVs. She grew calf muscles that no longer fit her jeans. Kavya rose to the helm of her own storied restaurant. For a while, it was all she needed: the comforting method of pizza-making, the smell of baking bread, her sous-chefs tossing and catching their great spinning discs of dough, graceful and sure as dancers. After closing every night, Rishi would meet her at the kitchen door and walk her home, Kavya smelling of warm yeast, the two of them holding hands on the quiet sidewalk, watching other restaurants tuck themselves in for the night.

All this time, she'd been living for the stolid delicacies of work and marriage, her tidy home, cocktail evenings and yawning holidays. Her grown-up life was fat with pleasure, but after three years, then four and five, the pleasure grew thin. She'd come to Berkeley to find herself, but found that her self was not enough. She wanted a self of her self. She wanted a child.

She'd been thirty-four when she came to this discovery. Her own mother had always seemed more irritated than fulfilled by motherhood, and for a long time, Kavya couldn't imagine how it might feel, this compulsion that seemed to possess so many. But one morning, she woke up, and like gravel in her voice, it was there.

She began to really look at children for the first time. Babies. Her chest ached at the sight of them. Her hands grew restless, like a smoker's.

She wanted to press one to the beat of her heart, feel the sweet, warm weight of a baby in her arms. She saw herds of children running, playing, frantic with joy, and wanted to run with them, to run like her life depended on it, her legs burning, her throat raw from shouting.

To love profoundly, and be loved. To shape her own blood and body into sparkling new life. She could be home to someone, a safe and soft place in a world of ragged edges. She could teach a little boy, a little girl, how to make their way.

It seemed simple at the start. Having a child, as she understood it, required a good deal of unprotected sex. Plenty of others had managed it. The goal was to have fun and not to worry. The path to motherhood would be wide and grassy, an open valley of possibility.

It had begun in their living room. They'd had a quiet meal that night—baked eggs and polenta, breakfast for dinner. She'd led Rishi to the living room, sat him down, and grew suddenly, unexpectedly nervous. So rarely did they say anything that meant this much. Her pulse ricocheted and her mouth went dry.

"I want to try for a baby."

Rishi had stared at her for a few long moments and then nodded, slowly.

She studied his face. "You want one, right? You want a baby?"

He squeezed her hand. "Sure. Of course I do." He assumed he did. Children had seemed like a project planted permanently in the future. A certainty about which he never thought he'd be asked. Had anyone asked his own father if he'd wanted a baby?

DESPITE THE CLARITY of her desire, Kavya had no real idea of what sort of mother she'd be. She'd decided this much: She would take her child to the ocean whenever she could, and she would teach him about trees. They would go to Muir Woods and she would guide her child's eye from the base of a tree—as big around as a bungalow—to the trunk that climbed and lost itself in green, tented pine. She would tell her child that the tree was taller and older than he could imagine, that the tree was taller than the Golden Gate Bridge, and the child would look right into her, his face just inches from her own, and tell her she was lying.

The parents around her seemed to take great pride in their work, like artisans of a dying craft. Jogging through parks and waiting in BART stations, Kavya had come across American mothers speaking French to their American children, fathers explaining the physics of underground transport to their preschoolers, property tax law to their eight-year-olds. At the farmers' market the week before, a little girl had fallen and scraped her knee. As she stood sobbing, inconsolable, her mother knelt down beside her. Here, sweetie, have some kale. The little girl had taken it, chewed on the tough, primordial leaf, and stopped crying. The stakes were high in Berkeley. The toddlers were eating their cruciferous greens.

There were things she couldn't know about being a parent without being one—this she sensed from the way men and women with children in tow seemed to have little to say to her. Parenthood was a members-only organization closed to freelancers and temps. Outsiders could visit for lunch, but they tended to leave quickly, overwhelmed by the demands of belonging. But Kavya didn't want to leave. Kavya wanted in.

FOR RISHI, the brilliant bonus of this new world, this procreative world, was a sudden abundance of sex. They were doing it every day, sometimes twice, like they'd done in the early days. They had sex for lunch, and ate burritos in the car. They had sex in the living room, and toppled the throw pillows from the sofa. They had sex in a restaurant once—in the bathroom—and once in a parking lot. But after two months, then three, these trysts began to feel inappropriate, like their control was slipping. He began to wonder what it was about, all the spontaneity. He supposed Kavya was trying to keep things fun, maybe even for his sake, to combat the impatience that lurked in the shadows.

For three months, Kavya refused to look at her calendar or take her temperature or do any of the things women did to track their fertility. "It shouldn't matter," she said. "It should just happen." But then it didn't just happen. After three months of trying and failing, the sex could no longer be casual. She began taking her temperature, tracking her ovulation.

Rishi had been on board with this. He would think of it as a project, he decided. Project managing was what he did, and driving his management approach was the Weebies principle—the Silicon Valley principle—that nothing was impossible. Impossibility was not an absolute, but as shiftable as a heavy boulder. Trial and error and a little cognitive daring were all it took to make the impossible possible. It had worked for PCs, the Internet, smartphones; it would work for his baby.

Sex whenever became sex on a schedule. Kavya felt a sense of purpose. Satisfaction, even. She was taking charge. Kavya began demanding sex as Rishi hurried from the house to catch the Weebus. She once actually drove out to the Weebies campus and showed up at his office door. "I'm ovulating right now," she'd said. "Like now." Rishi had found them a nap room, disobeying the strict single-occupant limit; they'd emerged flushed and rumpled in full view of his coworkers gathered at the espresso machine. Often, from across the bay, she'd text him in all caps, mid-meeting, mid-presentation, mid-epiphany, to say COME HOME. I NEED YOU NOW. What once would have thrilled Rishi stirred in him a sense of anxiety, futility, ingratitude. He felt less like a man and more like an indentured servant, keeping up his end of a shady bargain. And every time, every month they tried to get her pregnant, Rishi watched Kavya grow more brittle. He thought of himself as a rational person, good at compartmentalizing, good at avoiding flights of fancy. But trying to have a baby defied his powers of reason and strategy and desire. He'd bought into the idea that hard work bred success, but Rishi and Kavya were working hard. They were working unnaturally hard at this most natural of tasks.

SIX MONTHS PASSED, and still nothing. Nine months, and Kavya had found herself at Preeti's wedding. And now, ten. The gravel in her throat had grown to a stone. Every time she saw a baby or a woman with a luscious globe of a belly, the stone grew harder and larger. But Kavya knew this much: She was a woman. She was an Indian woman. Surely a country with one billion people had produced some capable wombs. She was going to have a baby. She and Rishi just needed to get away from the theater of failure that had become their bedroom. They needed to escape the chilly corners of their bungalow and have the sort of relaxed intercourse from which babies seemed to spring. Her ears buzzed with certainty, and farther inside, her ovaries winced.

She texted Rishi: *Napa Valley this weekend! Spa, B&B. I'm booking it.* The exclamation mark: so hopeful. She began to delete it, then decided to let it be.

6.

It had been five days since Soli had last seen Checo, and thoughts of him and what might have happened to him jangled inside her like shards of tin.

Soli and two other women sat on the bed of a yellow onion truck, with crates stacked high to shield them. Every now and then, a thin whistle of air made it through the slats of the truck and past the crates, and for those swift seconds, she sensed the sweet nearness of the end. With the air, the morning light, the company of calm women among whom she could—at last!—close her eyes, Soli felt that she would hold together, cohered by a single strip of hope, just long enough to arrive at Silvia's door. They stopped twice that day to piss on the side of the road and stretch their legs. Soli slept. For how long, she did not know. She did not dream of what had happened to her. She did not dream of Checo, or of the brutish men who came later. The cave between her legs was numb, but her thighs were sticky and began to blister in the day's heat. When she awoke, the air was still. The woman beside her was called Fatima, and Soli wondered if she'd drugged herself, because after saying "My name is Fatima," she fell asleep and didn't wake for six hours.

A woman named Luz squinted at her across the mound of onions. "Where are you going?" she asked.

"Berkeley," Soli answered.

"Where's that?"

"Close to San Francisco."

"You know someone there?"

"Yes, my cousin."

"Your cousin have money?"

"I think so. I think she has money."

Luz shook her head like she didn't see good things for Soli.

A few hours after dark, the driver stopped the truck and stuck his head out his window. "Get flat," he called.

"What's he talking about?" Soli asked.

Luz rolled herself into a ball. The truck slowed to a halt. The engine stopped. "Get down," she hissed, and pulled sleeping Fatima from the bench to the floor. Fatima grunted awake, blinked dumbly, and then burrowed behind them into an empty space, hemmed in by towers of onion crates.

"Are we here?" Soli asked.

"Quiet! Make yourself small."

Through the crates and the slats, Soli saw the flicker of a dark green uniform. The flicker spoke in English. He spoke in English!

"We're here," Soli whispered.

"Shut up." Luz was kneeling beside her, and she took Soli's hands in hers. She slipped her fingers along Soli's knuckles like they were rosary beads, and Soli prayed silently, thinking of her own lost rosary. Though his words were muffled by onions, she knew the uniformed man was questioning their driver. Shuffling paper, more questions. And before she could move, a stick shot through the slats. She gasped. It grazed her skull. Again and again, it rammed through the slats, a guard's iron wand, trawling for migrant flesh, hoping to hit something live enough to cry out and prove the truck carried more than onions. She held her hands to her head and prayed. She knew she was shaking, but luckily for her, fear made no sound. Moments later, she heard footsteps crunch away and vanish. The engine started up again and they rolled forward.

Luz released a tremulous breath. "Lucky," she said. "A lazy one." She looked up at Soli, grinned, and pushed her tongue through the gap in her teeth. "We're here."

"In the North?"

"America, m'ija. That's what they call it here. We're in California now."

Soli looked up to the sky. Same blue as the Mexican sky. She looked through the truck's slats. This was California. The United States of America. She had arrived.

And here's what she discovered. This place, this America? This new place, this streets-of-gold place? Looked a hell of a lot like the old place.

America streaked by her, stripped and tender with heat. She watched it all rush past through the slats of the old truck: the tin roofs, seas of broken glass, glinting and breathless like a fever dream. America was the dust in her hair, the wind in her throat, the sun that shouted against her eyelids. Between the slats of this truck, America was nothing but a high-tech, high-speed dream of trees and houses and fences, a sliver of interrupted light.

The old folks back home, those who'd been here and back, told Soli she would do well here, that she had the spirit. They told her to keep her head down and work hard and for God's sake keep her mouth shut.

After four more hours with sleepy Fatima and gap-toothed Luz, Soli was ready to jump. The man up front drove hard and fast, like he had someplace to go, like he wasn't hiding three people in a mound of onions in the back of his truck. This dream smelled horribly of onions.

They were entering a city, where the buildings rose like missiles from the ground, too tall to be seen completely. Minutes later, the buildings shrank down and grew dingy; the sidewalks streamed with walking life.

The driver pulled over and stopped. He called through the slats: "This is your stop. Get off here."

"You." He nodded at Soli. "This is where you get off."

She stepped off into a flurry of bodies, crossing paths and jostling, moving in all directions at once. It was cloudy here, and surprisingly cold. From where she stood that day, California was a gray road that lived for miles, sloping down, then up, dying into a sunstruck horizon. The horizon was where the earth turned, where it decided it had had enough of the same, and dove into something new. She wondered if the earth found what it was looking for, if it was happy with its new life.

She looked up: The signs were in Spanish. She looked around: The people looked like her. She opened her ears: All around her, Spanish. And her heart dropped. This wasn't America. She'd been cheated again. They'd somehow crossed back into Mexico. The truck was gone.

She turned a corner and walked. Her knees ached, her vision floated, and the taste of her own mouth was nauseating. She didn't think she could go much farther—she'd find a way back to Popocalco or she'd sit down where she was and never move again. She was still a fool, unschooled by the hardship of her journey. She looked up and saw a wide marquis: *Amnesia.* Under the marquis, young people gathered and smoked.

But they were white young people. And Chinese young people. And then—she rocketed with hope when she saw them—there were *black people.* She kept walking and saw more of every color, street signs in English, and on the side of the road, a line of cars with license plates. *California,* they said. A sunburst on each plate: This was California.

The sun above was cool, the ground littered with shriveled cigarettes. Soli kneeled before San Francisco and gave thanks. Because she didn't have her cross, she kissed her thumb. She kissed it again.

She wasn't a city girl. She walked and walked, but didn't know where the streets were leading. The houses here looked like frosted cakes, painted pink and blue and purple, rising and falling with the curve of the city's hills. So full was she with the thought of being in America that she had to remind herself that she had someplace to get to. She came to a crossroads. There were five corners, six, and people all around. People held mobile phones high, at arm's length, smiling to the sky. This was no place for a woman who'd entered the country beneath a pile of onions. People were all around, and mostly they looked up at the sky. She looked up, too—spires, wide gray bricks, cornices and turrets, more windows than she had ever seen, clouds the color of turmoil.

HER SHIRT WAS ON INSIDE OUT and backward. The tag stuck out from under her chin. Her backpack was gone, her water, her money. She could smell herself. She cursed herself for losing the five dollars, that bill of weathered hope that Papi had pressed into her palm. What she did have was Silvia's address, packed into her memory, recited and re-viewed so many times that it had grown limp with handling: 2020 Channing, Berkeley, California. It sounded high-tech and glamorous, an address like a disco ball. After where she'd been and what she'd done in the three weeks of her journey, finding her way from San Fran-cisco to Berkeley didn't scare her. She'd ask questions, point, and ask for help. She would say the word *Berkeley* many times, piecing together links of kindness, holding fast to the chain until it led her to Silvia. She came to a subway station, something she'd heard of but never seen. She asked a woman playing guitar what to do. The woman pointed at a sign on the wall with an arrow. "Go," she said. "There."

When the man in a booth turned his back, Soli hoisted herself over the turnstile and ran. He didn't chase her. It seemed that a disappearing Mexican wasn't worth his trouble.

Here's what Soli planned to do. She would go to her cousin Silvia, who had moved to the States nine years earlier. Silvia was high-tech. She was doing well. She had an apartment and two boys. She had her own business, and she had papers. She could get Soli papers. She would work for Silvia's cleaning business. *The people in these neighborhoods,* Silvia wrote, *they pay a lot of money to not have to clean their own houses. They give you cash gifts at Christmas. They are good people, a lot of them, and they know how to treat their servants.*

"Servitude lives in the heart." Papi had said. "Soli, you will never be a servant because you know your heart."

"Bravo, bravo, Trovador. Do you want your daughter to scrub floors all her life?" Mama had asked.

People called Papi Trovador because the things he said were beautiful.

"Soli, do you want to scrub floors?"

She said to Papi, "I want to go. Servitude lives in the heart, Papi."

"Not in yours."

"Not in mine."

The matter had been settled that day.

Arriving in Berkeley, she exited the station and stood on the corner of a wide and teeming avenue. This could have been any corner, anywhere. Behind a café counter, she found a Mexican man. This one looked at her kindly. She told him the address she'd memorized. It turned out it was not so far from that café. She walked down a cracked sidewalk. Garbage cans overflowed, and the place smelled of rot. In the thick and stormy air, there was nowhere for the stench to go. This is America, she thought.

As she approached, she could see that Silvia's building leaned slightly at an angle. Scaffolding rose up its side, and on it sat dark women, darker than Soli, in flowing silks, scrubbing windows. They watched her get closer to the building. She had seen plenty of smiling people in America, but these were the first to smile at her.

A label with a tiny doorbell: *Morales*. Soli rang it.

She heard the thump of heavy footsteps. The door opened. "Solimar."

"Silvia."

Silvia stood tall as a statue, so clean, so American. Soli stepped over the threshold and into Silvia's arms. She held her so long that Soli stopped feeling both her cousin's body and her own. Her legs gave out, and she began to cry. Not from sorrow or anger, but from wild exhaustion, the only thing she still owned.

"You smell like shit," Silvia said. "Where've you been?"

"I've been getting here."

"Come upstairs, girl. What did you do to your hair? Your papi's been calling. Every day. You've made him crazy. Why haven't you called him?"

Upstairs, two boys waited, Silvia's sons, five and seven. Before she could kneel down and smile, or take them in her arms, or ask them what they liked to eat, Silvia shoved a towel in her face and pointed to the bathroom.

"Shower," she ordered.

This was Soli's first shower. In Popocalco, they'd had baths and only baths. She would come to miss baths, of course, but that morning, the shower was what she needed. The steam kept her warm and the past sped down the drain. She was an earthworm in the warm spring rain.

Now that she had arrived, her happiness had time to establish its landscape. And it was not pure. Her happiness was terrain pitted with melancholy. The end of her journey brought with it the realization that Santa Clara Popocalco was behind her, perhaps forever, and that she would never again be the Soli she'd once known so intimately.

Silvia walked in while she was drying off. "That's better. Now I can see you." She picked up the *Soccer Players Do It for 90 Minutes* shirt and scowled. "I'll burn this," she said.

"No. I want to keep it." Soli snatched it from her. The shirt hung heavy with filth, and she let it drop to the floor again. She would wash away the stink and sweat and fear. It would be clean again, like Soli.

Silvia found Soli a skirt and a T-shirt. The shirt was fine, but the skirt slid to the floor as soon as it was on.

"You're too skinny," Silvia said. "You'll do good here, all right. Skinny here means you're smart and hard-working. And rich."

They laughed together.

Silvia found her a cotton dress with no sleeves.

"This'll do," she said. "I used to wear this before the boys were born. If this falls off you, we're both in trouble."

Soli took off her shirt and reached for the dress, but Silvia held it. Soli's hair dripped down her back and she winced. Silvia let her stand there, naked as a worm, and stared.

"The dress, please, Silvia."

Silvia's eyes cupped each portion of Soli—her breasts, her stomach. They rested on the two purple bruises that spread over Soli's hips. She sucked her breath in.

"It's nothing," Soli said.

Her eyes settled on Soli's face, and she gasped.

"What?"

"You're having a baby."

"Stop it. Dress. Come on."

Silvia shook her head. "You're pregnant."

And because Silvia was Silvia and never wrong, Soli looked down at her belly, as if searching for a stain she hadn't noticed. She saw the puff of hair below her waist, her small, sure abdomen, and her breasts, on most days as pointless as two unborn mice. Now, they seemed on the verge of waking.

"Whose baby is this?"

She felt no different. She couldn't be pregnant. And yet. The possibilities whirled and settled. "Checo," Soli said. "It could only be Checo."

"Who the hell is Checo?"

The answer felt foolish, so she said nothing.

"Soli, Soli, Soli." Silvia came closer. Soli saw something alive on her cousin's face that she identified as emotion. She hadn't seen emotion in days. She mistook it for love.

"*¡Idiota!*" Silvia slapped her across the face. "!Pinche puta! What were you *thinking*? This is how you come to America? This is your big plan?"

Silvia whipped the dress at her. The cotton caught her waist and stung.

"*Ai*, Silvia. Stop it! I'm sorry."

"You're sorry? *Stupid, stupid*, Soli. This is not what your papi spent all his money for!"

Daniel and Aldo stood in the doorway. They'd probably never seen their mother whipping a naked relative. Silvia shooed them away.

"Get dressed," she muttered, and slammed the door.

When Soli came out again, Silvia was in the kitchen, pulling something from the oven.

"Sit down, food's ready."

Silvia spooned rice and chicken onto her plate. And when she plopped down an extra serving of meat, Soli felt like maybe things would be okay. Her cousin tipped the boys' uneaten rice onto her own plate, then sat down to eat. She hunched over her food in the old familiar way, smacking her thick lips and frowning. Soli, for a moment, could have been back in Popocalco, in an old adobe hut with Silvia and her family. While they ate, the kitchen grew warm and her troubles cool. Silvia looked up once, in the old Silvia way. Then she paused, put her fork down, and picked up her napkin.

"We don't even know," she said, still chewing. "Have you done a test?"

Soli shook her head.

"So, we don't even know. Maybe I'm wrong."

But Soli knew Silvia, and Silvia was never wrong.

7.

HER FIRST BERKELEY MORNING, SOLI WOKE INTO A FOG OF remorse. If there was a right way to do things, she had missed it completely, and it was too late to start again. But the blanket was kind, the cushions forgiving. She lay still and took in the large television, a glass vase, the trappings of stability. In the other room, an alarm clock buzzed and the children came clamoring in.

Before breakfast, she used Silvia's calling card to phone Papi. She didn't know what she expected, whether he'd be overjoyed to hear her voice or whether some tornado of revolution had hit Popocalco, where nothing could possibly be the same after all that had changed for her.

"Solimar? Solimar!" Papi's voice was edged with fear. She'd never heard him like this, and she'd never, she realized, been so very far from him.

"Papi?" It was all she could say, stunned now by the realization that she couldn't just go back home, that her mother and father were part of another life.

"Why didn't you call me, m'ija?"

She tried to answer, but began to weep. She cursed herself for giving in like this, now that she'd arrived, now that her tears would only make Papi feel more helpless.

"I'm sorry, Papi," she managed, at last.

"You'd better be, Soli. You don't know what it was like over here."

"Is Mama all right?" She half expected him to say that Mama was gone, that she'd stopped eating or run away or burned the house down.

"Mama's fine. You want to talk to her?"

So she talked to Mama, and he was right, she was fine. Mama sounded as tiny and distant as Papi, but wearier. "I'm glad you got there," she said. For this small sentence, Soli was grateful.

"Have you eaten?" her mother asked. "Is the food there okay?"

Silvia tapped her watch.

"I have to go, Mama."

"Get a calling card. Silvia can get them cheap."

"Te hablo luego, Mama."

Mama paused and seemed on the verge of words, but said nothing more. Soli heard the click of the phone, the dial tone. *How are you feeling?* her mother might have asked. *How was the journey, and are you glad to be alive? Can you believe you made it? Was it all worth it and will you ever be the same?* Her mother had asked none of these questions, but how could she have known?

There had been a good deal she'd wanted to tell them about, like Manuel's big sweaty lie, his plan for Soli to pass not over the border, but under it. But a few details would have summoned more questions, and she didn't trust herself to keep her words at bay. Soli didn't want to pass on the wounds, not to her parents, who'd be able to do nothing but feel them. So she closed her eyes and felt for the wind on her face, the demonic rumble of the train below, the rush of the valley speeding northward. She felt for Checo, his dusty hair between her fingers, his skin rough and moist. Was she angry with Papi for believing Manuel? Or with Manuel for his lies? How could she be? Without them, there would have been no Checo.

Silvia was not wrong. Soli took her test the next day. She had pissed on many things during her journey, but never expected a reply. In Silvia's bathroom the next afternoon, she pissed on a very expensive little stick that answered her with a plus sign.

"Okay," Silvia said. She stood at the kitchen counter, peeling a garlic clove. "Now we know. Now we can take care of it."

Soli knew what taking care of it meant. And she wondered if she would have considered this back in Mexico, this simple solution to a life.

"What do they do?" she asked.

"We go to a clinic. There's one in town, and they won't ask for much. I'll pay, you'll pay me back."

Soli was quiet for a moment. "But what do they *do*?"

"What do you mean? You mean, what do they actually do?"

She nodded. Silvia put the garlic clove down.

"They stick a vacuum inside. They vacuum it out of you, and then it's done." She smashed the clove with the back of a wooden spoon. "Okay?"

Silvia was right, Soli knew. She couldn't start her American life with a baby inside. It wasn't in the plan, and it certainly wouldn't get her anywhere. And what would she tell Papi? If she were going to get pregnant, she could have stayed in Popocalco. The world was an ocean of opportunity for a girl seeking sperm. She could get knocked up anywhere, papers or no papers, no problem.

That night, Silvia presented Soli with a notebook. Inside were hand-drawn columns labeled "owed" and "paid." The "paid" column was empty, but soon it would contain Soli's share of the groceries, bills, and rent.

"I'll help you with the bills, Silvia, when I get a job."

"I know you will." Silvia softened, regarded Soli for several seconds, then rose and went to the fridge. She returned to the sofa with one glass of milk and one bottle of beer. She sat down.

"So. Tell me." The two sat across from each other on the sofa, like they had when they were girls and all there was to do in the world was talk and sit, sit and talk until the weak light of morning. Soli talked about Manuel and his car, Checo and the trains, the flour and the onions.

"You were lucky those gangsters stopped you," Silvia said. "You never would have made it through that desert."

"I think you're wrong about that, Silvia. I could have made it through anything with Checo by my side."

"And the baby inside you? You ever had a baby inside? Would the baby have made it?" Soli looked down again at the place where the baby lived.

Silvia had a job the next morning, but left an envelope with cash, an address, and directions. When Soli got to the clinic, they made her wait in line. They spoke Spanish, and they didn't look at her like she was a dirty stupid puta who'd ruined the plan.

Silvia had warned her about these places, how religious people hung around with pictures of dismembered fetuses. She didn't need a church-goer to tell her this was a horrible thing to do. In the exam room, a nurse asked Soli if she knew what to expect. Soli did half expect to see a big dusty vacuum cleaner, the kind Silvia hauled to her cleaning jobs. She half expected the nurse to stick a Dyson up her you-know-what and slam her foot down on the pedal. But instead, the nurse showed Soli the thing they'd use, as if she'd take an anthropological interest. It was smooth and white and gleamed beneath the ceiling lights. It looked like a rocket to the moon. And maybe that's what stopped Soli. Maybe if they'd trooped in a Mexican housecleaner with a big dusty Dyson, Soli would have gone ahead with it. But the thing they showed her? It was so clean, too clean a thing for the mess she was in. It didn't match. It didn't match her. The whole scene—the clinic, the nice people, the astronaut vacuum with its sterile, gaping eye. None of it was meant for her.

The realization began at a low hum. They'd be sucking something out of her body that she had put there—something, even, that Checo had put there. She thought back to the warm pulse of his chest, their first early morning together, his hands on her waist, the graveled cheek. A desirous ache shot down her side. She stopped herself. Her memories of him she'd have to fold lovingly away, to be brought out the next time and the next, for as long as they would last. But this, she knew: What lived inside her—and the mere thought of it sent through her a throb of energy—what lived inside her was all she had left of Checo. Their together-invention. Boy beast, night spawn, prince of the rails.

Already, she felt the thrust of new life inside her, the kick of her will. The answer rang between her ears. This was her baby, not Silvia's. This was hers.

And so she got herself out of there.

She made sure to get the money back, because Silvia would be pissed as hell if Soli forgot. She was already preparing for Silvia to call her an idiot. And possibly, she wouldn't have been wrong. But this wasn't about Silvia not being wrong. This was about Soli being right. Once Silvia pointed out the truth of what was inside her, Soli knew it as surely as she'd known anything. This thing, growing inside and filling her breasts with promise, this thing was the same as her. It matched her better than anything or anyone she'd known.

She spent that afternoon with Daniel and Aldo. They came home from school and she fed them cereal. Aldo and Daniel had a father whom Soli had never seen, in photos or flesh. Aldo looked like Silvia and Daniel looked like some man. Daniel's hair was golden brown, and fell to his shoulders like a prince's. He smiled easily and laughed at any joke Soli cared to lob his way. Aldo's hair was black, his eyes two drops of molasses. He liked to walk around with his pants off, and Soli was struck by his tree-trunk thighs. If Daniel was a prince, Aldo was a warrior. The boys knew where everything was; they'd been feeding themselves since they were in preschool. But it felt good to make them something anyway, even if it was only Cheerios with milk and chocolate syrup. They sat on the sofa on either side of her, bookends around their hidden cousin, and Soli told them about Popocalco. She liked the way their eyes fixed on hers and watched her lips move. They burrowed into her stories, chewed them up and swallowed them.

That evening, Silvia returned.

"Did you do it?"

Soli didn't answer.

"You did do it. You found the place? You took the money? Did you take the money I gave you?"

Soli rose and found her bag. Inside was the envelope stuffed with cash.

"Here," she said. She held out the envelope, unable to hide the shake in her hand. "Now I owe you nothing."

Silvia looked at it, looked at Soli. She blinked rapidly. Her eyebrows dove into each other. The silence palpitated.

There was nothing Silvia could do but take the money, count it, and fold it into her palm. Soli was certain she was angry, but there was no way of knowing whether to expect a hurricane or a silent freeze. So she locked herself in the bathroom to allow the reaction, whatever it was, to pass.

At dinner, Silvia said nothing of what Soli had or hadn't done. "I have a job for you," she announced. "It's with a family called Cassidy."

"What is it?"

"Housecleaning. Every day."

"Every day?"

"No weekends, unless they request it."

"Is that normal?"

"No. This is a good job, Soli. Normally? You'd be cleaning four houses a day. Five. You're my family, but you've still got to work."

She nodded.

"This job I would have taken myself. But you can have it now"—she nodded at Soli's middle—"because of that one."

"WHAT ARE YOUR PLANS?" Silvia asked the next morning.

Soli shrugged. She'd have two free days before the job began. "I'll walk around. See things."

Silvia stood with her hands on hips, trying to find something wrong with this. "Okay," she finally said. "But remember, 2020 Channing. All right? Don't forget that address. A lot of these places look the same at first. I don't want you calling me, lost."

"Okay."

"Write it on your brain."

"It's written on my soul, Silvia."

"And don't talk to the police. You need directions or something, ask in a store."

"Okay. Silvia?"

"What?"

"Where's the tortilleria?"

Silvia shook her head and laughed, then ushered the boys out the door.

Soli stepped out to the sidewalk later that morning, and for the first time since she'd left Popocalco, she had a sense of being in a place, a fixed and real place that wouldn't slide from under her feet with the next train or truck. The Mexican sun had slipped under the horizon to find a new life, and so had Soli. If what the sun found was Berkeley, then happiness was the only option. Everyone seemed happy in this green, misty place, and everyone as healthy as humans could be. How green the city looked those first days. How exuberant! Only later would she notice the smog that rolled between buildings in the humid autumn, the days when the fog refused to lift. For now, every breath was a surprise. Carbonated, almost, when a dizzying gust blew in from the ocean. The air in Berkeley sparked in her throat, awoke the hairs in her nostrils and whistled through her eye sockets until she was certain she could think more clearly than she'd ever thought before.

"I DON'T KNOW what you plan on doing now," Silvia said the evening before she started at the Cassidys', "but you can stay here as long as you want. This job is lots of money, and quick, so you'll have no trouble paying your way. And you'll look after the boys when I need you to. And then if you last, you might even have some money of your own."

Soli hadn't known when she'd left Popocalco that she'd be paying Silvia back, and she wondered if Papi had known. Family was family, she'd thought. Family didn't send one another bills. In any case, she was stuck, and before long, she would start to feel sick and exhausted, and she would have no one to turn to but Silvia. She feared she'd eventually be too big to reach a dustpan, much less scrub a toilet. But she couldn't think about that. The only option was to get started.

"And, Silvia?"

"Yes."

"What about the coyote?"

"What coyote?"

Soli told her about the onion truck, the man who'd gripped her arm and known her name and her hometown, the three thousand dollars. Silvia shook her head, as if Soli were to blame again.

"If they come," she said, "we pay them. If they don't, we don't."

Silvia had done well for herself. She'd always been more a woman than a girl, and now she carried herself with the authority of someone much older than twenty-seven. After nine years in the States, she had an apartment and a television and a microwave. Every week, women arrived at her doorstep with envelopes of cash, which Silvia counted out. They were from Ecuador, Honduras, Mexico, Colombia. Silvia had found them at different times, struggling, nearly homeless, and went about rescuing each one, finding her a place to stay and a cleaning job, making life livable in this America, all for the good of her soul and a tidy thirty percent commission. They relaxed a little when Silvia handed back their share. Some of them even sat down, crossed their ankles, and talked. Mostly they spoke about this family or that, the married couples who slept separately, the children who never deigned to pick up their own toys. And they talked about the people they knew—so-and-so who'd been joined by a sister or nephew, or who'd been picked up and sent to detention, or who'd been blessed with another baby, or who was jobless now and living with his aunt. But aside from these short visits, Silvia seemed not to have friends. "I don't have time for friends," she had said.

To Soli's ledger she added *$3,000*, written clearly. The amount seemed insurmountable. It dwarfed the other sums, the thirty dollars per week for food, the ten dollars for gas and electricity, the spurts of paltry expense that appeared for Soli's new shoes, for the two pairs of pants and three shirts designed to fit her expanding belly. Three thousand dollars.

"No big deal," Silvia said. "Let's wait and see if they come. And if they do, you'll start paying me an extra three hundred a month, and we'll take care of it in no time."

Soli was grateful for her levelheaded cousin, but there were things she never could or would tell her. Silvia had a visa, had arrived in America whole and clean. How would Soli explain the daily desperation, the ceaseless grapple of trust and fear, the prospect of crawling from one country to another in a suffocating tunnel, saddled like a burro with sacks of white powder? How to tell the story of what grew inside her those days on the trains—not the child, but the will to fight?

"Get a cell phone," Silvia said. "Pay-as-you-go." She bought one for

Soli, and added the cost to the "owed" column of her accounts. Silvia taught Soli English. Soli already knew how to ask for the nearest hospital and say that it was raining, but Silvia taught her the phrases she'd actually need. *Excuse me?* instead of *What?* "You say *what* too many times and you start to sound estupida." *Same time next week? Should I do laundry? Can I have a raise?* This one, she said, was not to be used right away. Or often. *Will you leave a key outside? Sixty dollars. Eighty dollars. Twenty dollars an hour.* This last one was Soli's favorite. It rolled from her tongue like pillowy thunder. She said it like an American. Twennydollasanowah. "Don't use that one yet," said Silvia. "You'll start at six." She taught Soli the names of the cleaning products the gabachas liked, taught her the gabacha methods of polishing floors, cleaning tubs, washing dishes, buffing bathroom fixtures. "Don't be leaving the kitchen sponge in a yogurt container full of water," she said. "Those were the old ways. The gabachas like their sponges squeezed *dry*. And set to the side. Parallel with the sink." She'd introduced her to the vacuum cleaner. This one looked nothing like a rocket. Soli played with it, flattened her hand to its belly, let it suck at the skin of her palm, until Silvia told her to cut it out.

Silvia had other instructions: "The police. The second they stop you for anything—*anything*—they can call immigration. Just keep your head down."

"Okay."

"Don't do anything wrong. Don't even pick your nose!"

"I don't."

"And don't cross the street unless the signal tells you to, okay? You don't want a policeman asking you questions. You know the signals?" Soli shrugged. "White man walking? Means you can go. Big red hand? Means you stay put. Just like in Oaxaca."

"I've got it," Soli said.

"You've got it?"

"Yes."

"Okay?"

"Okay."

"Okay?"

For weeks Soli would stand very still at empty crosswalks, waiting for the walking white man, certain that the police would come blaring around the corner the second she stepped off the curb. She stayed put while others streamed past her. At crosswalks without a signal, she stood perfectly still, unsure of what to do in the absence of the white man. In most cases, she waited a good long while, made sure no one was watching, and ran like hell.

THE NEXT MORNING, Soli got off the bus at a corner of the city canopied by oaks. People streamed by in pairs and trios. Soon, Soli would know this corner well. She would know it was Shattuck and Vine, that in one direction lay the university, in another the water, and behind her the hills. Around her spread the Gourmet Ghetto.

Let's make one thing clear. Soli had seen ghettos. This was no ghetto. All she saw were women pushing their babies in strollers, a few fathers who looked like movie stars, the young on bicycles and the old in sunhats, seated at café tables. The salty warmth of baking bread drifted over the rooftops to nuzzle her, like a cat on her shoulder, the moment she stepped off the bus.

In Popocalco, the young men had left. The town rattled with their absence, and only the newly built houses gave evidence that they still existed somewhere in the world. But Soli remembered them. And the roads, stretching empty, remembered them, too. In Berkeley, there were people everywhere. Students finished their degrees and dragged their feet, people left their high-paying careers and retired here. Streaming in constantly were the academics and vagrants of the world, with their doctorates and dogs on strings. Buying bungalows and hybrid cars were the young families who had good jobs and helpful parents and custom-built child-carrying bicycles. They all stayed and lived and took up room. They pulsed down the sidewalks and pushed into lanes of traffic. They stood in line at bakeries and pizzerias and surged through outdoor farmers' markets as if fresh herbs and homemade kombucha were all that could matter in the world.

She was learning that in Berkeley, even beautiful things were small. From the street, the Cassidy house was nowhere to be seen. It hid somewhere in a tumble of vines and crimson trumpet blossoms. She fought through the brush until she reached the front door, crossed herself, and kissed her thumb. Somewhere in that lovely mess of vines she found a doorbell, which she rang.

A rush of toenails on the floor, sharp barking. Someone scolding a dog. "Toto! Toto! Toto, no!" The door opened and before her stood Toto the elephantine dog, a lady, and a little girl. "Down, Toto!" Soli smiled at the profanity, even as the dog leapt for her shoulders. The woman, struggling to grab the dog by the collar, was tall, with red hair. From where she stood, Soli could smell the coffee on her breath, and the sweet waft of a blossom that she recognized but could not name. The woman caught hold of the dog and dragged him into the house, calling, "Come in! And shut the door!"

The little girl's name couldn't be pronounced. The mother said it easily enough, but it sat like a fuzz on Soli's tongue. The mother said it twice more, and spelled it—S-a-o-i-r-s-e—which didn't help. Soli worried for the little girl and her strange little name.

"It's Celtic," Mrs. Cassidy told her, "traditionally Irish. It's part of our heritage. We want her to be in touch with who she is, you know?" In Popocalco, women had names their grandmothers had, and their grandmothers before them. Only politicians spoke of heritage. She would call the little girl *m'ija*.

The Cassidys lived in a bungalow that smelled of green plants and wood. That first morning, it was plain to see why they wanted her every day. This house would need a strict daily purge, just to keep it from soiling itself. The bookshelves were piled with ceramic trinkets, things that seemed to be made by schoolchildren but which, she found out later, were really quite expensive. The kitchen was more of a jungle than a kitchen, with plants that hung from the ceiling and pots of herbs crowding the windowsill above the sink. The sink! The sink was a work of art, a surrealist sculpture of balancing pots and a chicken carcass, dishes upon dishes upon dishes, a leaning tower of refuse. It smelled of old food and damp cloth. Soli's stomach lurched and she feared she would be sick right there, that this house and the baby inside would not be getting along.

From the kitchen the señora led her to the master bedroom. "Every day," she said, "Every day? Yes?" Soli nodded. The señora pointed to the bed, the carpet, the dresser. "Questo," she said. "Questo y questo, ma no questo." She pointed to the closet. "Sí?"

Soli followed her finger, piecing together what seemed to be a mélange of Spanish and Italian, when the señora gave up and switched to English.

"I'm sorry about the mess, Soli. You can see why we needed you. Brett's been in Hong Kong for a month and things are getting just completely wacky. I'm not a messy person."

Soli smiled.

"But you can see that there's a lot of work to do. So take your time, help yourself to anything in the kitchen. Okay? Mi casa es su casa. Or whatever." She scoffed at herself and left the room.

"Thank you" was all Soli could say. She sniffed a curtain and frowned. This was most certainly not her casa.

8.

KAVYA HAD BOOKED THEM INTO A BED-AND-BREAKFAST. That Saturday they drove to Calistoga, a bottle of prosecco rolling in the backseat. In her purse sat a hopeful bottle of lubricant. That morning, Rishi had found her sticking an ovulation test in her bag. "Please," he'd said. "Leave that at home, will you?" She'd acquiesced, but soon after had snuck it back in. She was timing herself religiously now, waiting for mittelschmerz, that sharp ache in her lower abdomen that meant an egg was on its journey. She felt it that morning in the shower: The mittel had arrived, and she was schmerzing like a fiend.

"Let's get away!" Rishi had said, as he buckled his seat belt. She'd smiled. He was trying. But now as she watched him drive, his back hunched, his chin jutting up as he squinted past the steering wheel, Kavya thought a pep talk might be in order. But what to say? Chin up? His already was. Go Nads? She smiled to herself. Finally she settled on "Honey, we are going to have so much sex. This is going to be the most sex . . . filled . . . weekend ever."

Rishi smiled—sadly, she feared.

"It's going to be amazing," she tried. "Sexoballistic."

Surely, this level of wordplay deserved some excitement. Rishi answered: "Does the exit have a number?"

. . .

SEXOBALLISTIC. When Kavya had first messaged him about the trip to Napa Valley, he'd indeed been excited. Kavya was the planner. Without her, Rishi would have spent the rest of his life going to work, eating pizza on weekends, attempting little else. The spa's website featured a courtyard with a pool, a dimly lit dining room, and a couple holding hands across their pool chairs. He thought of driving into the sun, of swirling wine between his cheeks and sleeping in a bed that wasn't his, after his own had grown creaky with child-making, with worry and apprehension and the gray chill of weekday mornings. The promised change filled him with lightness born of freedom, neutrality. He even sensed the old Kavya coming back. After months of fruitless effort, his wife had become a slave to a nonexistent child. Her cool independence had curled and blackened and burned away. The woman in his home wasn't Kavya. His Kavya wasn't helpless. He could have had any number of women who blew this way and that with gusts of fate, crying out to be rescued. He'd fallen for Kavya because she moved straight and strong as a bullet. And so, this trip to Napa felt like a step in the right direction, a refortification of Kavya's will. Yes, they were taking the trip in order to have the sort of relaxed intercourse from which babies seemed to spring. But within this plan lay a reassuring sense of confidence, a certainty that if anything could conjure a child, it was wine stored in oak barrels, an afternoon of whirlpools and steam rooms.

But when she'd turned to him in the car like that, squeezed his knee in that motherly way—*Honey, we are going to have* so *much sex*—he saw the hollow at the heart of this trip. She was hoping, without reserve. The bed in which they'd sleep—or not sleep—wasn't neutral territory. It was a petri dish, acidic with expectation, doomed even before its covers were thrown back. If this trip didn't conjure a child, he didn't know what would become of Kavya, the girl he knew.

Suddenly the prospect of spending a whole weekend alone with Kavya, in the compression chamber of a sauna, a hotel room, with nothing to do but stare into each other's eyes, was more daunting than he'd expected. Better, perhaps, to spend their weekend crossing paths at home, stepping out to run errands, losing themselves in solitary Internet forays. But as rows of grapevines flashed past, the day started to feel right: the open sky, the reliable warmth of the valley, the roads growing wide and the wineries appearing, one after another, each with a stately sign at its entryway. His hesitation trailed off with the morning mist.

RISHI PULLED UP to a low stucco building with a Spanish-tiled drive. Inside, enormous wood chandeliers hung from the ceiling, and the lobby was lit with candles. It was meant to be romantic, and it was. A woman at the counter greeted them and led them to a sitting room, where a server brought glasses of cucumber water. This room too was candlelit. The sofa they sat on was velvet, soft, enveloping. Rishi sat back. Kavya sat upright. "Sit back," he said. "You look a little tense."

He was right. She sat back.

"This is nice," he said, and reached out to smooth the crease from her forehead. She grabbed his wrist and brought it to the couch. It was like they were holding hands, but weren't. Other couples moved in and out of the room. Through the gloaming, Rishi nodded at another man and woman. The other couple sat on a sofa on the opposite side of the lounge, linked hands, and gazed at each other.

Rishi leaned in. He couldn't help himself. "This is one of those places."

Kavya realized he was right. It was a place people came to save their marriages and conceive their children. Of course no one talked about it that way. What they called it was relaxation. A relaxation destination. She didn't care what people called it. She'd try anything. She'd try a full-price room booking, expensive dinners, and inscrutable wine tastings, if they brought about a baby.

In the name of relaxation, they booked a couple's massage. In a darkened room that smelled of hot stone, they lay on parallel tables. She lay on her front, her eyes closed. Rishi's eyes rested on the pale, small cushion of her breast that pressed against the table. He thought back to a much earlier vintage of his wife, the one he'd known in college.

"Hey," he said, his eyes fluttering to her breast.

She followed his gaze. "Get lost," she said, but smiled.

It had been a very long time since they'd lain quietly, side by side, free from the racket of plans or worries or the clamoring unspoken. The failures of the past year had turned Kavya's spine to a scepter of fear, and it took a good deal of work to get her to release. But when she did, the fear spilled out of her. It slid off her shoulders and trailed in quiet tears from her eyes. She saw him notice, and smiled at herself, extracting a hand from the white sheet to wipe at her nose and eyes. Rishi wanted to climb off his table and gather her up. Joint by joint, he would fold her together if he could. But Kavya's eyes were closed now, the massage therapist working on her calves. All he could do was reach a hand out. She sensed this, eyes still closed, and reached out to meet him. For the rest of the hour, they held hands across their tables, like the couple on the website.

BEFORE DINNER, back in their hotel room, she slipped her arms around his waist. He had tweezed the center of his browline. His jaw was clean-shaven. He smelled of cedar. A drop of shower dew rested in the divot of his lip.

She whispered, "I feel like I'm ovulating. Should we try now?"

Rishi's arms clenched. He let go of her, just slightly, but enough for her to notice.

"What's wrong?" she asked.

"I don't— I don't— Never mind." In Kavya's eyes he saw a tremor, in her smile a lopsided incline.

"What's wrong?" she asked.

"I thought we would just see how things go, you know? Maybe go to dinner first?"

"Really? This is a problem for you?"

"Well, no—"

"You're really saying this?"

"Yes. No." He pressed his palms to his eyes. "No. I don't know." He cursed himself now.

He didn't want to think about conceiving, he told her. And he didn't want her to ask him if he was ready. He didn't want to make babies that weekend. He wanted to be with her.

"Maybe this was a mistake," he said.

A long pause followed, during which neither of them moved or made a sound.

It was quite clear, in that moment, that nothing would happen easily for them; that wasn't the way Rishi and Kavya worked. They wouldn't get their happy surprise, their unexpected blessing. Perhaps the happy surprise had come when they found each other. Easy gifts had come and gone, and left them only with each other.

She stepped away from him. She'd put on a red dress, low cut, her hair still slick with massage oil. She wore lipstick and her skin shone. But at her center, she was dried out, empty. Her eyes had lost their luster, two wood chips sunk deep in their sockets. When he took her hand, he felt the quake in her fingers. She slumped to the bed, as if her legs had given out. She sat hunched. Hollow.

"I'm sorry," he said. His wife. Wounded. He felt cruel. She wanted nothing more than to give love. He wanted nothing more than to bring her back.

He picked up her limp hand. "Can we start over?" he asked.

She neither spoke nor pulled away, but let him wrap his arm around her. He hugged her harder, and her head fell to his chest. They sat this way for longer than they should have and let the clock tick past their reservation time. When they descended to the dining room twenty minutes later, they sat at the bar and Rishi ordered two glasses of champagne.

After dinner, they went back upstairs. The afternoon sun had baked the room's interior, and by nightfall it was stifling. "We're going to have a baby, Kavya." His voice cracked, something that normally would have made his wife laugh. "You hear me?"

She shook her head and lay down. He followed, and they lay on the covers, shoes on, facing each other. They spent many minutes this way, gazing at the walls, at each other. She seemed hardly able to look at him. He studied the plain of her cheek, watched as the words, the ones they'd been avoiding, found their way into her mouth, rolled over and under her tongue, and dropped out of her, at last: "Fertility treatments." They weighed a ton, those words.

He took her hand. "That seems to work for some."

"I know."

"Let's start there."

She searched his face. "Are you sure you want to try? Can we afford it?"

Rishi couldn't fathom the depth or the cost of such a project. He knew he wanted Kavya back. He knew she needed him to say yes. That was all he knew. "Yes."

"Okay." She nodded. She hoisted herself onto her elbows and looked a long while at Rishi. "Okay." She rose to her feet and walked to the mirror. He watched her smooth down her hair, straighten her dress, and throw back the fine sweep of her shoulders.

They made love wordlessly, heavily. Rishi succumbed to soft snores.

Fertility treatments. When she'd spoken the words, when Rishi took them in hand and said yes, her hope awakened. Now, it shimmered up her spine and across her scalp. She would not sleep. She settled for lying still, so as not to wake Rishi, letting her thoughts course past. She listened to other couples slipping keys into doors, to the chink of a room-service tray, to splashing, around midnight, from the courtyard pool. And before she was aware of having slept, she woke to the morning light that winked between the curtains.

9.

EVERY MORNING, SEÑORA CASSIDY LEFT THE HOUSE IN running shoes and black leggings, and came home with fresh bread from the bakery around the corner, and a scone that she ate with her tea. "Fresh from the Gourmet Ghetto," she beamed, and held the baguette high.

It wasn't clear if the señora had a job. She took Saoirse to preschool and returned in the afternoons, then spent the remaining day wandering from room to room, or sitting on the front porch with her arms wrapped around her knees. She seemed, much of the time, to be thinking very hard, to be lost in a cloud of a plan, sipping from her blue goblet.

But this was a good family to work for. Yes, they hoarded like rats and there were times Soli wanted to tour the house with a garbage bag and throw out everything she saw. And Mrs. Cassidy tried most days to speak her incomprehensible patois, ending every attempt with a laugh and an explanation that she'd never taken Spanish at school. The upside was that Soli was learning English and even a little Italian. And most important, she had a job.

She also had Silvia's rules. "*Never* throw a piece of paper away," Silvia had told her. "Even if it looks like trash, even if it stands up and begs you to end things. Just straighten it up and make it look neater. You

never know what it is these people want to hold on to. Believe me." She
wasn't wrong.

There were other rules to remember: "Lift everything off the countertop and clean under it," Silvia instructed. "They'll check and they'll
know if you got lazy and cleaned around things. Always bring your own
food and your own water. Never—NEVER—open the fridge to help
yourself, no matter what they say. Think of it!" Silvia said. "If they saw
you with your trasero sticking out of their fridge? They won't like it if
they see it, no matter what they say." So every day, Soli brought some
bread and meat and fruit.

Soon the bread and meat and fruit were not enough. As her child
grew inside her, he demanded more. She wasn't sick with pregnancy—
she was the opposite. She ate like a beast in a cave. She found herself
addicted, thinking only of her next meal, where it would come from,
what it would taste like, how much of it she could cram down the hole
before anyone saw her. If she could have smothered herself with bread
and meat and fruit and yogurt, she might have stopped praying altogether, certain she'd found paradise.

And so it was hard to stick to, this rule of Silvia's. Sometimes the
señora would leave her morning scone uneaten, resting on a plate by the
sink like it was ready for the garbage. It wasn't easy, but every day Soli
covered that scone in plastic wrap like it was a holy relic and left it where
it was.

"My trasero," she announced to Silvia, "is staying out of trouble."

The baby raged inside her. He raged inside her and sent her to the
fridge with a wet yearning. Wiping down the shelves, she gazed at what
she could not have. Every morning she played this game with herself.
Then one day—it was bound to happen—she found herself reaching for
a tinfoil parcel on the low refrigerator shelf. She watched, as if in a
dream, as her hand yanked fingerfuls of meat from the foil bundle. She

chewed, her lips slipping with grease. Chicken. Lemon. Garlic. Before she could stop herself, she grabbed again at the meat, and again.

"That happened to me, too," Silvia said later that evening. "It must be a thing with our family, you know? We don't get sick, we turn into warthogs."

"I know this baby's appetite," Soli confided. "It comes from the father. From Checo." Checo's hunger had been incessant, born of days and days on a train. The wind, the air, the ceaseless sun, made them all hungry as animals. But Checo had eaten more monstrously than any of them.

La Bestia, the great freight train, had moved through Mexico like an angry python. It had sucked the open air into its belly; it would have sucked the dozy traveler beneath its wheels. But the beast in Soli was a different sort of monster. Its only menace was its hunger, and its hunger was insatiable.

THERE WERE THINGS she got used to in the Cassidy house. Like the dog. Toto. She was greeted each morning in the most profane way, with Toto digging his nose between her thighs. But soon she grew accustomed even to this. "It's just me, Toto," she'd say. "Same old Soli." She learned to live with him and, eventually, to like him. The little girl grew fond of Soli as well, began to hug her around the waist when she came home from school. She followed her from room to room as she cleaned, introduced her to her toys, of which she had many; but the toys she had most of were Barbie dolls. She carried them through the kitchen like an armful of kindling. As Soli picked muck from the corners of the windowsills, the little girl lined them up against the wall to balance on their gruesomely angled feet.

"See this one, Soli? See? See? See? See?"

These people probably believed that in Popocalco they had one Barbie doll, Soli thought, and that they all shared it, and that one summer when the corn wasn't growing they fried the one Barbie and shared it among the hungry village. In fact, the citizens of Popocalco had a wealth of Barbie dolls. They were brought by a missionary who visited the school, and by some miracle had enough Barbie dolls for all the girls, and enough baseballs for the boys. Where he got them and why he bothered coming to Popocalco, nobody seemed to know. They were Catholic enough without his help. But for the Barbies, they were grateful.

"This one is Malibu Barbie."

"Malibu?" Soli asked. Some of the names she understood, others were only sound.

"This is Doctor Barbie," she continued. "And Fireman Barbie, and Pet Vet Barbie and Teacher Barbie and Bride Barbie and Pizza Barbie and News-Lady Barbie. She has a microphone."

"And Mexican Housecleaner Barbie?"

The little girl bent over with little-girl laughter. "There's no Mexican Housecleaner Barbie!"

"M'ija," she said, "I could have told you that."

"You're a silly lady," the girl pronounced, and trailed from the room, chattering.

The señora was Mug-of-Tea Barbie. She was a Barbie doll brought to Earth and wrapped in wool, holding a rough-hewn blue mug, the sort of thing Soli's grandmother had drunk from. Her eyes were round and stricken and as blue as the mouth of her cup. They took up most of the space on her thin face; they were the most voluptuous things on her body. She had red-brown hair and always wore a sheen of gloss on her lips. She was taller than the fridge. Soli could tell that she'd once possessed the sort of beauty that inspired a twinge of pain, and that she had gotten used to this beauty, taking it for granted even as it began to wither. Her eyes had sunk into deep sockets and her lips spewed creases like cascading vines. Soli wondered why she didn't get them taken away by a doctor. In Mexico, the women with real money didn't have to grow old.

"Nobody here has any goddamn money," Silvia told her. "Even the people who have money don't have money."

Soli asked why.

"It's their houses, their houses are vacuum cleaners that suck up all their money. Those pretty trees? Money. Those nice flowers? Good paint, no water stains? Money and more money."

"But they have *homes*. That's something."

"Mortgages," Silvia said. "They don't have homes. They have mortgages."

Soli grimaced at the word. The syllables themselves stuck in her throat.

"Mort. Gage," Sylvia repeated. "And don't look so worried. You'll never have one."

Mort. Gage. It was a word that got in its own way. It was a word that held within itself a sense of its own limits, an echo of death.

AFTER TWO MONTHS, Mr. Cassidy returned from Hong Kong. Soli had grown so used to their little household of three people and one animal that she'd forgotten about him completely. With no man in the house, there were no men's undershorts to pick up, no shaven hair peppering the bathroom sink, no clouds of aftershave hanging over steamy morning bathrooms. But then, one Monday morning, there he was. She sensed, even before she opened the house door, that something inside it had changed. An odor of the faraway greeted her, mingling with the smell of baking bread that followed her in from the street.

He sat at the kitchen table, unshaven, with the deep tan of a foreign sun. He had the hair of a romantic hero, a thick sweep of it. "¡Hola!" he called. "¡Solimar! ¿Com'estas?" He spoke Spanish, this man, faster even than Soli did. Before him spread an array of teacups and a small black teapot on a stand. On a plate sat a mountain of scones. Her hunger thrashed inside her.

"Where are you from?" he asked in English.

"Mexico."

"Right, oh-*kay*, excellent." He switched back to Spanish: "Where in Mexico?"

She told him.

"I went backpacking through southern Mexico one summer, after college. It was amazing! The mezcal is something else, isn't it? It's really another world out there."

"Sí, señor."

He fell silent, but she stayed put.

He cleared his throat. "So what do you think of the Chiapas situation?"

"Chiapas is very nice," she said. "Very beautiful."

He considered this.

"But the situation? The Zapatistas?" He lifted his hands to the air, as if the situation were beyond his understanding. "What do you *think*?"

Mister, she could have said, I don't think a thing.

Instead she said nothing and stared dumbly at the plate of scones. She didn't know how to speak politics. She'd seen people doing it, men at the cantina in Popocalco who pounded their fists and believed ferociously in what they were saying. But she didn't speak that language. Tossing up an idea would mean having to catch it again, having to actually understand what it was she believed. And what made him think Soli knew a thing about the Zapatistas?

Later, she told Silvia about it.

Silvia clapped her hands and threw her head back with laughter. "No manches! Oh, no no NO! He did not say that to you!" She fell back on the sofa laughing, wiping at her eyes.

"What was I supposed to say to him? Was I supposed to answer?"

"Stop it. The Zapatistas? Stop it!"

"What would you have said?"

"Don't ask me, bruja. No one's asked me a thing like that. He must think you're smart."

"Well, that's his problem if he thinks I'm smart."

"So what did you do?"

"I stared at him like a donkey."

"And what did he do?"

"He gave me a scone."

Maybe because he felt bad for asking her questions she couldn't answer, maybe because she couldn't pull her eyes away from the mountainous plate, Mr. Cassidy had picked up a scone and held it out.

"Have you eaten today?" he asked, the way you'd ask a homeless person or a runaway. Of course she'd eaten that day. The scone was gold-crusted, and red berries pushed through its doughy boulders. She took it. Inside her, the baby leapt for joy. She took it to the other room before she crammed it in her mouth, because she knew that no matter what anyone said or did, no one in that house would truly want to watch her eat.

SOLI LEARNED A NEW WORD that year. Housekeeper. She was the quiet mesh that contained the Cassidy home and kept it whole. Two months passed, and then three. They didn't have time to make a mess when she was there every day. She felt like the house, in some very small way, belonged to her. She was its day nurse, and without her, it would have suffocated, forgotten, beneath the Cassidys' colonies of material possessions.

Now and then, Soli caught the señora watching her through the archway that led from the kitchen to the living room, her arms folded, her head cocked forward. She tried to ignore it, but the woman's eyes sent a current through the house that chilled Soli's arms and quickened her heart. She stuck to her work and didn't look up. She hummed to seem at ease. Every evening, Mrs. Cassidy did a tour of the kitchen, peeking at the dusted shelves, nodding at the spray-cleaned stove. Every evening, Mrs. Cassidy stood before Soli, said *Gracias*, and blanketed her in her ponderous gaze. After Soli gathered her things and left, she could feel the woman's eyes follow her steps down the drive, down the street, until she escaped around the corner.

The Cassidys were waiting for something. Soli just didn't know what. She went over her list of daily tasks with Silvia, to see if she'd been missing something vital.

"You could polish their shoes, I guess," Silvia said. "But it all looks good to me."

Even when Mrs. Cassidy wasn't watching, Soli felt that she was. Watching and waiting. Expecting a miracle of service, of cleanliness? Expecting the saints themselves to rain down their praise? But no. Soli sensed that what the Cassidys wanted had nothing to do with her work. They approved of her in one sense; they seemed to approve deeply of where she'd come from, how she'd struggled. Mrs. Cassidy asked her questions about her life in Mexico, and sometimes received her answers with a slow nod, open lips, wells of empathy. Other times she met her with a quizzical smile, as if Soli's answers had missed the question.

SOLI WAS BRINGING HOME two hundred forty dollars a week. And after Silvia took half of it (For your food and for your passage here, she said. You have no idea how much you eat!) she was left with an acceptable chunk to send home every month. A few hundred dollars could do a lot in Popocalco, and she liked to think that she was giving her parents a home. Working while pregnant was getting harder every day, but she knew how it was for other people—slaving in factories, getting cheated and beaten. On the train, she'd heard stories of how workers were treated and Silvia told her more, about the women in factories who'd been raped, about workers locked indoors for twelve hours a day and paid for only six. "Consider yourself lucky," she said, "to be working for me."

When the baby had been in her for five months, it started to get harder to bend. A weight pulled at her back, anchored her to the ground, and bore down on her knees and feet. She began to sit down—to wipe the table, to wipe the counter. Washing dishes, she leaned on her elbows. She began to sweat in a way she never had before, covered throughout the day in a moist film. It sprung fresh on her face and trickled down her neck, it bloomed in the dip of her back and streamed quietly into her panties. Even the backs of her knees perspired.

One morning, Mrs. Cassidy found her sitting at the kitchen table, her head in her hand, her eyelids drooping.

"Soli!"

She shot to her feet. Too fast. Her head spun and she had to catch herself on the table's edge. She sank back into the chair.

Mrs. Cassidy set her mug of tea on the table. "You're sweating, Soli. Are you ill?" She lay a hand on her forehead. "You're clammy!"

Soli's heart beat faster when she realized the woman wasn't going to ignore this. She wanted an answer.

"Do you need to go home? I'll make you some tea. Stay there."

"¿Señora?" She didn't know how Americans turned this particular phrase, but the señora sat before her and she had to say something, so she stated what she knew.

"I have a baby."

Mrs. Cassidy frowned. Soli pointed to her stomach. "Baby."

The señora covered her mouth and chirped like she'd swallowed a bird.

"You're pregnant?" she said. "You're pregnant."

She leaned closer, looked right into Soli's face. Soli cowered, waiting for the slap. None came.

"Soli, you're *pregnant*." A smile bloomed, and she was beautiful. "But where's the father?" The smile fell.

Soli laughed inside when people called Checo *the father*. To her, a *father* was Papi. A father was a man who scratched his belly and talked back to the radio. Checo was no more a father than the wind was. He'd blown through her, woken her up one day and kept her breathing. And then, as quick as the wind, he was gone.

Señora Cassidy picked up a notepad and started flipping through the pages. "What are you going to do, Soli? What are you going to do? Is your sister helping?"

"My cousin."

"Oh." She stopped flipping. "Does that mean something in your culture? I mean, will she help you still?"

Help me to what, she wondered.

"Okay, let's plan. We'll have to plan." At the far end of the house, the little girl was belting out a song. "You don't have kids, Soli, do you? Do you have kids back in Mexico?"

"No, Mrs. Cassidy."

"My goodness, Soli. Oh, honey. You have no idea, do you? You really have no idea what you're in for." She sat back and shook her head and looked like she might start crying. "Is the father in the picture?"

She didn't understand this at first.

"Is the father here?" She rammed her finger into the table. "In Berkeley? Does he live with you?"

"No, señora. He does not."

10.

Soli had started to enjoy her walks home in the evenings, when the autumn air was welcoming and the soft chill drew a finger up her spine. Around her, the city bloomed. Rosebushes rose above aeoniums, beach grass tickled the trunks of Japanese maples, princess plants sheltered yuccas. In Berkeley, the plants grew over one another like the people did, around and under and in between one another. They held each other up and kept each other down, and all the while they seemed wholly encased in their own private ecosystems.

When she left the Cassidy home each day, crossing Shattuck Avenue to the bus stop, she noticed how soft the sidewalks were. Here in Berkeley, the ground forgave, and through these hills the people walked softly, like angels. They shopped and laughed and sat on the grassy median between lanes of traffic to eat their gourmet pizza. She boarded the bus that would take her home and pushed her way into a window seat. Always, she pressed her forehead to the window and searched the faces that streamed past, slowly first, then faster as the bus picked up speed, and slower, slower, slower, as it came to another stop.

Sometimes she thought she saw Checo. She saw him in the young men who clustered around coffee shops with wild hair and stony shoulders. Some wore headbands and bracelets made of string. She imagined that Checo would end up somewhere remarkable, not as a fruit picker or factory worker or gardener, but a groundbreaker. A world-changer. Or else the companion of a rich young woman with short hair who hated her father. He would be taken care of, or he would be extraordinary. If she saw him again, would she claim him? What if she saw him right then and there, on a crowded strip of sidewalk? Would she drag him into her life of babies and buses and houses to clean? Or would she leave him to be young and blanketed in sun, lounging in the legs of a fairy-haired girl?

The day she'd told the señora of her pregnancy, she left the Cassidys' with a stronger sense that her child was coming.

"What happened to *you*?" Silvia sprang from the doorway and un-buttoned her coat, then landed on the sofa next to her, breathing heavily. "You feeling all right? Bueno." She placed a hand on Soli's belly and called into it, "Bueno, que tal?"

"I told them I'm pregnant," she said.

Silvia sat up. "No, you didn't. What did they say? I told you not to tell yet. What happened?"

And so she said to Silvia what the señora had said to her. Soli would work for them for as long as she could, and then she would stop. Silvia grunted at this like they'd conned her. She rubbed her cheek and sighed.

"And then," Soli said, "I'll be their nanny."

Silvia had always been beautiful to Soli. She was her strong-armed and lusty-haired cousin, her eyes fierce with life. She moved like a woman who'd woken up and figured out how to live this dream. But now Silvia let out a small laugh and grew very quiet.

"Housecleaner to nanny. That's a big step up, Soli." Silvia stood still, considering her. "You know a lot about children, do you?" There was something in her voice that didn't make sense. "Okay, then. You'll keep working. And you'll pay me back. For the coyote, if he comes. For all the rest."

"Silvia."

"What."

"You're not angry?"

She looked into Soli's face like she was trying to read her. "You are lucky, Soli. Do you know how lucky?"

At the time, she didn't know. So she said the thing that she did know: "She said something about yoga."

Silvia frowned.

"The señora, she wants me to do something called yoga for pregnant women. She wants to take me."

The corner of Silvia's mouth quivered, a smile that she tried to fold away. But the laughter boiled up inside her and sputtered out, first low and then high-pitched, a guffaw, a hooting like a drunken owl. Silvia laughed for a good long time.

As Soli's middle began to expand, sleeping on the sofa became impossible. "We'll move you to the boys' room," Silvia said. "They can sleep out here for a while." Daniel and Aldo lit up at the prospect of trading their double bed for sleeping bags and the room with the television. The switch was made. Waking up two, three times a night now, Soli would catch sight of the flickering television in the living room, its volume turned low, the boys sleeping before it or lying awake with eyes glazed over at three in the morning, four.

One night, Soli lay in bed, staring into the darkened room, when the door opened. In the faint light stood a boy. Daniel. He entered, dragging his sleeping bag behind him. Aldo followed. The thrill of all-night television had worn off, and the boys wanted their room back. Daniel laid out his sleeping bag, then helped Aldo straighten his. The boys stretched themselves out side by side, parallel to Soli's bed. Soon they were asleep, the three of them to a room. And that's how things stayed.

. . .

SHE DREAMT ONE NIGHT of trains, trains slowing to a halt, trains stopping, at last. She stumbled in her sleep and jarred herself awake, just as she'd first tripped over the solid earth, stepping from a train onto stationary ground.

"I found you a truck going west," Checo had told her. "It'll be here in the morning."

"And you?"

"I'm going east, amorcita. We're leaving tonight."

"I'm coming with you."

"No. You can't."

"I will."

"You won't make it through the desert, Soli. I can't be responsible for you."

"Who says you're responsible for me? I can take care of myself."

He grinned, then looked very sad and said, "Okay. Come along if you want."

They piled onto the bed of a truck. Around them, sacks of flour rose in solid stacks, higher than their heads. Pepe was gone, and now they were five: Soli, Checo, Flaco, Mario, and Nutsack. The boys had stopped treating her differently—they talked about women and passed gas. When they needed to, they angled themselves through the truck slats and pissed with the wind. All of them but Checo, who was apparently above such biological requirements.

The sacks were packed in tightly enough not to avalanche when the truck made a sudden brake, but the air was thick with flour. Opening her backpack, she drank down one bottle of water, then two. With each bump in the road, clouds of flour puffed and settled in her throat. She drank three bottles of water that morning, which was the wrong thing to do.

Soli had to go. What's a girl trapped on a truck bed to do? Does she piss on herself? Does she squat in the corner and endure the stares? Does she angle herself through a slat and hope for the best? These were all possibilities, but they weren't her possibilities: She wouldn't be pissing in front of Checo and the others. She banged on the wall of the driver's car. She yelled. Her bladder burned like a lit stove.

Checo, then Flaco and Mario, stood up and joined in the banging and shouting, but they soon gave up.

"I'll find something for you," Checo said. He rummaged in her backpack and came up with an empty water bottle. Soli shook her head. "Flaco," he ordered, "give me your hat." Flaco grunted and pulled his cap over his eyes.

"Checo, please," Soli said. Checo shook the backpack, emptied it of everything, and handed it over. Soli began to weep and laugh, and then bent over with pain.

At a certain point, a girl loses hold of her possibilities. So Soli stood where she stood, her head pressed to a flour sack, and because she could not stop it, she let it go. The urine gushed between her legs. It announced itself more loudly than the engine or the growl of the road. It spilled with joy, its own private gusto. The boys listened too, their heads down. Their eyes hovered on the pool that formed at her feet. Only Checo walked over, put his hands on her shoulders, and pressed his cheek to hers. She cried tears as hot as the piss that streamed down the truck bed and caked the flour and fell through the cracks to the road. Her thighs burned against the soaked fabric of her pants, but in slow, halting steps she walked back to her seat, and for minutes, there was silence. To escape their eyes, Soli closed hers.

THE MORNING OF THE SECOND DAY, they stopped outside a massive yellow building. "It's a tortilla factory," Checo explained. Soli had never thought of tortillas made in factories. If pushed, she would have accepted that they existed, somewhere in the world. Just not in her world. The thought of warm, fresh tortillas brought desire dancing through her.

"What food do we have?" she asked Checo.

"Almost nothing left. A little bread. I'm saving it."

"That's all? What are we supposed to eat?"

He glanced at the others, then back at her. "I told you this wouldn't be easy."

When the door of the truck bed rolled open, three men jumped in. They each grabbed a flour sack and hurled it off the bed, where another man caught it and stalked off to the factory. They grabbed and hurled, grabbed and hurled, until the bed was empty. And for a good two hours, Soli and the boys had the truck bed to themselves. They stretched out. Soli slept in Checo's arms. They awoke to Mario and Nutsack playing a balancing game, each trying to stand on their hands as the truck sped along the bumpy road. Flaco was turning cartwheels, falling drunkenly at each landing. And then the truck stopped again.

Onions were loaded on, crates and crates of red onions. The boys groaned at the smell.

"You don't smell much better," Checo said to them. "At least now we don't have to smell *you*." And so they set off, riding among onions. Soli's pants had dried by now, and she began to think that it wasn't so terrible, this northern voyage, that the stories of danger and death had come from those too cowardly to make the trip themselves. This was an adventure, truly. She was choosing her own path, alongside Checo's, and she'd never been happier.

When the truck slowed again and came to a halt, she called out, "What's next, muchachos? Garlic and cheese?"

The boys grew still, peering through the crates to the door.

"Nutsack, you're in luck," she tried again. "With the garlic and cheese we won't even smell *you* now!"

Checo shushed her. He stood. The others stood as well, searching for something to see, when all there was to see were crates and crates of onions. The truck grew absolutely silent. And then she heard it: the shuffle of footsteps outside, gruff voices she didn't recognize, followed by the truck driver's voice. He was answering them, and though she couldn't make out his words, she heard each statement end with an upward inflection. And then she heard shouts, a hasty stampede of feet from the front of the truck to the back. And then the truck bed rolled slowly open. Next to her, she heard Checo swallow.

She whispered, "What is it?"

"Shh!" He squeezed her hand so hard she nearly cried out, but the look on Nutsack's face silenced her. Nutsack was breathing hard in the still air. His chest heaved and sank with every breath. They heard voices again.

"How many?"

"Just some men. No money."

"How many?"

"Four. Five."

"Well, which is it?"

"Four."

They waited through a long silence. And at last, they heard a low rumble. Soli sighed. The rumble of an engine, she thought.

"We're going," she said.

Checo shook his head. He looked at Soli now, as he never had before. He looked like he was very, very sorry for what he'd done.

The rumble continued, and then grew closer. They listened, as floods of onions tumbled from their crates, barrelled across the truck bed and onto the ground. The crates moved out from around them, and she was blinded by the glare of a flashlight. Checo shoved her into a corner of the truck bed. "Hide!" A row of onion crates formed a low wall, and she scrambled down behind them.

Heavy hands seized her by the shoulders: Flaco, trying to pull her out.

"No!" she hissed, and sank her teeth into his wrist. Flaco cried out and cursed. And then he froze, the beam of a flashlight trained on his back. Slowly, he turned, shuffled to the mouth of the truck.

"This is all?" a man snarled. "Four fucking men?"

"Look, señor, you're stopping every truck on this road. I don't know what you think you're going to find—"

"Shut up!"

A burly man stomped onto the truck bed and yanked the boys by their shirts. She watched from behind the crates as they were lined up, Checo farthest from the truck, Nutsack closest. In the dark of night, in the glare of the headlights, she could see that the ground was covered in sand. They were nearing the desert. They were almost at the end of their journey. The man who stood before the boys was bald and muscular. He seemed to be wearing a tight black shirt. But no, Soli realized a few moments later—he was shirtless, and covered in a complex collage of ink. She'd never seen a human like this before. Two other tattooed men stood beside him, holding up flashlights, guns slung across their chests.

Her friends were ordered to empty their pockets, and Nutsack fumbled with a watch on his wrist. He handed it to the man and received, in return, a kick in the gut. Mario pulled some pesos from his jeans and shrugged.

"*Pinche baboso.* Don't shrug at me." The man snatched the pesos from Mario's shaking hand. "How about your friend?"

Beside him, Flaco pulled out the linings of his pockets, then held up his wrists.

It was Checo's turn. He stood with his hands on his hips. "I've got nothing for you," he said.

"Empty out your pockets." Checo reached in his pockets.

"I don't believe you," the man said. He called to his cronies, "Get his pants off."

Checo didn't wait for the men. He undid his own zipper, let his jeans fall to the ground, and stepped out of them. He stood in his underwear as a man with a gun riffled through the pockets and came up with nothing.

The first man cocked his chin at Checo. "Okay, then, take off your underwear. We'll see what else you've got."

Checo straightened, his hands behind his back, his chest thrust forward. He didn't move. The tatooed man drew closer and stared him down. Checo stared back, unblinking. For several moments, they waited, each considering the other. The tattooed man let his eyes drift from Checo's face down to his crotch. Then he took a slow stroll and stopped, his face just inches from the back of Checo's head. He stood there a good long while, breathing down Checo's neck and saying nothing. As the seconds ticked down, Checo seemed to grow stronger and more firmly rooted to the earth. He was a boy no longer. He was a man.

And then he ran. Soli almost screamed at the sudden bolt, the drum of his feet and the crack of the rifle. Checo vanished. The three men fired their guns into the dark, but Soli heard nothing—no screams, no indication that Checo had been hit. Either he lay bleeding on the desert floor or he was charging through the night on his own. Either way, he was gone.

She watched the other boys fall, kicked to the ground, kicked in the head, and spat on. When the men finally left, the driver of the truck reappeared. Grunting and muttering weakly to himself, he tossed the crates back onto the truck bed, gathering armfuls of onions from the ground, dropping a few and watching helplessly as they rolled away. Soli stayed hidden behind the crate, until the driver salvaged what he could and rolled the door shut. The engine coughed to life and they took off, leaving the boys behind.

When they stopped again, hours and hours later, Soli was nearly unconscious with hunger. The meager collection of food was gone. The boys had left their backpacks behind, and she'd ransacked them, found and devoured the bread. The other bags had nothing to eat, just bandages and gum, a notepad. The truck door rumbled open, and this time she didn't have the strength to hide. She sat at the center of it, and the driver cursed when he saw her.

"How long have you been here?"

She had no real answer. "Where are we going?"

"North."

"Where north?"

"Denver."

She'd never heard of it. "Is that in the States?"

"Where do you need to go?"

"California. Berkeley. Can you take me?"

He was chewing on something. Whatever it was, he spat to the ground. "I can get you there," he said, and began to shut the door.

"Wait! Do you have any food?"

He disappeared to the front of the truck and returned with more people and more crates of onions. Soli sank inside.

11.

KAVYA AND RISHI WERE KEEN BUDGETERS—THEY HAD TO be, living in Berkeley. The cost of this baby was not in their budget, nor could they have squeezed it into their budget. But still, the checks were written, the credit cards swiped. Their first step was an updated fertility workup: a series of blood tests and an ultrasound. The next step, a hysterosalpingogram, a word that rattled and dinged like a slot machine. A technician threaded a catheter into her cervix and up through the rails of her reproductive system. A contrast dye was injected. With Rishi by her side, one hand on her shoulder, she watched the dye on-screen course through her insides, pass through her fallopian tubes, and signal that they were open for business.

Back at home, Rishi fell to the bed, exhausted. He pulled Kavya down beside him.

"It's beginning," she said.

"It is." They listened to their breath fall in and out of sync.

A week later, Kavya was scheduled for an endometrial biopsy. She barely noticed the spear-ended salad tongs they stuck inside her to pinch away at the inner lining of her uterus. These were simply instruments of the step-taking. And this particular step proved what she'd hoped: Her uterus was the consummate hostess. And the money that bled from their bank account and soaked through their solvency simply gave her permission to push ahead; the more they spent, the sillier it felt to stop. The fact that their insurance covered none of it didn't matter.

And neither did the daily shots. The first time, Kavya quaked at the thought of jabbing herself. Rishi, bravely, offered to give it a try, but the act produced in him such heaving anxiety that Kavya took back the needle. Soon, the quick jab before her shower grew so routine that it seemed she'd begun every day of her life by gathering a roll of belly fat and stabbing it with a hypodermic. The one egg a month her body had always known was amped up to twelve, twenty, twenty-five eggs. She became a very busy chicken.

It didn't matter that she was sticking herself with needles; it didn't matter that the medicine seeping out of those needles cost hundreds of dollars per half-milliliter. What mattered was that she was *taking steps.* She was doing something that could result in a baby.

And finally, the queen step, for which all other steps had been preparing, was IUI. In the doctor's office, with Neil Diamond playing over the speakers, a wave of Rishi's semen was spewed into her through a needle-less syringe. Rishi's sperm would search out Kavya's egg in the dark disco of her womb. This was by no means their last chance, but to call it a good one was a stretch. They had a ten to fifteen percent probability of conception, the doctor said. Kavya had tried not to see the funnel clouds of cost analysis erupting from her husband, but they were hard to ignore. In all her Indian-offspring-model-minority life, she'd never felt such pressure to succeed.

Kavya was supposed to wait for a blood draw at the clinic to test for pregnancy. Twelve days after her appointment, she couldn't stand it any longer and bought a three-pack of home tests. But all home pregnancy tests come out positive: Rishi's voice, which she ignored. She just wanted the tests on hand.

But the thing was, she felt pregnant. She could see the plus signs even without the tests. And what was the harm in affirming what she already sensed? She could try one stick, she decided, just to see. She'd save the others for the right time. She unwrapped one test and took it to the bathroom.

A minute later, all three sticks sat unwrapped and peed upon, lined up on the bathroom counter. Now she could only wait.

Slowly, one by one, two plus signs bloomed on each stick. "I knew it," she whispered.

She stood in her bathroom for many minutes, watching these plus signs, waiting for them to change back to minuses. She listened to the nasal hiss of her breath, and for those many minutes, this was all she heard. Twelve days. It was possible, she dared surmise, that she, Kavya, was twelve days pregnant. In the soft light of their Spanish-tiled bathroom, she blinked at her success, until slowly, very slowly, she accepted that life, at last, would begin.

Two more days until the doctor's office. She would wait. Her certainty was stronger than medicine. She would treasure this secret knowledge. For two days, it would be hers alone. Three sticks, three promises, six little plus signs, her ducks in a row.

That night, she lay in bed and let Rishi stroke the flat plain of her abdomen until she fell asleep. Kavya didn't need Rishi or a doctor or even three dripping sticks to tell her she was pregnant. She felt the same as she'd always felt, physically, but a certain light-headedness, born of elation, had emptied her mind of all thoughts but the idea that she, Kavya, would be a mother.

She packed the thought away. She wouldn't let herself believe just yet.

"AWESOME!" THE DOCTOR SAID. "You did it!"

Kavya jumped to her feet. Joy rose from her gut. Thirteen months of trying and failing had tamped it down, but now it bubbled over in laughter she couldn't control. She wheezed each breath, unable to catch it, her laughter and inhalations tripping over one another. Rishi picked her up, like he would a child, and she wrapped her legs around him. He held her for so long that the doctor left the room. When she looked up, they were alone.

"What happens now?"

"I don't know. Where'd he go?"

"I want to scream, Rishi."

"Do it."

She laughed again. "I can't!"

The doctor returned soon enough, grinning widely. Kavya took Rishi's hand in hers.

"When can we see it?" she asked.

"Nine weeks. We'll do an ultrasound and you'll get a neat little picture for your Facebook page."

For Rishi, the indentured servitude seemed, at last, to have paid off. Rishi became a man again—a husband, holding Kavya's hand in the OB's office. And if all went well, a father. The world around him felt rarified, thin but life-giving, like mountain air. Maybe this was happiness. From the soles of his feet came an electric charge, and in his chest there gathered a deep, warm well. No, this was purpose.

In the car, driving home, Rishi turned to Kavya. "We can do it here."

She turned to him, then squeezed her eyes shut and let loose a horror-movie scream. She squeezed her hands into fists and screeched, then fell into laughter. Rishi opened his mouth and let out a howl. Their lives had been barreling toward this day. Joy, at last, had found them.

That evening, they walked down Shattuck and sat in a sidewalk tapas bar. It was autumn, and the leaves had gathered the season's fire. Orange, red, yellow: An old oak tossed them down as if it had had enough. Together, they searched for menu offerings Kavya couldn't eat anymore: tuna tartare, soft cheeses. "Are you craving anything?" Rishi asked. Kavya ordered fried potatoes and flan. They sipped on lemonade with mint and watched the sidewalk course past. People seemed to move more slowly than usual, bathed in the waning sun. It grew late, but they weren't tired. It grew cool, but neither felt the chill.

LATE THAT NIGHT, Rishi's eyelids grew heavy and he began to drift off, when he was woken by a rustling inside. In the depths of his chest, he felt a murmur. His heart had been a tornado shelter, stocked and sealed off to the world, waiting patiently for imminent disaster. But now, rapping at its wood was a tender hand, a slow-growing promise. As he lay still and felt the small taut push of Kavya's belly against him, a drop of longing coursed through his bloodstream, minute but terrifyingly potent.

He slipped his hand beneath her shirt to her waist, where the skin was incandescent, hotter than he'd ever felt it. He ran his fingers along her belly, still modest and supple, and moved up to her breasts, fuller now—definitely fuller. He cupped one in his hand and she gasped.

"Sorry," he said. "Do they hurt?"

"No." She breathed deeply. "No." She guided his hand over her breasts and down her abdomen. She reached back to slip his pants from his waist, and though a small part of him worried that they shouldn't be doing this, invading their blessing with the rampant impulses of their own bodies, he followed Kavya's lead.

FOR THE WEEKS THAT FOLLOWED, Kavya did what pregnant ladies did. She did the yoga, she bought the vitamins. She read pregnancy timelines to keep track of her baby as it grew from a squiggle into a complexified tadpole with round black eyes. She tried to feel it inside, to press her senses against the quiet formation of head, mouth, and hand-buds. But mostly, she felt the same, exhausted at times, more bloated than usual, and then nauseated. Around week six, she started to carry plastic bags in her purse, should the urge to vomit overtake her in an elevator or checkout line. She couldn't tolerate the smell of coffee or basil or garlic, and the thought of chocolate brought on an angry surge of nausea. The streets of town became an obstacle course of miasmic offense.

Rishi watched her through these weeks, fascinated by this newly contented and incredibly sleepy version of his wife. She took a nap after work each day, rose for an hour or two, and went straight back to bed. Her weekends were spent in a nest of pillows, watching television, reading books, dozing. He felt powerless against the hormonal workings that had taken her over. He'd done his part, in a cramped room at the fertility clinic; the rest was on her shoulders.

Now Rishi picked things up for Kavya and rubbed her feet at night and danced for her in the living room to Janet Jackson songs when she was feeling especially sorry with sickness. She longed for her mother's cooking, its rice and rasam with hot peppercorns that stung her tongue numb. But they hadn't told her mother yet. They hadn't told anyone, had decided not to until they were ultra-sure. So she lived her life feeling green, happy, but particularly alone.

She went about her business at Gamma Gamma Pi, avoiding garlic like a vampire would, ignoring demands for low-fat yogurts and cheeses—which, she was surprised to discover, smelled distinctly like Play-Doh—and sticking her head out the window every few minutes to escape the odorous steam clouds that hung about the kitchen.

KAVYA WOULD ALWAYS REMEMBER her pregnancy as the first time she was owned by someone else. She became an apartment of liquid and light, of distant blood rush and nutritional delivery. She was glad to give. But then:

"Gosh," the doctor said. And Kavya knew. "Gosh darn." The doctor muttered this, moving the fetal heart monitor from one spot on her belly to another. Kavya wrapped her arms around herself. The doctor looked from her to Rishi. "This happens sometimes."

Kavya didn't need to ask how or why. She knew enough. Somehow, what she'd offered in two months as a mother hadn't been enough. What started out as six tidy plus signs had somehow lost its positivity. The fevered patter of the heart was gone, had petered into nothing more than a spot, very faint and very still. Kavya didn't remember much else of what was said, only the buzz of the overhead light, the question she asked five times, six or seven: *What do we do with it?* The answers were crowded out by a new truth, repeating: I lost my baby. I lost my baby. I lost.

Rishi explained to her—three times, even after the doctor explained them—the methods of removal. Each time, she gazed at him like she'd forgotten the question. "D and C," she said the next morning, "that's what I want to do." She spoke so quietly that Rishi didn't hear her at first. She blew on her tea, eyes downcast, and said the words again.

The drive to the clinic was long and quiet. They listened to a story on NPR about the 9/11 memorial, as if the radio were trying to soothe their bad thing with a reminder of worse things. There were worse things that could have happened, yes, than losing a pregnancy. Kavya greeted the doctor with tremulous control. As she sank into anesthetic rest, Rishi's own mind quaked with a question that wouldn't and couldn't be answered: What if this child was the one?

The one what? The devoted son or astonishingly successful daughter? The answer to their worries about growing old? What if this child was a sort of secular savior, the one to answer the amoebic burgeon of the world's problems? The words from the old book came back to him, transformed: One child to rule them all, one child to find them, one child to bring them all and in the darkness bind them. This child might have been the one.

And these were the sorts of thoughts—injurious, wildly unshareable, and who needed his opinion, anyway?—that coursed through Rishi's head as his wife was undressed, prepped, and anesthetized.

On the drive home, Kavya was still groggy. She sat silently, with her eyes closed. When Rishi turned on the radio, she reached out and she switched it off.

12.

THE SEÑORA PAUSED THE VIDEO. "HERE'S THE THING, SOLI. You're in for a serious shock. With the birth, with the delivery." And here she stopped herself, tilted her head to the side. "Or are you? Have you been at a birth? Back home? In your   your village?"

"No, señora, I have not."

"This isn't going to be pretty. But it's what you need to know." She wrapped her hand around Soli's and pressed play. On-screen, the señora on a hospital bed. A clear tube ran from her hand to a bag of liquid on a stand. The on-screen señora kicked off her sheet to reveal her bare bottom and legs, her feet covered in a chunky pair of socks. She turned and revealed an ivory globe of belly. From Soli's own belly came an anxious flutter of kicks. A doctor walked in and shook her hand. As if this were a real movie, the camera focused in on her face, her closed eyes. She writhed in a mild, dramatized sort of pain. It wasn't pretty, but it was prettier than Soli's delivery would be. Of this she was fairly certain.

On-screen, the doctor gave a thumbs-up. He was as handsome as a doctor on a telenovela. In Popocalco, a comadrona with hefty arms and hanging jowls brought babies into the world. From the television came a glottal moan; Mrs. Cassidy arched her back, spread her knees.

Soli was beginning to feel queasy again. This was her sixth month, and nausea should not have been an issue.

On-screen, from between the señora's legs grew a conflagration of tissues, distended and purple and open to the world. When the camera zoomed in close, Soli ran for the bathroom. In the toilet, the toilet she had just cleaned, her stomach emptied in an angry and orange cascade.

If Señora Cassidy had noticed her run out, she was too transfixed now to notice her return. She sat cross-legged on the sofa, focused on the screen.

"This part gets samey," she said, fast-forwarding through high-speed writhing, high-speed tight-lipped breathing. Soli stood in the doorway. "Here we go. Here's the money shot."

She pointed on-screen to a pair of thighs, knees raised high, feet held aloft by husband and nurse, and a cavity bulging, opening, glistening with a slick sort of liquid, and finally, the wet-matted hair of a newborn's head. On-screen, she let loose a scream that ripped through the television and caught Soli by the throat. She screamed again, like a dying animal.

"Señora!"

This was Soli. The señora turned. Soli couldn't stop her words. She was shouting.

"Señora. This. I cannot do this. This is enough."

Soli bolted for the kitchen. The sound of the señora's scream followed her. Even filtered through a video camera and a television screen, the pain was more real than anything Soli had known. It clung to her, a vibration of fear. She thought about picking up her coat and heading out the door and never returning. But the señora stood in the kitchen doorway, still clutching the remote.

"But, Soli, you missed it. You missed the birth!" She crossed her arms. "Get back in here, Soli. There's stuff you need to see."

"¿Señora?" She steadied her breath. Inside, the baby held his. "Señora? There is a line."

The señora shook her head.

"Do you understand? There is a line. This is the other side."

Mrs. Cassidy opened her mouth to protest, and then closed it. She was about to fire her, Soli believed. Or report her to the police. The señora was searching for the right words with which to send her back to Mexico. Soli wondered, Did other housecleaners have moments like this, when the loudest sounds in a room were the tick of the kitchen clock and the wind-rush of knowledge that her words, her act of simply refusing to watch what she could not watch, had thrown her livelihood, her very ability to remain in a country, into danger?

The señora began to speak, but stopped. She fixed Soli to the floor with a long and steady gaze. "I'll turn it off," she said.

Soli nodded. But she couldn't imagine herself getting back to work, donning rubber gloves to wash the dishes or mop the floors. So she said, "Forgive me," and gathered her purse and coat. "I'll be back in the morning."

The señora grabbed her wrist and Soli stopped breathing. What now? The woman didn't let go, but instead looked down at her own long, thin fingers wrapped around Soli's arm, twisting the skin. She seemed not to know they were hers.

And then she let go. From the living room drifted the crow of a newborn. "I'm sorry, Soli. And, gracias." One side of her mouth rose to a smile, the other stayed put. And in the blue waters of her gaze, Soli saw a dark flick, a shark fin of disenchantment. She wanted to explain. She did want to. But what could she say? The señora had a husband with a video camera and a handsome doctor who gave a thumbs-up. Who would Soli have? The only person who was truly hers would be the one trying to get out; he'd be the one making her scream.

"Goodbye" was all she said, and in slow steps, she moved through the kitchen, picked up her coat and handbag, and walked to the door. If she was doing the wrong thing, she had no choice. If she'd stayed, she might have slipped and sunk into those shark-infested waters, pulled under by the current of her ignorance.

Outside, winter had settled gray and still over the town. As she walked home, the cool afternoon began to wash away some of the day. Soli was six months pregnant, and bulged with certainty. After months of being told where to sit, when to wake, and what to eat, she had had enough. Today she'd met a new part of her self—the part that knew what was right and what was wrong, and could go ahead and say it, the part that could walk out on her boss one day and walk back in the next, as if nothing at all had happened.

She opened the apartment door to find Silvia on the sofa, flicking through the channels. She sat up straight and fumbled with the remote control. "What are you doing home?" The TV switched off. "Did they fire you?"

Soli was too tired to lie. "I walked out."

"You quit?"

"I left for the day"—she sighed—"that's all."

Silvia squinted. "Something happened."

And so Soli sat on the sofa and told Silvia about the birth video. "That isn't a normal thing to do," Silvia said. "There's something wrong with that woman."

"She was trying to help me, I think," Soli said.

"Hmph." Silvia looked her up and down, then turned the TV back on, and lost herself in a talk show. Soli sat with her, just as she'd sat with the señora. Silvia was quiet for the rest of the evening, even with the boys. After dinner, she yawned and stretched and left the table, shutting her door behind her, leaving Soli to clear the dishes and send the boys to bed.

. . .

THAT NIGHT, FROM THE SILENCE of her room rose a thin whine. A nearby telephone cable to anyone else, but as it buzzed through Soli's waking mind, it gathered body, velocity, and grew to a wail. It was the señora's wail, and it was Soli's, from that day by the roadside that neither her new life, her new job, nor her many American showers could wash away. That night, she left her bed and returned to the dry desert road, alone.

"Get out." She could still hear his voice, cavernous and dim. It was the driver. She'd ridden alone for a day, the truck bed echoing with worries for Checo and Nutsack and the others. And then, like a warehouse, it had been restocked with more people, women and men and children she'd never seen before. Now the others struggled off the truck bed, their legs bowed at angles, their shoulders and spines warped. Even the children walked with crooked backs after days of hunching down in the truck.

She toppled off and one of the women helped her up. The driver pointed to another truck, this one open to the air, boarded by wooden slats. "That's yours," the driver said. "California."

Before she climbed aboard, a man grabbed her elbow. This one wore a cowboy hat. "Not so fast, señorita. This is going to cost you. You know that, don't you? We'll be expecting payment." Soli had neither peso nor penny.

"Not *now*," the man said. "When you get there, you'll be paying us three thousand."

Papi had given all he had to Manuel. There was no way she would get three thousand pesos.

The man squeezed her arm: "Three thousand dollars. Okay?"

She'd never heard a number like this. She couldn't imagine three thousand dollars.

"If we don't get it from you, we'll get it from your family, Solimar Castro Valdez of Santa Clara Popocalco." He grinned. "Got it?"

She nodded once at the man, then pushed past him, irritated. She didn't have time for his scare tactics. She needed to piss.

The man broke off from the group and walked behind her. Soli heard his footsteps but thought nothing of it, until two others began to follow. Any other day, she would have pissed her pants and run. But today, Soli was too bandy-minded to think, and cradled in daylight, she felt she had nothing to fear.

One man. Three men. They shoved her down, the ground a hard shock. They pinned her arms to her chest and pulled every thread of clothing off her, there on the stony earth. The first man ordered her to take her piss. He pulled a pistol from his pocket and ordered her to do it. She might have run, but the gun emanated its own heat, a promise to follow and find her. She had nowhere to go, so she stayed where she was. One knee, then the other, on the ground, where rocks and sand ground into her skin.

"Go ahead," the man said. His voice was calm and deep. "Take a piss. That's why you came out here, right?" The tears wouldn't come, but she heaved nonetheless, propping herself onto her feet and squatting. Her thighs were bare, splayed wide. Her thighs shamed her, their fleshy flanks the most naked things she'd known, and the dark gutter between them. It gaped at the ground, grinning and open to the wind. She was too frightened to piss, and the wave of relief stayed bottled up inside. She shook her head, and was pushed down.

The evening was nearly silent, the desert sands swallowing sound. First, second, third. One by one, they rammed into her and did their animal thing. She placed an arm over her breasts and they laughed and shoved it away. Her throat was dry and she tried to scream, but the sound only wheezed out of her. She saw then the barrel of a gun, pointing down at her like a camera lens. When the last one finished, he got to his feet and zipped his pants, tugged his shirt cuffs over his wrists. Through the tremble of her own legs, she watched him diminish in the thickening dark. When he was out of sight, a gush of urine drenched her thighs and buttocks.

Soli found her clothes strewn around the base of the tree. She returned, dressed, parched and shaking, to the group that had gathered around the second truck. The men who'd done it to her gathered around, sucked on cigarettes, gazed up to the darkening sky. They chatted quietly, like they were waiting for a bus. All three wore cowboy hats. Some vaqueros they were. When the truck bed opened, they herded the passengers on. Soli sat on something hard and even, crossed her arms over her stomach, and rested her head on her knees. Her thighs smelled sour.

When the door clanked shut, she let loose a wail. Her shoulders shook with a force she couldn't control, as if her grief had turned against her, as if the horrors within were taking charge and shutting her down, having decided she would die. She made sounds she'd never heard, and they droned for hours, maybe days, born from some canyon of loss. They churned up her throat and vibrated through her teeth. She did not know these sounds.

But she didn't die. She felt a hand on her back. It belonged to the woman beside her. Soli grew silent, until the hand on her back brought her back to the truck, back to the hum of the bench on which she sat. The hand, solid and still, brought her, in its quiet way, back to the world. When she felt down her shirt for her rosary, it was gone. She sat up, looked down her collar and saw nothing but brown skin, her breasts. No beads, no cross. That's when the door to the truck slammed shut and the engine coughed to a start. She hunched back down, her head between her knees, and stayed this way, never looking up, as the truck lurched forward. The earth rumbled low and surged from under her. She knew she was on her way.

. . .

AND HERE SHE WAS NOW—it was almost beyond belief—in her warm bed, the Berkeley morning a cool white blush. After haunted dreams, the sun had brought silence. She moved through that morning a few inches from the ground. She had built a castle of light, with walls that dissolved as she passed. This place was not hers. These homes— Silvia's apartment, the Cassidy bungalow—were refuges lent by a gentle fate, but she held no claim to them. The life she knew could slip from beneath her with hardly a moment's notice.

Soli had told no one about those men, and would have wiped her memory clean if she could. But she couldn't. Three men. Three cowboy hats, all white, like they'd bought them together. They'd used her like a latrine, taking turns, each moving methodically like a dog fucking a dog. By the time the third had jammed himself inside her, she could stare into the sun's glare and think of herself as a dog, and them as dogs, and nothing more. When all of them were animals, the spikes of pain deadened and she felt nothing. She'd felt nothing when they ground her shoulders into the dirt. She'd felt nothing when the third man held a knife to her throat, smiled, and pulled the blade away. Three more paternal possibilities for Soli's child, three more gambles in this land of infinite chance.

A hardness had taken root in her that evening, out among the desert rocks. And now, as she listened to kitchen clatters and the rush of the shower, a sense of disgust welled up inside her, radiating through the room. She began to sweat through her clothes, hot now with rage. She crammed her eyes shut and forced herself to remember again the sickly, spastic thrust of their bodies, the sight of a rigid penis, the veinous alien. She reminded herself of these things so that she could live with them. They had killed a piece of her, those men. Now that she could be still, safe in the light, she sensed something heavy and dead within. She would use it one day, that heavy dead thing. She would care for it like a baby. She would relish its violence. And one day, it would serve her well.

SILVIA HAD BREAKFAST WAITING. Normally, she was out the door before Soli woke up, but that morning she lingered, setting a plate of hot tortillas and eggs before her and smoothing down Soli's hair. Perhaps she knew, Soli thought, about the visions that had stalked her through the night.

Silvia set down a cup of dark coffee. "Your mama called early this morning."

Her stomach clenched.

"Everything's fine."

"Papi?"

"Fine." Silvia paused. "Have you told them yet?"

"About?" But Soli knew what about, and no, she hadn't. And in an unfamiliar fit of authority, she set down her cup and said, "You don't tell them either, Silvia. Do you hear me?"

Silvia shrugged.

"Please. Silvia. Please."

Silvia arched an eyebrow over her coffee cup, smacked her lips, and before Soli could drop to her knees as one would before a village saint, Silvia said, "Okay. I won't tell."

"I'll tell them myself. I promise. I just need to do it at the right time."

"You *have to*, Soli. How can they not know?"

"They'll know."

"Okay."

And when would they know? Before the birth or after? Would Soli return to Popocalco one day twelve years in the future, with a tall and gangly stranger, a flamingo-legged boy she called her son? Or would she call her parents immediately and say Mama-Papi, I'm having a baby.

Whose, I can't be sure. It could be a wonderful young man who is either dead or mowing lawns, or one of three rapists with flamboyant taste in hats. Oh, yes, and by the way, I was raped three times but also made some very nice love by a railroad track. And so it happened that Soli did not get around to dropping this news bomb on her parents, though she did speak to them every few weeks, for fifteen, twenty minutes at a time, nuzzling into the warmth of their improving humors (sending money home, it seems, does wonders for parental moods). Mostly she let her mother talk. She told Soli about Doña Alberta, her brand-new home built right in front of the old one, with tile floors, an air conditioner, an indoor toilet.

"And a shower, m'ija! And above the shower, there's a square in the ceiling with a window in it, just in case she wants to look up at the sky!" Mama said.

"Have you been to visit?"

"No, no. She's taking no visitors," her mother said and sniffed. "Not us, anyway."

When her parents asked Soli about her life in America, she told them everything she could think of about the Cassidys and Berkeley and how well she was being treated. But when it came to such key pieces of information as their impending grandchild, she told herself that she had enough to deal with. She had, for instance, the señora to deal with.

The day after the birth video, she walked into the Cassidy house at 8 a.m. exactly. Mr. Cassidy sat alone at the table, sipping his tea. He smiled, said good morning, and asked her to sit down.

"Señor?"

"Call me Brett."

The truth was, Soli couldn't say the name Brett, not the way he said it, and the way it sounded on her lips shamed her. "Can I call you Mr. Cassidy, please?"

His eyebrows jumped. "Sure."

Soli took off her coat, hung it on the laundry room rack, and returned to the kitchen to begin the dishes. Over the past two weeks, dishwashing had grown nearly impossible. Reaching the sink was no problem, but levering heavy pans against the weight of her belly produced a new kind of strain in her neck. She picked up a frying pan and held it high to scrub it.

"Soli," said Mr. Cassidy. "Soli, sit down!" He sounded upset. "Don't do that now. Look how pregnant you are! Have a seat, please."

She couldn't so easily slide a chair out and relax.

"*Sit.*"

When Soli did sit, she feared another question about the Zapatistas. Or that he was angry she'd walked out the day before. Or perhaps this was about the food. They might have noticed their Tupperware growing lighter, the bread loaves shrinking, the missing containers of yogurt, the sandwich meat, the milk. As if reminded, her stomach sang out with a throaty, three-beat gurgle.

Mr. Cassidy smiled. "Stay there." He got up and went to the fridge and came back with a stack of creamy pastry on a plate. "Have you had a Napoleon before?"

No, she had not. Soli didn't know where to begin with the concoction. She knew from what drifted to her nostrils that it was sweet and rich. It rose before her, a castle of pastry layers topped with a solid pane of sugar, a candied cherry. The fragrance of cream sent a willowy ache up her jaw.

She looked at the man sitting before her. There was a smudge on his glasses that she wanted to wipe. "Is the señora home?"

"She's in bed today, Soli. You won't need to clean the bedroom."

"Is she sick, señor?"

"No, no. She feels awful about yesterday, though. She was worried you'd never be back."

"I'm back."

He smiled. "Soli, you'll be a mother soon." He cocked his head, searched her face. "Are you ready?"

"I have to be ready?"

He laughed at this. "I suppose not. Do you know yet? Boy or girl?"

"No. But I feel that he's a boy."

The truth was, Soli hadn't been to a doctor. Silvia hadn't wanted to spend the money. You're so young, she'd said. You're getting so big, the baby must be growing, right? You think our mothers went running to the doctors like the gabachas do?

Silvia was right, of course. Soli felt the life that kicked inside her, and that was all she needed. In Popocalco, she would have seen a comadrona, and she would have had her mother. Here, she had Silvia.

"Who's going to help you, Soli?" he asked, as if he'd read her thoughts. "Do you have a lot of family?"

She shook her head. "Only my cousin."

"Uh-huh. And have you thought about the time you're going to take off?"

She shook her head. She'd assumed Silvia would pull out the baby, towel her off, and send her back to work.

The señor rapped his fingers on the table, pinkie to thumb, making a sound like rainfall. He looked at Soli, and Soli, who should have felt uncomfortable, who should have risen from her chair or stared at her feet, simply looked back. She sat frozen in his gaze.

"Well, listen," he said. "We're prepared to give you a month off, to rest and heal and what have you. But then we'll need you back. All right?"

A month seemed like a long time to go without pay.

"You'll be paid," he said, a step ahead again.

"Señor?"

"We will pay you, okay? For that month, you'll get money." He rubbed his thumb and forefinger together. "But then we'll need you back. You can bring your baby, and start a few hours later if you need to. You'll watch Saoirse after school, and you'll clean while you're here. You'll be our nanny, like we said before."

What could she say? She almost refused. The people here were too kind; she felt that she didn't deserve them. No one got treated like this, did they? To be paid for doing nothing? For a whole month?

Mr. Cassidy got up and opened a drawer. "I forgot to give you a fork," he said, and, handing it to her, sat down to sip his tea.

Cutting into the thing was not easy. Every press of the fork caused a layer to slide off. She felt Mr. Cassidy's eyes on her, and feared she was doing it wrong. The harder she sliced, the more the pastry slipped across the custard. When she did cut through the Napoleon, it collapsed into a thousand flakes. She had to scrape them up and mix them in with the cream, until she gathered on her fork a mouthful of something that looked nothing like the original. When she placed it in her mouth, the custard was cool, and the layers broke coyly on her tongue. She had trouble swallowing, for the lump that had formed in her throat. It was a beautiful gift, more than she could have asked for, and impossible not to destroy.

13.

MOST LIKELY, IT WAS FINDING KAVYA CRYING IN THE CAR outside her house that made her mother suspect something was wrong. And because Kavya had no other answer—what else could be wrong?—she told the truth. She told Uma half the truth anyway, the truth as it had been eleven weeks earlier, when all they were doing was trying for a baby, and trying and trying. Perhaps she hoped to erase the baby who'd died inside her by keeping it out of the minds of others, forgetting by ignoring, starving it of attention until it shrank to a limp skin of memory. So she cried and told her mother that she wanted a baby. Uma stooped at Kavya's open car door and held her around the shoulders. Kavya, still in her seat belt, sobbed into her mother's chest as she hadn't since she was small.

And then, because it poured out of her without stopping, she went ahead and told Uma. She revealed the pregnancy, the failure, the removal. Uma held her at a distance, surveyed her daughter from eyes to ears to chin, and drew her back into an awkward embrace.

"Be patient," Uma said. "Don't rush yourself." Kavya didn't blame her for not being helpful. The thing about patience was that it couldn't exist without impatience. Impatience, desire, the irksome passage of time—these were what kept her from sleeping. Patience was the act of holding impatience at bay, of keeping it, like an impudent lover, from wearing her down.

WORK WAS A REFUGE with its high ceilings, its instruments comically large. The colander measured two feet across, the salad tongs were as long as her arms, the rice cooker was the stuff of her mother's dreams, the wok an ominous dome hung high on the wall, which only Miguel could reach. It was a giant's wok in a giant's kitchen. When Kavya entered each day, her troubles shrank away and left her with her habits and her hands. She tore, mashed, rubbed, and sliced, and her materials moved to her will. Within these walls, she could rely on the rules of cause and effect.

The doctor had said to wait six months to try again, though there was no harm, he added, in trying naturally. After six weeks, her body regained its monthly cycle. She didn't tell Rishi.

A WEEK AFTER HER MISCARRIAGE, the clinic had e-mailed her a list of couples therapists. She'd tucked it into her junk-mail folder, and said nothing to Rishi. They didn't need therapy. They needed a baby.

She felt utterly dulled, leaden at the prospect of more clinic visits, more shots, more nerve-addling drugs, more scheduled, wordless sex, a prolonged fight for what should have been her unquestioned, naturally granted right. All of it would end again—again and again—with brutal failure. And when would they stop? And what would stopping mean?

Now, lying alone in bed, she thought of Rishi. She tried, overcome now and then by gratitude, to be kind and rational with him, even when—especially when—she was screeching inside. The effort, most of the time, was monumental. Together, they had braved the cycles of hope and despair, the hope growing more tenous and perilous with each passing month. Together, they had maintained a deliberate show of calm, held aloft by an undercurrent of torrential desire. They'd be in for months of this, probably years, with more IUIs and IVF.

And if it didn't work? Kavya wouldn't come out the same. She had known damage in others, the way it changed their faces and pulled them a step back from the world. She didn't know if she—if they—could withstand it.

She couldn't do it anymore. Or maybe the truth was that she wouldn't. That's what Rishi would probably say. Either way, she knew this with sudden clarity: She was done.

She'd never had to truly give up on herself before, having always had a trust fund of potential—untapped, hidden, wasted—to fall back on. It was early evening, dark already in the first week of December. Outside, she heard voices passing, restaurant patrons and market-goers. She was hungry. There was no food in the house, but the thought of stepping out onto a populated sidewalk struck her with deep fatigue. She'd never been prone to cramps or menstrual trauma, but on this evening she could feel the actual sloughing of her tissue. And from the shredding, the shedding, the loss, came an unexpected discovery. Her body was no home for a baby. But her lovely bungalow was, her charmed life. She'd gotten everything she wanted, and this left little room for the deep, transformative joy of having her own child. Her life, already, was too good.

"My life is too good," she said. She said it again, aloud, to the ceiling. "My life is too good."

It was perfectly rational: Kavya had everything she wanted, and the laws of karmic accountancy stipulated that one could only experience so much fulfillment before having to pay the piper. The cosmic piper. If Kavya had had a baby to add to her wonderful life, then something terrible would have had to happen to rebalance the scales. The baby that was almost hers had martyred itself to save its mother from being blindsided by disaster down the line. Kavya felt herself filling with knowledge. Her baby, yes, the lost one, had been part of the great universal whole, and it knew this—it *knew* this, the veinous little bundle. Her child had been a genius of the most unpredictable order. The thought left her positively apostolic. She rose, filled with light, to share the news with Rishi.

But then she stopped herself—what did it mean? He would ask her this. Rishi always had a follow-up question, and she would need an answer. She lay back down, her hand on the plain of her abdomen. She thought about karma. Something bad had happened to someone out there. Kavya had to correct that badness, by taking it on and making it a goodness. Kavya stood. The idea had occurred to her before, of course, but only in this moment had she truly awoken to it.

She would adopt. Kavya and Rishi would adopt a child.

She found Rishi in the living room. He sat mangled in an armchair, his elbows on his knees, a book wedged open between his fingers. A stranger would think he suffered some degenerative dystrophy, but really this was just Rishi, with his terrible posture, reading a book.

"Rishi, I want a kid."

He didn't look up. "I know," he said. "I know, babe. I'm totally with you."

She said nothing, stood still in the doorway. He put his book down, at last. "What do you mean you want a kid?"

"I can't wait. I can't wait like this. I want a kid now." She realized she sounded like Veruca Salt demanding an Oompa Loompa, but there was no way but the direct way to say what she meant. She sat down next to him. "I want to have a child as soon as possible, Rishi. I want to adopt."

Rishi stared blankly into her face, almost as if he hadn't heard her.

Under normal circumstances, Kavya would have assumed he'd not been paying attention. But this time, she knew he'd heard. She said it again for him, softly.

They sat for a long time, Rishi kneading the skin of her hand.

"I know you haven't thought about this much—we haven't really talked about it."

"M-hm."

"It kind of just dawned on me, you know? Like I finally just . . . knew."

More silence followed.

"This isn't like adopting a cat, Kavya. This is serious."

She resisted the urge to snap at him. Of course he was hesitant. Who wouldn't be? It would have worried her more if he'd stood up and said hurrah.

"This is going to take you a while," she said. "It took me a while, but then it seemed really clear. Like this was the plan all along."

"Let's get some information."

She pounced and flung her arms around him.

"It's just information," he said. "We can't decide anything yet."

It was too late for Kavya. Her mind was made up. Had Michelangelo tried dentistry before he painted the Sistine ceiling? Had Joan of Arc weighed the pros and cons of listening to her angels? Did the Queen of England send out résumés, in case something better came up? Kavya knew what she was meant to do, and it was only a matter of time before Rishi knew it, too.

Almost every seat on the Weebus was taken, but Rishi found one near the front. No one spoke on the bus. They operated under the tacit understanding that the bus was an extension of the office, minus the big pink stuffies and the espresso bar. The quiet was alien to Rishi, who actually enjoyed small talk. It seemed, however, that no one else did, and so normally, he was left to check his e-mail and his news feeds and his Clash of Clans updates and whatever other time-wasting maneuvers would have whittled away his morning's productivity. But that morning, neither news nor social media nor the maneuvers of warring clans could hold his attention. The memory of what he'd agreed to—adoption, the possibility of it—pinged him endlessly, like a bothersome coworker. Adoption. The word itself was overpowering, especially when turned on him.

Rishi had always been a diligent worker, if an indecisive one—it had taken two years of abandoned premed courses, an unused business school degree, and a two-year fizzle at law school before he discovered his interest in renewable energy and got the Ph.D. that landed him the job at Weebies. Going to work in Silicon Valley made Rishi feel like an active member of his age. It affirmed all the wrong turns he'd made in his career, to finally be part of a successful company, even if he was merely a cog, and a nearly invisible one at that.

Meeting Sen five months earlier had stirred in him the excitement of meeting a celebrity, only this celebrity had shaken his hand. This celebrity was the new husband of his wife's supposed onetime best friend. This celebrity would remember him.

His inability to father a child didn't have to seep into the rest of his life. Except that it did. Rishi's ambition was flaccid, his heart pummeled.

Adoption. The word hogged the armrest and leaned into his breathing space. He tried to return to his laptop, to shove the word out of his morning, but it was hefty and stubborn and would not budge. So he watched the passing streets and did his best to think of other things.

They arrived at the Weebies campus and everyone filed off, preoccupied and orderly. There had been a time, during his first weeks and months in the Valley, when he could stand very still, listen very closely, and hear the air buzz with invention. He could feel it in the soles of his feet, reverberating up through the immaculate sidewalk. At the center of the buzz sat Vikram Sen in a massive office Rishi might never see. He thought back to the wedding and felt a tug of regret.

What would he say to Sen, if he did work up the courage to call? Sen would have to call him. Of course, he most likely would not. A year earlier, he'd been named one of *People*'s 50 Most Beautiful, and *Esquire* had done a full-page spread on his office, a lofted mirrored expanse that took up a sizable wedge of the main Weebies building. He'd been photographed in a tux with the tie undone, reclining on his white sofa, ankles crossed, arms splayed over the cushions. Rishi had read it with amusement, admiration, and aroused ambition.

And then, one afternoon, his laptop pinged. He looked around to see if anyone in his open-plan office was watching him, smirking, perhaps. He checked the name again. On his screen, an instant message from Vikram Sen.

Got a minute to talk?

Sure. His phone rang. He picked it up, waited for the snorting laughter of an office prankster.

"Rishi Reddy! Are you ready?"

"Hi there."

"How's it going, man. Listen."

Rishi waited, still convinced that this was all going to end in laughter at his expense.

"Are you there?"

"Hi. Yeah."

"Great. I'm calling in a favor."

"Okay."

"Did you read the *Journal* yesterday?"

"The journal?"

"Yes. Apparently, Rishi-bhai, good air helps people think. Did you know this? They did a study—scientists, that is, not the Wall Street guys—they did a study that showed that clean air improved the cognitive ability of children in classrooms."

Rishi leaned in. The speaker's accent was precise, Indian, with a British boarding school lilt. It seemed to actually be Vikram Sen.

"You know about VOCs, right, man?"

He knew more than most people did about VOCs, volatile organic compounds, the bad guys of the air quality world, the stuff of sick building syndrome and carcinogenic buildup. "Sure."

"The clean-air craze has started, Rishi-bhai. And already we're lagging. Everyone's getting rid of their VOCs, cleaning up their air. All over the Valley. But I want to do it better. I want to create a room for our software guys that contains *the cleanest fucking air anyone has ever breathed.*"

Rishi waited.

"I'm calling it the Stratosphere."

"Okay. Sorry. Calling it what?"

Sen paused. "Come to my office. Can you come right now? I'll let Sally know."

Rishi hopped on a blue-and-pink Weebike, rows of which were stationed around campus for employees to ride among buildings. He didn't need to ask where Vikram's building was—it was the largest and loudest, painted fluorescent, sky-piercing purple. On its roof sat a gigantic fiberglass infant, diaper clad, with glassy blue eyes that surveyed the valley, a rattle held aloft.

"The Stratosphere," Vikram picked up exactly where he'd left off, "is what I plan to call the programming center." Rishi had removed his shoes at the office door at the secretary's request, and was immediately glad he had. The carpet in Vikram Sen's office was thicker and softer than any he'd ever felt. As he sank into the white leather and wrapped his fingers around a warm cup of chai, he couldn't imagine saying no to the man before him, whose very carpet left Rishi nurtured, nourished, ready to conquer. In a bid to hang on to its headier start-up days, most Weebies buildings were furnished with a studied shabbiness—scooters and cardboard boxes stacked against the walls, dorm room futons, formaldehyde-leaching beanbags and plastic tables in the common areas. But Sen's office was fully grown-up, at once minimalist and lush, the domain of a man who'd come to terms with success. Sen sat in his own armchair, a wider, higher-backed version of Rishi's. A stack of black binders rose beside him. A framed photo of Preeti Patel sat tastefully on his desk. Behind him hung a tiger pelt.

"Good chai, isn't it?" Sen asked. "None of this hipster nonsense. None of this nutmeg bullshit. I trained Sally to grind cardamom." He smiled mischievously into his cup.

"So what exactly do you want to do with—the Stratosphere?"

Sen slurped with gusto and smacked his lips. "I want a room that is completely free of VOCs. Completely."

"No VOCs?"

"Zero." He slurped again. "How do you see that happening?"

A Weebies newbie would have said that a zero-VOC programming center would be impossible, that between furniture, tech equipment—clothing, even—no modern office could be absolutely free of VOCs. But Rishi had been in the Valley long enough to know that no one respected a pessimist.

"I guess," Rishi said, "we'd start by testing the paint. We could strip the paint and repaint with no-VOC stuff if we had to."

Sen shot to his feet and headed for his door. "Come with me."

Rishi rose, regretfully set down his chai, and put his shoes back on. He followed Sen down one hallway and then another. They came to a glass wall. Below them spread a field of programmers, hundreds of them, hunched around tables, their heads motionless as their hands churned over keyboards.

"Babies," Sen said, and sighed. "You have babies, Rishi-bhai?"

You have no idea, he wanted to say. He had everything but a baby, and nothing but a baby. A baby couched in shadow. A baby that had filled their home, ceiling to floor, corner to corner, a vapor. "No."

"Those are my babies, those fellows down there." Rishi followed his gaze, and it took him a few moments to realize who Sen was talking about. And yes, there they were. All male. Bouncing baby boys. Most programmers were fresh out of college, milk-fed, softened by free snacks and office ping-pong. "All those fucking idiots are my babies, yaar." It was jarring to hear Sen swear. Wrapped in the soft curl of his accent, the word came out especially obscene. "They're not idiots of course, they're highly intelligent, too intelligent, some of them. Some of them can't have a bloody conversation, they're so intelligent."

"I see."

Sen turned to him. "I don't think you see. Yet. These are the company's babies, Rishi-bhai. Everyone in this company who is *not* a programmer works for the good of the programmer. Including you. Including me." He crossed his arms. "Well. No. Not including me."

Rishi was beginning to understand what Sen wanted from him. "So the clean air is for these guys."

"That's right."

"Because you read that cleaner air enhances cognitive function."

"That's it."

"And the cleaner the air, the better *they* do." He took a deep breath. "Which, of course, is better for the company."

"You hit it! Think, Rishi-bhai, what might happen if those brilliant minds down there had nothing but the finest air filling their lungs? Already they practically live here. When they sleep, they sleep in the nap pods. When they shower—if they shower—they do it here. If they exercise, they go to our gym. And when they eat, what do they eat but the free fucking food we give them in our canteen? Do you know our people have walked out of Starbucks without paying because they've actually forgotten that the rest of the world pays for its food?"

Rishi stroked the windowpane with his finger. It buzzed faintly. "I can't strip the paint, can I?"

"No. You can't."

"Because there's no way you'd move all these guys to another building, or make them work with painters and construction guys hanging around."

"Would you do that to your babies?" Sen wrapped an arm around Rishi's shoulders. "See those fellows over there?" He pointed to a group of heads, curly black hair, dark skin, Indian. "I could have been one of them. IIT. H1-B. Easy. But I refused. I wasn't going to be a worker bee, you see. Those fellows, they make a hundred K, which to them may as well be a million. They live like modest people. Nothing flashy. Their hearts are in India still. And their mothers are in India, and that's where they send whatever money they can spare. Fair enough. But that was not for me." He sighed, rubbed a hand across his chest. "I did my time at IIT, then I got my business degree and then I went to every bloody tech conference I could find, and I started to meet the right people. And finally, at last, I got my green card. And here I am." He paused, then took Rishi by the shoulder. "Look at me," he said. "When you decide what you want, don't settle for anything less."

Rishi nodded. "I think we can do this." The possibilities of this project were beginning to reveal themselves. He'd have to source new furniture, figure out how many plug-in air filters he could possibly cram into the center, and whether they'd really make a difference. Rishi felt fortified now, with Sen's arm around his shoulder. "I'll have to put together a proposal," he said.

"By Monday."

A week. That would be enough time, if Rishi started right away.

They stood together, watching the hive of industry below. "The

Stratosphere," Rishi said. It wasn't the most appropriate name—there was nothing inherently pure about the earth's stratosphere, which was defined more by its distribution of hot and cold. But it had the right ring, and Vikram Sen, if nothing else, knew how to work a ring.

"I was going to call it the Nursery. But then I'd have to explain to these guys that I think of them as babies."

If Rishi could create the Valley's first VOC-free programming center, he'd begin to feel that all of it—organic chemistry, law school, the years of Ph.D. labor—was worth it. "If we could do this for Weebies, we could take the zero-VOC concept out to the world, couldn't we? To real nurseries, even. The purest air for babies."

"It's like we really are brothers." Sen sighed.

"We could make a lot of money."

"This would mean more than that for you, Rishi-bhai. You could really make a name for yourself here." He paused.

"I'd like that," Rishi said, nervous about revealing this desire. "I'd like to make a difference here, Vikram."

Sen nodded, and grew solemn. "But really, what we're trying to do here, what we are all trying to do, is make this world a better place, isn't it?"

Back at his desk, Rishi closed his laptop. He had a sudden hankering for the scratch of pen on paper. He was generating something absolutely new, and after nearly two years of trying and failing at the creation game, the thought of his plans coming to fruition—faraway as that day was—froze him with anticipation. He spent many minutes drawing squares on paper, letting a mild electric charge course up his elbow. He would plan out phases and experiments. He would plant his seeds, the seeds would grow. He began.

14.

As far as Soli could gather, the señor worked for a government office that worked with the university, and that's why the Cassidys lived in Berkeley. He called her Solimar, never Soli, and he offered to make her tea if he happened to be in the kitchen and making a pot for himself. Soli always said no. The stuff he drank smelled like sour tree bark, and Silvia had warned her not to eat or drink with the Cassidys, and even though she'd already wildly disobeyed, with the tree bark, she could stick to the rule.

If Soli had been someone else, or perhaps just a different version of herself, she might have fallen for Mr. Cassidy. He looked her straight in the eye when he spoke. There was no way Soli could meet the straight shot of his gaze, and so she spent a good deal of time scanning the other segments of his face—his nose, his cheeks, the full bow of his lips. Even if she liked what she saw there, Soli knew the señor would take no physical interest in his seven-months pregnant and boarishly hungry housecleaner, no matter how much attention he paid her.

He asked for her story, he wanted to know how she'd arrived on his shores, and what had happened to her on the journey. Soli, without papers and pregnant, and hanging by a thread to this happy, healthy place, considered telling the truth. With a sharp slap to her inner chismosa, she slowed down and shut her mouth.

At first she gave him shreds of detail, sparse and scattered enough to keep him from linking them into a whole. She told him about the trains and the changing scenery, about arriving in the Mission and thinking she was back in Mexico, which made him laugh. But she told him nothing of the border, the trucks, the weeks she spent making herself small.

Because he seemed less invested in her answers, she found him easier to speak to than the señora. And soon she found herself telling him how it was back home, where everyone knew she was an Indio, a hill girl with brown skin whose family had wound their way down to the valley and started up a farm. Her Indio papi knew everything about every type of corn that grew in every mountain cranny in the whole of Oaxaca. He liked this detail, she could tell. She told him about living surrounded by adobe, crumbling at its corners, in a house that sheltered as many birds as people. The palomas would perch in the cyclet nooks that peeked below their roof, where the corrugated tin didn't quite meet up with the hand-flattened ridges of clay. She told him about their nests, round as baseballs, arrayed along the town's power lines, and about the time she found a baby bird fallen to the ground, too young still to fly, its legs no thicker than dandelion stems, its head the size of an almond.

She told all this to Mr. Cassidy, because when you find success, even the most modest success, it gets easier to talk about thinner times. The poor times feel as far away as an abandoned train. You don't know poverty until it's you who has to feed and clothe your children, her papi used to say. Poverty is a pit that rumbles in your gut. You squash it down and pack it over with family and drink and music, but still it rumbles, threatening any day to erupt and send you and everything you know careening down a hillside. These details, Soli kept to herself.

One day, the señor called her into his study. "Solimar? Could you come in here a minute?"

"Señor?"

"Call me Brett." He smiled and motioned for her to sit. He sat back in his office chair. She liked to stroke this chair when she cleaned the room, its tight, smooth hills of leather punctuated by round buttons. It was the richest thing she'd felt in her life. It felt to her like salvation stretched and sewn, and she wondered how creatures like the moody old cows she'd known in Popocalco could have produced such leather. Maybe, she thought, the cows that made this weren't like the cows in Popocalco. Maybe they were happy cows, and healthy.

She sat.

"Solimar?" He smiled even wider. "You strike me as brave."

She'd grown weary of people telling her what she was. She said nothing.

"Solimar, here's the thing. I'm a consultant. Most of my work is for the government. You know that, don't you?"

Say the word *government* to an immigrant with no papers and all you get is a system-wide shutdown: silence, and the faint hum of fear. Her throat went hot and dry. All she could see was Mr. Cassidy and his wide, wide smile.

"Right, so. Here's the thing. When we hired you, your sister-in-law—is that right? Is she your sister-in-law?"

"My cousin." She remembered then that even happy, healthy cows ended up at the slaughterhouse door.

"Right. Your cousin told us that you were in the country legally—and of course we trust you both completely." He tapped his palm on the table. "Now. I'm going to ask you something, and I don't want you to take it the wrong way."

That was when Soli began to panic. Why the big toe of her right foot was the first to sniff out the trouble, she would never know, but it began to hop around like a lightning bug right there inside her shoe. Its tremor passed like a current up her leg, to her knee, and her bouncing knee got her hands riled up, and the quake surged up her torso, through her shoulders, and right up to the tangle between her ears. Soon she was shaking all over, and in response, for the first time in a very long time, she began to weep.

"Please, Señor Cassidy. Please don't send me away!"

"Solimar!" He rolled his chair over to hers, and took her hands in his. "Just hold your horses. Don't get upset, all right? I'm just going to need your Social Security number. Okay?"

He looked her straight in the eye. "You have a Social Security number, don't you?"

She stopped shaking and sat very still. Her hands grew hot, hot enough, surely, to make him pull away. But he looked at her steadily— what was it about that look?—and she knew that one way or another, she'd be getting that number.

THAT EVENING, Soli left the Cassidy home on feeble ankles. She didn't know whether to feel scared or stupid. Stupid, for thinking that she could dream and live with no one noticing. And scared to think that she might be caught. That the simple, functional life that she'd been blessed with might be yanked away. Already, she wondered how she'd give birth in jail.

And yet, looking around her, she saw it: proof that the life she sought was possible. On the bus, walking down the crowded sidewalk, carrying backpacks, pushing strollers. She saw women who were dark like her and foreign, living their American lives, pushing ahead without fear, none of them doubting for a second that they belonged. Did they have numbers? Did they have papers? Had they ridden to the border on a freight train? Some of the women around her were as old as Popocalco grandmothers. They could have been the women who ran alongside the tracks when the train slowed down for stretches, slow enough for bystanders to hand off water bottles and parcels of tortilla. Now, Soli ached for these women. She still could see their worried squints, the awkward thrust of their elbows as they ran. She could see Checo taking the bottles and waving, like a president on a motorcade, his smile coaxing theirs to the surface.

"They look like they need the water more than we do," Soli had said. "Why take from them when we have enough to drink?"

"They give these to us because they have people out there, and they can only hope that someone else is handing bottles to their kids and their husbands." He'd steadied his gaze on her. "Don't ever assume you have enough. Okay?"

She'd taken Checo's word as the infallible truth, as did they all, Soli and the boys, as they laid and relaid their plans. Plans were very important and everyone had one. "We're going to be mojados!" Flaco threw his fist in the air, as if farm labor were a great adventure. Pepe, who was only eight, was looking for his mother. She worked in a factory somewhere in Arizona. If he didn't find her, he'd decided to be adopted. If any of them could be adopted, it was him. His eyes were dark puddles. He seemed to imagine an American fairy-woman who would take him in and love him and feed him all he could eat. "I'm going to get fat like an American," he said. "I'm going to get so fat they'll have to wheel me in a wagon. The next time you see me, you won't even know it's me." Nutsack taught the other boys the words they'd need to know. Un jornal was *daily wage*. Un camion was *truck*. Una pala was *shovel*, and la tierra was *mud*. The boys practiced the sounds, stretching their lips around *daily wage*, laughing at the word *mud*. "Tierra," Nutsack said. "Mud." The boys slapped their knees and laughed at the sound of it. Mud. Mud. So oafish on the roofs of their mouths, so dead.

WHEN SILVIA GOT HOME with Daniel and Aldo, Soli was slicing onions at the dinner table, glad at least to disguise the tears that streamed down her cheeks. On the chopping board, a hillock had grown, and it toppled over itself every time her knife hit wood, sending onion shards snowing to the ground, a few each time, to gather in drifts around her toes.

"Why the tears, muchacha? Not so happy to see me?"

Soli told Silvia that Mr. Cassidy had asked for her seguro.

Silvia sighed. "This was going to happen eventually, I guess." From a kitchen drawer she pulled a book, small, its cover printed with unicorns and stars, the sort of book Soli kept as a little girl, to write stories and list her dreams.

Carefully, Silvia copied some numbers onto a blank page.

"Is this the seguro?"

"No, tonta. That's called a phone number. But to tell you the truth, it probably won't work. You'll have to go there."

"Go where?"

Silvia didn't answer. Below the phone number was what looked like an address.

Marta, the slip of paper read. "Who's Marta?"

Silvia shrugged.

"Who's Marta? Will Marta get me a number?"

"I don't know any Marta," Silvia said. She picked up the chopping board and carried it to the kitchen, moving swiftly, without spilling a single onion.

The next day was Saturday. Since Silvia wouldn't talk to her about it, Soli had to find her own way to the city. The address, on Mission and 14th, was obvious enough. She took the BART train to the city, paying this time for a ticket.

She remembered her first day here, how convinced she was that she'd never left Mexico. Now she could see between the brown, familiar faces, to the others that teemed down the street, young Americans, tall and thin in big glasses, girls with tattoos and piercings in their eyebrows and chins (how her mother would have beaten her!) and boys with beards, storkish legs encased in jeans, holding hands. Girls and girls, boys and boys, girls and boys and boys and girls. This was no Popocalco.

She found the address and looked down at her paper to check the number. This was a vegetable market. She didn't know what she was expecting, but she didn't think they sold seguros with cabbages. She went in, and almost immediately walked out. The people inside were not Mexicans, not even Sudamericanos. They were one hundred percent unfiltered *Chinese*. Or maybe Japanese? Soli couldn't tell the difference. She was finding there were as many types of Chino as there were Mexican. In any case, the woman scanning her from the counter looked nothing like a person who supplied seguros.

"What do you want?" she called to Soli.

"I am looking for Marta." Soli approached the counter. "Are you Marta?"

The woman pointed to the vegetables. "Buy something."

Soli was about to protest, and then she understood. She picked up a banana and brought it to the counter. The woman muttered something. She dropped her coins on the counter, and the woman gestured down the aisle again. "Through that door," she said. "La puerta!"

La puerta. It opened into a short hallway that ended in a doorway hung with heavy black flaps. Soli pushed through these. She heard a deep voice call from the dark.

"I see the belly first, and then I see the woman! Ave Maria purísima!"

She stepped carefully through the dim room; it was dark enough that she could not see the floor, and she didn't entirely trust her feet to take her where she needed to go. Where she needed to go was to the very back, where a man sat at a small table. A lamp shot a pool of light onto his desk.

"¡Pasale! ¡Pasale! ¡Pasale!"

The room smelled of onions, and she could make out a shadowy mound of them rising from a stack of crates. "I'm looking for Marta," she said.

"And Marta is me."

"What kind of name is Marta for a man?" Soli heard the words before she realized she'd spoken them.

Luckily, he was too fixated on her middle to notice. He walked over to her, his arms reaching for her belly, and Soli backed away.

"¡Tranquilo!" He stopped where he stood, his arms still reaching for her.

If she'd had Manuel's knife that day, she might have used it. But it turned out that Marta had little interest in anything but the circumference of her belly. He charged back to his desk, pulled a measuring tape from the drawer, and to Soli's amazement, he began to measure the width and length of her abdomen.

He returned to his desk, jotted a few numbers, whipped out a fresh sheet of paper, and began.

"Name?"

"Solimar Castro Valdez."

"Is that your real name?"

She nodded.

"Date of birth?"

She answered.

"You got a picture?"

Soli would have a state ID and her Social Security number. Nine numbers, nine dainty steps to the dream. Wadded into her bag was a roll of bills that would have gone to her parents. Four hundred seventy-five dollars. Now, she counted the limp and clammy things into Marta's hands. The bills stank of bus exhaust. He printed something out, then disappeared into another room. A few minutes later, he emerged with something that looked like a credit card—her California ID—and a piece of paper of roughly the same size, this one a somber blue and gray. On it were nine digits, separated by dashes. Where they came from, she didn't know and didn't want to know. They proved, however humbly, that she belonged.

That Monday she found Mr. Cassidy in his study. He sat holding a pair of glasses to his face, squinting his eyes and relaxing them, squinting and relaxing. She would do as he said and call him Brett, his first name, though to her it sounded like a belch. "Señor Brett?" she began, standing in his office door.

He looked up and smiled. "Come in, Solimar. Have a seat."

"Señor Cassidy, I have the number for you, the Security Number."

"Good girl! Let's have a look."

He took the folded paper and held it at arm's length, squinting again, and wrote the numbers on a form. Then he rolled the paper into a ball and flicked it into the trash can.

He picked up the glasses again and wiped them with the end of his sweater.

"Would you like me to clean those for you?"

"These? Nah, don't bother." And he tossed them to the desk.

She sucked in her breath. "Please be careful."

He grinned. "You know value when you see it. You want to hold them?" He placed the glasses in her hands. "Real glass. Feel how heavy those are," he said. They were, indeed, heavier than she expected. The lenses were perfectly round and framed in gold wire. "Now, these belonged to my great-great-great-grandfather." The lamplight winked through them.

"Go ahead. Put them on," he said. She did.

"Killian Cassidy of County Cork. Ireland. That's how the man himself saw the world."

To Soli, Killian Cassidy's world was a dense and painful blur. She blinked and squinted.

"He arrived in New York harbor in 1880. Back in the days when the Irish weren't wanted here. We found him in the arrival records last summer."

"So he had a Security Number, too," Soli said.

"I suppose he did." He smiled.

"You should put them on," she said.

He smiled sadly, took off his own glasses, and put on the round gold frames. He cleared his throat. "How's that?" His eyes had turned as big and round as an owl's.

"Beautiful," she said.

He smiled wide, crossed his arms. Soli didn't get up then. Maybe she should have. Instead, she stayed put, and looked at Señor Cassidy. And Señor Cassidy looked at her. And it felt good to feel at ease. And so she stayed in her chair, in the dark heart of this house, with its owner and his poetic possessions. She knew that she was part of the poetry, part of its maintenance, at least. It had been a long, long time since she'd been a part of anything.

He smiled. "You've come a long way, Solimar. I'm proud. You should be proud."

"Thank you" was all she could say. How could she tell him that his words were stronger documentation than the nine-digit number now etched in her memory? She looked up, and he seemed to be waiting, had grown very serious.

They heard a step at the study door. Señor Cassidy whipped the glasses off. In the doorway stood the señora, her arms folded across her chest.

"Everything all right, you two?" she asked.

Soli sprang to her feet with a sudden, acute awareness that she'd been sitting in a comfortable seat. Mr. Cassidy's smile stretched wide across his face. "Yes, señora," he said. "Thank you."

In the doorway, the señora stood, arms still folded. She didn't step aside until Soli whispered, "Excuse me." And "Thank you."

The señora's smile deepened, but only her lips moved. Soli couldn't see the woman's eyes in the dark hallway. In the living room again, she picked up the vacuum and switched it on and ran it over the carpet once, twice. She watched the avenues of awakened fiber bloom and dull, until the hammer in her chest subsided.

15.

Rishi was rehashing his proposal. He'd sent it off to Vikram Sen ten days before, as promised, only to have it returned a week later with a two-word reply. *Rehash, please.* What exactly needed to be rehashed, Rishi couldn't say, but rehash he would. He was creating a software model of the programming center; then he'd add windows, air vents, sticking on and plucking off the variables like parts of a Mr. Potato Head. His laptop pinged. As if he'd sensed Rishi's uncertainty, Sen sent another one-liner: *Healthiest fucking babies in the world, yaar.* It was meant to be inspirational, and for the moment it was. Vikram Sen was good at his job. He was very, very wealthy for a reason.

Healthiest fucking babies in the world. Rishi examined each word on his screen as if it held an answer to a greater question. Healthy babies were what Kavya wanted. Healthy babies were all anyone wanted, in the end, whether they knew it or not. A healthy baby was what he wanted.

When parents gave birth, Rishi realized, they got to picture their child before it arrived. They could try on the possibilities, pairing a mother's eyes to a father's nose, hoping for the father's height but not his eyebrows. When Rishi tried to picture the adopted child, the child Kavya seemed already to feel with such conviction, he came up with nothing. When he imagined a boy with black hair, he could see only a blank plain of face. When he imagined a girl with blue eyes, they floated in nebulous flesh. His theoretical children lined up like a row of unfinished dolls, in turns hairless, eyeless, mouthless. And race—he hadn't even begun to chip away at race. So instead of eyes and mouth and hair, he imagined a presence that came to his knees, a well of desire, a spike of ambition. He imagined chatter in a child-high voice, the clammy grip of a hand across his neck.

Rishi was the first to bring up the race question. He was still in the tentative phase of this adventure, but to his credit, he spoke of it often in the days since Kavya decided she wanted to adopt. All his questions bore the conditional tense. The *if* roamed liberally, while the *when* stood staidly by. The idea of adopting hadn't appealed to him at first— had in fact come with the cold shock of a slap. Most unattractive ideas he tucked into a mental recess until they were forgotten. But this idea wouldn't stay in its corner. And so, the thought took up residence. He spoke of it with Kavya most nights, sitting on the sofa after dinner.

"Would it be an Indian baby?" he asked. (Would it even be a baby? he wondered. The possibility of an actual, sharp-elbowed *child* only arose on the tails of this question.)

"Why would they have to be Indian?"

"Well, it wouldn't. I guess."

He knew that Kavya was ignoring race, that she would have already concocted a corny truism that she'd be too embarrassed to say aloud, but strongly believed, something to the effect of love not having a color. So it was Rishi's job to draw her to the pool of reality and ease her into its cold waters.

"*Are* there Indian babies to adopt around here?" she asked.

"I don't know. Maybe. If an Indian teenager got pregnant. It happens, right?"

"Yes. I think. I mean, it must, and it's not like an Indian teenager's going to keep her baby."

"Not with the SATs coming up."

"Ha."

Kavya chewed the corner of her lip. "Would you want to adopt from India?"

Rishi lay back on the sofa. The thought of adopting from India—from anywhere outside of Alameda County—was overwhelming. Just the thought of parking near the social services office in downtown Oakland had nearly put him off the project.

Rishi shook his head.

"You're right," Kavya said. "It's way too expensive, right? Even in India. I mean, I don't actually know. Gold is cheaper there, so maybe adoptions—"

"We're not adopting from India." This was the first time Rishi had said anything definite about their adoption. And in the silence that followed, a new understanding gelled.

"Okay," Kavya said.

"There are kids who need help in this country," Rishi said.

Kavya beamed, and laced her fingers into his.

Rishi was not one to forget a line of questioning. "So what about race?" he asked. "How would that work?"

"I don't know."

"It's mostly black kids who need to be adopted, right?"

"You don't know that."

"I'm probably right."

"I would be honored to adopt an African American child," Kavya said.

"And what would your parents say?"

"My parents would hate me adopting, anyway. They'd probably have a problem with an Indian baby."

There was too much they didn't know. They would have to pursue actual channels of information, which, Rishi was very aware, could plunge them into a real-life adoption. Going to an agency meant they couldn't turn back. Even if they decided not to adopt, they would find themselves at a frightening new level of certitude. Rishi missed already the nebulous world of *maybe* being a father. His thoughts flitted to couples gleefully bonking and finding themselves pregnant. As he took Kavya's hand in his and said, "Let's make some calls in the morning," he knew that the life he'd known was falling into shadow. A new life would begin—possibly a very good or even a better life—but before it did, he and Kavya would have to journey there; they would cross a no-man's-land of uncertainty, parched and dark and crawling with vigilantes. The possibility of emerging unscathed felt slim. The search for a child would take them through stifling obscurity, and already Rishi was finding it hard to breathe.

FEW INSTANCES IN Kavya's family life had proceeded according to her wishes. Her childhood was happy enough. Her parents paid for violin lessons, and read stories to her at night. But like all well-fed middle-class children of professionals, there were things she could—if she put the rest of the world out of mind—manage to complain about. Like the time she'd begged and hoped for a Cabbage Patch Kid, only to be handed a knockoff, a waxy-faced creature that smelled of gasoline, its face a crude assimilation of the adorably pintucked real thing, its butt cheek a blank. This, she'd overcome. Even the revelation that Santa Claus was a fake—spat at her by her overtired mother who couldn't stomach the idea of making Christmas Eve cookies for an already overweight Christian deity—was tolerable. And later in life, the sixteenth-birthday party that ended at 9 p.m.; the quiver of disappointment in her parents' smiles when Kavya proudly announced she'd been accepted to Berkeley, but not to Stanford or Harvard or Yale; the wedding ceremony—*her wedding ceremony*—that had to start at 7 a.m. on a Thursday because her parents' temple priest had determined that this was the only Vedically appointed time that would save her marriage from ending in death and disaster (only later did it occur to Kavya that every marriage ended in either death or disaster). This series of parent-child deflations had prepared her for this moment. She picked up the phone and dialed.

After a few minutes of stilted small talk: "And this is why you called?"

Kavya tried to read her mother's mood, acutely aware of the confessional cliff on which she perched. "No."

The voice grew tender. "What is it, Kavya? Why you're sounding so sad?"

"Well, I'm not sad. Not anymore. I don't think."

Her mother waited.

"We're thinking about adopting."

Her mother remained silent. The phone line crackled.

"Mom? Are you there?"

"You know what I think, Kavya?"

"What."

"Don't get mad when I say this. I think you are putting too much pressure."

"On who?"

"On yourself. On Rishi. On your body. Too much, Kavya. You are working too hard, isn't it? Try to go easy."

"Try to go easy?" This was a phrase Uma Mahendra had never used. Uma Mahendra was not a woman who liked to go easy. "What do you think of us adopting?"

"I think it's a stupid idea."

This was the Uma she knew.

"Adopting is okay, Kavya. It is a good thing to do. But not for us, no?"

"Why not?"

"You don't know the kind of problems, Kavya. This baby could have any kind of problem. Drug addiction. AIDS. Psychotic behavior."

"*Mom.*"

"Mom, pom. Listen to me. When you and Rishi have a baby, when you have *your* baby, you will know what's coming. You'll know this baby comes from good family, with smart brains, with good healthy body, no alcohol, no drugs . . ."

Kavya began to imagine how this might have gone for another woman, one with parents whose outlook wasn't rooted in the absolute necessity of genetic reproduction. She imagined a mother with white-blond hair, feathered—Florence Henderson, specifically—weeping with joy into the phone, weeping with pride, that her child would give of herself so deeply and nobly, that her child would pledge her heart to the child of another.

"You know Moti Uncle's sister? She lives in Michigan. She is doctor. She worked too much and couldn't have children. You know what happened to her?"

Kavya braced herself for whatever travesty had befallen Moti Uncle's sister.

"She adopted one child, some child, I don't know who. And now? You know what is happening? He is doing drug, he is not studying. She kicked him out, and he comes to the house and yells from the driveway. Why, Kavya? Why you want to do this to yourself?"

"You're right, Mom. That's precisely what's going to happen to me. Thank you."

"Don't be fresh."

"Well, I'm doing this, okay? And Rishi wants it, too."

"That Rishi. Put him on the phone."

"We can talk about this later. But it would be nice to have your support." Her nose stung with impending tears. "This is a big thing for me, you know?"

Uma's voice grew high and tight, a sign that she too was close to tears: "You talk like I don't support you. I have only supported you. That is all

I have done in my life, supporting you, and this is my reward? This is what I get?"

"Well. I don't know what to say." Kavya was crying quietly now.

In the long silence that followed grew a mutual realization that this was one battle neither woman had prepared for.

"I have to go," Kavya whispered.

Uma hung up.

When she married Rishi and fell into the forgiving rhythms of her adult life, Kavya assumed all this—the aggressive molding of an identity, the repeated questioning of her choices—would come to an end. But now that she'd decided to adopt, she felt them coming again, the people who believed she was doing something wrong, the people with their questions and doubts and scrutiny, and she bristled. Kavya felt a fight, and in response, her spiny old shell began to emerge.

She curled into the crook of Rishi's arm.

"Well, of course she doesn't like it," he said.

"What do you mean?"

"Think about it, Kavya. Indians. They're, like, crazy for eugenics, right? Think of how much time and energy they put into finding the right matches for their kids. And for what?"

"For money and social status."

"And for offspring. Why do you think Brahmins are so bent on marrying Brahmins? So they don't have some other caste's genetic code souring the batter, right?"

"I guess."

"So, if our families put that much effort into choosing spouses for their kids, they're not going to be cool with an interloper loping in from who knows where and calling themselves family."

"And this interloper would be the innocent child we're adopting. Correct? This would be your interloper?"

"I'm just telling you what they're thinking."

"You're talking to me like I'm either stupid or not Indian."

He smiled. "I know you know." He picked up her hand and kissed it. "Fuck 'em."

"Well, look," she said, softening now. She raised their conjoined hands. "There's been so much inbreeding in India that you and I are probably cousins and don't even know it. I mean, you have what, like four knuckles on this middle finger?"

"Yeah."

"We could use a little fresh air in our gene pool."

He pulled her close and she dug her face into the crook of his shoulder, where he smelled of sweat and skin and waxy soap.

16.

SOLIMAR WAS DOOMED. AND HERE'S WHY. NORMALLY, WHEN we fall in love, it feels at first very much like we're falling, like we're plummeting down a well shaft of desire. But as time passes and we come to know our lovers, we see that there are things about them that are less than dreamlike. Okay, we say, so he spits his rice when he talks. So she snores like a tractor. So he wears a mouthguard at night. These are things, we tell ourselves, that we can live with. And these are things that slow the fall, that bring us to a nice comfortable drift, where we can love without aching, and shift our gaze from the abyss below to the road ahead.

But Soli. Poor Soli. Soli met and loved and lost her man in a matter of seven days, and before she could learn that he had a villainous mother or waxy ears or an insurmountable fear of bees, he was gone. She fell in love with the pure essence of Checo the train rider, Checo the pioneer. And before she could settle into the normalcy of their attachment, he had vanished among dust clouds and a spray of bullets. Whether he'd made it to safety or fallen there on the valley floor, Soli could not know.

She had fallen for Checo and was still falling down and down and down. Most days, she could lose herself in the dusting of shelves, the washing of dishes and making of beds. The love that should have cushioned her was black and fathomless. But it was love. She'd felt it when she was crammed in a truck. She felt it when her baby kicked. She'd even felt it that day, when the three men had taken her, had battered her from the inside. Not even those animals had rid her of her love. When they had torn her panties off and pushed her down, she'd lost herself down that black hole. And that time, for the first time, she felt the darkness catch her.

The day after she'd held Killian Cassidy's glasses, Soli encountered Señora Cassidy in the kitchen. The señora stood before her, a tower of certainty, a hefty book in her hands. "This," she'd said, "is for you. Read it." It was a book on pregnancy and childbirth, written in Spanish. Soli studied it that night, and was stunned to find a list of things she shouldn't have been eating, and even more stunned to find that papayas weren't on the list. What she remembered most clearly about pregnancy in Popocalco was that pregnant women were never, ever to eat papayas. The señora had also teased from Soli a few worrying truths: that she hadn't been to a doctor, that she hadn't found health insurance, that she had no semblance of what the señora called a "birth plan." Soli didn't want to tell the señora that she was being a silly gabacha and that no one in the history of Santa Clara Popocalco had come up with a birth plan, and still managed to give birth just fine. Soli's birth plan was to wail and curse herself and lament her womanly burden until the baby found its own way out. So, "No, thank you, señora," she said. "For me, no birth plan." She did let the señora give her a number, jotted on a piece of paper.

"I'm not sure exactly what your situation is, Soli," she'd said. "But this place will treat you very affordably. Promise me you'll go?"

La Clínica, the señora had written.

"I don't know . . ." Soli trailed off. "My cousin, she can't drive me. . . ."

"It's right by BART! Have you been on BART?"

And so, one evening, Soli found herself outside a clinic splashed with color, a mural on its front wall, bright lights within. She waited in a chair for two hours. She was learning that being rich in this country meant never having to wait. And being poor, even just a little poor like she was, meant steeping in impatience.

Eventually, she was taken to an exam room by a nurse with tired eyes and a young voice. She lay down, and for the first time, a human hand touched her belly. No one had touched this part of her, not with her baby inside. The nurse's fingers, soft and firm, found the baby's elbow and his knees. She rubbed an uneven curve and said, "Here. This is the head. Baby's facing out into the world, Soli." Soli placed her own hand where the nurse's was and felt, undeniably, the curve of her baby's head. She pressed down, just slightly, and it was like pressing a button. She cupped her fingers to his head and gave in to sudden, deflating sobs. "*Oh,*" the nurse murmured, and rested a hand on Soli's shoulder. Soli had noticed this mound before, but had no idea it could be a specific portion of a body. She wept at this small and silver slip of knowledge. She wept for all that she didn't know.

"This is the forehead, I think," the nurse said quietly. "The head is up still, but that's no reason to worry. Baby'll find its way down, soon. It'll be ready when the time comes."

And the nurse said to her, "You'll have to go to social services. For the baby. Understand? Not for yourself." She stared good and hard into Soli's eyes. There was a message in there.

The message came to light the following Monday when Soli rushed from the Cassidys' to the social services building. She'd found the office on her own; her ability to navigate tall gray buildings was making her feel like a sharp and wily woman of the city. She met with a social worker who said, "Come back when the baby's born, okay? With his birth certificate. We'll need to know his or her status. Not yours. It's the baby we're talking about here. The baby's status. Not yours. Got it? I don't need to know where you're from or whether you're a citizen." She gave Soli the same look the nurse had given her. Soli rode that look back to Berkeley, back to Silvia's apartment. It seemed she was carrying precious cargo now, an entity with its own status. It had become an asset of this country, and Soli merely its vessel.

THE NEXT DAY, SHE RETURNED to the Cassidys' filled with the pride of her bureaucratic triumph, for this was how it felt, to have officially declared her unborn child. He was only a fetus, but now he was a fetus with status. She set to cleaning the kitchen and said goodbye to the señor and señora, who left in separate cars, one with Saoirse. When she finished there, she moved to the bedrooms, and finally to the study. The room sat as she'd left it the day before. Soli liked to maintain, among the señor's paper stacks, a few rectangles of absence, spaces on the wooden desk that stayed polished and empty. No pens, no sticky notes. Just a field of smooth brown wood. But today. Today.

Today what she found was a strip of white paper—familiar to her, but from another time. It sat curled and wrinkled, as if it had once been scrunched in a ball. The paper had been smoothed out, but still flailed upward at the ends, like a bird attempting flight. She knew this slip of paper. And when she picked it up, she knew the nine numbers written on it. She knew the writing, because it was hers.

But the señor had thrown them away, her nine numbers, her seguro. Who had resurrected them? She imagined him fingering them, frowning into the telephone as he recited the digits and found out, once and for all, that she was a fraud.

Her vision went gray. The room jolted. *Never throw out a piece of paper,* she remembered. She wasted no time, picked up the paper and tore it to shreds. She flung them in the trash can and pulled out the plastic bag, nearly empty. From the front door, she could hear the trash collectors on their rumbling rounds. The Cassidys' garbage bins waited on the curb, and Soli dropped into them the trash bag, the numbers, her security. She hurried back in the house and slammed the door shut, listening to the quiet buzz of the refrigerator as she waited to catch her breath.

The rest of the day passed as normal. The señor and señora came home, set their bags down, and released her for the day. By evening, thoughts of the number had receded to the uncharted caves of her memory, only to resurface later that night, in a series of muddled dreams.

THE NEXT DAY, SOLI STOPPED outside the Cassidys' door. For the first time, she could hear voices from the sidewalk. The Cassidys were shouting at each other. No. They were speaking very loud and very fast. She couldn't understand them, but she did hear this: Soli. Soli. Soli. Three times, her name popped from the froth of sound.

A woman next door stepped out of her house, spotted Soli, and stared. It was time to go in. As usual, she went to the kitchen door. The voices churned. She turned the doorknob—the voices stopped. She stepped inside.

There stood the señora, the señor, facing her now, their cheeks a high Irish pink, their eyes bright with conviction. They did not smile at first, but as they stopped to catch their breath and register who she was, their smiles began. First with their mouths, moving slowly up their faces but never finding, not quite, the light switch to the eyes. "Hello, Soli," the señora said. They stepped away from each other, and Mr. Cassidy left the room. The señora's eyes followed him.

It was only then that Soli noticed Saoirse, perched on the arm of the sofa, swiping at a cell phone screen. The señora swooped past her and snatched the phone from her grasp. "Enough!" she called above the girl's wails. "Soli," she said. "Mr. Cassidy would like to speak with you.

In his office." She dropped her teaspoon and cursed. The woman was shaken. The room was shaken.

In his study, Mr. Cassidy sat at his desk, his fingertips resting on the very spot where her number had sat. She couldn't pull her eyes away from the desk. For a few moments, they stayed silent together, gazing at the empty patch of wood.

"Solimar."

"Yes." She looked at the floor now, the tips of her shoes just visible beneath her belly. She barely breathed, but her child moved inside her, sliding one way and then the other, like a great fish.

"Solimar, I think you might know what this is about."

"Yes, señor."

"I had a number? On this desk? Your Social Security Number?"

"Yes, señor."

"Do you know what happened to it?"

"No, señor."

He waited.

Soli looked up at him, and gave in. "Yes. I'm sorry. I thought it was garbage."

He smiled sadly. "It wasn't garbage, Solimar. I think you knew that."

She waited for him to stand up and tell her to leave, to take her things and go home and not bother them again with her store-bought number and her teetering half-truths. She waited with both dread and impatience, like waiting for a slap.

"Okay," he said.

"Señor?"

He sighed. "Okay. You can go now. You can get back to work."

She watched him tug at the cuffs of his shirtsleeves. His eyes seemed to shrink beneath their lids, and then shifted away. Rising on shaky knees, she left the study, shutting the door behind her. The hallway was dark and quiet, the kitchen covered in breakfast crumbs, tea-stained and empty. And so she began her day by filling the sink with soapy water, the run of the tap drowning out the whine in her head, the feeble alarm.

"It was the wife," Silvia said later that night. "She wanted to check up on you. I can tell."

"You hardly know her."

"*You* hardly know her. I've worked for enough of these women to know, Soli. They treat you like their prize pony, until you do something that could get them in trouble." She turned from the stove and crossed her arms. "What have you been doing over there?"

"What do you mean?"

"Have you been behaving yourself?"

Soli only stared back at her.

"That señor isn't so rough on the eyes, is he?"

Soli stood. "I didn't do a thing," she said, and sat back down.

"She's watching you, Soli. I'll bet my soul on it. Just watch where you step, okay?"

"Okay. Even though I don't know what you're talking about. And he's old."

Silvia snorted at this. Soli might have pretended, even to herself, that she felt no attraction to Mr. Cassidy, that the thought hadn't even crossed her mind. But a seed planted begins its life underground, Papi used to say. By the time we see it, its roots are down, its buds are calling to the world.

The evening passed and the boys went to bed. Silvia poured herself a glass of diet soda, and handed Soli what was left in the can.

They sat sipping, listening to the hiss and pop.

"Unless you take things the other way," Silvia said. It took Soli a moment to catch her cousin's meaning.

"With the señora?"

"With the señor. You could make him your ally. When you spend so much time with one family, Soli, you need your allies."

"I don't know what you're talking about."

Silvia glared at her now. "I think you know."

Feigning ignorance, she was realizing, was not her strongest move. Yes, there were many things a woman, even a pregnant woman, could do to make her life more complicated. There were plenty of games she could play. But the trouble with games was that games could be lost. And losing, in her case, would be a painful burden to bear.

She returned to work the next day with a newly hatched conviction to be the señora's ally, not her husband's. She became, in Silvia's words, the señora's prize pony. Indispensable, loyal, an entity that moved through the house like an ancestral ghost, giving everything and taking nothing. And rather than feel the burden of this, she found comfort. She sank into a purity of purpose that she hadn't known before. If she'd known the phrase *model employee*, she would have called herself this, without a shadow of irony. She managed to avoid the señor most days, cleaning his office with blunted eyes that didn't see, treating his possessions as motley forms of the same generic matter. She worked quietly and left quietly, letting the señora hold her hands at the end of each day for as long as she wished, returning her gaze only when she said her heartfelt *Gracias*. In this way, the winter passed and the year neared its end. Soli let loose the memory of those nine numbers, the shredded paper, and they floated away, like ashes from a campfire. Three days before Christmas, the Cassidys gave her an extra week's pay and sent her home for the holidays. It was more money than Soli had ever held at one time. She thought back to Papi's five dollars. How rare it had seemed, that single pale bill.

. . .

THAT EVENING, SILVIA CAME HOME with a three-foot tree, and brought down from a closet a small box of ornaments and a string of tiny bulbs. The boys hung them carefully, and the family—for they felt that night like a family—sat on the sofa and watched the glass orbs catch the light.

On Christmas Eve, Silvia refused to go to church. "I haven't been to a church in years," she said, "and I won't be starting now." In Popocalco, the Templo de Santa Clara would be abuzz with services. Soli told Daniel and Aldo about the Three Wise Men and the boy with the poinsettias, who made his way to the manger with nothing but some branches to give the son of God. Silvia picked up tamales and an apple pie and a liter of fancy-looking soda from the expensive supermarket, the one they never went to. The corn casings of the tamales were fresh and warm, but the chicken inside was dry. Even amid their bounty of food, the gratifying hunger of the boys, the sparkle of the tree and the presents beneath it, Soli couldn't help but think of home: Mama patiently grinding and mixing her mole, the wafting scent of romeritos, the rich and potent bacalao, the syrupy rosca cakes that lined the shelves of Señora Garza's tortilleria.

On Christmas Day, they opened presents. Soli bought race cars for the boys and Silvia bought them basketballs and books. Soli bought Silvia a box of soaps shaped like hearts, and Silvia bought Soli a pack of cloth squares. "Burp cloths," Silvia said, "for when the baby throws up down your back."

"Thank you."

The day passed slowly, with little to do. Soon enough, it was dark, and they went to bed. Christmas was over.

17.

KAVYA WAS HOME ALONE ON A SUNDAY AFTERNOON. SHE'D been imagining a child. A dangerous game, she knew, but once invented, the child refused to leave. She imagined him—for he was a he, in this game—an infant tucked into the crook of her arm, his face hidden from view. She imagined him, slightly older, sprawled on the floor with a pile of blocks. She imagined him, school-age now, standing in the doorway, a briefcase in hand. Why a briefcase, she couldn't say, except that the child in this game had become a sort of Alex P. Keaton, earnest and precocious and prim. The doorbell rang and she gasped. She sat and stared at the door. She had conjured something, surely. But could she have? On unsteady feet, she made her way to the front window.

Preeti Patel. Kavya breathed again, and reached for the door but stopped herself, searching for some reason not to answer. She had none. She hadn't thought Preeti even knew where she lived. They'd said exactly ten words to each other at the wedding. Ten words in ten years had felt sufficient. She looked around her living room. Rishi had left a stack of papers strewn across the coffee table. She hadn't vacuumed in possibly weeks.

"Kavya?" Preeti called. "Is that you?"

The curtains hung an inch open and Preeti peeked through them. Kavya cursed herself and opened the door.

"Hi." Preeti stood fresh and tidy on the porch. Her ski jacket—San Franciscans seemed always on the verge of heading for the mountains—was a flattering fuchsia, its collar upturned. She was smaller than Kavya remembered her.

"What are you doing here?"

"Hi," Preeti said again. She stood with her hands on her hips, her eyes wide.

"Hi." Kavya paused. "How are you?"

"Can I come in?"

If Kavya had done the calculations, she would have realized that she and Preeti Patel had not been alone in a room together for eighteen years. Now Preeti found Kavya's sofa and fell to it like she was desperate to stop moving.

"How's it going?" Kavya began. "How's married life?"

Preeti groaned and dropped her head to her knees.

At a loss, Kavya turned to convention. "You want some tea?" She switched the kettle on and found a place on the sofa a few feet from where Preeti sat, head in hands. "Are you okay?"

Preeti looked at Kavya like she was surprised to find her there. "Oh my god," she said. "You're probably like, What the hell is she doing here?"

This was precisely right.

"I've totally fucked up," Preeti said.

"Okay."

"So, I mean, you've fucked up a few times before, right?"

"I guess I'm the local authority."

"Sorry. There aren't many people I can talk to about this."

"About what?" Kavya got up when the kettle whistled. Preeti followed close behind, tailgating her to the kitchen.

Preeti Patel had been having an affair. Preeti Patel was not in love with her own handsome and rich and very new husband. *Preeti Patel was in love with a married man.* The depravity of it sunk Kavya into a pool of such warm redemption that she barely remembered to swallow her smile. His name was Huntley Macaulay, and he was a professor of epidemiology. Kavya had questions, of course, but couldn't get past the name.

Preeti went on: "So he calls me the night before my wedding and tells me he can't live without me. And I tell him to fuck off, of course. I mean, I'd given him like five years of my life, I wasn't about to call off my wedding for him."

"Uh-huh. And Vikram?"

"And Vik knew nothing about him. And he wouldn't have ever known anything about him, except that this morning, Huntley shows up on our doorstep. Drunk. And tells me he's left his wife for me. I mean, what the fuck, Kavya?"

"Yeah. Yeah." What else could she say?

"So then Vik knows everything, or figures out enough, you know, to know. And he leaves. Vikram left and I don't know where he is!"

"Wow." And Kavya meant it.

Preeti burst into tears, right there in Kavya's kitchen. She leaned against Kavya's fridge and spilled wet and snotty tears onto a paella recipe that Kavya had stuck up with a magnet.

"Hey," Kavya said. "Um, okay." A hug seemed to be in order, and Kavya circled her arms around her friend. Preeti gripped Kavya's shoulders and cried into her neck, and Kavya stood with her for as long as she needed to, wondering what Rishi would do if he walked through the door right then.

"God," Preeti croaked, pulling away after soaking the collar of Kavya's shirt. "I'm so sorry. I completely just barged in here and unloaded on you—"

"No," Kavya said. "It's okay." She waited for silence to settle on the room. "So what are you going to do?"

Preeti shrugged.

"You must have other friends. I mean, other friends who'd know where Vikram is." She'd imagined the couple spent their time with a coterie of tech magnates.

Preeti nodded quickly. "Sure. Sure." But looking at her now, Kavya had her doubts.

"Do you still love—Huntley?"

She shrugged again. "I don't know. It's been so long. You sort of get into this—routine—when you're in love with a married person, like you're always ready for disappointment. And the disappointment becomes so normal that you forget what happiness feels like. I mean, I *should* be happy, right?"

"But what about Vikram? Do you love Vikram?"

"I do. I think I do. He's kind of my only hope, you know?"

"And Huntley?"

She shook her head. "Anyone named Huntley can pretty much suck my balls."

Kavya laughed, and even Preeti was moved to a sort of weepy chuckle.

"So it's Vikram, then."

She shrugged. "If I ever find him."

"Well, go find him."

She looked up at Kavya and seemed to reconsider her. "You're right."

Between the two friends hung an understanding that things were not so simple, that love wasn't always about free will. Kavya walked to the sofa to pick up Preeti's jacket. The strange detour from her strange afternoon was over. "Do you want to call me?"

"Yes. Yes, I'll call you." She took the jacket from Kavya and held it to her chest.

Kavya knew how ancient friendship worked, and was very aware that Preeti might never call at all. When Rishi got home less than an hour later, he walked in, stopped short, and gazed at Kavya.

"Are you smiling?" he asked.

She shrugged. She smiled.

"What're you smiling about?"

"I don't know." And she didn't. "Preeti Patel came by today."

"Excuse me?"

"Preeti Patel. Stopped by."

"Why?"

"I don't know," she lied, silenced, surprisingly, by an ancient sense of loyalty.

"Was it—nice?"

"She's got a filthy mouth." Kavya placed a hand on Rishi's neck, and felt there the clinging sun. "Let's celebrate," she said.

It didn't matter what they were celebrating, only that they felt celebratory at all, only that the evening celebrated with them. The imaginary child, she left at home. They stepped out onto Shattuck, and thoughts of Preeti drifted away. The air popped with ocean salt. A salsa band played outside Green Pizza and a couple danced on the sidewalk. At the streetside florist, peonies caught the sun and blazed orange, and sweet peas rose from their metal pails with a purity that verged on joy.

18.

ON AN EVENING IN MARCH, AS SOLI WALKED THROUGH the dark from her bus stop, a new kind of pain sliced through her. It gripped the lower band of her abdomen, wrung her out and didn't let go. She doubled over right there on the sidewalk until it ended. She made it home, and it grabbed her again. Silvia found her leaning against a table, straining against her own breath.

"Silvia," she said. "I think it's starting."

Silvia lay her down on the carpet, with a sofa cushion beneath her head. She sat with her cell phone, timing the contractions, stroking Soli's forehead. The pains felt like terrible gas cramps, and Soli wanted nothing more than to sit on a toilet and get them out. But that wasn't what this was. This delivery was going to rip her body in two. She would die, surely. When Soli couldn't stop herself from crying, Silvia let her cry. She seemed to know that this labor was not just physical.

"Listen," she said, taking Soli's hand, wiping the hair from her wet face. "You know what happens, Soli? You know how parts of you go to the baby? Through the placenta? Your blood and your cells and your vitamins?" Soli knew none of this, but nodded. "Parts of that baby go through to you, too. His cells and his blood. He leaves pieces of himself inside you, and they'll be there forever. It's a two-way street, Soli. You live in each other. Forever."

Three hours later, Silvia drove Soli to the clinic. She waited at the check-in desk, barely able to stand on her feet, while Silvia confirmed repeatedly the price of the service, demanding it in writing, refusing to fill in paperwork until she had documented proof that she wouldn't be paying more than she'd budgeted for this birth.

"Just pay!" Soli finally shrieked. "Just pay!" Someone—she couldn't see who—lowered her by the elbows into a wheelchair and wheeled her to a delivery room. A woman in blue clothes came in and introduced herself as Nurse Camila. She explained to Soli what she was about to do. Soli heard none of it, and allowed her feet to be guided into stirrups, her knees pushed apart.

"You'll feel some pressure now," the nurse said. Her hand shoved into Soli and she gasped. The hand prodded her insides, explored her like a hard little animal, and she began to weep. She was back on the rocky roadside with the men in cowboy hats. They shoved themselves inside her. They ground her down to a dusty pile of sand. She closed her eyes to the fluorescent lights above, her ears to the nurse's murmur. The nurse pushed deeper and she screamed.

"Whoa! Okay, Solimar. I'm done for now. I just checked how open you were—your cervix. Okay? So we know how far along you are. How close to delivering."

Soli let out a long, low hum.

"Nice work, Solimar. You're three centimeters. You're on your way."

Silvia came in, at last. "I'm late for a job," she said. "I have to go."

"Go." Soli lay on her side, parsing out her breath like the nurse had shown her. She shut her eyes against a fresh contraction.

"Try to relax," Silvia said. "You can do this on your own, Soli, you understand? I could lose this client if I don't—"

"Go!" Soli growled. She kicked out feebly, her foot smacking Silvia's side. She turned onto her other side and did not watch her leave. The door clicked shut, and a cascade of liquid gushed from between her legs.

"No," she gasped. "Help!" she called. "I need help!" She continued to gush, no matter how she tried to stop it, and she was back on the flour truck, piss running down her thighs, the boys around her silent and staring.

The door opened again, and Nurse Camila walked in.

"Who closed this door?" The nurse spoke to her in Spanish, and Soli began to cry.

"I need help," she answered. "I'm sorry. I didn't mean to do it."

The nurse stopped when her foot slid. "*Ai*," she said. "Okay."

"I didn't mean to. It was an accident!"

The nurse gathered towels from a cupboard and spread them on the floor, then took a seat next to Soli.

"That's your fluid," she said. "Your water broke. That's all, Soli. Nothing to worry about."

Alone in the delivery room, Soli labored for eight hours longer. At times, she wanted nothing more than sleep. Other times, she was certain the pain would kill her, that she was doomed to a life alone with her burdens, that being alone would be her death. Camila came and went, monitoring her blood pressure, offering her plastic cups filled with ice cubes. Soli was hungry and weak. Her face and neck were soaked. She sucked on the ice until a late, thunderous contraction made her chuck the cup at the wall. A team of medical personnel trailed in, as if summoned by this last contraction. More nurses, a doctor, a man setting instruments on a tray.

The doctor stepped to her side and began talking, but Soli heard nothing but the last part: "You're going to start pushing now. Are you ready? Push down like you're going to the bathroom."

Soli did just this; it was all she could do, and through the waves of pain and a fear of shitting came the relief of knowing she was doing what was right and real. She closed her eyes and the earth charged forward, the trees rushing by. She felt the wind against her eyelids, Checo's arm around her waist. Checo's eyes, their walls of intent. She focused on his eyes. When the trees vanished and the earth grew dark and close, the thought of Checo wrapped around her and he pulled her through. For twelve more contraction cycles, she breathed and pushed, tunneling endlessly.

And then: "Do you want to feel your baby's head?" Camila guided Soli's hand to a spot between her legs, where she felt the small globe of flesh, warm and wet and foreign. At last, with a tearing scream, she bore down and pushed and felt the solid slide of a body pass from hers.

The people around her leapt into action. "You did it!" someone cried. "He's here!" The nurse held the baby up for Soli to see. He was crimson and shone with slime, his eyes trapped shut. He was barely human. An alien cord extended from his navel and disappeared somewhere between her legs. She stared, appalled. Above the cord she caught a glimpse of a miniscule, very human penis. A boy. Her boy. He thrust his fists into the air and wailed. Moments later, still slick with fluid, he lay on her naked chest, his small lips churning, searching for her breast.

HE WAS SMALLEST AT NIGHT, when shadows lapped at his edges. In the dark, he was magically small, a miracle, a sprite. It was easy, in the hours before dawn, to think Ignacio might die, only because it seemed impossible that such a creature could live a whole week and then two, then three and four. It was impossible to think that four weeks could grow into a lifetime.

Love wasn't a word that meant anything to Soli, not when she looked at her boy. Love was a television word. Soli held her sleeping son, his fists balled and eyes shut tight, clinging to a dream. What she felt for him was epiphany. She had awakened, sprouted a new layer of skin, pink and raw and wholly vulnerable. For the first time since arriving in

America, she was well and truly scared. And so she named him Ignacio, for the patron of retreats.

At times, the fear consumed her. Fear that Ignacio would stop. Simply stop. That each breath, the revelation that it was, could surely not lead to another.

Fear that should anything happen to her child, she would be obliterated. She was at the world's mercy now, in a way she'd never known.

Fear that should something happen to *her*, her son would never know who his mother was, this woman whose every inhalation raked with desire. Awakened, fearful, Soli had room for little else. Room, barely, to think of Checo. Room, barely, to think of her baby's other possible fathers—the roadside vaqueros who'd left her balled up like a trodden insect. Lucky Ignacio. Lucky boy. Not all fathers were trovadors.

But in the end, there was only one possibility that she could live with. In a clinic recovery room, at her core a punctured and spewing volcano, Soli locked eyes with the parcel in her arms. She had spent many nights worrying about how this moment would play out, whether the creature she birthed would resemble a rapist, whether she'd live out her days with an angel-skinned reminder of three devils by a roadside. But there in the clinic, an hour after she'd given birth, she awoke to the sight of her son, swaddled and placed in the wheeled transparent bassinet. She'd picked him up, placed him against the bump of her belly, and took her first long look. She felt herself falling again, this time faster. From her son's head rose a brief tremor of hair, and planted in the center of his face was a fine razor of a nose, Checo's nose, rendered by some miracle in sweet, picayune perfection.

19.

A TUNE, A HUM FROM SOLI'S LIPS, EACH NOTE A PINPRICK to sensitive ears. She hardly knew she was singing.

"Ignacio El Viento Castro Valdez," she whispered to the bundle in her arms. "I will call you Nacho, and so will your cousins and friends. If only we knew your father's family name, you would have that, too." She couldn't name him Checo; to Soli, only Checo was Checo. And so, to combat the primal, heart-crunching fear, he would be Ignacio. "And El Viento for your father, for the wind," she said. Digestively, at least, he was living up to this.

So far, like a good son, he had given Soli everything she wanted: for Ignacio to guard her thumb in the curl of his fist, for him to reach for her in that baby way, his hands trembling, as if air and light were his own phantasmic inventions. She wanted him to search the sky for her, to kick his legs and struggle for her breast, as if milk were air and suckling, breathing. All she wanted was that he stay this way for a good while longer. As long as he stayed the same, she could stay the same, wrapped in her room and sheltered from the do-this and do-that of the world beyond the door.

His shit smelled like baking bread. His lips were hardly lips at all. The button of his chin, the porcelain poppy cups of his ears. The sturdy fat of his hands.

"I will tell you about your father, Ignacio," Soli said, but she fell asleep before she began. She sat propped up in bed with eyes closed and mouth open, cradling him in one arm. She would wake again and continue: "I will tell you about your father, the wind. I'll tell it to you now, when you're too young to have to understand." She would speak quietly so as not to invite the snatching spirits.

"How to explain La Bestia? It was a monster train. You don't know what monsters are, but being a child, you soon will. Your father and I rode La Bestia together. He protected me. There were bandits on that train who would throw you off it, send you down to the slicing wheels, if you didn't give them all you had. There were hit men and con men and some downright no-good majaderos. But we won't talk about them. We'll talk about your father the wind. He was one of the good ones. There were many good ones, people who would rather leave the place they loved than stay home to ruin it.

"Your father said he was going to be a gardener. He could name every tree we passed. He would probably move on, he said, start off with a boss but build his own business." Checo had said this only to Soli, on one of their few mornings together, when they lay wrapped in his sweater in the predawn chill. Around his braying, bragging boys, he kept his mouth shut, pretended along with the rest of them that nothing much mattered.

Here Soli paused, because she thought of Pepe, the loudest of all, and the smallest. Checo had kept an eye on him. He did it in a way, of course, that Pepe would never have noticed; and, likewise, Pepe sought out Checo, hovered beneath his protective wing in a way he thought Checo would never suspect.

Pepe was tonto enough to play the sorts of daredevil games the big guys did. Lying down on the train, dozing, running and jumping when they had room, playing kick-me-in-the-chest, just to pass the time. One afternoon, as the sun burned low and orange on the horizon, Pepe lay on his side, watching a small town rush past. His voice was lost under the roar of the train, but from the way he opened his mouth and held it, the way he jutted his chin just so, Soli knew he was singing.

He sat up. "I see it!" he'd shouted. "I see it!"

Soli had turned to find a few tall towers in the distance, as long and thin as cigarettes.

"It's Arizona!" Pepe cried. "I know it is!"

He jumped to his feet.

And BAM. Like a gun had gone off. Pepe hit a tunnel. Soli screamed. Everyone screamed. Only Checo had the sense to grab in the dark for Pepe's arm. He caught it. When they emerged from the tunnel, the boy swung like a pendulum, batting against the train's metal flank. He was silent. His head hung down so that no one could see his face to know if he was alive. "Pepe!" Checo had shouted. "Pepe!" It was a miracle that Checo had caught him, but sometimes miracles don't amount to much. Pepe wasn't answering, and Checo himself was falling from the train, dragged down by the boy's dead weight. The others, Mario and Flaco and Nutsack, were calling, *Drop him! Drop him!* They pulled back on Checo's legs. But Checo held on until the last thin finger of the boy's hand had sidled from his grip. And Pepe fell beneath the train. They felt barely a bump below, and then he was gone, as if he had never existed. Not everyone would have tried to save Pepe. Some would have been too slow, others too tired. Soli wondered, in the silent and horrified hours that followed, if Pepe had had a moment to realize that the tall buildings were not Arizona, that America was still a long way away. She hoped he hadn't. She hoped that when he'd died, all he'd seen was the great city against the sunset, a quivering filament of glory. What a thrill for a little boy, to discover America.

"But you want to know where your papi is, Nacho." She paused. "Nacho. We don't know." The last time she'd seen Checo was outside a factory in northern Mexico, running for his life, Soli exploding inside, more certain with every second that letting him go would be the worst decision she'd ever made. But she'd had no choice. There was no long goodbye, no final kiss. At the edge of the Sonoran desert, shots rang out. Whether they were bandits or drug traffickers or drug-trafficking bandits, she would never know. What she did know was that the whole group ran—Mario, Flaco, Nutsack, and Checo. They scattered in all directions. What she did know was that she was safe, and so was her hidden baby. "I made it," she told Nacho. "I made you.

"I didn't know what I was doing when I did it, but it turns out I survived for you. I might tell you all this again someday. I might tell you about your father when you're old enough to know. I may tell you about my voyage some years from now, when you've grown and you've known a little of the bad stuff of life. Just when you think you know what's what and you can't be touched, I will tell you everything. And when I do, Ignacio El Viento Castro Valdez, you'll know what you are made of."

THE FIRST MONTH PASSED in a flash. Soli did not grow bored. She did sit for hours before the television, but spent most of them watching Ignacio work at her breast. When you have just one possession, you guard it with your life. The *you* that once centered your universe becomes nothing but a keeper of the one precious thing. As the weeks passed and Ignacio proved increasingly that he would live, Soli's fear shifted to the newly formed knowledge that she was now tied more fiercely to fate and luck than she'd ever been before. Having a child was like turning inside out and exposing to the world the soft pulp of her heart. If something happened to Ignacio—if illness took him or an accident, she herself would never recover. If the night stole his breath away, as sometimes happened to the very very young, her own breath would never return. At night, thoughts like this sat vigil around her bed. She woke every few hours to look at him, lying next to her in a nest of blankets. She felt for his breath, touched a hand to his forehead, and tried to sleep again.

But those were the nights. The days were a different story. The days brought her light and comfort and the eager Berkeley spring. And amid the uncertainty of new motherhood, the sleepless fog that hung over her days, Soli felt, at last, that she had a home. Motherhood was her dwelling, the boy at her breast her hearth. After a month of heavy dawns, Soli returned to the Cassidy bungalow, this time with a basket full of boy.

20.

Rishi arrived fuming, after an hour of trying to park in downtown Oakland. The lobby of the social services building was as bleak as he'd expected. A guard who'd fallen asleep on his perch pointed him to a partition in the lobby's far corner.

Every head turned to watch him take his seat—twenty, maybe thirty people who looked like they wanted to be parents, and two at the front, who looked like they worked for social services.

Kavya nudged him. "Where were you?"

He'd come straight from work. He was sweating and had expected snacks. The Department of Social Services apparently didn't budget for snacks. The private agency they'd been to had set out sushi and bottles of wine and sparkling water infused with a variety of subtle fruit flavors. The private agency had shown them a video of testimonials from the parents and children they'd matched. What Rishi remembered most were blue skies and sprinklers. The room they'd sat in was wood-paneled, a sauna of central heating and perfume. The meeting had felt like a two-hour infomercial, capped off by the sticker shock of the estimated cost of private adoption. They had spent their money, nearly all of it, on trying to get Kavya pregnant. It was a gamble that had seemed entirely worthwhile, at the time.

And so he found himself here, in the beige florescence of the social services building, with an empty stomach and a sullen wife.

Kavya crossed her arms and gripped her elbows. He felt her deltoids recede and knew she was trying, quite literally, to give him the cold shoulder. What went on for the next hour was the distribution of checklists and training packets. Before him lay a pamphlet titled "Foster Care Facts." Rishi liked facts. In a financial panic, he had called the DSS to find out about state-run adoptions. It turned out that the state ran foster-adoptions, meaning that fostering came first, and if the circumstances aligned, adoption followed.

THE ENTIRE UNDERTAKING still felt distant to Rishi, but the meeting facilitators spoke of their decision like it was a foregone conclusion. Here, the need, not the price tag, was overwhelming. The county at the time had 1,400 foster children and 251 participating families. Children were in need of a safe place to live.

Rishi came away from the meeting with a heightened awareness of how children paid the price for adults and their calamitous judgment. He looked at the couples streaming past him, men and women, men and men, women and women. They all looked terribly sure of themselves. They walked like they knew what they had come for, like they could say for certain that their homes were better than the homes from which children were being taken. Such confidence worried Rishi. He doubted himself. How could a warm home and a hybrid car guarantee anything? And good intentions? These scared him the most: People with good intentions tended not to question themselves. And people who didn't question themselves, in the scientific world and beyond, were the ones to watch out for.

That night, Rishi lay awake. The heat was up too high. He listened to his thoughts course past. Fostering, adoption's slimmer cousin, lay on the pillow beside him now, blowing in his ear. Kavya had said she was cold and now her body was a campfire next to his. She lay awake beside him. Neither could sleep.

"Should we have sex?" Rishi asked.

"That's not the solution," Kavya said.

"Do we need a solution right now?"

The numbers had been running through Rishi's mind, and they seemed to present a pretty tidy equation. Fostering paid for itself, especially if they fostered to adopt. The meeting had left him with a pit in his gut, but it was the right sort of pit. For the first time in a long while, Rishi sensed that the planning and talking and thinking about a child would result in something real, and possibly something wonderful.

He'd heard about bad foster parents, and he wanted to be one of the good ones. The life he'd envisioned for himself was changing. The future was being reborn. Rishi and Kavya's conversations stepped up to a new level of complexity, a higher pitch of possibility.

"I think it sounds smart," Rishi said. "Fostering."

"I don't like the sound of it."

He knew she wouldn't. He knew she'd bought into the wood paneling and party trays at the private agency.

"It's not like the kids would be better there," he said.

"Where?"

"At the private place. It's not like you're buying a better kid."

"And?"

"So why not go with kids who really need us?"

"All these kids need us, Rishi. All of them."

Yes, all those children. All those children needed them, and there was only one Rishi and one Kavya. The thought of making his own child, when there were already so many others, seemed suddenly obscene.

"I don't think you're thinking, though, Kavya. I mean, the price for the private—"

She sprang from her pillow. "The price! You're thinking about the price!"

He sat up: "Well, someone has to. What do you want, Kavya? Do you want to spend everything? All of it? Do you want to go into serious debt when we don't have to? Do you want to take away all the money that we might have spent on schools and—"

"I don't want to lose the child."

The sentence shot cold and clear through that overheated room.

"What?"

"I don't want to foster a kid, and get attached to him, and then have to give him up when his mom gets her act together."

"Oh."

"That would be too much," she said.

"But what if we go concurrent, and we end up adopting him?"

"That may not happen."

Logic was Rishi's weapon, and Kavya was using it against him.

The discussion continued for days. It skirted around fostering, adopting, the elusive day when they'd finally have a child. It never swelled to an argument, but rumbled with the persistence of an underground train. What resulted was this: a home inspection appointment with a licensing evaluator, an enrollment slip for four weeks of six-hour training sessions, twenty-four hours of training in all.

The social worker drove up in a Chevy Cavalier with government license plates. Her name was Joyce. She was, as Rishi had privately predicted, a rotund woman with a soft brown face and a hard, official edge that could shing like a switchblade. The first thing she asked to see was the child's room; foster children couldn't share a room with their foster parents. Kavya took her to the small guest room, still occupied by a double bed and squat bookshelf. Welcoming afternoon light filtered in through the window. Outside grew an old and abundant magnolia tree.

She'd envisioned a nursery in here, with walls painted sage green, a white changing table and crib.

"And where would a child sleep?" Joyce asked.

"We'll get a crib," Rishi assured her. "One with organic wood, I was thinking. Hardwood, not composite. The composites leach formaldehyde."

Joyce looked doubtful. "You know you might be getting a child, right? Not a baby?"

They'd signed up for a zero-to-five-year-old, and were hoping to land somewhere closer to the zero. "The crib would fold out!" Rishi said. "I mean, the ones I've seen—" He paused, cleared his throat, looked down at his feet. "I work at Weebies, and the ones on our site have sides that slide down and turn into little beds." Joyce seemed to be watching more than listening. Rishi looked to Kavya. "But we could get something bigger, right?" He turned back to Joyce. "We saw this fire engine bed the other day. It was, like, in the shape of a fire engine, but with a—"

"That's fine," Joyce said.

Walking out the front door, she softened. "I think you two will do just fine." She paused on the threshold. "We need more people like you."

21.

THE CENTER OF THE UNIVERSE WAS SITUATED AT THE CORNER
of Shattuck and Vine. Solimar spent her afternoons with Saoirse and
Nacho, Green Pizza on one side, Chez Panisse on the other. And all
around her, children, infants, strollers and carriers, mothers wrapped in
layers, fresh cheeks blooming in the shade of tired eyes. And the fathers, men with saintly faces and childish bellies.

Soli might have lost herself in the stream of happy, healthy mothers
who made their way down Shattuck Avenue, past the bakery, pausing at
the florist, stopping for coffee. She went out each day with Nacho in a
folding buggy, a bag slung over her shoulder (stuffed with diapers and
wipes and a small stack of folded onesies, should the baby's bowels grow
volcanic) and a new pair of sunglasses (a gift to herself, from herself).

"Look at you," Silvia said. "You look like one of those ladies. Like a
Berkeley mother."

Soli clicked her tongue. "I'm no Berkeley mother. I'm a mother in
Berkeley, but I'm no Berkeley mother." Fair enough. Her sunglasses came
from the drugstore, her sweater fortified with rayon, not mountain-ready
down fill. Her skin, flawless, was a product of youth, not of a go-to es-
thetician. For the most part, the mothers of Berkeley had a good twenty
years on her. In Popocalco, they would have been grandmothers. And
for the women around her, the afternoon was a time to stare through

their sunglasses at the street, managing sippy cups and tamping down the flaring tempers of their toddlers. While they weren't exactly relaxed, they weren't exactly at work, either. But Soli was on the job.

At her side walked Saoirse, her strawberry hair in a high ponytail, the sweetness of sunscreen wafting upward, her limbs as fawnlike as her mother's. There was no mistaking Soli for the mother of this Celtic fairy child. More obviously hers was the sleeping infant, his mouth slightly open and his wide swathe of cheek pressed to her chest.

Nine months had passed. And how do nine months pass? With sidewalks blue with rain. With an Easter, a birthday. Soli turned twenty, and her parents acquired a phone line. They called to tell her that she had given them more than they could have hoped for. Talking to them brought a swell of hot tears.

As she spoke, Ignacio reached for the phone, his wet lips churning, wanting not to talk, but to cram the thing in his mouth and suck. Soli twisted away from his reach, fearing that he'd cry if she put him down, revealing himself at last.

She had not found the courage to tell her parents that she was pregnant—the cojones, so to speak, and her ovarios were still catching their breath. And after she'd given birth and discovered the torrent of her own love for her child, and realized that the father was exactly who she'd hoped he would be, she cowered at the thought of explaining to them the grandson they might never see.

Popocalco, Papi, Mama, home—these receded even farther into the past, and Soli found herself living a life that was, more than ever, her very own. Returning to work at the Cassidys' meant finding a newly negotiated rhythm. Her days pre-Ignacio had been quiet and calm. Cleaning every day meant not having to clean much, and she could stretch her mornings over a sparse list of things to do: after-breakfast dishes, wiping down surfaces, sweeping the floors or mopping them, checking the windows for spots, the toilets for spots, the mirrors for spots. She'd once had hours at her disposal to pick up the señora's Delft figurines, to examine the passage of light through her finely buffed windowpanes, to rub a washcloth over faucet handles, just to see them shine.

But now, but now. Who knew this about children? They take up all your time. Even when they're not doing a thing. What was Ignacio but a fleshy bulb of human growth? What could he possibly ask of Soli?

Only for her everything. Only for her every drop of time, of milk, of sight. To look away from Ignacio was to abandon him. To put him in a bouncy seat, catastrophic. To leave a room that he was in, unthinkable.

Soli couldn't buff the windowsills. She couldn't hold a ceramic figurine in the palm of her hand without Ignacio, clinging chimpishly to her chest, grabbing for it. So she carried him from chore to chore and grew used to him screaming. She tried to do the two-handed chores—the dishes, the mopping—when the Cassidys were out, so the shrieking wouldn't disturb them. In a matter of months, the baby would need real food, more clothes, more shots. Getting fired was not an option. So Soli held Nacho over the toilet while she scrubbed it, she pressed him to her chest as she sprayed and scrubbed the stove, the oven, the cupboards. He fed at her breast as she ran a Brillo pad over the seams of the kitchen sink.

The señora came home early one afternoon. She stopped at the bathroom door and found Ignacio screaming on the tiled floor, Soli scrubbing furiously at the shower drain, leaking tears of her own.

"Soli!" the señora cried, her eyes perfect platelets of alarm.

And that's when things began to change.

First: The señora bought a baby-carrying contraption. An *Ergo.*

Ergo, Soli began to work with her boy strapped to her chest. This solved the problem of the screaming, the one-armed scrubbing, and made things easier, in some ways.

Soli had seen other women, the Berkeley mothers, carry their babies in these things. She'd seen a woman carrying what must have been a three-year-old in one of these things. With Nacho strapped to her chest, and then her back, she returned to work. Still, she wondered, was this all that lay in store for her? Mornings and workdays and exhausted nights?

Soli was not tortured. Soli was not abused. So no, Soli didn't have it so bad. She wasn't cheated of pay, overworked, or starved. She was never actually threatened with deportation; never from the Cassidys' tea-warmed lips did she hear the word *ICE*. She didn't have to clean with materials that corroded her nasal passages or coated her intestines with toxic sludge. And for this she should have been happy. But the uncertainty of Soli's happiness remained, a permanent raised eyebrow on the face of the great green woman she'd equated with America, the supposed mother of exiles. Soli had arrived tired, poor, a huddled mass indeed, and had been given a bed to sleep in and a place to work, money in hand, the outlines of a life. But Soli longed for more—and wasn't this the American way? She could hear Checo laugh at her. *More! Give me more!* She couldn't put a name to her hunger, and America made no promises. It was she, and the others like her, the fools with stars and stripes in their eyes, who imagined such rewards.

For a time, her working life became systematic. She cleaned in the mornings, made a snack for Saoirse and took it to preschool pickup. She washed dishes and sprayed countertops and folded toilet paper ends into sweet rosettes. Ignacio was fond of open windows, liked to grasp and turn the crank, liked to place his palm against the screen and feel the air pass against it. When she was alone, she'd pull her breast from her shirt and let him feed while she worked. Against the warm cushion of her breasts, Ignacio spent most of each day snoozing. His breath rattled when he slept. It was the sound of the wind within him, Soli told herself, the ebb and flow of his life source.

And one evening, Silvia had news. "The men came today," she said.

Soli had no idea what she meant, but it was never a good thing when men came. She clarified: "The men for the money. The coyote's men."

Soli slumped into a chair. The apartment around her hadn't been touched. Silvia was calm. Nothing had been moved, nothing harmed. "And you had the money?"

"I did," Silvia said. "Of course I did." She brought out the notebook where Soli's expenses had been tallied. "And now," she said, "we begin the accounts." Soli sat down with her cousin to decide how she'd pay back the three thousand dollars. There was no ideal plan; every option seemed to take too long or ask for too much. Choosing how to pay Silvia was like choosing which of her fingers to slice off. But eventually they settled on one, and Soli settled into the reality of having less to send home and to spend on her boy, of watching the colors of this dream fade, for a time, from brilliance.

A SEASON PASSED, and before Soli could pause to count the teeth on his gums, Ignacio turned one year old. She planned an evening with Silvia and the boys. The days were getting longer, so they'd spend an hour or two at a playground, and then take the boys to ice cream. Real ice cream, Soli promised them, with many scoops and chocolate sauce and fake cherries. It was a Thursday.

"Soli," the señora said that morning. "We have a reception to get to this afternoon. Any chance you could watch Saoirse an extra hour or so? Till six or so? It's just on campus. Just a show-your-face kind of thing."

Soli liked that expression. A show-your-face kind of thing. She would use it herself one day.

The señora left at three in a current of perfume, a silk scarf trailing behind her. Saoirse, sitting on the living room rug with Ignacio, looked up when the door closed. "Where's she going?"

"To a party, m'ija."

The girl's face crumpled.

"Not a fun party. Don't worry."

Soli's thoughts turned to her own party, due to start in three hours. She'd meet Silvia at a park near their apartment. Silvia would bring a Tupperware of food, and they'd spread themselves over a picnic table beneath the last rays of the afternoon sun. Soli had seen other Mexican families celebrating in parks, with throngs of cousins and uncles and aunts. Paper lanterns hung from the trees, and piñatas. Music blared from radios. Someday I'll have that, too, Soli told herself. Thoughts of an ideal future bobbed to the surface now and then. But because she didn't know how this would come about, she tamped down her hopes of a sprawling and joyous throng. And when such thoughts popped back up, she let them float by, until they'd traveled out of sight again.

She made Saoirse a grilled cheese sandwich with the Gruyère her mother had set out. She chopped some carrots and poured a glass of soy milk. She would wait to feed Ignacio in the park, his birthday dinner, followed by his first taste of ice cream. At 5:30, Soli cleared away the dishes and fed Ignacio a snack, just a small one, just two crackers. Silvia was making tlayudas with fresh salsa. At 5:45, she changed Ignacio's diaper and buttoned his sweater. At 6:00, bags packed, Ignacio in the Ergo, she waited by the door. The Cassidys owned a car that made hardly any noise, but Soli would recognize the tick-tick-tick of its approach.

At 6:10, she sat back down, bag in hand, and waited. Saoirse was watching television. She thought about turning off the television then, to let Saoirse get her whining out before her parents returned. Six fifteen. Soli turned off the television to Saoirse's wails. Six twenty. Soli scanned the sky. The sun was losing its verve. Her phone rang and she grabbed for it. Silvia.

"We're on our way," Silvia said. "Are you there already?"

"We're leaving any minute. Any minute now."

Six thirty came and went. Six forty-five. Seven.

Saoirse yawned. "It's time for bed," Soli told her, not at all sure of what time the girl went to sleep.

"I need to have my bath."

"No bath tonight. Get in bed." Soli helped her into pink pajamas, watched her scrape a toothbrush over her faded pebbles. Into the sink she spat a thin bubbly stream, then turned her teeth to Soli for inspection.

"Muy bien."

In the darkened bedroom, she held Saoirse's hand and willed her eyelids to close. The weight of Ignacio pulled at her shoulders, so she unsnapped the Ergo and lay him down next to Saoirse. He sat up and examined the fair-haired girl who lay before him. When he grabbed for her face, Soli whisked his hand away. She thought of leaving the girl, of letting the Cassidys find her asleep and safe, without her nanny. Soli never did bedtimes.

Seven fifteen passed and the sky went gray. The sun would retire for the evening, and within minutes, the day would be dark, the parks deserted. From the other room, she could hear her cell phone ring. It would be Silvia, asking where she was.

By 8:00 Ignacio lay asleep against her chest, unaware that he'd been alive a whole year.

Silvia, on the phone: "We'll do it another day."

"This weekend," Soli whispered.

"This weekend."

It was 9:00, and Soli sat staring into the living room, Ignacio asleep on the sofa, when she finally heard a key in the door.

"We're home!" the señora called out, too loudly. She clicked into the kitchen on high-heeled boots, teetering in the half-dark. "Did you miss us? Is Saoirse in bed?" She was still speaking too loudly. Mr. Cassidy followed her in, handsome in a suit and tie, his hair swept gallantly off his forehead.

Soli stood on trembling knees. The señora dropped her smile. "What happened?"

Soli only shook her head. She didn't want to make trouble.

"Is Saoirse okay?" She clicked across the kitchen. "Soli, tell me what happened."

"Today is Ignacio's birthday," she managed to say. "He is one year."

The señora brought both hands to her cheeks, and beamed. "Oh, my little boy!" She lurched forward and smeared Ignacio's cheek with a badly aimed kiss. Soli caught the sharp tang of liquor. "Happy, happy birthday, my beautiful boy! Buon compleanno!"

She stumbled into the hallway, called good night to Soli, and shut her bedroom door.

The señor poured himself a glass of water, then headed for the hallway. He stopped, turned. "Oh," he said. "Did you have something planned? For Ignacio?"

Yes, she wanted to answer. Yes, we did and we had to cancel it. A simple statement of fact, but even this felt like a battle cry. Soli tried to force the words, any words, but instead her lip began to tremble.

"Ah, jeez," Señor Cassidy said. "Ah, jeez, Soli. I'm sorry. I— We didn't mean it. No, we didn't think. Shit. Shit."

She stared dumbly at the door, doing all she could not to cry.

"C'mere." His words ran together and his voice was hoarse. He stepped toward her and before she could move, he pulled her into a loose sort of hug. And from the warm wall of his chest rose a cloud of soap, of liquor, of whatever lay beneath the cloth of his shirt. In spite of herself, she let her head rest.

"I could give you a ride home," he offered.

Soli looked up at him. His eyes focused on hers. He'd been drinking but was not drunk. From the hallway, a door clicked open.

The señora, sleepily. "Brett? Brett."

He looked down at Soli. "I guess I can't. I'm sorry."

She picked Ignacio up from the sofa and balanced him on her chest as she fastened the Ergo. The señor reached into his pocket and pulled out his wallet, counting out a fan of twenties.

"For your extra time," he said. She stared at the money but couldn't bring herself to take it. "Take it, please. For your time." Three twenty-dollar bills. Pride was expensive. She opened her palm and let him place them in her hand. Never had she suspected that so much money could make her feel this small.

"I'm so sorry, Soli," he said again.

She was glad now that she could not speak. *It's okay*, she might have said, if she had had the words; she never would have forgiven herself.

Soli rode the bus home, Ignacio sleeping soundly against her chest. She wished she'd brought a heavier blanket for him; the bus windows were open and the wind lashed and stung her ears. She wrapped the front of her coat around her son and squeezed him tightly, almost too tightly. "These beautiful people," she whispered. "Their beautiful lives. They're just people, Nacho, aren't they?"

She lay in bed with Nacho tucked against her arm. She had no gifts for him, only dreams. She gave him the best she could muster. She tried to stay up until midnight, to mark the silent passage of one year to the next. But the street outside was quiet, her shoulders heavy, and by midnight, she too was asleep.

The next day, Soli arrived early at the Cassidys'. She wanted to establish herself in the kitchen before the señora vanished out the door. She'd woken up at dawn and lay thinking, certain that she'd have to say something to the woman—so certain that she didn't bother asking Silvia about it, for fear that her cousin would try to dissuade her. She was equally sure that this was not the behavior of a model employee, of a benevolent domestic. When Soli arrived, the señora sat at the kitchen table with her head in her hand. Beneath clouds of rouge, her cheeks were pale. She hadn't managed her lipstick yet, and her mouth was tinged blue at the corners. She spoke barely over a whisper.

"Margaritas are evil, Soli. I don't know how your people can handle them."

The chair screeched when Soli pulled it out and sat down across from her. The señora looked up, looked at the microwave clock. "You're early."

"I want to say something."

She sighed. "What is it, Soli?"

Soli lost all sense of her skin. Her bones and her face seemed to hang in midair. It was what happened when she found herself about to do something risky and foolish and absolutely necessary, like climbing onto a moving train or confronting her boss lady about her drunken late arrival the previous evening.

"Señora? Yesterday was my Ignacio's birthday."

The señora raised an eyebrow. "I remember. I did wish him a happy birthday, didn't I? I'm planning on getting him something, of course—"

"Yesterday it was his birthday, and we were going to have a party. For Ignacio. In the park."

The señora's face sank into itself. "Shit," she said. "Shit, shit."

"Sí."

"We were late."

"You said six o'clock, señora, and I waited."

"And you missed it."

"We will do it another day."

The señora sat upright. "This is so typical."

"Señora?"

"The one day I go out and have a little fun, Soli, and it turns out to be this, this *debacle*. I mean, look at me! Do you realize how long it's been since I wore heels?"

Soli blinked.

"And had a real drink? You have no idea, Soli. You have no idea what motherhood is like."

Soli had heard enough. The moving-train impulse was urging her now to stand up, pick up her her bag, and quit. She pushed her chair out and picked up her purse.

"*Wait*. Wait. Hold it. I'm sorry. I'm sorry for saying that. Of course you know what motherhood is. That was totally out of line."

The woman got to her feet, picked up her mug of tea, and left the room, clomping back down the hallway, shouting for her daughter. When Saoirse emerged, carrying a backpack and water bottle and lunch box, the señora led her out the kitchen door, without another word to Soli.

Soon after, the señor entered the kitchen, his hair slick with water, shower heat still steaming from his neck and hands. He nodded at Soli, who stood now at the kitchen sink.

"Doing all right, Solimar?"

"Yes, señor."

"Gretchen seemed a little upset. Everything okay?"

"Maybe she's upset, señor. I told her that Ignacio had a party yesterday. That he missed the party."

"And she wasn't happy about that."

"No."

"Did she apologize?"

Soli wasn't sure.

A long pause followed, during which no one said what they wanted to say.

And then: "Being a mom hasn't been easy for her, Solimar."

She turned off the tap and waited.

"Come here a sec. Have a seat."

She picked Ignacio up off his play mat and brought him to the table. It felt good to sit down.

"You probably don't want to know all this," he said. "But she's had a hard time of it, overall. Getting pregnant, which took a long time. Years. And then depression after Saoirse was born. Mild depression, but it was still hard. And then not getting to get back to work for a good long while. And then, you know, she's *tired*, Solimar. She's almost fifty, you know. You probably can't tell. But we just don't have the energy someone like—like you would have."

This must have been a category of hardship that Soli simply didn't understand because, quite simply, none of the señora's difficulties sounded terribly difficult.

"And to tell you the truth," he spoke in a stage whisper, "we can barely afford you. But in the end, you're cheaper than divorce."

Soli didn't want to know what she was cheaper than. A hard spike of anger was pushing through her now, and only by focusing all her strength on the soft whorl of Nacho's hair did she manage to keep herself quiet. She kissed the top of his head and sang Caballito, Caballito, no me tumba, no me tumba, as the señor continued to talk. The soft spot on his head was hardening now, with every passing week. He remained wholly unaware that his birthday had come and gone.

"But none of that matters, Solimar," he continued. "The point is, we let you down. We said we'd be home by a certain time, and we weren't. And that was our mistake." He wrapped his hand around hers. She pulled away. Pride, like a cornstalk, had grown inside her.

"Thank you, señor."

When Brett Cassidy made his way around the kitchen and said goodbye for the day, Soli found her way to the living room sofa and sat there for a good hour, watching Ignacio crawl around the room, press buttons on the television, and try to bend his feet into his mouth. She thought back to that day she'd sat on this very sofa, watching the señora's birth video. There's stuff you need to see, the señora had said. Soli realized now what she had meant. Motherhood, from its first seconds, is woven with hurt. But what else had she meant? That Soli would be alone? That she'd face it all without a husband, without friends, without the support of either partner or parents?

"You're overreacting," Silvia said.

Overreaction or not, her dissatisfaction was planted and sprouting quickly.

"But why?" Soli asked. "Why didn't she say sorry?"

Silvia stood in their own family room, coiling the serpent of her vacuum hose around her elbow.

"If I knew how these people worked, they'd be doing my laundry."

Silvia had started calling her Soli Poppins, and Soli expected to hear it now, *Pobrecita, Pobre Soli Poppins!* But instead, Silvia put down the vacuum. She walked over and placed her hands on Soli's shoulders. "And listen up, Miss Muy-Muy. Don't walk around judging these people. And if you do—and you will, of course—don't let yourself think about it. They'll sense it. If you think they're lazy, they will know. If you think a husband is cheating on his wife, he will know. They don't like to be judged by the people who scrub their pots. Okay?"

"Okay."

"Even if they want to know, they don't want to know."

"Okay."

"Don't be anyone's conscience."

"*Okay.*"

Mama called that weekend.

"Soli, let me tell you. Doña Alberta's house? The new big one?"

"Did you go?"

"No. And I'll tell you why. The house? It's a dud."

Soli could hear her mother's smile.

"It turns out, the Doña's still waiting for her plumbing and her light. No electricity, no water. The municipality hasn't got around to it yet."

"But did she bribe them?"

"Of course she bribed them!"

"You don't know that," she heard Papi say in the background.

"Imagine it, Soli. Every day she sweeps her new house, looks up at the window to the sky, sits on her new front patio. And then at night, she goes back to her old hut out back. It's too heartbreaking to even think of!"

Her mother didn't sound heartbroken. Nacho began to wail, and Soli said goodbye.

22.

Kavya and Rishi were instructed to make a book. "Put your best foot forward," the private agency had said. "Think of yourselves as a vacation destination and this book as your brochure."

Rishi had never thought of himself or his wife or their life as a vacation, though by some standards it was. Their mission was to create a book with pictures and descriptive captions that would give a bio-mom (the counselor's term, not Rishi's) a good idea of what life with the Reddys would be like for her child. This was Kavya's territory, not his.

"Why is this any more my job than yours?" she'd asked.

"You're the creative one."

"Who said I'm the creative one?" And then as they sat outside the Cheeseboard, Kavya had started to cry. The corn-cherry scone had turned to sand in his mouth.

Since they'd decided to adopt, Kavya's sorrow and her elation could boil up in an instant, sometimes the same instant. She was more erratic than she'd been during her hormone treatments, and Rishi was getting tired. He had no desire to pretend that life in his home would be a vacation.

But for the sake of a pregnant, luckless bio-mom, and for his teetering wife, Rishi was willing to create a work of fiction. But where to begin? With himself? Not the best idea.

Rishi had a good cocktail-party job. In response to the inevitable
What do you do? he'd say he worked in healthy buildings and energy, that
he managed energy efficiency and air quality in the buildings at Weebies. In a town with a Prius problem and a crush on all things tech, this
won him smiles, admiration, nods and more questions, shared stories,
opinions, drinks. When people inevitably asked for specifics, he started
to run into trouble.

"I work in indoor air quality," he'd begin. And then he'd try to syn-
opsize his work with Contam, window-opening behavior, particulate
concentrations and their impacts on occupant health, until his voice fell
from party volume to an almost conspiratorial whisper, his descriptions
growing increasingly complex, his synopsis getting less and less synoptic
as his listeners leaned in, their brows furrowing, their eyes darting to the
exits. What he needed was Kavya by his side, minding his verbal spe-
lunking, keeping him concise. If not for love or lust or financial code-
pendence, he needed Kavya for her tidy summations of his life's work.

"He uses software to measure air flow at Weebies," she'd say, "to make
sure they ventilate enough but aren't wasting energy." If the connection
seemed worthwhile, Kavya would proffer one of Rishi's business cards,
a few of which she kept in her wallet. And yes, the business cards read
"Ventilation Engineer," and yes, she and Rishi both agreed that the title
sounded like a trumped-up name for an a/c repairman, but Rishi could
tell that Kavya was proud of him nonetheless, and this made the cleaving
of his heart to hers all the more intractable. When his wife took charge,
his listeners leaned back again, unfurled their brows, visibly relaxed.
They understood. Rishi was a scientist. Rishi was saving the world.

And because it made things easier for everyone, Rishi stuck to
Kavya's version. He wouldn't trouble her with the truth of what he did, a
truth which didn't involve lab coats or clipboards. He worked in airflow,
yes, but rarely did he encounter an actual gust of air in his beige building. What he really worked in were borders, the passage of air across

them. He worked also in illusion, the brash belief that such borders could be patrolled, that the passage of something so essential and free as air could be managed by a mortal with a laptop. And these days, he worked in possibility, weighing the expectations of a man like Vikram Sen against the limits of physical reality. He hadn't told Kavya about this new project, or even that Sen had reached out to him, for so many reasons that he had trouble pinning one down.

HE TURNED BACK to his computer screen. He would filter the best of everything, and compile for Kavya, for the bio-mom, for an unknown child, a cohesive and neatly bound life. For Kavya, he did this: He burrowed to the back of their bedroom closet and pulled out a file box that he'd been always vaguely aware of, but never expected to open himself. It held stacks, surprisingly weighty, of photographs. He looked through pictures from Berkeley, from their wedding, from their honeymoon and early years of marriage, and soon realized that the photos they'd taken of each other had all started to look the same: sun-splashed, toothy, drinks in hand, at weddings, on deck chairs, their own faces clustered like peonies with the faces of forgotten friends. He compiled pages of pictures, and beside them, in a logical, if not esthetically inspired sequence, he listed their accomplishments and bullet-pointed the highlights of their lifestyle and their neighborhood. The Gourmet Ghetto was mentioned, and so were playgrounds, schools, and farmers' markets. He chose pictures of them at their happiest. He chose the winningest of their winning smiles and plastered them across that book, so often that the volume as a whole took on the slightest breath of desperation.

Looking through his finished work, he began to understand: He and Kavya had ridden their youth to its final conclusion, wound their days together over a spool of parties and friends and travel. It was time now to take the next step.

23.

"Nacho," she'd sing every day into the crown of his head, almost without noticing. "Naaaaacho . . ." Late mornings at the Cassidys', when no one was home, she held Ignacio to her chest and sang him the songs from home. She'd carried them with her, lodged in her throat. Popocalco seemed unreachable now, a corner of another galaxy. And though her parents phoned her and she phoned them, her unspoken child had closed a very heavy door between Berkeley, California, and the place called home.

That afternoon, they made their way up a small hill, to Gooseberries, the preschool. In the yard, the mothers and fathers gathered in clusters, waiting for the front doors to open, and for the teachers, like plump ringleaders, to raise their arms in greeting. Soli stood at the edge of the gathering; they knew one another well by now, the pickup parents, and they chatted and let their children run circles on the concrete.

When they saw Ignacio, the mothers gasped and cooed, they spoke in squeaks and whispers. The fathers called him buddy and poked gentle fingers into his grasp. To Saoirse, they gave big hellos, high fives. The younger fathers gave her fist bumps.

What Soli would have given for a fist bump.

It's not that they didn't smile. It's not that they didn't say hello. The first day she'd shown up at Saoirse's school, the parents had smiled at her. The second day, the parents had smiled at her. The third day, a mother had walked over to her.

"So you're Saoirse's nanny?"

"Yes," Soli had said, and smiled.

The woman smiled sweetly, nodding. *"Wonderful."*

Soli smiled again.

The woman smiled back. She was a nanny to Saoirse, and sometimes it seemed among this crowd, a nanny to Ignacio, as well.

A moment later, another nanny arrived, this one clearly Salvadoran, followed by a Venezuelan and another, whom Soli immediately pegged as Mexican. The nannies clustered together, spoke in rapid Spanish, darker and shorter shadows of the parents. There was one nanny who spoke no Spanish; she was Asian, with long black hair and a clear smile. She smiled at them. They smiled at her, before turning back to their conversations. Soli took a few steps over, until she hovered at the outer edge of the Spanish nanny circle. She listened more than she spoke, happy just to have a place to stand.

When Soli complained that the preschool parents never spoke to her, Silvia shook her head. "There's a name for that," she said. "It's called a First World Problem."

"Okay, so it's not such a big deal." But it was, in the way that very small things could be a big deal within the very small orbits on which they spun.

24.

A MORNING IN JUNE. THE DAY STARTED WITH A BOWEL movement from Nacho that exploded from his diaper and shot up his back, browning the sheets of his crib. Later that morning, the broken showerhead plummeted off its bracket and clocked Soli on the head. It landed with a heavy thud on the shower floor. "What was that?" Silvia shouted.

"Nothing."

"What?"

"Nothing!" Soli reconnected the head, but not without soaking the floor of the bathroom. In the kitchen, she dropped a glass that broke around her toes. And after breakfast, when she opened the cupboard to put back a cereal box, she discovered a bottle of syrup, overturned and missing its cap. Syrup oozed from the head of the lady-shaped bottle and pooled on the shelf. Worse than this, it swarmed with ants. The smarter ants stayed at its edges, and a single file of emissaries marched off to gather more troops. The stupid and greedy ants trudged to its center, got stuck, struggled vainly in the dense golden pool. They gorged themselves, the idiots in the middle. They would eat themselves to death. At this point, Soli should have given up and gone back to bed.

She should have stayed out of the way of this day. She should have let this day pass, like an overcrowded bus, and waited for the next one.

But instead, she hopped on. The Cassidys expected her, and Silvia was honking from the car downstairs.

The rest of the morning passed without incident. Nothing broke, nothing burned, Nacho's stomach seemed to settle, and so did Soli. It appeared that the day's tilt-a-whirl of minor disaster had slowed to a rest. That afternoon, Saoirse came bounding from the schoolhouse door and informed Soli that they'd be playing with Paloma that afternoon. The children, one by one, were turning five and taking it upon themselves to arrange their own social plans. Parents laughed about this at the school gates, trading stories of their hilarious and intelligent children, lobbing anecdotes about each other's offspring, to add a sheen of munificence to their boasting. For Soli, these charming little social planners presented a dilemma. For four- and five-year-olds, playdates almost always included parents. It was assumed, therefore, that the parents would get along and want to spend time together. It was assumed, also, that parents were parents, and not nannies. It was rare for a parent to socialize with a nanny, particularly one whose English was only passable. Soli knew the mother of this Paloma. The woman dressed in scarves and swept a severe fringe of gray hair across her forehead. She spoke incessantly at the school gates, with a sort of focus that permitted no interruption. She addressed herself to whomever would listen, but ignored Soli and the few other nannies. Soli couldn't stomach the idea of spending an hour with this woman, and she was pretty sure the woman wouldn't want to spend any length of time with her.

The little girl, Paloma, sprinted from the door herself, swinging a large metal lunch box. "We're going to the park with Saoirse!"

The mother gazed up at Soli, and Soli waited for her to say something, anything, to get them out of the arrangement. Surely, this woman who couldn't stop talking would be able to come up with an excuse to keep the date from happening. But the woman's lips parted, and no sound came out. She seemed to be waiting for Soli to act. And so, Soli

said, "I can take the girls. To the park. I can take them both." Ignacio
yelped in protest.

The mother brightened and said, "Fantastic!" It was the first word
she'd spoken to Soli, and for a moment, it felt like conversation.

And so Soli took the two girls to the park. It was a big one, with
three separate playgounds, and a wide, steeply sloped hill that led off the
sports courts of a local middle school. The mother walked her daughter
over to the park, just half a block from the school. "See you in an hour?
Okay?" She bade the little girl goodbye and winked at Soli.

Saoirse took one hand, and Paloma, without hesitating, took the
other. Soli was glad for the simple weights and measures of a child's
judgment. At the park, she settled onto a bench, Ignacio snoozing in his
carrier, and watched a hummingbird hover over a wall of freesia, making its promise to every blossom. Paloma planted herself in the shade of
the slide, while Saoirse leapt from slide to ladder to swing, unfettered by
height or gravity or the scrape of sand on skin. Soli clucked and called
out to her to stop. She feared for this child with no lashes, with skin so
pale she could see the indigo streams beneath.

At last, Saoirse came to a rest beside Paloma, and the two busied
themselves with the quiet intricacies of being girls. Girls are not like
boys, everyone said. They don't have kick-fights on the playground or
step on one another's necks. They don't delight in yelling or throwing,
in discovering new avenues of destruction. Girls swing from monkey
bars. They talk and plot and plan and play. They are quieter. They hold
hands. They sit. They make dolls from twigs and rocks. They make
cradles from bark and grass. They are quiet. They are sometimes a little
too quiet.

Soli looked up from her sun-struck daze. She'd fallen asleep on the
playground bench. On her phone, twenty minutes had passed. It was
a warm day for the season, and after days of rain, the playground was
crowded, the children frenetic. Ignacio nestled into her chest. Around

her, children swarmed anonymously, building a wall of noise. She looked for Saoirse. She didn't see her. No Paloma, either.

The last time she'd seen them, the two girls had been tucked beneath a wooden drawbridge, sticking sandy twigs between the slats. She turned one way, then the other. She turned a full circle. She searched under the bridge, around the bridge, on the other side of it. The girls were nowhere. She called their names, and then she shouted them. Children stopped playing. Parents turned to stare. The girls were nowhere to be found.

Kind strangers offered to help. Soli felt the questions before she heard them—*How old? What do they look like? What are their names?* She couldn't find the words to answer. Around the playground, she saw blond and brown and black heads. No pale amber. No Saoirse. She tried to remember what Paloma was wearing; she didn't know the girl well enough to be able to spot her from afar. Any of them could have been Paloma. All of them were. And none of them.

To lose a child, even for a few moments, sends a panicked ring from ear to ear. To lose a child for several minutes—to lose two children— can cancel the air altogether. Soli crossed the playground, her throat sucking and closing, her vision going gray. She found herself in the parking lot, weaving between cars and peering in their windows. She ran to an open soccer field. Ignacio laughed as she ran, and held on to her cheeks. She crossed the soccer field to search in the bordering bushes. She found a discarded tricycle and a single dirty white shoe.

"Nacho," she pleaded. "Nacho, where are they?" Nacho swung his head around, searching wildly for the source of his mother's distress. She rummaged for her cell phone to call Silvia, forgetting the numbers at first, then whispering them aloud to stoke her memory.

"Bueno," Silvia answered.

"Silvia!"

"What happened?"

"I can't find them. Las pequeñas. They're lost!"

"Where are you?"

Soli told her. "We're at the park," she said, "the one by the school."

Silvia cursed. "Soli," she said.

"I can't find them! Help me, Silvia, please!"

"Soli."

Soli began to shriek into her phone, panicked now, beyond words.

"Soli! Calmate! Stay there. Don't move. Where's Nacho?"

"Here, with me."

"Stay there. I'll bring the car."

In the distance, Soli spotted the park office. She would find help there. But if they called the police? If the girls were missing, they would call the police. And Soli couldn't risk the police. She had to think of herself, her boy. So she walked to the window and looked in. A woman at the counter looked back out at her. The rest of the room was empty. She had a better idea: the nannies. She scanned the playground for brown skin. The nannies would help her look and they'd know well enough not to call the police. She ran for the slides and the swings.

"Soli!" At the head of the parking lot stood Silvia. "Get in the car. We'll drive around the arca."

Together, they drove slowly around the park, coursing along ever-widening circles, Soli calling *"M'ija! Paloma!"* from her window. Silvia joined in, her hands on the steering wheel, her face out the window, yelling to the street, the occasional pedestrian, the rows and rows of closed doors. They circled onto Shattuck, its wide avenues a wilderness of cars and buses.

And then Soli's cell phone rang. It was a number she'd never seen.

"Is this So-lee?"

"This is Soli."

"Soli!" She heard the little girl's voice in the background. "Soli, where are you?"

"We have two girls here who say you're they're caretaker?"

"Where are they? Who is this?"

It was the woman in the park office. Soli laughed with relief and marveled at the resourceful little girl she was raising, a little girl who remembered the number Soli had taught her, sung to the tune of "Pajarito." When she saw Saoirse again, she would twirl her through the air.

"I've got 'em here in the office," the woman said. And then her voice sank doubtfully. "You are coming, aren't you? To pick them up?"

"I'm coming. Yes, I'm coming."

"I'll just give her mom a call, too. Just in case."

"No, no! I'm coming."

"It's no trouble," the woman said, and hung up.

Silvia was already driving back to the park. "So?"

"They're calling the señora."

"*Ai*, mierda." She leaned in, and the car jumped forward, speeding down Shattuck now, through one yellow light, then another.

Soli slammed her fist against the door and cursed. Silvia breathed a high whistle and chuckled.

"I didn't ask to be their nanny!" Soli nearly shouted at Silvia. She'd never shouted at Silvia before.

Silvia smiled at the windshield. "Soli Poppins, Soli Poppins," she said, and shook her meaty head. Soli wanted to bop it with her fist.

"You're supposed to be my friend," Soli said. "Aren't you?"

Silvia shrugged.

"Aren't you?"

Silvia let out a yelp that startled Nacho and sent him wailing. "You want me to hold your hand and tell you they were wrong, Soli? You lost their babies at the playground! What were you doing? The little girl calls her mama crying? From a stranger's phone? And you want me to tell you they were wrong? You'll be lucky if they don't fire you."

Soli sat back, closed her eyes. "I know that."

Silvia calmed. "So don't tell me I didn't support you."

"I know."

"A lot of people have it worse than you," she said. "You're lucky you work for people who look at you like you're a real human. Most of us get treated like dogs in this country. Worse than dogs."

Soli had seen how dogs were treated in this country, and she knew that Silvia was right. "I'm sorry," she said quietly. She sank into her seat, helpless under the weight of two lost girls.

"Don't tell me I'm not your friend," Silvia muttered, her eyes on the road. "Pulled you out of that mierda-de-burro village."

"Yes," Soli said. "Thank you."

Silvia turned, frowned, and took her hand off the steering wheel to wrap it around Soli's.

And that's when Sylvia ran the red light. She zoomed through the intersection of Shattuck and University with hardly a thought.

Horns blared around her. "Why're they honking?"

Soli turned around. A cyclist launched an empty plastic water bottle at their back window.

"Culero," Silvia muttered.

"*Silvia*. The light was red!"

"What? No. Psh. Nothing to worry about."

"Silvia, turn here. I see police. Please."

Any other day, Silvia would have been right. But on this day of days, she could only be wrong. If she'd believed Soli and turned a corner, then maybe the cop on the motorcycle would have lost interest. Maybe the pedestrian who pointed out their car would have given up and shrugged them off. But their blue Honda ambled stupidly down Shattuck. It seemed not to know that pedestrians were pointing, that cyclists were grinning, that the cops had caught their scent. If this had been a television show, the streets of Berkeley would have opened up and let them zoom through, lady-rebel style, leaving the cop on his motorcycle buzzing and lost like an injured bee. But this wasn't television. This was Berkeley, and Berkeley on this day, as on every other, was full of people. People and bikes and cars and babies and students and dogs and even an alpaca standing, inexplicably, at a crosswalk. There was no room for a high-speed chase or even a low-speed chase, and the blue Honda was running out of options.

Silvia glanced up at her rearview mirror. "Mierda."

A police car joined the motorcycle. The red lights of the cop car swept left-right-left. It bleeped three times. They sped through another red light, missed an oncoming car by inches.

"They're giving up!" Silvia cried. But the cop car was right behind them. And then there were two. With barely a glance at oncoming traffic, she swung left at the next intersection, zoomed down the street, past houses, past a stop sign, swinging right and right and left.

Soli shrieked and hid her head in her arms. "Stop it, Silvia. Stop! Just stop!"

"They can't get us," Silvia said. Silvia ripped down the narrow avenues, but the police car roared right behind. A loudspeaker was telling them to pull over, but Silvia kept on going. Soli thought only of Ignacio, strapped in and helpless in the back of the careening vehicle. She craned back to find him staring wide-eyed out the rear windshield, his two teeth bared. Back on Shattuck now, they burned down the main strip.

"Stop it, Silvia! Stop the car!"

Silvia swerved to miss a cyclist. She swung back into her lane. She chipped the curb. The tire screeched, the hood leapt skyward, the car spun one revolution, two. They crunched, at last, into the side of a tall concrete barrier. Through the window, the hood of Silvia's car had bent in half, and smoke began to seep out its side.

Cyclists. In the weeks to follow, Soli would think most bitterly of the cyclists, smug in their helmets and slick shorts. From her side mirror, Soli saw a cyclist slow to a stop, pull out his water bottle and suck from it, watching, cold as a shark. Three police cars crept in close. Walkers gathered, students with backpacks, a man with a stroller.

Ignacio set off a shrieking cry.

From behind, a robotic loudspeaker: "Step out of the car."

"Don't move," Silvia said. "Callate, Nacho."

"STEP OUT OF THE CAR. WITH YOUR HANDS UP."

Silvia leaned into the steering wheel and stared straight out the windshield at her smoking, mangled hood.

"Silvia."

Behind her, the doors of the two police cars opened, all four of them at once, as if they'd driven into a television show.

Soli sucked in her breath and opened her door. She stepped out, slowly. She raised her arms above her shoulders, as she'd seen on cop shows. This was something she never thought she'd do. The lights of a siren whirled round and round behind them.

The policeman closest to her had been reaching for his holster, but let go of it when he saw Soli. Her hands trembled by her ears. From the corner of her eye, through the filter of her fingers, she watched the dance of red lights on a white wall. She watched this dance as if there were nothing else to see, as if officers were not approaching, extracting handcuffs from their belts, pulling Silvia, limp and sullen, from the driver's seat, and stooping, peering through the backseat window, at the little boy, at her Nacho, who waited and watched, shouting syllables, one small palm pressed against the window.

"They've got a baby!" an officer barked. Ignacio, startled, began to howl.

Silvia stood by Soli, heads held high, wrists behind their backs.

"Nacho!" Soli called. "Estoy aqui!" Silvia hissed her quiet.

"He's all right," the cop said, chewing his gum and crossing his arms. "You got guns in there?"

"No."

"No guns? You got drugs? Drogas?"

There was no reason for him to ask. Already the large blond officer sat on the passenger seat, opening the glove compartment, spilling the contents onto the floor, poking his fingers in and baring his teeth with the effort. "You can't do that," Silvia spat. Soli cowered. "You can't search our car like that." He would find nothing but a map of San Francisco, a Lila Downs cassette tape, a ChapStick, and a maxi-pad.

"You got drugs in there?" the officer asked again.

"No," Silvia said.

He turned to the car. "Search the baby seat," he called, pointing to the back window. "The car seat. Whatever it's called."

He turned back to Silvia. "You illegals?"

"What?"

"Illegals? Are you illegals? Inmigrantes? Illegales?"

"No," Silvia answered. "We have papers."

He called to another officer, the third, a woman who'd been keeping watch all this time at the border of the scene. He said, "Get their bags for them." Turning to Soli: "Let's see some ID. Tienes ID?"

"Sí."

People paused on sidewalks, slowed their cars, stood and watched with their cell phones held aloft. From the crowd, a woman pushed her shopping cart toward Soli. She was ash-toned and no taller than the mound of her dusty belongings. She was barely a whisper of a woman. She peered at Soli through oversized glasses, looked her up and down, and sneered. "Get the fuck back to Mexico," she said.

"Ma'am." The policeman placed a hand on the woman's elbow and she yanked her arm away, cursed at the officer, and trundled off. Later, weeks and months later, Soli would wonder if this was not so much an insult as a morsel of sound advice.

No one asked whose child Ignacio was. It was obvious, maybe, when he cried out and reached for Soli. He watched as his mother was shoved, a heavy hand on her head, into the back of the police car. Silvia was shoved in after her.

"My son!" Soli said.

Silvia shushed her. Ignacio was still in their car.

"My son is in there!"

"He'll be fine. He's going in another car."

Soli was handcuffed, and so was Silvia. Soli wept and could not wipe her tears away. They streamed down her neck and onto her chest. Silvia stared at the seat back in front of her and said nothing, not even when Soli asked what was happening. Silvia was elsewhere. No one had re-membered to buckle them in and they lurched forward and sideways with every turn of every corner, with every rough and poorly measured stop.

At the station, their names and photographs were taken. Ignacio was nowhere. "Where is my son?" Soli asked the police officer who was fill-ing in her papers. "He's on his way" was all she'd say.

"Where is my son?" she asked another officer, when Ignacio hadn't surfaced. "Where is my son?" she asked passersby, an hour later, when Ignacio was nowhere to be seen, and she sat, handcuffed to a chair, her chest an aching drum.

25.

THERE WAS LITTLE LEFT TO DO. KAVYA HAD BEEN HELD aloft for weeks by a stream of paperwork and state-stipulated tasks. She'd ticked all the boxes. Now she could only wait.

She'd been waiting for weeks, and each morning she woke to a shiver of possibility. Her waking breaths tickled with the thought that the phone would ring that day and it would be Joyce. But every evening, the clock ticked past five and the sky dimmed and she knew there wouldn't be a call. She imagined Joyce packing her briefcase and sailing from her office, head up and bosom held high. She went to bed each night a little duller than the night before. But always, hope reawakened in the mornings, a bedraggled servant.

Kavya had been calling, twice a day sometimes. "Just checking in!" she'd say, trying to sound casual.

"Nothing today, Kavya," Joyce would say. "When something happens, I will call you immediately. Okay?"

"Sure!"

"No. Kavya? Are you listening?"

"Yes."

"I strongly encourage you not to call me. I'll call you. I promise."

In the evenings, Kavya and Rishi curled into the sofa and watched television. Rishi knew better than to leave her with her thoughts, so his work went untouched, and they binged on drama and comedy and the comforts of fiction.

It was Tuesday, the end of an endless evening. She could barely speak that day, and Miguel noticed. "You all right?" he asked. "You forget your V-8 today?" What would she say? I want a child so badly it hurts to talk. Have you diced the onions?

After dinner service, she told Miguel to go home and leave the cleanup to her. He tended to bang pots and zing around the kitchen in a whirlwind of maximal efficiency. That evening, she wanted quiet. She cycled home in a light rain, the drops falling like confetti through the glow of every streetlight. It was only six thirty, but the night had made its wintry entrance. The rain didn't bother her as she sped down the hills and onto the flats of central Berkeley. Her face gathered no more than a sparse dew.

At the front door, Rishi stood, cell phone in hand. "Call Joyce now. She'll be there until seven," he said. "She left me a message."

"She did? She called you? She called *you*?"

"Call her now."

Kavya grabbed the phone and sat down on the front porch. The rain smattered the knees of her jeans. Rishi sat beside her, his arm around her shoulders. She shivered as she dialed.

"Joyce?"

"Kavya? I'm glad you caught me. I called four times—"

"Do you have any news?"

Silence, hushes and clicks on the phone line, and then, "Yeeeesssss. Hold on, just getting . . . Okay. Kavya, we have an infant, a little girl. We'll call her Baby A for now. Would you like to meet her?"

"Baby A?"

"She's in a foster home currently, but we're looking to place her elsewhere. Are you free Saturday?"

"This Saturday?" She looked to Rishi. "Yes? Yes! Yes."

Times were arranged. Kavya and Rishi would meet Joyce at the foster home. "Thank you, Joyce." She said it too many times, so many times that Joyce had to raise her voice.

"See you then, Kavya. Okay? Kavya?"

"Yes, Joyce."

"Kavya? This is for temporary placement. You got that?"

Kavya nodded into the phone. She felt good. Temporary or not, this felt right. She hung up and rammed her face into Rishi's chest. She squealed when he squeezed her tight. That night, they ignored the television and stayed up long into the night, drinking tea at the table, Kavya's hands folded into Rishi's, laying out the details of how they'd get to Joyce's office, what they would need for the baby's room. Kavya ignored the worried cleave in Rishi's brow. He was being cautious, she knew. Nevermind, she told herself. Let him be the cautious one.

26.

SOLI AND SILVIA SPENT THEIR FIRST NIGHT IN A SMALL jail in Berkeley. Ignacio had come to her, at last, after four hours and thirty-seven minutes. She'd heard the familiar rattle of his breath before she saw him. He appeared around the corner, head up and back straight, in the arms of a white woman in uniform. The woman was short and thin-armed, with wide gray eyes. She whispered to Ignacio as she approached the cell. He listened, his chin alert and aloft. And when the officer handed him over, he fell limply into Soli's arms, as if exhausted. She held him, opened her shirt to feed him, whispered in his ear.

"He's been searched," the officer said. "You can keep him for the night."

A few hours later, the female cop sat Soli down and asked questions, many questions, sometimes the same question twice: "Where were you born? Do you have papers? When did you arrive in the U.S.? Was your child born here? What is his date of birth? How old is he? He was born here? Do you have a visa?"

Soli lied exactly three times, all in response to the same question. She did not have a visa. She didn't even have a passport in which to put a visa. By the end of the interview, she'd convinced herself that she at least had a state ID, that this had to count for something. She knew that most people got their papers in offices, in big white buildings like the one she was sitting in now. She knew not everyone bought their papers from a man named Marta in the back of a Chino grocery. But as far as she could tell, what she had were papers. She wasn't sure why she lied about having a visa; it was something she was meant to have, of course. Before she could stop it, the lie fell out of her, and it sat between her and the female officer, a wobbling egg fallen from its nest.

"You have a visa?"

"Yes."

"Is this visa at home? With your passport?"

"Yes."

"You have a Mexican passport?"

"Yes."

The lies hatched and cheeped and demanded feeding. But the lies seemed to be working. The officer was writing things down, nodding. And then she rose, picked up her papers.

"Follow me," she said, and led her back to the cell.

Soli was breastfeeding Nacho when Silvia returned. Silvia's eyes rested on the back of his head. "The boys went to their dad," she said quietly.

"Are they letting us out?"

"No."

"What about bail? Don't they let us out with bail?" This too she'd learned from television.

"Not me. Probably not you." For the first time that Soli could remember, Silvia looked helpless. And on Silvia's broad and soft face, helplessness looked a lot like stupidity. Blinking bovine ignorance.

"So now what?" Soli asked.

"I'm going to court, I guess. I'm staying here. I'm a criminal now."

"You're going to jail?"

Silvia shrugged. "I get a lawyer."

"Do I get a lawyer?"

She stared at Soli. "How should I know?" She sat back and closed her eyes. "And then I go to jail, or something, and then they deport me."

"What do you mean they deport you?" It seemed a sort of over-punishment. "But you have papers. Why're they punishing you so bad?"

"I was driving without a license." Silvia sat up and counted the offenses on her fingers, as if laying them plain for the first time. "Driving without a license. Not stopping for the police. Crashing into some mal-dito street barriers. And not having papers."

One beat, two, three.

"You don't have papers!" Soli whispered. She whisper-yelled, the way schoolchildren do, the way people in big stupid trouble do. Silvia only shrugged.

"You told me you had papers. You told everyone you had papers! In Popocalco, they said, *Silvia Morales? She's got papers.* That's what they said!"

"They were wrong," Silvia said.

"You were wrong. You lied to me."

Silvia glared. "I never said a thing about papers."

But Soli had made up her mind. Silvia, who'd always been right, was wrong this time, in the biggest and most terrible way. Silvia, who'd always been a landmark for Soli, was now a pile of bricks. Soli felt the ground slip from beneath her. She felt that she could have turned to vapor and floated away and not even known it.

Only Ignacio was keeping her solid, his head heavy against her shoulder. In his sleep, he pressed his nose and mouth against the curve of her neck, forming a well of sweat and heat. He smacked his tongue, dreaming of feeding. She closed her eyes against his damp temple. Only that morning, things had been fine. She sensed the weight of night around the windowless room. It was nine o'clock. She should have been bathing Nacho now, rubbing his limbs with baby oil, squeezing with her thumb and forefinger the strong flesh, the nascent muscle.

They spent the night in the holding cell. The next morning they were given breakfast, and it seemed to Soli that a morning with breakfast could only bring good things. She felt the sun through the walls. Ignacio was in good spirits, laughing when she bumped her forehead against his, tracing with his fingers the ridges of her nose. When the female officer approached, Soli waited for some happy news. A release, an error, the buzz of an alarm clock, an end to this bizarre waking dream.

"Van's here," the woman said. She was the one with the gray eyes, the soft voice. She held her hands out, nodded at Ignacio.

"What do you want?" Soli's mouth went dry.

"I'll take him." Behind her, a male officer approached, two pairs of handcuffs dangling from his fingers.

"Where are you taking him?" Silvia asked.

"He's going with you, don't worry," the woman said in her kitten voice. "You can't hold him with your cuffs on."

"Where are we going?"

"Come on, now," the woman urged. "Hand him over, now."

Soli would reconsider this moment many times in the future, thinking she should have run while she could. Should have yanked the officer's gun from her belt and bolted from the station, firing. She might have escaped, might have hidden herself and Ignacio under a bridge somewhere, or by a creek in the hills. She might have become a homeless woman, pushing a shopping cart full of clothing and cans, camouflaging herself against the sidewalk, against the burnished silver of the morning sky, where she and Nacho could be invisible. The officer settled her gray gaze on Soli. She had rosy lips and a soft nose. She didn't have the face of a cop. And because she knew nothing of the future, and because the officer had small, fair hands, Soli gave up her child. He screamed for her.

"We'll meet you at the van," the officer said, and headed down the hallway.

Handcuffs clamped down.

"Nacho!" Soli called.

Ignacio was waiting, as promised, in his car seat. As the van coursed through Berkeley, Soli pointed out the window to the playground, the corner store, and their very own street. Their apartment lay empty. The remains of breakfast had been left out the day before, and would still be on the table, crusting over. But she'd be back soon enough to clean it all up. Soli felt sure of this.

Sunlight shot through the window and warmed her cheeks, and she was able, for a few moments, with Ignacio's hand on her shackled wrist, to feel the pleasure of this. A guard sat in the back of the van, his club at his side.

The ride was short. Once again, Nacho was pulled from her arms. "You'll get him back," the guard said. They were yanked from the van, walked across a yard, hissed and yelled at by other women in yellow jumpsuits, and before they could process or protest, Soli and Silvia stood in yellow jumpsuits themselves, stripped of their possessions.

"What are we doing here?" Soli asked. "What are they doing to us?"

Heavy footsteps, a guard approached.

Silvia's breath grew heavy and urgent. "Soli," she hissed. "Don't sign anything. Don't sign anything they give you!"

The guard gripped Silvia by the elbow and pointed her to a room, prodding her in the back with his club.

A few minutes later, a guard came for Soli. She was led, once again, to an airless interview room. A fluorescent beam lit the space and warmed it. A man knocked on the door and entered.

He threw a folder down on the table, pulled his chair back with a screech, and sat.

"You Thelma or Louise?" he asked.

"Excuse me?"

'Your name is Solimar Castro Valdez, is that correct?" He spaced his words out now, so that Soli could understand.

"Correct."

"Would you like me to speak in Spanish?" he asked. "Español?"

"Sí. Por favor."

He proceeded to ask the same questions she'd heard the day before.

"How long have you been here? Do you have a visa? Where were you born? Where was your child born?"

And then he put his pen down, leaned forward, tented his fingers.

"Who is Preston Chiu?"

"What?"

"Who is Preston Chiu?"

"What?"

"Who is Preston Chiu?"

27.

PRESTON CHIU WAS AN AMERICAN, IT TURNED OUT. PRESTON Chiu was an American with a Social Security Number, a driver's license, and a driving record. Preston Chiu was the rightful owner of Soli's Social Security Number. Soli was not Preston Chiu. Soli was in trouble.

She believed that a female officer might have sympathized. A woman would be easier to speak with, but Soli had no choice. With the discovery of Preston Chiu, she felt herself unmooring from the reality of her home, her life, her crusting dishes, her Ignacio, all of it shrinking rapidly away. She clasped her palms together and said, "Please, señor, I have a boy. And my cousin. We both have small boys. I take care of a child. We made a mistake on the road because we were going to her."

"It wasn't running the red light that got you in here," the man said. "It wasn't even that sad little chase you led the police on." He crossed his arms. "Your cousin was driving without a license. And that's why we brought her in. We did a little research, and we found out you are both here on false docs. Your Social Security Numbers didn't check out."

Soli felt she might blow away at last, even in that airless room.

"And what will happen to us?"

"You're about to find out. We're deciding that."

"And what will happen to my child?"

He sighed so heavily it turned into a cough. "We'll have to see about that." He crossed his arms and gazed at her for several long moments. "You're an illegal," he said in English. "Is that correct?"

And in English, she replied, "That is correct."

SOLI DIDN'T SEE SILVIA AGAIN. She was led to a cell where four women stared at her. When Ignacio was brought to her, she buried her face in his soft burgeon of hair.

"What is happening, Nacho?" she whispered in his ear. "Where do we go from here?"

It was a question that would vibrate in his ears for weeks, just as it echoed, never fading, in hers.

An officer arrived again, slid open the grated door, and said, "Good news."

They weren't pressing charges against Soli. She had technically committed no traffic offense. She wouldn't be a criminal. She wouldn't be on trial. For a moment, she was overjoyed. For a moment, she saw the world as a righteous place.

"You're letting me go," she said. "You're letting me go?" She hugged Nacho close. He wound his fingers through her hair and tugged.

The officer raised his eyebrows and said nothing. From around the corner, footsteps.

A woman turned the corner wearing neither a uniform nor a jumpsuit. Her skin was dark, Cuban brown, and she wore chunky abuela shoes and a light blue sweater. From her glasses hung a chain.

"I'm Joyce Jones from the Department of Social Services," she said. She held out her arms, nodded for Ignacio.

Soli held him tighter. "What do you want?"

"Give me the child, please. He'll be just fine."

"No."

The officer stepped forward.

"Miss Valdez," he said, "we'll need to take your child. Just for now. Okay? Just for now."

"No!" She kicked him in the knee. He doubled over, cursed, then straightened. He reached for his belt and lunged. Fire jolted through Soli's arm, and she tumbled to the floor. Ignacio held her by the neck, fell with her, and began to scream.

When she tried to scramble away, she couldn't. The muscles in her arms went dead as cardboard, and Ignacio was lifted away. In the brown woman's arms, he vanished around a corner, still screaming. She wailed for him. Her arms came to life and she tore at the air.

She was hoisted by one elbow, then the other, and dragged down the hallway, legs out, head down, like a sack of flour. A door opened, and she was thrown into a small room, hardly bigger than a closet, with concrete walls and a hard floor. A single window let in light from the hallway, but no sound. She lifted herself to her feet, pressed her hand to the window, and wept. "Please," she cried. "Bring him back to me!" But no one heard her. No one passed. And if anyone did, they would probably not have noticed the hand against the window, the fleshy palm pressed flat and featureless against the pane.

There is a beast in all of us. Only the worst things can bring it ripping through the human veneer. On that cold linoleum afternoon, Soli's screams vibrated through her abdomen and up her chest, relentless and pure, and broke from her lips in a swarm.

Hours later, she awoke. She'd fallen into a stupor and now that she was conscious, her body ached with thirst. She sat up, shaking. The front of her blouse was drenched with milk. Feebly, she knocked on the door. It was too much to stand and bang on the windowpane and if she had, no one would have heard. "Help," she called. But her voice was too hoarse to even penetrate the room around her.

Hunger wended its way through Soli. She grew weak. She waited, but no one came. Hours passed, and she lay forgotten. "I am brought to this," she whispered. Her vision turned gray, then cleared, then clouded over again. "I am brought to this."

From a high corner of the room, a CCTV lens trained its red eye on her. If he'd bothered to watch, the guard in the control room would have seen this: a woman, gray and grainy, her pupils aglow in the darkened room, hunched against the door, lifting her shirt, curling into herself, and drinking from her own breast. They might have gasped and pointed, they might have shaken their heads and called others to watch. And if Soli knew about the cold red eye trained on her from above, she was past caring. What mattered was the moisture on her lips. What mattered were the droplets of milk, warm and sweet, inching down her throat.

SHE WAS MARCHED down a corridor, out into the blinding sun, where an old blue bus sat idling.

"Spread your feet!" she heard. "ARMS OUT. SPREAD YOUR FEET."

And what she wouldn't do herself was done for her, her arms yanked akimbo, her feet pulled in two directions. The handcuffs clamped on. The wind stung her sodden cheeks.

"What are you doing?" she asked.

"Quiet."

And then, around her ankles, rings of iron, sharp and crude. Shackles. The officer was shackling her feet. Soli gaped. Only slaves had their feet shackled, and the worst criminals. She dug her heels in and turned to the guard.

"What about my boy?"

"He's in care," she said. "He'll be fine." She shoved Soli up the stairs. Later, Soli would realize the miracle in the guard's words. That she was willing to answer a question would feel, months later, like profound kindness.

Many times that year, Silvia had said to Soli: "You can make it here, Soli. All you have to do is work hard and keep quiet. And if you do, you'll make it."

Making it was a concept of which Soli had never required a definition. She assumed that she would discover one day that it had happened, when she had money for food, a place to live, maybe even a man to love. She would know making it when she saw it, and until it revealed itself, she would work and wait. But she knew this much: Calling her employer from the Alameda County Sheriff's Office, the skin on her wrists still sore, was no signal of success.

Mrs. Cassidy would be home because Soli wasn't. She'd be irate. Soli listened to the ring and waited for the tremor of poorly contained indignation.

"Hello? Hello?"

"Hello—"

"Hello?"

"Señora? It's me!"

A pause. "Soli? Is that you? What happened?" Her voice was clipped and strained.

"I am in prison," she said. Silvia had taught her this sentence, just for the call. "I am in prison."

"You're *what*?"

"I need help," she said. "Please, the señor?"

"Hold on."

Señor Cassidy's voice crackled through the line, but even through the static it was deep and calm. "¿Qué pasa, Solimar?"

With her Spanish came a release of tears. "Please, señor, I'm in a prison somewhere. I've been here since yesterday. They took Ignacio from me. They took him!"

"But why? They arrested you? Why?"

"I did nothing!" And she explained about the car chase, the police, the crash.

"But why'd they arrest you? What did *you* do?"

She clamped her feet to the floor and gathered her courage. "I lied," she said. "I don't have papers. I don't have a visa."

From the señor, silence.

"Señor?"

"Solimar."

"I need someone to take care of my Ignacio. I need help."

"Solimar." He sighed deeply. "I need to think about this."

For Soli, the answer was clear: These noble people, people who understood her and her struggle, these people would save her in the end.

"I can't do it," the señor said. "We can't, Solimar."

She waited in silence for him to correct himself.

"You understand, don't you?"

"No."

"It's my job. It's very tied up with the government. And if they knew—if they knew I'd been dealing with a—"

Soli heard no more. The room rushed around her ears until all she heard was static, cracked and lonely, like wind over a barren field.

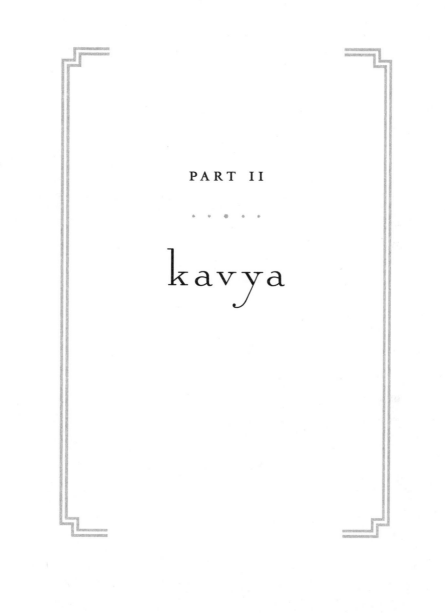

PART II

· · · ● · ·

kavya

28.

Rishi ducked into the Prius and shut the door.

In the driver's seat, Kavya looked fresh and ready.

"Hi," she said.

"Hi."

For a moment, they looked at each other and were silent, more silent than their silent car, and Rishi remembered what he'd almost forgotten—that this was the day they were going to see about a child. This was a small and brilliant beginning.

The house had four windows, two up, two down, and a pointed roof, a house from a kindergarten drawing. From the outside it looked only slightly larger than their own bungalow, with a patch of blanched grass at the front.

"Six kids?" Kavya asked. She and Rishi followed Joyce up the short walkway.

"Six kids," Joyce said. She cleared her throat and rang the bell.

Footsteps thundered above, the steps of twelve feet, the steps of a hundred, it was impossible to tell. Voices called out, a voice called back, and then came silence. Silence greeted them and silence made them wait, until Rishi cleared his throat.

Joyce smiled. "Six kids."

They stood on the porch for another three minutes, until Joyce rang the bell again. Rishi lunged forward and knocked hard. *"Rishi,"* Kavya hissed.

Again a thunderstorm of footsteps, and this time, a woman's voice. "Just—*Just* a minute!"

The door opened. Rishi had expected a harried mother, overwrought and milk-stained, haggard, becardiganed. But the woman who stood before them was clean and crisply dressed. She smiled, she wore makeup. She showed no sign of the ruckus that had preceded her.

"Sorry about the wait," she cooed. "Come on in."

Toys littered the living room carpet, but the house was clean, filled with light, and smelled of lemons. Rishi worried how their own house compared. The foster mom was giving up the foster baby, Joyce explained, because a grown bio-son had graduated from college and was moving back home. "Majored in *French*," she muttered.

Rishi didn't comment on the grown son with the impractical major. He was too busy noticing the heartbeat, the tripping arrhythmia, that filled that house. It was his own heart, or possibly Kavya's, or more likely both their hearts beating in nervous asynchrony as they were led to the family room, where a gathering of children waited. The foster mom stayed in the kitchen, running water in the sink. One, two, three, four, five. Rishi counted them. And in the center, sitting on the lap of a teenaged girl, was Baby A.

If there was a baby out there who looked less like him and Kavya, Rishi hadn't met it. Baby A—"This is *Agatha*," Joyce announced—had flaming orange hair and blue eyes with stony blue pupils, a mouth that lost itself in imperious pillows of cheek.

"Wow" was all he could say.

Agatha was eight months old—old enough to sit up, young enough to be sucking on an entire fist, but alert enough to look alarmed when Kavya leaned over her.

The teenager thrust the baby into Kavya's arms, and Kavya took her.

She rounded her shoulders, held her gingerly. He sensed a quiver in her arms. From behind, Rishi placed his hands on her elbows. When Kavya turned to look at him, he didn't see what he'd expected—and what had he expected? Joy? Relief? Terror?—but an opacity that told him nothing. Kavya's eyes had gone solid brown and the face that Rishi could read so easily was inscrutable to him now.

"Sit down," Joyce said, as if she knew.

Kavya sat down with the baby, who whined and clawed at the air. She began to howl.

"Does she want me to stand?" Kavya asked Joyce. Kavya turned to the teenager. "Should I stand up?"

"She's fine," said Joyce.

Tiny tears streamed down the baby's face. Rishi looked around for the foster mother, but she'd kept to the kitchen. Agatha's wail rose to a full-blown screech and Kavya jiggled the bundle in her arms, shushing it, clicking her tongue, wincing with every cry.

The teenager stepped forward and scooped the bundle from Kavya's arms. She held it to her shoulder and the crying stopped.

With a gasping sort of laugh, Kavya crossed her arms and legs. And when she looked at Rishi, he saw it: sadness, like a frog breaking through the surface of a pond.

"Well, that went well," Rishi said. He couldn't stop himself. Kavya glared.

"Can I bring anyone a glass of water?" the foster mom called from the kitchen. Nobody answered. The room fell into silence.

"Perro." Rishi looked around. The chirp came from the corner of the room. "Perro. Perro." Like a heartbeat externalized. A bigger baby, a year old, maybe two, stalked on his hands and knees to Kavya's side. He was dressed only in a diaper and blue socks, one of which had slipped halfway down his foot to reveal a silken heel.

The boy grabbed her shin.

"Who's this?" Kavya asked.

The foster mom came in with two water glasses. "That one's Ignacio," she said. "He thinks he's a dog." She handed the glasses to Rishi and Kavya, and sat down on a corner settee. "He's been with us for a week now."

Ignacio pulled on Kavya's pant leg and lifted himself to his feet. Rishi watched her lower her water glass. Ignacio leaned in. He lapped at the water with one, two, three flicks of his slim pink tongue. When he looked up at her, a rogue drip trickled from his chin to the plain of his bare chest.

"I think he's cold," she said. She scooped Ignacio into her lap. Rishi turned from adult to adult, from adult to teenager, looking for disapproval, for someone to tell his errant wife that she couldn't swoop into a foster home and pick up any child she wanted, that this wasn't a yard sale or a petting zoo, but no one seemed to mind her picking up the boy. Maybe, Rishi thought, no one else knew her well enough to know what was happening. She didn't bother looking at Rishi, but from a distance, he could see this much: The fog in her eyes had cleared. He could see quite plainly, because he'd seen it before, that Kavya was falling in love. Ignacio lay in her arms now, his cheek pressed to her chest. She'd wrapped the ends of her sweater around him, to guard against the chill.

From somewhere in the house a breeze was born—a heavy sigh, a closing door. It passed through the living room and raised a sheet of goose bumps on Ignacio's back. This was what she noticed first about the boy: the wakeful, tender flesh. She heard the faintest rattle in his breath. It angered her that he'd been left to grow cold, that the foster mother, now settled on the sofa, could fail to see that the sun had set and evening was approaching, that the bay winds had begun to whistle through her single-paned windows.

When he rested his head against her, she found herself consumed. The essence of Ignacio grabbed her by the ears. She lowered her nose to his skull and breathed him in, the hair there soft and brown and slightly unwashed. When she pulled him closer, the cavity that she'd been carrying around for so many months—for so many years, she realized now—opened itself and was filled.

Kavya and Ignacio weren't born in that room on that evening. An outline of her desire had been building for years now; it was clearly delineated and multidimensional and lacked the one thing, the real thing, the child at its center. Ignacio climbed quietly into that outline, and Kavya knew she was his.

Rishi had to end it. She knew he would. When he cleared his throat and suggested they go, it took her several minutes to give Ignacio back. The room waited in respectful silence, as if Ignacio were already hers, and hers to give up. Joyce waited. The other children played quietly. Agatha had fallen asleep. Even Rishi kept his trap shut.

And when she found them prying the boy gently from her lap, ushering her into the moonless dark, she twisted to peer at the closing door, into the winking sliver of light, thinking, perhaps, that Ignacio would follow.

Rishi put his seat belt on, but didn't start the engine. "Wow," he said.

"I know."

"What *was* that?"

"He was amazing, wasn't he?"

"What?"

"What?" she asked.

"You couldn't see what you were doing?"

"You didn't get to hold him, did you? I was just so caught up, I didn't think to hand him over to you—"

He stared at his wife for a long minute. "No. Listen. We were *brought* there to meet a baby. We'd asked for a baby and they gave us one. And then you—you—like—*dissed* the baby for this other kid."

Kavya stared back. "Excuse me?"

When Rishi swiveled his head to look at her, she saw something familiar and distasteful there. It was the lawyer look. An argument was roiling inside him, and he was gathering his militia, readying for the attack.

She breathed deeply. "Can we talk about this at home, please?"

"Yes. Sure."

And they drove through Berkeley in silence.

At home, Kavya stripped down to her underwear and pulled her husband into bed. With her legs wrapped around him, she knew she had the upper hand. She wasn't using sex as a weapon, or even as a coaxing mechanism. Sex, it turned out, wouldn't factor into that night. She was operating on the belief, recently discovered, that naked skin begged for understanding. She had never wanted one person as immediately as she wanted Ignacio, and the fact of this wanting made her wholly vulnerable to the fickle step of circumstance. When she wrapped herself around Rishi and slid her hand beneath his T-shirt, she felt him soften. The brace of his abdomen slackened, and he sighed.

"So what are you saying?" he asked.

"I want to be a mother to Ignacio."

"Ignacio."

"Yes. If you could just hold him like I did—"

"Would you listen to me, please? For two seconds?"

"Yes."

He inhaled deeply. She could feel from the punctuated drop of his belly that he was measuring his words. "You can't. Just. Do that."

"Yes I can."

"What was wrong with the baby? Why were you holding it like that?"

"I don't know. I just didn't— I felt something for Ignacio."

"You can't just choose him because you feel like it. It doesn't work like that."

"Yes it does. I'm choosing. I'm calling Joyce in the morning."

Kavya shut off the lamp and lay in the dark. She hadn't showered or brushed her teeth. The lights in the house were still on. But she was done for the day, and though she didn't sleep for more than an hour at a time that night, she wanted nothing but to meet the morning.

SHE WOKE UP SHIVERING in the gray light, still in her underwear and nothing else. She'd pulled her comforter tight around her chest in the night, and now her knuckles ached from the strain. It was Sunday morning. Joyce wasn't answering her cell. Kavya would have to wait. And think. She knew that Rishi would view this weekend as the cooling-off period, the delay before she changed their lives forever, but Kavya didn't want to cool off. She'd spent most of the night hyperalert, a pot of water mad with heat and longing to boil. To her, the situation was simple. She couldn't have a child. And then she met a child she wanted. The child, quite possibly, needed a better home. This was *easy*, she decided. So much easier than the waiting and the loss she'd known already.

29.

SOLI BEGAN HER RETREAT, BURROWING A TUNNEL TO THE inside of the inside of herself. It was safer there, where no one could see her truly, where she could keep things small and dark. There were hundreds in the camp, maybe thousands—hard to tell from the outside, when they marched her along the barbed wire, hands shackled to a chain around her waist. From the outside, all she saw were fantastical domes, ivory-white beneath the blue sky, surrounded by never-ending flatland. The domes were like nothing she'd seen before. From the outside, they were pleasure castles. On the inside, she found rows, dozens, of bunk beds, like in an orphanage in a children's book. Prisoners slept head to toe, and at night, they shivered. She had a single purple blanket. She would never forget this blanket.

Nothing feels lonelier than not knowing where your loved ones are. Ignacio. Aldo, Daniel. Even Silvia. She'd filled with ache on the inside, and had no room left for food. She was saturated with sorrow.

At night, the winds gathered speed across the land, unbridled by buildings or trees. The cold of the open land was spiteful. She'd assumed she was in a building, but soon it became clear that this was no more than a tent, a very large one. The night wind hissed through the cracks and folds, circled the dome until it found her. She spent the nights gripping her blanket, stretching it as best she could around her bare feet. The prisoners shivered and their teeth clacked. Imagine two hundred sets of clacking teeth. Soli kept herself together by thinking about Ignacio, replaying him again and again. Sometimes she'd think of Berkeley, the people eating pizza in the middle of the street, the lazy music that trailed from restaurants. And other times—she couldn't help it—she'd remember the night she first saw the ivory domes glowing from within, the sky smeared with stars, and she couldn't help thinking that this was a beautiful place, a dream arrayed on a naked plain.

She rarely slept at night. If she did doze off, a shriek usually yanked her back. She heard men in pain, and women. But she got used to this, as people get used to struggles of any measure—the guards who behaved like insolent children, the mildew smell of the food, the roaches that scurried beneath the beds at night. She got used to the hands that slid down her pants, past the loose elastic waistbands. She got used to the feeling of never being warm or clean. In that first place, she wore a baggy gray sweatshirt, jogging pants, and sandals. Even with the residual paunch of pregnancy, Soli's pants slid down when she walked, unless she bunched the waist in her hand. Silvia would have slapped her chest and laughed.

Solimar was Alien 127676. The beds on either side of hers were occupied by Aliens 127677 and 127678, also known as Serena and Salma. That first day, Serena and Salma were already deep in conversation when Soli arrived at her bed, but they spooled her into their discussion as if she'd always been there, because what else was there to do? They remarked upon the fact that all their names began with *S*, which was a comfort. Days later, when the three of them were moved from the dome, marched to the main prison building, and shut together in a cell, they were grateful. To be grateful, in such a place, was a small surprise.

They called their room la juala, the cage. Its only openings were a door, kept locked most of the time, and a small high window in the wall, no bigger than a piece of notebook paper. It was too high to look through, but they could see if it was gray outside, or blue. It kept in them the old habit of looking for the weather, of expecting to go outside and feel it.

Criminals lived in the adjacent cells—real steal-and-rape types, arsonists and con men and drug dealers, more varieties of evil than Soli cared to ponder. They trailed through the yard and down the corridor. She passed them when she went to the cafeteria. She heard them howl and wrangle at night.

Because such men occupied the public spaces, they kept the women locked in their rooms. Women were treated like criminals, while thieves roamed the yard like bison, and men were as free as children to play and fight. Soli was no angel. She was fairly sure she wasn't a criminal, either. Still, kept with criminals, though she'd stolen no more than a number, some water bottles, and a jug of wine in all her life, Soli started to believe that maybe she was one of them, that some evil resided within her and the people in uniform had been the first to find her out.

At night, she cradled the microscopic slips of her son that had passed from his body to hers. She foraged for memories of him. In the mornings, they rose with the blast of a horn and said to each other, Today is Monday, Today is Tuesday. They kept track of the days like this, because it seemed to them—to Soli, at least—that if the days could be counted, then they'd have to come to an end. At times, the three women found themselves laughing, and this place on the inside didn't feel so terribly bleak, just ludicrous. Soli shut off a part of her mind so she could live. In the mornings, the guards walked down the corridor, opening doors, yelling for them to stand up and be counted. They were counted, lined up, and herded to the cafeteria. After breakfast they were given twenty minutes to mill around the yard. This was where Soli felt the most watched, out in the open air. The eyes behind darkened windows were palpable. Once they were taken back inside and locked in their rooms, they sat on their beds and gazed up at the rectangle of light. She could stand up and move to the other side of the room, if she wanted. She felt her behind spreading and fattening, weighing her down with every passing day.

One night, Soli had a dream that the door opened and a man came in to take Serena away. "Where am I going?" Serena asked. "Am I getting out? Am I out? Where are you taking me now? Where are we going?" She went on squawking like a frightened crow until she was slapped into silence. Soli tried to get up and stop them, to say *Serena, wait*. Or *Serena, goodbye*. But sleep pinned her to her bed.

When she did wake to the blast of a horn, she sat up and said, "Today is Tuesday, Serena, and I had the strangest dream." But when she looked across the room, Serena was gone.

Serena was gone, and then Serena became Jeanette.

And there was nothing to say about Jeanette, except that she kept to herself and said nothing at all. They'd wake in the morning and Salma would say, "Today is Wednesday." And Jeanette would look at them as if to say, Of course today is Wednesday.

And even when Soli asked her if she spoke Spanish, she didn't say a thing. But when Salma and Soli spoke, Jeanette seemed to follow their words, even when they led to nothing. Even when they spoke purely for sound.

"Walls," Salma would say.

"Balls."

"Calls."

"Falls."

They could spend an hour or more this way, throwing rhymes back and forth, in English, to see who the poet was, the trovador.

"Fly."

"High."

"Goodbye."

Jeanette stayed out of this nonsense dance of theirs. Sometimes Soli wondered if words inside a cage meant anything at all. Sometimes they spoke about their children. Salma had three at home in Chicago. They were born in America, and living with their aunt. And if Salma got deported, she'd lose them. They would stay behind, and she'd be back in Mexico, childless, her children motherless. "But I'd find a way," Salma said. "I'd come back across to get them. Or I'd find the money to bring them with me, back home. We'd be poor as hell—I don't know what we'd do. It's not safe anymore in my old town. But we'd be together. And any place, even the worst part of home, is better than this cage . . . Don't get offended," she said. "You're the only good thing."

And Soli told her about Ignacio, how she didn't know where he was, just that he was somewhere in Berkeley. In care, she'd been told, which sounded like nothing, like the passage of air through barbed wire. He must have had another mother, another father, maybe a sister and brother and piles of toys, and perhaps he was even happy, and perhaps he was with a señor and señora who had their own Mexican housekeepers, who drank tea and did yoga just like the Cassidys. She told Salma about the Cassidys too, but found that after a while, she didn't have much to say about them. So mostly, it was Nacho, things Nacho had done, how he liked to open windows, how he liked being propped on her knees and pony-bounced, how they'd dance together in the empty living room of the house on Cedar Street.

And Salma said, "At least I know where my children are, at least they're safe at home. If I were you, Soli—if I were you I don't know what I'd do. I'd be hanging from the bars of this cage, wailing like La Llorona until they let me out."

"And what's the use of that?" Soli asked. "If I didn't shut my own mouth, they'd do it for me." Through all of this Jeanette said nothing about her children, if she had them, where they were, where her regret resided. Sometimes Soli would wake in the night feeling hot, and thoughts of Ignacio would scuttle into her head and scare away the sleep.

She'd look over and see Jeanette staring at her, her eyes two beacons from a lighthouse.

There was only so much loss a person could take, and once Soli reached her fill, her head, or maybe her heart, said *Enough's enough.* And it spun a web, thin as a whisper at first, but thickening with time. As the shock dulled, her old life, dreamlike, began to slip from her grasp. Her new existence stepped forward, and Soli followed, held together by the paltry web inside. Life in jail grew nearly tolerable for a while, for a few weeks, until something new happened and kicked into her head the idea that *No, this is not for me.*

One day she woke up and said, "Today is Wednesday," and went about her day until it was time for dinner. She sat in the dining hall with Salma and silent Jeanette. They'd been served a thin slice of bread and a concoction in a bowl, something like pozole, a sludgy grain of some sort, some mashed-up beans mixed in and at the base of it, an unseasoned tomato sauce. This was a good meal compared to most—most of what they ate was overcooked and starchy; it filled them up but left them dull and bloated. Salma had been talking so long that Soli had lost track of what she was saying, and happened to look down into Salma's soup.

"Salma," she hissed, and pointed.

Salma stopped talking, looked down, and cursed. What she saw there was as long as her thumb, its sides littered with legs. Two pincers sprang from its head. Even Jeanette leaned over and stared into the bowl.

"What should I do?" Salma asked.

"Tell them," Soli said. "That's some haunted soup. They can't make you eat that haunted soup."

"They won't give me more."

Jeanette leaned in farther. And then she said, "That is one nasty. Shit. Bug."

They both looked up. Jeanette had spoken. For a moment, they forgot the bug. Jeanette's eyes grew wide, still staring down.

Soli looked back at the soup.

The insect surged forward in the soup and Salma shrieked. *Shrieked.*

The dining hall fell silent. Salma started whispering, cursing, praying.

A guard approached. Soli counted every footstep.

"What's going on?" he called.

More than anything, Soli was angry. This small offense, this misdirected insect, was the bug that tore the web inside.

When the guard arrived, she spoke up. He looked at her like she was about to shit on his grandmother's grave.

"There's an insect in this soup," Soli said. "She can't eat this soup. You can't make us eat bugs."

And his hand—his hand went to the gun at his side. Imagine getting shot for a bug in Salma's soup. But Soli would have taken a bullet for that buggy soup.

The guard leaned over to look into the bowl, his pale shaven head just inches from hers. She could have bitten off his ear. Salma kept her head down, breathing heavily.

"You got a bug there?" he said loudly, too loudly. "You got a big old bug in that soup, huh?"

Salma nodded. Soli could tell from the clench of her cheek that she was holding back tears.

Soli spoke up again, "She doesn't have to eat that soup."

The guard looked up. "You're right. She doesn't. Better yet, she could take the bug out." He leaned over, picked up the bowl.

"Here go," he said. "I'll do it for you." With that, he raised the bowl high. The women watched as it tipped forward, ever so slightly at first, then farther, until the red stew peeked over the vessel's lip, creeping forward. It cascaded down. Salma cringed and squeezed her eyes shut. The stew splashed down onto the crown of her head, dripped down her hair and past her brow. It dripped to the tip of her nose and onto her

T-shirt, chunks of cornmeal stuck in her hair. Her hand shook as she wiped the sludge from her eyes, from her nostrils and lips.

Soli had had enough. With her better judgment gesticulating wildly, growling at her to stop and take one second to *think*, she spoke. "You can't do that to her." She leapt to her feet. She came as high as the guard's chest, her body just inches from his. The guard grabbed Soli's shoulder and shoved her to the floor. And then he leaned over and told her to get up.

"Get up!" he shouted. "Get the fuck up, you fucking moron!"

He yanked her up by the elbow and they walked out of the dining room. Arm in arm, Soli and the guard. She would carry the bruises for weeks.

Where he took her, she'd never been before. First, though, he searched her, inside her pants, his dirty claws inside her panties, up in her armpits and beneath her breasts. He called her a terrible name. He did the things he'd wanted to do in the dining hall, but couldn't with all those eyes on him.

"I thought you Mexicans liked that shit," he said. "Crickets and shit." And when his hands had finished hurting her, he pushed her into a room and shut the door. The room was no bigger than the señora's closet. It was big enough to take three steps forward and three to the side. Its walls were padded in foam, and it was semidark, but she could see her hands. They kept her there for hours and hours, maybe a day, maybe more. When she slept, she dreamed of Berkeley, a version of the old playground cast in shadow. She thought back to a day with Nacho and Saoirse. She'd walked Ignacio around the concrete border, guided him down the slide, and kept her third eye on the little girl. Saoirse stood on the wooden footbridge that swung between the play structures and tossed Barbie dolls from the chained precipice. One by one she let them plummet, and spent a few moments considering each new victim, facedown on the ground, its strands of flaxen hair mingled with the rough sands. During these forced suicides, Soli saw in her eyes the señora's shark-fin flicker of sorrow. The little girl carried with her a shadow of a woman's pain. But what did she know of pain? Soli tried to look down into Nacho's face. I'm here, she wanted to tell him, but he wouldn't look at her. She clasped him by the shoulders until her forehead met his, but still, she could't see his face. His eyes were a blur. Don't be scared, she said to the blur. I'm coming to get you.

Time passes differently in twilight. They didn't feed her. She didn't go to the bathroom. She held her urine because she feared what they'd do if she pissed in that room, if she made a mess.

When they let her out, she was limp with hunger, with lack of sleep. Her side ached with backed-up fluid. Back in la juala, Jeanette was asleep on her bunk. Salma lay awake and sat up when Soli entered. She'd been cleaned, with just a faint orange stain on her shirt. She blinked at Soli, looked up at the sunlit window. "Today is Friday," she said.

30.

July in a county courtroom, just big enough for two slim tables and a modest lectern. Around the table sat four women—one a judge—who'd gathered to discuss a child named Ignacio El Viento Castro Valdez. Ignacio himself wasn't there, and neither were Kavya, Rishi, or Soli. At the end of the session, the judge declared the boy a dependent of the state of California. A permanency plan would be compiled, along with a list of tasks that Soli would have to complete, to prove her ability to mother. In the meantime, Ignacio would stay in temporary foster care.

Joyce's voice broke through the cellular static. Kavya had to squint to hear her. She asked her to repeat what she said once, and then twice, until Joyce was shouting from her end.

"I HAVE GOOD NEWS."

Kavya sat down.

"THE FOSTER MOTHER SAID YES."

Kavya placed her forehead on the table. This got Rishi's attention. He pushed the speakerphone button.

Kavya nodded into the table, breathing heavily.

"However"—here the static vanished, Joyce's voice snapping clear—"this placement comes with risks. Kavya? Can you hear me?"

"Yes."

"The child has a mother who's very much alive and very much willing, but in immigrant detention, for identity fraud, and there's a chance—a good chance—that she'll be back for him soon. Long-term placement here is not a certainty."

"Okay," Kavya said. "Okay."

"So you understand that."

"It's not a certainty," she repeated. "But there's a chance."

"I can't commit to anything, Kavya. These situations never come with certainty. And let me tell you something *else*." Joyce was starting to sound peeved. "This requesting one child over another?"

"Yes?"

"Highly irregular. Normally, we don't let it happen. Foster care is for kids who need families. Not for families who want kids. You're not shopping for purses here. You get that?"

"I do."

"No. I don't think you do." Joyce sighed. "But look, the foster home was a much better setup for an infant. Ignacio was frankly a little more than the foster mother could handle. So we made an exception. Consider yourself lucky."

Kavya was speechless, and before Joyce could rescind the offer, she gently disconnected the phone. When she looked up at Rishi, he raised his brows and smiled.

"We're getting him," she said.

"We're getting him."

Before Rishi could get up and wrap his arms around her, Kavya rose and went to the bedroom. She climbed under the blankets, closed her eyes, and fell asleep. She slept for six hours that morning. It was a Tuesday. Rishi called the sorority.

The woman on the phone asked him to repeat himself. She was quiet for a few long, dry seconds.

"You can't get takeout?" Rishi asked.

"No," the woman said. "We cannot."

Joyce's news had come on a Tuesday, and Ignacio was due to arrive that Sunday. The process had been so painless that Rishi began to worry. His inner lawyer was searching through the night for a loophole, a prediction of regret, sniffing every corner for the proverbial little rat.

"What if he's more difficult than he looks?" Rishi asked.

"All kids are more difficult than they look," Kavya said. She was cramming plastic plug protectors into every outlet in the house. Now she crawled across the living room on her hands and knees, past the mound of toys that occupied an entire corner.

"I've got to get diapers," she said. "I was going to do that today. Is that all right with you? Are you on board with that?"

Kavya had been asking him a lot lately if he was on board with things.

She gazed at him then rose and walked to his side. She wrapped her arms around his waist and pressed her face into the dip between his chest and arm. "Are you happy?" she asked. "I'm happy."

He held her hard. "I'm happy, too." He smoothed down her hair. "Do we have to tell your mom?"

RISHI AND KAVYA had been dating for six months before he met her parents. It was during their third year of college, when they were due to separate for the six-week winter break, a length of time that had once felt luxuriant, but that year stretched before him like a sexless desert. He would miss Kavya herself, even without the sex, though this was not something he was ready to admit, even quietly. His plan was to go home to Ohio for the break, but he'd managed to say yes to a trip—a week in Lake Tahoe with six of his premed friends, four of whom were old enough to buy alcohol.

"Why don't you stop by Sacramento on your way back?" Kavya had asked. "It's a good rest stop for Berkeley."

"Stop by? At your parents' house?"

She stood in the kitchen, peeling cucumbers, her hip pressed to the countertop, one foot resting gently on its toe. She was making tzatziki. In the oven, pita bread was warming. In the blender, a volcano of home-made hummus sank into itself. Over midterms, she'd taught herself to make tahini, and a fresh bowl of it waited at her elbow.

I like to cook, she'd told him on their first real date. He'd thought this was something Indian girls said because their mothers told them to. He'd had no idea of the truth.

He watched her work, and considered the prospect of six weeks of not watching her. He wondered if she cared that they wouldn't see each other. If she did, she didn't let on. Even now, she seemed to focus solely on her cutting board, rinsing cucumbers and swiping away their tough green skins. But technically, she'd been the one to suggest the visit. It was her idea.

Going to Sacramento meant meeting her parents. Moreover, going to Sacramento meant meeting her Indian parents. He knew from his own pair that Indian parents never settled for a quick and forgettable how-do-you-do over cocktails. Meeting the Mahendras meant that assessments would be made, prospects tracked, and errant dreams of a red and gold wedding would waft through their living room. The heavy iron stamp of officialdom would be thrust upon Rishi and Kavya. They, as a couple, would exist.

But they as a couple did exist, and something about Kavya's fierce focus, the silken plain of her wrist, the silver bangles that jangled at her arm as she stirred the hummus, and the inch of brown skin at her waist that peeked between her jeans and white T-shirt, compelled him to stop thinking and simply say yes.

"Okay," he said. "I'll stop by."

"Okay," she answered quietly.

The visit had almost not happened. Rishi hadn't brought himself, during his week in Tahoe, to tell his friends that they'd be stopping for tea at his girlfriend's parents' house. Their group didn't plan—they simply did. They found themselves doing. And so, he ended up waiting until they'd reached the series of Sacramento exits on Highway 50, on their way back to Berkeley, to bring up the Kavya situation.

"What?"

"Who?"

"Heeeeeeeellllllll, no!"

"No way, man. No."

The chorus of dissent was unanimous and passionate. So the driver slowed the car at the mouth of the Mahendras' driveway, and Rishi ran around the back of it, grabbed his backpack, closed the trunk, and gave it a whack to send it on its way.

Kavya opened the front door. She looked at him blankly. It occurred to him then that maybe her invitation had been a half thought, something he was supposed to pursue and solidify himself. It occurred to him that he might have failed in some stage of the planning. But then, as if to compensate for the poor greeting, an aromatic cloud slunk out the door to meet him. He grinned at Kavya, and stepped forward. She stiffened, turned her face away, and leaned in for a feathery non-hug, a veritable pat on the back that Rishi, for the moment, did not understand.

Then, through the window, he saw two faces, two pairs of black eyes, as hard and lustrous as rune stones. He cleared his throat and followed Kavya in. Kavya's mother stood short and broad in her kitchen. He bent to give her a gingerly long-distance hug, before wondering if he should have shaken her pincushion hand instead. "Hi, Aunty," he said.

"Okay," she replied.

Kavya's father was startlingly tall, taller than Rishi, with sleepy eyes and stooped shoulders.

"Hi, Uncle." He saw in her father's face Kavya's cheekbones, the stubborn jut of her chin.

Almost immediately, they were sitting down to eat, a pot of lamb curry at the table's center. Kavya's mother asked questions about his degree, his plans, his parents. Kavya barely ate. Her father barely spoke but to offer a line of information, a morsel of commentary on the very-goodness or very-badness of things. The mother's eyes bore into him like lasers, incising his intention, assessing his moral and perhaps his monetary worth. Rishi's thoughts sought refuge in the mountains he'd been on that week, his skis slicing snow, their clean parallel lines.

And then it was over. His stomach was heavy, his eyelids heavier. He wanted nothing now but to sleep, his face burrowed into the peaty warmth of Kavya's skin.

"Rishi, you would like to lie down?" Uma asked.

"Yes!" Rishi nodded, grateful.

"Kavya." Uma signaled to her daughter, then turned her hard gaze back on him. Laser eyes.

Kavya led Rishi to a room down the hall. In the dark hallway, away from her parents, he felt his shoulders unlock from his neck, his arms slacken. He took a good long look at Kavya, and she looked new to him again. He'd grown used to her at school, he realized. Over the break he'd forgotten the strength of her back and the patrician angles of her face. She had a force that he craved. He wanted to belong to her.

She brought him to the guest room. Kavya leapt for the bed and landed outstretched. "Come here," she said.

Rishi stopped to close the door.

"Don't! If they hear the door close they'll think something's happening!"

"But something *is* happening."

"Trust me," she said. "Come here."

Rishi lay down on the bed in a stiff line, hands on his stomach.

"I missed you," she said, and covered his body with hers. "Put your arms around me."

They lay like this for a long while, Rishi holding Kavya, nervous and grateful and sleepy all at once. He began to drift off, but felt her lips on his neck, her lips on his lips, and woke again. He'd lost her scent, and now it came back in a storm cloud of soap and skin and something like warm bread. He forgot about sleeping, about the open door. He let Kavya run her fingers into his waistband, undo his fly, and yank down the denim. His hands went to her waist, to the fevered bare skin of her back. He longed to be alone with her, and then he was. He was lost in the world of Kavya, and they were, at last, absolutely alone.

And then they were not.

"Kavya!" A shuffle at the door. "Kavya!" Uma stalked in, a fire-breathing bull. *"Stop it now!"* she roared, and smacked at her daughter's back. Rishi flipped onto his stomach, cringed, and waited for the blows. But there were none. Uma chased Kavya from the room, still swatting. Her voice faded down the hall. *"What he will think, Kavya? You are my daughter? Who taught you this business?"*

He sat up, catching his breath and listening to their distant shouts. He grinned in spite of himself. He would have to find a way home, he realized. He certainly wouldn't be spending the night.

An hour later, Kavya had gathered her keys and purse to drive him to the train station. Rishi could hear her from the other side of the house. "I know! Okay! O-*kay! I know! Mom!*"

Rishi stood in the entryway, his ski jacket on, his duffel bag in hand. Before him, Kavya's father was silent, his cheeks sagging glumly from the lower rim of his spectacles. He smoothed his hair down over his forehead and cleared his throat.

"Rishi," he began. "You also are Indian. Are you not?"

Rishi nodded.

"You know the values?"

The values, Rishi thought. There were just so many of them. He nodded.

"Our daughter, Kavya . . . our daughter is not this kind of girl."

"I'm sorry, Uncle."

"It is very bad, Rishi."

"I know. I'm sorry. Thank you for having me here, Uncle." Rishi's stomach turned, and spikes of sweat sprung to his forehead.

Kavya drove him to the station in her parents' beige Lexus. They said nothing until the first stoplight, when she turned to him with a miserable sort of grin.

"So that went well," Rishi said.

Kavya rolled her eyes.

"Shit," he said.

"Indeed."

They rode in silence and merged onto the highway.

"Let's go to Berkeley," he said. "Forget the train station."

"I wish I could."

"Am I, like, an untouchable now?"

"You?" She sent him a sidelong gaze. "No, you're not the untouchable."

"Oh."

"It's a good thing you're premed, though. I think that saved you," she said. "I, on the other hand, will have plenty to answer for."

"Sorry."

Kavya was silent, then turned, saw he was staring at her, and frowned. "What?"

"Who taught you that business, Kavya?"

She started to laugh.

"You're not that kind of girl."

And Rishi was glad he came. He was almost glad that it had gone badly—it had gone badly and he still wanted to be with Kavya. She was worth the worry and the trouble, the anticipated strife of future parental meetings, the shadow of that afternoon that would forever darken his encounters with Uma Mahendra. He was glad that he knew this, glad he'd stopped for tea, glad for old Laser-Eyes, and glad, most of all, that Kavya, his Kavya, was that kind of girl.

AND NOW, the day of Ignacio's arrival. The sun pounded its welcome through the bedroom window.

Kavya stood in the doorway, still hunched with sleep. She wore an old T-shirt of Rishi's with the sleeves cut off, and her arms dangled from them like jungle reeds. Her legs were bare. White panties stretched across her hips.

"I'm speaking to my mom today."

"That's nice."

"I'm speaking to her about Ignacio," she said.

"Oh." He studied her face. Kavya was right to be worried, and Rishi didn't envy her task; breaking unfavorable news to Uma when there was nothing that Uma could do was like swatting a wasp.

Uma Mahendra had made her position clear. Offspring sprung off the family tree. Adoption was trouble. Adopted children were shadowy variables in an otherwise finely wrought equation of marital eugenics. Adoption itself subverted what Uma saw as the very purpose of existence: to marry, to mate, to give birth to caste-navigated, elder-sanctioned, blessed and bouncing bundles of reproduced hope. To adopt, to take a child from some *other* union, some union of whose nature they had barely an inkling, was an act that uprooted the very foundations of family.

The phone rang. "It's her," Kavya said. "I can tell."

She did not move, and let it ring until Rishi rolled out of bed, crossed the room, and picked it up.

"Hi, Mom. Sure. We were up. Uh-huh. Uh-huh. Uh-huh. Uh-huh."

Kavya snatched the receiver and pressed the speakerphone button.
"Hi, Amma."

"What you're doing?"

Her mother sounded suspicious already, at eight on a Sunday morning. Rishi stretched, put on a T-shirt, and headed to the kitchen to make their morning tea. From the doorway, he watched his wife. He watched the woman he thought he knew try to reason with her mother. Her skin was still powdery with sleep, her voice raspy. As she listened, her jaw sawed to and fro. She picked at the rug and rubbed her eyelids, quiet, listening despite her best intentions. This was not his wife. The wife he knew did not ask for approval. Nor did she weave crisis, drawing it from her palm like spider silk. The Kavya he knew wouldn't be seeking her mother's pardon on a day like today. Her pursuit of it was nothing but self-destructive.

But Kavya, this new Kavya, seemed to need it badly. She submitted totally to her mother's rattling tirade, her body sprawled at angles like a homicide outline. When Uma met the kid, she'd fall in love, as all grandmothers did. Or she wouldn't. But there was no reasoning with an angry wasp. He filled the kettle and put it on the stove. When he returned to the bedroom with a mug in each hand, he found Kavya lying flat on the floor, her palm pressed to her forehead, still on the phone. "Uh-huh. Uh-huh. Uh-huh."

When she saw him, she put the phone down, rolled onto her side, and took the mug of tea. Rishi lay facing her on the carpet, listening to Uma squawk through the room. He wondered if she'd always sounded like that, or if her voice changed with age and wear. Kavya's face was slack with defeat, her cheeks drooping to the floor. Her eyelids fluttered as she listened. It angered him, suddenly, that this day, of all days, should have to begin like this. He listened to Uma's litany. It was a thorough one. She remembered it all: the mistakes they'd made in trying and failing to get pregnant, the recklessness of their decision to foster, the hassles they would inevitably face, the perils that lay with the little boy who, at that very moment, was eating his breakfast, watching his foster mother pack his bag, and preparing for the car ride that would bring him to their door. He hoped that maybe, in her pre-tea state, Kavya was too sleepy to detect the condemnation that saturated the airspace of their bedroom. He wanted this to be a good day for her. He set his mug next to the telephone and pulled her close. He took her mug from her hand and placed it next to his. He pressed the speakerphone button, shrinking Uma's voice to a distant buzz.

His fingers moved up Kavya's shirt and found her breasts. She drew closer to him, looped her arm around his neck, and kissed him. And then, they proceeded to do what had come to feel like an exercise in failure, but on this muggy Sunday morning, with their future eating its breakfast, their tea steaming on the carpet, and maternal disapproval still rattling from a nearby mouthpiece, proved to be the essential thing, the only thing.

It was nearly ten. A ring of steam misted the windowpane where Kavya pressed her forehead. Rishi wanted to tell her to relax, to come away from the window. One of them had to be calm. But he wasn't calm and couldn't pretend to be, so he pressed his own forehead to the window and gazed out onto Vine. Their French toast grew cold and wet. The air was heavy that morning, the sky bereft of color, waiting for rain to break. Outside his window, the bougainvillea hung lushly off their gate, the grass grew wild, overfed that spring with rain. Rishi thought of trimming it, but couldn't bring himself to leave the window. The time was 9:47.

The phone rang.

Kavya grabbed it, said three words, put it down.

"They're almost here."

What Kavya and Rishi hoped to project, from under the eaves of their Berkeley bungalow, was an air of parenthood. An air of belonging where they were, of knowing what to do with the little stranger—for that's what he was, a stranger, as foreign to them as they were to him. Parents were people who knew what they wanted. It fell to Rishi and Kavya, the parents in this game of make-believe, to do and say the things that parents were meant to say and do, until pretend became real, and they found, one day, if all went well, that the little boy was theirs and they were his, that the three of them did indeed belong to one another. Pretending, at this point, was the most they could do.

31.

AND THEN, ONE DAY, SOLI WOKE UP AND SAID, "TODAY IS Sunday," and Jeanette was taken away. But that was okay. "Maybe they'll send someone new," Salma said. "Maybe her name will start with *S*, or maybe she'll at least have something to say." They waited for two days, three, but nobody else showed up. It grew cold in the yard as summer hinted at fall. Though they could see no trees with crisping leaves, they felt the sadness and the vigor that would ride the currents of autumn. La juala wasn't heated. Soli knew a request for heat would get no more than a chuckle. The guard would laugh and go and tell the others, and they would laugh, too. Without a third person to heat the room, the nights grew even colder, and one night Salma and Soli kept each other awake shuffling in bed, groaning with cold. The only way they could sleep was to lie side by side, Soli's arms around Salma's waist, knees curled into knees. Soli climbed up to her bunk before daybreak, because if the guards found them lying like this, lying like sisters and keeping warm, there would be a price to pay.

Later that morning, Soli awoke on her top bunk. "Today is Thursday," she said, and from below, she heard nothing. Not even the rustle of sleep. She looked down. Salma was gone.

That afternoon, the guard found Soli. "You have a visitor," she said. Salma, she thought. Salma was out and coming back for her, coming back to tell her about her life outside, the miracle that had freed her. Or else it was Nacho. The possibility left her breathless.

The room contained rows of small tables, each divided by a pane of glass, inmate on one side, visitor on the other, speaking by telephone across the glass. Some chatted as if nothing at all were wrong, others held the receivers and stared in silence. Waiting at a table was a man Soli had never seen before. He wore a gray suit and red tie.

He picked up the phone and introduced himself. "Adrian Alvarez," he said.

"Excuse me?"

Against the pane of glass he pressed a small card:

ADRIAN ALVAREZ

WILEY, WITTGENSTEIN, ALVAREZ, AND JAFFREY

It meant nothing.

"I'm a lawyer. I'm your lawyer."

It took her a few moments to decide what this meant.

"Where's my son?" she asked.

He smiled a tight, horizontal smile.

"You're Solimar Castro Valdez," he said. "Is that correct?"

She said nothing.

"We only have about ten minutes, Miss Valdez—"

"We're supposed to have thirty. Thirty for visits."

"I know. I think they took their time getting you here. I've been waiting awhile."

She shrugged.

"Okay. So we'll need to get started, all right? I'll need as much of your story as you can give me, okay? Should I speak in Spanish?"

"Yes," she said. And in Spanish she leaned forward, in Spanish she stared him down, in Spanish she asked, "Where. Is. My. Son?"

"Your son is with foster parents. That's all I know right now. All right? He's fine. Can we agree on that? He's being well taken care of, I'm sure."

"How would you know that if you don't know who he's with? And without his mother? How could he be fine?"

"I promise." He sighed. "I promise to try and find out for you. And I'll tell you next time."

She looked him over. Alvarez. He looked barely old enough for his suit. "Who are you?"

"We don't have a lot of time, Miss Valdez. I'll need you to be totally honest, okay? I'll need to know all your mistakes, everything that happened to you, everything you understood to be true."

She looked at the timer on the side of their table. "Are you with the police?"

"No. Absolutely not."

And so she began, haltingly at first, because she had no reason to trust the man. But soon it began to feel so good to tell her story to someone who was willing to listen, laying it out and remembering that, yes, she had existed, that she couldn't stop herself. Her story poured from her lips like sand. In the five minutes that remained, she told him everything she could about Manuel, Checo and La Bestia, the truck with the men, the men with the hats, the onions. The timer buzzed and she hadn't even got to America yet. From behind, she heard the heavy footsteps.

Adrian gazed up. "I'll be back tomorrow, Miss Valdez."

"Find Ignacio," she said. "Ignacio El Viento Castro Valdez. Ignacio El Viento Castro Valdez!"

From behind, she was yanked from her seat to her feet, pulled across the room almost faster than she could walk. She looked back, and Adrian was saying something through the glass partition that she couldn't hear.

. . .

THE NEXT DAY, NO ADRIAN. The day after, he still hadn't come. There were no visits on Sunday and by Monday she'd decided he had given up on her, or had found out something terrible about Nacho and didn't want to tell her. Sunday night, she hardly slept. Two new women were in her cell, and they seemed to know each other, but neither spoke Spanish. One was fat, the other thin. They were Chinese, or something like it, with paler skin than any she'd ever seen. They spoke to each other without stopping, with hardly a breath between words. They talked so tiresomely that she began to miss Jeanette. The thin one snored like an industrial machine.

On the third day, at last, a guard called her to the visiting room.

"Adrian Alvarez."

"Hello, Miss Valdez." He didn't smile. She would learn that Adrian Alvarez rarely smiled.

"Where is my son?"

"Ignacio's with a couple in Berkeley. They don't have any other children. They have a comfortable home. That's all I could find out. All right, Miss Valdez?"

"Call me Soli."

"Now listen, you've got to finish your story for me, and faster this time. If you cooperate, we'll get you out of here, and you'll be able to find your son on your own."

"On my own? What about you?"

"I'm an immigration lawyer, Soli. I don't do family court."

"And you can't help me find my son? Then why the hell are you here?"

From his folder, he pulled a sheet covered in writing. He signaled to the guard, who looked it over and nodded. The guard walked the paper around to her.

"I've translated it for you," Adrian said. "It's your reunification plan."

She read it aloud, a list of tasks set out by the court.

Family counseling upon release, it read. That was number one, and the thought of her release was enough to make Soli smile. Number two: Parent education training. Sure, she thought. She could have used some of that. Three: Substance abuse evaluation and adherence to all court approved recommendations. Four: Psychological evaluation and adherence to all court approved recommendations. The list went on and grew murkier by the line, until she came to the final requirement: Visitation with your child.

She would see Ignacio again.

"I'm going to visit with my child? I can see Ignacio?" She sat up. "Where is he? I want to do this now."

Adrian cleared his throat and looked at her long and hard over the rim of his glasses. "Listen, Soli."

She waited for him to clear his throat once, and again, more vehemently than the first time.

"Listen. This list was issued by a dependency court judge."

"And it's a way to get my son back. I know."

"The thing is. The thing is, dependency court and detention centers don't work together."

"And so?"

"And so you won't be able to get out of detention to go to counseling, or to go to class."

"And Ignacio?"

Adrian Alvarez pursed his lips and shook his head.

She stood to leave.

"Sit down," the guard called. "Sit down till you're told to get up."

She sat down. "Why are you here?"

"To get you a supervised release. My priority is to get you out, so you can work things out for yourself and Ignacio."

"I have nowhere to go."

"You'll find something. You'll figure it out. The point is, in here, you won't be able to do a thing. When your custody hearing comes around, they won't let you out of here. Got it? They don't care about your son in here, Soli. You've got to get out."

Adrian Alvarez was getting red in the face, and this made her feel like maybe he wanted to help.

"Who sent you?"

"Brett Cassidy."

"Brett Cassidy who wouldn't take my son in, you mean. That Brett Cassidy? Is that the one?"

Adrian ignored this and flipped open his yellow writing pad. She kept talking anyway.

"I took care of his daughter for almost two years, Adrian Alvarez. I was her second mother. And he let my boy go to strangers. Brett Cassidy didn't want anything to do with me. He said he couldn't. I just can't, he said. Like he couldn't be blamed. Like he was just too good to get himself involved. And then he sends you, like a hero, right? He sends you so he won't have to show his face. To take care of my problem so he won't have to touch it himself." She sat back, crossed her arms. "I've had a lot of time to think, Adrian Alvarez. Don't talk to me about Brett Cassidy."

"You asked."

She almost got up then. She almost decided she didn't need the likes of Brett Cassidy and his lawyer.

But of course she did need him. And she needed whatever Brett Cassidy could toss her way. She was flailing in an ocean, losing strength and swallowing saltwater, and Adrian Alvarez was the only boat in sight.

"So," Adrian said. "Can we continue?"

She told him about Silvia and the Cassidys, the abortion clinic, the social worker, giving birth to Ignacio, the money she sent back home, the preschool pickups, the day at the playground, the red light, the police. She told him about the day the señor asked for her social security number, the trip to see Marta, the money she paid him, the strange man's cheek against her belly.

Many times, Adrian stopped her and asked questions about what she'd paid, where the shop was, what Marta told her about her Social Security Number, what Mr. Cassidy said about her number, if he ever mentioned it after she threw it away.

"Hm," he said, and rubbed his chin, stared down at this notepad.

"What?"

"He must have known. He had to know the number wasn't real."

"How could he know? It was just a number."

He looked up. "It would have come back to him, eventually. Even if he hadn't checked up on you. At tax time, or when he filed the papers. He would have known that you didn't have papers, Soli."

"But I didn't even know I didn't have papers."

He peered at her. "Really? You didn't know? You thought the man in the grocery store was selling legal numbers?"

She stopped to consider this. She'd painted her days with a veneer of falsehood—her very existence in the country a falsehood, a secret, an unknown—and had been doing so for so long that the reality of what she knew and didn't know lay hidden. Here, sitting before Adrian, she let herself emerge, just a little, and exposed a slim sliver of truth. "I knew," she said. "Of course I knew."

"You didn't want to think about it."

She shook her head. "So the señor knew, also. That I didn't have papers. But he didn't kick me out."

"No, he didn't."

"So what happens now? With Ignacio?"

"Well, okay. There isn't much policy around this, Soli. Around getting children and parents like you back together. There's no *you-must-do-this* for the courts to follow. Do you understand that?"

"No."

"So, it'll depend on the people who handle the court case. On the judge. On how they see you. You're only twenty, right? That could work in your favor, or it could work against you. The important thing is that we get you out of here."

"I have another question."

"Yes?"

"Where am I?"

"What?"

"Where am I? Am I in California?"

Adrian blinked. "Yes. You're in central California. Didn't you know that?"

"How would I know?" she asked, gazing at the gray wall behind him. The buzzer buzzed.

"Time's up."

"I'll be back tomorrow."

"I'll believe you when I see you."

AFTER SOLI GREW USED TO the nightly commotion, she had learned to sleep deeply, sunk to exhaustion by the endless and empty days. Now, Adrian dropping occasionally into her days, and constantly into her thoughts, was enough to keep her awake at night, staring into the dark until morning. She comforted herself by remembering Ignacio, cataloging her memories of his body—the birthmark on his chunky thigh, the sprouting of two teeth, how he liked to chase the broom when she was sweeping. When she couldn't stop herself, she thought of all the times she'd put him on the floor and ignored his cries, when she had dishes to wash or onions to chop, when his twenty-pound heft was just too much for her, when all she wanted was to move without impediment, to be free to lie down on a sofa with a glass of cool water and the slow meander of her thoughts. She thought of his small arms reaching out to her, his tendency to press his forehead to the ground and weep theatrically, inconsolably. Those nights, when she let herself, she dreamt of his body pressed to hers, pillowy but firm, the weight that made her shoulders ache.

THE FOLLOWING WEDNESDAY, she was led to a room at the front of the compound. It was no bigger than la juala, windowless, with fluorescent beams running overhead. She sat down at a table. A female guard sat across from her.

"Is this my hearing?" she asked.

"Is this your what, now?"

She'd never seen this guard before. She'd answered a question, which made Soli think she had to be new.

"Is this the hearing, for my son? I'm phoning the court today?"

The guard smiled, frowned, cocked her head to one side.

"We'd like you to sign this, is all. This is for you to sign, okay?"

"Is this for my release?"

Soli looked down at the English words and knew them immediately. Adrian had warned her of this, had made her repeat the words aloud until she knew them by heart. *They'll let you out,* he'd said, *but only to be deported, Soli. Do you get that? They'll send you back to Mexico, and you won't be able to find Ignacio.* Stipulated Order of Removal. Silvia too had told her not to sign anything.

"That's your voluntary departure agreement," the guard said. "You seen one of these before?"

"I will not sign this."

The officer cleared her throat and scooted her chair in. "Miss Valdez," she said. "I'm a mother, too."

Soli waited.

"I know you're trying to get your son back. I know what it's like to worry for your kid."

Don't let them fool you, Adrian had warned her. *They'll make it sound like a good thing. Just push it away.* She waited for Soli to return her gaze, for some acknowledgment that they were kindred spirits. Soli gave nothing. Under the sharp light of the ceiling lamp, a pale coat of hair covered the woman's face.

"The thing is, you sign this? You'll be able to fight for your child. The longer you stay in here, the more likely you'll miss a hearing, miss a court date. If we get you out of here, you'll be able to get to those things."

"But my lawyer"—a smile leapt across the guard's lips and vanished— "my lawyer said he would get me released. With a monitor."

"M-hm. That's one way to do it. It *could* not happen at all. And then you'd be stuck in here even longer. Months, maybe."

Months, maybe. The thought of it pushed Soli back in her chair. The days to come, the weeks. The woman was calm, not hot with aggravation like some of the other guards. She acted like a woman, not a malicious sibling. She acted like a mother. The woman sat very still, as if she were posing for a portrait.

Soli dropped her pen to the floor.

The woman's eyelids began to flutter. "Your choice," she said at last, her smile almost gleeful. Parentheses sprang from her lips and hung there even when the smile fell away. What lay within those parentheses, Soli wouldn't know until it was too late.

Her mood changed after that day in the interview room. It didn't lift. She wasn't happier. She just cared less about everything that wasn't

Nacho. She'd lost her focus for a few weeks, distracted by bugs and chitchat, but now she had it back. She found freedom again, even between those four tight walls, even with no one but the two Chinese women to talk to. She tried speaking Spanish to them, at them, which of course they didn't understand. But it was something to do. And it interrupted their chatter, forced them to pause for a moment and wonder what was happening, which was worth a little something, too.

She'd decided not to make any more friends in that place. Making friends would make things tolerable, and if she could tolerate a place, she'd be in danger of staying.

There were matters she didn't want to broach with Adrian. Why was he there? Why, really, had the Cassidys sent him? And how would she end up paying?

One question she did ask: "Can you find out about Silvia? Can you tell me what happened to her, her children?"

"I'll see what I can do. She's not your problem, though. You realize that."

"Yes. I have another question."

"Yes?"

"When I get my Nacho back, what then? Will they send us both away?"

"If you win custody of your child, Soli, you'll most likely be deported. You'll have your removal hearing, but I don't see anything particularly compelling or unique about your case. To them, you're just another illegal."

"But I'll have my Nacho."

"You'll have your child."

32.

We've made a mistake.

It wasn't Rishi's first thought, but it was his strongest and clearest.
The boy—the baby—the creature in between (it seemed wrong to call
him a toddler, as he hadn't toddled yet) lay on his back, writhing and
shrieking.

That morning, Joyce had arrived and carried him into the living
room. He was subdued and observant. His hair had grown since they'd
last seen him, and a few curls fell over his forehead and grazed his brow.
He wore a yellow T-shirt and red pants that stretched across the bulk of
his diaper. This was the boy he remembered, and to see him again—his
mop of dark hair, his dimpled knuckles—stirred in Rishi an unexpected
longing.

"Hi there," Rishi said to Ignacio.

From Joyce's arms, Ignacio leveled his gaze on Rishi, and neither
cried nor smiled. He seemed to be developing an image of his new father through the filter of his lashes. Rishi took the boy's hand and ran
the pads of his fingers over Ignacio's miniature nails. Rishi wasn't sure
what a sixteen-month-old would want to hear. This one still looked
babylike, with pillowy cheeks and skin so soft it vanished at his touch.

"Would you like to hold him?" Joyce asked.

Rishi turned to Kavya, who was bringing a warm bottle in from the kitchen. She stopped. She smiled. "Hold him," she said.

"Maybe I could—um—" Rishi pointed to the floor.

"Let's sit down," Joyce said.

So they sat on the floor together, the four of them, like they were at a picnic. Ignacio turned to the mound of toys that waited in the corner, reached for a wooden hammer and cobbler's bench, and began taking drunken swipes at its blue and yellow pegs.

"He's not walking yet," Joyce said. "He's a little late, nothing to worry about. But he crawls like a champ."

"He's doing well," Kavya murmured as Ignacio whacked away. The women nodded gravely at each other.

"Hi, Ignacio." Kavya leaned in. "Hola, Ignacio," she cooed. Ignacio looked up and a flutter of recognition passed over him. He stuck his lips together and made a sound, a nonsense sound, and handed her the hammer. Kavya laughed, her eyes glistened. They played quietly with Ignacio while Joyce, in her practiced way, retreated from the scene a few inches at a time. Finally, she rose to her feet.

"Ignacio," Joyce said. "I'm going to say bye-bye now, okay, sweet boy?" Ignacio looked up. He blinked, not comprehending. He reached an arm up for Joyce. "Okay, now. Okay, now, you be good, now. Bye-bye, Ignacio." She backed out of the room and vanished into the front entryway. Ignacio watched her, craned his neck to find her again. They listened, the three of them, as the door opened and clicked shut.

Rishi had read about crying in an article Joyce had given them. There was the angry cry. There was the attention-seeking cry. There was the tired cry. And there was the sad cry. The article was called "The Grieving Child." At first, he hadn't understood why grief would have anything to do with the boy's arrival. There was nothing grievous about the situation, as far as Rishi could tell.

As it settled upon Ignacio that Joyce was gone, he looked at Kavya, then Rishi. His lip trembled, and with a deep inhale, he let loose a blaring wail. It tightened to a scream, a steady siren. Then the cry halted, his mouth hung wide open and silent. His eyes bulged.

"Oh my god," Kavya said. "Ignacio?" He sucked in a breath and set off on a new howl, this one longer and angrier than the first. When Kavya reached over to pick him up, he shrieked and clawed her away. His uncut nails left a long scratch down her cheek.

"Hey," Rishi said. "Hey, you okay?" Kavya touched a hand to her face, blinking. Rishi reached out to grasp Ignacio beneath the arms. Ignacio kicked out with broad-footed, astonishing force, and Rishi leapt back.

Kavya knelt beside him. They sat and watched the child for several minutes.

"What's wrong with him?"

"Nothing's wrong with him. Maybe he's sad," she said. "How would I know."

She tried again to pick Ignacio up, but he twisted himself away. "Hold on," she said, brightening. She jogged to the kitchen and returned with a cup of water. Kneeling before the boy, she stuck her tongue in the water, flicked it back and forth. "Perro!" she said. "Ignacio, perro! Woof woof!" She lapped at the water, wagged her tongue. Ignacio stopped crying, took the cup, and dumped it on the ground, wailing again, louder than before. Kavya rose to her feet, her hand over her mouth, and walked to the kitchen. Through the open doorway, Rishi watched her stand alone, one hand on the refrigerator door, motionless.

The boy had crawled to the corner, and now lay flat on his back. He screeched rhythmically, his legs pounding out a steady beat against the wall. Then, on a wave of fresh indignation, he began to yell. He yelled. He yelled. He yelled.

"Ignacio," Rishi said as gently as he could. *"Ignacio."* He tried it loud and firm, as he'd seen dog trainers do. "IGNACIO."

The boy paused, turned to Rishi, and his yells juddered to whimpers. His arms went slack, his tears spilled quietly to the rug. Keep a grieving child warm, the article had said. Sadness precipitates feelings of cold. Rishi picked a blanket off a neat stack in the corner and draped it over the boy.

They met in the kitchen.

"What are we doing?" she asked. Her forehead rested on the refrigerator door. It's what Rishi had wanted to say, but he knew very well that he couldn't have said it.

"He's okay," Rishi said. "He's in there, he's just—" The word escaped him.

"Catatonic?"

"Sure. Yeah. He's fine. He's just catatonic."

Kavya didn't smile. "Should we call Joyce?" she asked.

"I don't know. Let's give it some time."

"You don't want her to think we're already screwing up, do you?"

"No."

"Me neither."

They stood in the kitchen together for a long while, until Kavya opened the fridge.

"I'm hungry," Rishi said.

She pulled out a loaf of bread. "This is for Ignacio."

"Can he eat bread?"

She looked down at the loaf. "He has teeth."

From the cupboard she pulled a tin of formula—expensive formula, organic, sustainably farmed, snowy pure. "He doesn't need that," Joyce had pointed out. "Plain old milk is fine after a year." But Kavya had researched this formula, with its promises of DHA and iron; she felt reassured by its label, a hand-drawn child, diaper-clad, tromping through a wood.

When Rishi and Kavya approached the boy, he lay coiled into his blanket, a cotton-swaddled nautilus.

"He's asleep," Kavya said.

Indeed, Rishi heard the elongated snuffles, caught the rise and fall of his back.

Ignacio woke up twenty minutes later, and Kavya fed him formula. He accepted a bite of buttered bread and two spoons of mashed banana before turning away.

"You should ask Joyce what he's been eating," Rishi said.

"Why?" Kavya scowled.

"Comfort food. Eating what he ate at his old house could be comforting." He'd read this, and was surprised that Kavya hadn't.

That night, Kavya slept next to Ignacio's crib, rolled in a duvet, her index finger clasped in his fist through the bars of the crib.

"It was good," she said to Rishi the next morning. "He held my hand all night. He wouldn't let go."

Rishi nodded, sipped his coffee. "He's attaching."

But Ignacio returned that day to his corner. He sat in a heap for much of the morning, gazing wet-eyed at the door. Now and then he picked up a toy, turned it over in his hands, and put it back down. His gaze flitted constantly to the door.

Rishi was packing his satchel for work. Rishi would come and go as he always had. His schedule wouldn't change, and Kavya wondered if he understood how spectacularly their lives had. When Kavya sat next to Ignacio and picked up the cobbler's bench he'd so enjoyed the day before and said, "Here, Ignacio, *mira*, Ignacio," he snatched it from her and flung it against the wall.

"It's magical thinking," Rishi said.

Kavya threw him a look.

"He thinks that hammer thing is what made Joyce leave."

Kavya squinted at him. "That's ridiculous."

"Uh, no. It's not. It's how they think."

Kavya had the maternal instincts she needed. She had the love, she had the faith and the food and the granite force of her will. But she'd ignored almost all the reading material Joyce had given them. It's so pessimistic, she'd said, and handed the articles to Rishi.

"But why Joyce?" Kavya asked.

"Well, okay, maybe the first foster mother. Or his real mom. But Joyce was the final link to them. Or something."

"Or something. We're not part of the chain. At all."

Rishi went on. "Ignacio thinks it's something he did that made Joyce leave. He equates that toy with Joyce leaving him here. So he won't play with it. He thinks if he doesn't play with it, she'll come back. And take him away from here."

"Really."

"It's called magical thinking."

"Oh."

Ignacio looked from Kavya to Rishi, from Rishi to Kavya. Rishi picked up his backpack, opened the door that had swallowed Joyce, and left. On the patio, he listened for a moment for Ignacio's cries, but heard nothing.

KAVYA WATCHED RISHI mount his bicycle, straighten his backpack, and ride off, shrinking with distance, until he looked more like a school-boy than a father. She'd taken three weeks off, with a cut to her pay, to adjust to life with Ignacio. She had found a daycare center for him. And yes, she'd wondered why she was bringing a child into her life, only to leave him in daycare. But the thought passed quickly: This is just the way things are, she told herself. Mothers have to work.

She called Joyce. The shake in her own voice surprised her.

"Don't worry about it," Joyce said. "He's letting go of his old home, and the crying shows he's able to attach. I'd be more worried if he wasn't upset. Just be with him, and he'll come around. Okay?"

She hung up and turned to Ignacio. He sucked on his lower lip and watched her.

"Stories," Kavya said. "Libros."

Books worked. Ignacio didn't throw books. And the way he watched her lips move made her feel that he was listening. His attention grew sharp, wide-eyed, when she was in the midst of a story, and she felt, for extended periods that morning, that she was doing something for him—that she was filling a need rather than signifying an absence.

Still, the easy, affectionate clasp with which he'd held her at the foster home was gone. Or it was hiding, waiting to see that the coast was clear. While she read, she stole glances at his eyes. From black pupils sprang amber coronas, riotous with light, fenced in by solemn mahogany. She read *Goodnight Moon*, *The Very Hungry Caterpillar*, *Jamberry*, and *Each Peach Pear Plum*. She started *Stellaluna*, the story of a bat adopted by birds, but closed it when it became clear that a bat was not meant to be with birds.

When they finished with the books, the house grew quiet again.

One day, she would look back with longing at these first endless mornings. She'd see this as a period of tranquility that she should have savored. That first day was a valley abandoned, murmuring and dry, punctuated only by mealtimes and diaper changes, Kavya's stories and one merciful nap. Kavya read to Ignacio until her voice turned to rust.

The next morning, when the door clicked shut and Rishi was gone, Ignacio picked up a book and handed it to Kavya. The morning after, he crawled to her lap as she read, and rested a sturdy elbow on her thigh. On the fourth day, Kavya picked up a book as soon as Rishi left. She began reading, when Ignacio broke the quiet with a scream. He pointed to the door, tears streaming. There seemed to be words in his cries. It seemed he was genuinely trying to tell her something.

"Come here," Kavya said, and picked him up. This time, he let her. She cradled him in her lap. This time, he burrowed his face into her chest and seemed to find solace in the warm valley between her breasts. She picked up a stack of books and began to read. The rhythms of the prose calmed her, and seemed to calm Ignacio as well. The longer she read, the more solidly he sank into the curve of her body, until his head rubbed up beneath her chin and she could smell the wheaty warmth of his scalp. And when the phone rang and she tried to put him down, he struggled against her, and she stayed put, letting the line ring itself into silence.

That night, as Kavya dozed off by Ignacio's crib, she felt a yank at her hair. She turned to find two copper pennies, wide awake. She sat up. "Iggy," she whispered. "Ignacio." And then, as babies do—as babies *must* do—Ignacio sat up and reached up with both arms, asking to be held.

Kavya had read the parenting books on sleep and food and discipline. She'd read them all and promptly forgot them. Those first raw days and nights played out on a separate plain, where discipline and sleep patterns didn't factor, where all that mattered was the sealing of a crack, the winning of Ignacio's acceptance. For this, Kavya didn't need rules. She got by on sheer desire.

She spent every night that week hunched in a duvet next to Iggy's crib. When she sat up, he sat up, and vice versa. He was a nervous sleeper. If she tried to leave, he cried out for her. If she had to pee, she did it with Ignacio sitting on her lap. In the space of those few days, he'd gone from not wanting her to not wanting to let her go. Only when he slept did he release her from his sight.

Surely, his real mother lived in his memory. What did he think had happened to her? Sometimes sitting on the living room floor, he looked up at Kavya, questions hovering like bumblebees at his lips. "She's all right," Kavya answered. "She just can't be with you now." Kavya knew little more than this—only that Ignacio's mother was alive and well and in a detention center. "And that's all," she said aloud. "We're taking care of you now. This is your home. Your good home." She spoke the words that she was willing to hear, and didn't venture further. The truth was a fragile thing.

And early one morning, before the first flush of day, she sat on the floor by Ignacio's crib, half asleep. The boy lay cradled on her lap. She felt the riffle of his hand on her belly. As she looked down, he pulled up her shirt, exposing her belly, its one narrow roll, to the twilight chill. She tried to pull the shirt back down, but Ignacio was adamant. In a flash, his hand pushed the fabric up to her shoulder. Her breast hung forth, a soft and bronzed cupola. It took her a moment, in the fog of sleep, to realize what he was doing.

"*Ignacio,*" she said, and pushed him away. Ignacio whined and clawed at her chest. She picked him up and set him on his rump. He sank into himself then, and lay on the floor, his face buried in an elbow, his shoulders shaking. Kavya had finally done some reading on adopting toddlers. This was the sad cry, and it ripped into her more deeply than the shrieking or clawing had. She watched her boy weep, defeated. She would give him what he wanted. She would have to try.

For the sake of comfort, she took off her shirt. Sitting cross-legged, she picked Ignacio up again, and placed him in the well of her lap. He stopped crying and wrapped himself around her middle, his head by one breast, his knees by the other. He took her nipple between his lips, latched on, and began to suck. Kavya gasped at the force of it. Ignacio's jaws worked at her breast. Kavya hunched over and bit her lip against the pain of cutting teeth, wondering all the while if maybe— anything was possible, where his desire met her hope, his mouth her glands. But eventually, he stopped sucking and unlatched. He frowned at the nipple, glistening now with his saliva. He rolled to the floor, then crawled to the bedroom door. That was it. He'd given up on her empty breast, and would never bother with it again.

RISHI WATCHED THE BOY grab one Cheerio at a time from the small bowl before him: breakfast. Ignacio picked up a chunk of banana and pressed it between his fingers until the yellow flesh caved and squelched between his knuckles. There were times when Rishi found himself staring at the boy with a sensation he had trouble naming. It was something close to surprise, but closer to incomprehension—of who and how this small child was, sitting opposite him in a high chair, cramming banana in his mouth. There were times when he looked at Ignacio the way one might look at a sculpture: for the fine curve of his nose or the sweetly turned petal of his bottom lip or the warm opalescence of his skin. And then, of course, there were times when Ignacio turned all too human, shrieking and banging, caught in a tempest. These moments, thankfully, fell under Kavya's jurisdiction.

I love you, Ignacio, he imagined saying. But Ignacio was another parent's child. He hadn't realized this until the day the boy arrived. Ignacio hadn't signed on to Rishi's love, not even to Kavya's, who seemed already to have fallen, irretrievably. Rishi didn't know when or if he'd be allowed to love the boy. He did know this much: He wanted good things for Ignacio—food and kindness and a clean, safe home. He wanted to be a haven for the downy head, the proud, elfin shoulders. He didn't want to let him down.

It was for this reason, Rishi told himself, that he was spending ten, twelve, fourteen hours a day at Weebies, pricing supplies for the Stratosphere, calculating, anticipating, building theory into reality in a manner, he hoped, that was authoritative enough to convince Vikram Sen that

Rishi was more than a ventilation engineer—that Rishi was both capable and destined to be someone important.

He began stopping by Vik's office nearly every day. Sally knew how many sugars he took in his chai, and he had a throw pillow on Sen's sofa—one with an elephant embroidered on it—that he liked to wrap his arms around when thinking or talking. During these visits, a piece of his old self returned to him.

It was a Thursday afternoon now, their usual meeting time, and Rishi stepped into the office, shoes off. Vik was lying on the ground, his head on Rishi's special pillow.

"Should I come back?" he asked.

"Rishi-bhai." Sen tossed him the pillow. "I have a bad back. The floor helps."

"When my back acts up, Kavya walks on it."

"Of course." He exhaled, turned to Rishi. "Are you ready for Tuesday?" In four days, Rishi would be presenting his plans for the Stratosphere to the Weebies management team, most of whom he'd seen only in magazines.

"Sure. I'll just have to know everything I'm going to say. And then say it. Right?" He was shooting for zero, halving his distance from his goal with the implementation of each new technological gadget. But halving distances would never get him to the coveted number; he was still maddeningly far away.

TUESDAY CAME QUICKLY. At two in the afternoon, Rishi stood before the Weebies management team: Vikram Sen, Topher Timmons, Mike Li, and William Reynolds, CFO, CEO, COO, and marketing director, respectively. Valley start-ups waited months—years—for meetings with these men. Rishi tried to still the tremble in his hand by repeating the mantra *I work here. I already work here.* He was simply a colleague with a PowerPoint presentation, he reminded himself. These were his coworkers. They were his age. His hand calmed. Watercooler guys. Guys at the company Christmas party, photocopying their asses. But the truth was, these guys had their own party, to which Rishi, if deemed worthy, might one day be invited.

He took a deep breath and began. "WeBreathe. Weebies' first exclusive consumer product. For homes, schools, businesses. For healthy babies, healthy workplaces, healthy families." Topher Timmons grinned. "And smart kids." Timmons's grin grew. Rishi went on to summarize the *Wall Street Journal* article that had birthed the idea. He explained his software simulations, showed the group the on-screen modeled version of the Stratosphere, and what happened to the air inside it when he manipulated, through the magic of simulation software, the strategically placed air filters, the air vents, the organic paint and furniture. As he proceeded, he tried not to look at Vikram Sen, whose left eyebrow quivered with excitement. He focused instead on the faces of the other three men, who, after ten minutes, began to look limpid, pudgy, serene. Anything but intimidating. He was good at this, he remembered.

When he finished, Rishi felt so good that he forgot that his presentation had comprised, if one stopped to think, twenty-seven minutes of bullshit. The ideas he'd come up with were predictable, rudimentary, the stuff of science fairs. He needed more. Timmons, Sen, and Reynolds showed no understanding of his failure. Li had looked a little suspicious, but said nothing.

He wasn't daunted. Air quality data was clear and quantifiable. It could be summoned and charted. Children and wives could not. Acceptance couldn't be graphed. Nor could love.

Kavya wore love like a wool cloak, wrapped it around herself, around Ignacio, until the two were securely bound. How her love could be so immediate and complete, Rishi didn't understand. Ignacio was another woman's son. Loving him couldn't be simple. His own child, he would have loved without question. But Ignacio—the boy asked with every movement, every syllabic babble, to be embraced, but there had to be limits. Didn't there?

With love lurking, he would sink deeper into the Weebies project, and leave the other one to Kavya. He would give in to the Stratosphere. An idea would drop, splat, like a dollop of bird shit. He would wait for it, and work tirelessly.

33.

She would take him back to Popocalco. Soli and Nacho, they'd live with Mama and Papi in the house that Soli had saved, with its phone line and new sturdy door and wall-to-wall roofing. She could see him, a fully fledged boy, a child without worries. He'd spend his afternoons playing escondido, sprinting down dirt roads and around adobe corners with other children (for in her imagining, the village had children again). On festival days, they'd stay up past midnight to watch the fireworks. Nacho would go to the school that his mother had gone to, with the same ancient teachers. He'd blend in among the locals with their proud faces, their noses straight and sharp, and skin like the buttered bark of a cinnamon tree. He'd know Torta, the madman in the village square; with the other children, he'd see Torta as a certain sort of hero, the only adult who behaved worse than a child. Nacho would grow to be a man, a Popocalteco who drank mezcal and argued about corn strains. He would stand broad, he would have children. The children would have wild hair that blew in the valley wind.

She lay on her cot and spoke to the ceiling: I'll take you to the fireworks, my Nacho. En la Noche del Maíz. Los castillos de luces, great towers with sparking crosses, with spinning wheels of flame, and Christ himself popping and banging. The happiest Christ on a cross you ever will see. The fire will talk in tongues and the crown of thorns will spin so fast you'll think it might spin right off and fly to heaven. And just when you think that the blazing and banging, the sparks in your hair, your eyes, your teeth, can't get any closer—just when you think the whole glorious high-rise contraption might topple flaming to the ground and send you running home, the square will calm. Silence. And then, an explosion. Blossoms of fire will fly and fall and fly and fall, until the sky gets dark and the crowd thins. And you'll go home, back to your kitchen, a glass of milk, and bed. And the night will be still again, except for smoke that trails through the village, except for the sprinkle of remembered light that spills down your eyelids as you drift away, to sleep.

A guard opened Soli's door. "Let's go," he said. The thin one slid off her bed. "Not you. The fat-ass Mexican. Get your fat ass out here, Mexicana," he said.

So she got her fat ass out of that cell and never looked back. She had a feeling she'd never see them again, but she didn't wave goodbye. The guard who'd covered Salma in stew handed Soli her old clothes and her purse in a clear plastic bag. Everything was inside, except for her forged ID card. "Good luck," he said, as if he'd never pushed her to the ground.

34.

AFTER THREE WEEKS WITH IGGY, KAVYA RETURNED TO work. On her first day back, she dropped him off at a home-based day-care, sat in the Prius for ten minutes, cried, then started her engine and drove to work. She'd never driven to work before—she couldn't risk a bike wreck with Iggy on the back—and it took longer than usual to get there, now that she had to obey the one-way street signs and road barriers that guarded the streets of Berkeley. When she got to the sorority, it was as if she'd never left. The house was still dark and hoary, the kitchen equipment still comically oversized. Miguel offered a fist bump, and she accepted. Martina McAfee stood in the kitchen doorway with the lunch numbers and instructions about gluten-free pasta, and didn't say a thing about Kavya's family leave, didn't ask her if she'd gone anywhere or had a good time or taken in a child. No one seemed to know that she'd revolutionized her place in the world, that she was now, of all things, a mother.

When Martina left the kitchen, Kavya turned to Miguel. "I have a kid now," she said. He'd just opened the dishwasher, and he stood swallowed in a cloud of steam. He didn't move. She saw only his feet, planted firmly, toes pointing out.

"You what?"

"I have a kid now. We're fostering a little boy, and we might get to adopt him. I hope."

"For real?"

"Yup."

"Really? Had you planned this?"

She rolled her eyes. "No, it was totally spur of the moment. We were having brunch and it sounded like a good idea."

"Hey, hey! You're a mama now, girl! Come here!" Miguel wrapped her in a hug, binding her own arms to her sides. In his warm arms, the sun angling through the window, the kitchen steeped in butternut steam, Kavya was freshly convinced that what she'd done was an okay thing, perhaps a very good thing, and maybe even the right thing.

EVERY FEW MONTHS, their weekends fell victim to emergency preparedness. It was easy, in Berkeley, to forget about earthquakes. No one seemed overly worried about them. It was generally understood that one day soon, the two plates that flanked the Hayward Fault would give in to pressure so intense that the cities of the bay would come crashing down. Destruction would march through their beautiful lives, bringing down their walls and trees and telephone polls. The quake would be an eight or a nine, maybe even a ten. The Big One, they called it. The Big One was coming.

About once a month, Rishi found himself unable to sleep, hyperalert to the catastrophe that could strike any moment. Now, for example.

Or now.

Rishi's earthquake kit, a coffin-sized Tupperware—weatherproof, verminproof, raccoonproof—sat waiting outside the back door. In it were first-aid supplies, water tablets, granola bars, a tent, a wrench, a shovel, toilet paper, extra clothes, matches, a fire extinguisher, a crowbar, a flare, a knife, and two adult-sized gas masks.

Kavya had objected to the masks at first, thinking they were too apocalyptic, that they would never need them, that Rishi was being an alarmist. These weren't the masks that surgeons and gardeners and people in Beijing wore. These were netherworld devices, heavy goggles with vinyl snouts and hollow air chambers. Rishi had tried his on first for Kavya. You look like a Tusken Raider, she'd said. It had impressed him that she knew what a Tusken Raider was.

They didn't have a mask for Ignacio. On an afternoon four weeks after Ignacio had come to live with them, Rishi set off for the camping stores scattered through Berkeley's west side. "Going out!" he called to Kavya, and left. He was gone for four hours and was driving home with three cardboard boxes full of survival gear (but no child-sized gas mask), when he realized it was 6:30 and time for dinner. He called home to see if dinner was waiting. The phone rang and rang. He cursed quietly her habit of ignoring the phone when she was busy. He felt like burritos.

He stopped for burritos. He would get one for Kavya. After standing in line for twenty minutes and ordering two burritos, he remembered Ignacio. He stood in line again and ordered a child's quesadilla. He got home to the sounds of Ignacio's bath.

"I got him food," he called from the kitchen.

No reply. And then, "He already ate."

"Oh. You all right in there?" It was the wrong thing to ask. She didn't answer.

A steam of discontent rose from the bathroom and trailed to the kitchen, drawing Rishi from his chair, from his plate, from his still unopened foil-wrapped burrito.

In the bathroom, Kavya, a vision of motherhood: She kneeled on the bathroom floor, the front of her shirt soaked with water, her hair in limp strands around her face. Ignacio walloped the surface of his bath, sending high arcs of water raining down. Ignacio himself: a slippery little beast, shiny as a seal, his hair foaming with soap, a trail of suds running down his back. Bubbles gathered at his elbows. He was a strong boy, wide-chested, with shoulders that could be described only as manly. But the manliness was nascent, bubble-wrapped in fat, in sweet soapy-slick skin.

"Yes?" Kavya turned a cold eye on Rishi. "Do you need something?"

"Uh. No. I was just seeing when you wanted to eat." He paused before leaving. "I've never seen him in the bath before."

She turned, unfurled a small, tight smile, and said nothing.

"I get now why some species eat their young," he said, and grinned.

"Excuse me?" She scowled, shook her head. He'd meant it as a compliment. In any case, it was the wrong thing to say.

Back in the kitchen, he wiped down the counters, swept the floor, and let the burritos sit on their plates, wrapped in foil, waiting. From the far corner of the house he heard the bathwater draining away, Kavya passing from bathroom to bedroom, chattering high and bright to Ignacio. He could hear her narrating what she was doing, singing songs with only a hint of melody. He heard the side of the crib slide down, Ignacio's squawks of protest, and Kavya's soothing reply. He heard her sing to the boy. And then he heard her wait. She'd be standing by the crib, waiting for him to drift off.

Anyone who knew burritos knew they had to be eaten immediately. The longer they waited, the greater the likelihood of a soggy tortilla, pasty beans. Within a twenty-minute window, a burrito could turn from a parcel of life-giving heat to a mealy and humid corpse. Everyone in Berkeley knew this. Anyone who cared the tiniest bit about food would know better than to let a burrito sit.

Forty minutes passed. Rishi swept the floor again. He sat, began to unwrap the foil, then remembered Kavya's scowl. He would wait. He wanted her to walk into a clean kitchen, an attentive husband, a table with two plates and two whole, gleaming bundles of satisfaction. Being caught mid-burrito would deepen the cast of his failings, whatever she found those to be.

By the time she walked in, the kitchen was spotless. Rishi sat down and picked up his burrito, thinking now about eating, about the first, best bite of the burrito, the way the steam funneled up his nostrils and the top morsels of rice and beans broke away from their base, landing lightly on the tongue. He was thinking about this and nothing else when he looked up to find Kavya, seated but staring past him.

"Hungry?" he asked, and took, at last, his first bite. It was cold, yes, but still a benediction of texture and flavor. He looked up. He finally *looked* at Kavya, and the food turned to mulch in his mouth.

"Hey," he said. "What happened?"

She shook her head. "I'm hungry," she said. "I'm tired."

He waited. "Is that all? That's all that's wrong?"

She'd picked up her burrito, but stopped to glare at him. And she slammed the burrito down. He cringed. Burritos were delicate.

"Okay," he said. "I just thought there was more to it."

"No more to it. I'm hungry and tired and that's all. That's all there is to it. Just me. Just me doing everything."

He breathed in, exhaled loudly.

"Oh, shut up."

He took another bite, and another.

"I know you think I'm being dramatic, but you know what?"

"What?"

"Fuck you."

"Jesus."

"You haven't done a single thing for Iggy this weekend. All weekend. Or ever! I'm back at work now and I'm still doing everything. Where were you all day today?" Her voice was getting higher and shriller than he'd ever heard it.

"At camping stores. I told you."

"At camping stores. Earthquake preparedness."

"Well, someone's got to think about it." He was getting angry now, his volume rising. "I've never seen you take an interest in our earthquake kit."

Kavya guffawed and dropped the burrito to her plate. Rishi ate in silence. Before Ignacio, they'd sometimes disappear from each other for hours on the weekends. Rishi had liked the fact that marriage hadn't shackled them together. He had four cold beers waiting in the fridge. He rose to get one, and brought one to the table for Kavya. She didn't open hers. She began to eat again. The tortilla and beans would be plastering the roof of her mouth by now, but he didn't open her beer for her. He didn't get her a glass of water. He'd hoped faintly for sex that night, but now even the small possibility of it had sunk to a negative value. When Kavya finished eating and rolled her foil in a ball, her hands were still shaking.

"Hey," he said. He got up and brought her a glass of water.

Twenty minutes later, the kitchen sat in a gel of silence. Rishi had tried to tell Kavya about his day, to ask a few safe questions about what she and Iggy had been up to. She snapped at him the first time, her mouth twisted and sour. Then she ignored him and stared at the table. He gave up, loaded their plates into the dishwasher, and opened his laptop. On Weebies.com he typed *child gas mask*. Child. Gas mask. The uncanny pairing of terms almost made him close his laptop. But if the world was ending, Iggy would need to breathe. Please choose a size, Weebies prompted. He'd have to measure Iggy's head. He thought of ordering something for Kavya. A parenting book, maybe. But he had no idea what sort of advice he could shop for that wouldn't cause even deeper offense. He used to have a number of wife-pleasing maneuvers to choose from, but after Ignacio arrived, her pleasure receptors seemed to have shifted. He didn't know, these days, where he stood on the newly calibrated spectrum of her approval.

In the nursery, Rishi slipped a tape measure around the boy's skull. He slept deeply. Even when the metallic end of the tape pulled at his hair, he swatted absently and then settled. Rishi watched him sleep. They'd brought a child into their home. The thought ran in circles and he watched it go, run into the distance and close in again, rounding the corners of his mind. They'd taken in a child to treat as their own. He'd said all this before, but what did it mean?

Ignacio began to cough cavernous, wet barks. They went on for so long that Rishi wondered how the boy was breathing. He'd picked up the bug from the other foster home, they thought, but it had worsened, each cough rocking his small body.

"What're you doing?" Kavya asked from the doorway. Rishi turned. She looked smaller now than she had in the kitchen, her shoulders stooped. Her body had exhaled its anger and now stood tired, perhaps contrite, ready not to fight.

"Measuring his head," he whispered. "For a gas mask."

"You and those gas masks."

"You'll thank me."

"Hopefully, I'll never have to." She walked to him and placed a tentative hand on his back. He pulled her in, and her head dropped to his chest.

"I'm sorry you were so tired," he said. "I'll try to be around more on the weekends."

She shrugged.

"You really do a lot. More than anyone I know."

"Well," she said. "I feel better now." She straightened up and they locked eyes. She kissed him lightly, once and again. Taking him by the hand, she led him out the door, stepping nimbly over the room's one creaky patch of wood, and Rishi did the same.

. . .

BY THE LIGHT of their bedside lamp, Rishi watched Kavya lie awake, eyes closed. She was naked still, the bedsheet gathered at her feet. He wanted to touch her, to run his finger along her borders, the patchwork of colors that comprised her—a wash of warm earth along her abdomen, her legs scaly and dry, the Aurelian valley from her breasts to her neck, the shades of her body warming and cooling, as variegated as a map of air currents. Rishi had been thinking all day of this time, when they could be together and alone with a whole night stretching before them, nakedness untrammeled. But what had happened—failure on his part, unprecedented flaccidity, like cramming a wand of string cheese into a parking meter—Rishi had no explanation for. He'd tried to forget the first half of the evening, and bring the second half, its feathery kisses, the easy reconciliation, to the end he'd been anticipating for days—for weeks, now that he stopped to count.

But it wasn't working. *It* wasn't working. He'd been charging forward for so long, gathering steam, thriving on work, that when the time came for release, his body refused. His body was home, but his mind was slung with workplace burdens. He could feel them still, his abdomen wrung tight with nervous energy that had gripped him for days, interrupted his sleep, chained him to his desk at the office, followed him home at night. Thinking about earthquakes all day hadn't exactly eased him into weekend mode. That evening, he hadn't been able to focus mentally on either Kavya or the very pleasant task at hand; his penis, truly an extension of his brain, proved correspondingly dissolute.

"Don't worry about it," Kavya said, staring at the ceiling.

"Let's try in a few minutes."

She sighed loudly and closed her eyes, but he could see she wouldn't sleep. Her eyelids pulsed with tension, her shoulders ground with dissatisfaction into the mattress, her lips pursed and peeved. She whipped her head around to face him. "What happened? What's wrong?"

It was an accusation, and Rishi recoiled. "I— Nothing happened."

She rose to her elbows and searched his face.

"I was distracted. I'm a little overwhelmed right now."

She raised an eyebrow.

"Not with Ignacio"—though, yes, he did feel sunken by sudden parenthood—"mostly with work."

"What's happening at work?" She was trying to soften her voice, he could tell.

"Well." He paused, reconsidered. She cocked her head to the side, waiting. "I've been wanting to talk to you about this, actually. I'm on this *pretty* interesting project now. It could be big. Vik Sen and I are heading it up."

"*Vik* Sen? Since when?"

"Since a while ago now. He wants me to do this—thing. I can't actually talk about it."

She scoffed. "What, it's top secret?"

"Kind of."

"So that's why you're never here anymore." She tilted her head as if considering him anew. "Is it for the government? Like a WMD thing?"

Rishi laughed. "No—it's more a clean-air thing. That's all I can say."

"So why the secrecy, then?"

Good question, Rishi thought. The only apparent answer: "It's going to make them a shitload of money."

"Them?"

"Weebies."

"Vikram Sen."

"Yes. Vikram Sen."

She crossed her arms.

"Oh, come on. Are you jealous? Yes, Vikram Sen. Yes, Preeti Patel. So if I do this for him, Weebies will be, like, even bigger than it is. And yes, Preeti Patel will have more money to play with. More money than you."

She shrugged. "Who said anything about that? I wasn't even thinking that."

"Right."

"No, really."

"What, then?"

"I was thinking that you are like, a—a wizard of clean air—you've done a Ph.D. in it, and clean air is *valuable*. It's *important*. And you know how to get it. How to keep it. Most people don't. You have this great gift, you've done all this work, you have a Ph.D.! And you're *giving* it away to Weebies. For what?"

Rishi shook his head, shook it so vigorously that it seemed he would shake an answer out. "It's my work, Kavya. I work for Weebies, so they get my intellectual property. And Vik said—" He pressed his palms to his eyes, summoning the promises of *big things in store*, promises that felt hopelessly vague now, and tried to weave them into an answer eloquent enough to convince his wife that he wasn't, for lack of a better term, Vik Sen's clean-air bitch.

She placed a hand on his knee. "Hey."

He waited.

"Listen," she said. "If you ever want to go out on your own? Start your own business? I would totally be fine with that. You could be a consultant, you could start your own company . . ."

He brought his hands to hers. "Start-ups are a ton of work, Kavya. Like, nonstop work. It wouldn't be a kitchen job."

"You're right," she said quietly, stiffening. "It wouldn't be a kitchen job."

"You know what I mean. I wouldn't be home, like ever. And with the adoption—who wants to give a kid to a family with an absent father? With no money?"

She lay back and pulled a sheet over her middle. "Maybe you're right. I wouldn't be able to take on an extra job, not with Ignacio."

The question was nixed before it was truly posed. Rishi felt his head grow heavy. "Are you going to sleep naked?"

She shrugged. "I don't know. Why?"

"Nothing."

"What? Why?"

"It's just— Nothing. I'm going to put something on."

"Oh." She smirked, tried to fold the smile away.

"What's so funny?"

"Earthquakes, right?" She dug her knuckles into his side, laughing now. "You think I'll run out to the street naked?" She wrapped herself in the sheet, a sculpture under protective cover, and laughed into her pillow. "If there's a massive earthquake, my friend, we'll have more than nudity to worry about."

35.

THE NEXT MORNING, RISHI WOKE TO KAVYA, HER ARMS splayed, her impressive wingspan covering most of the bed, still naked, blinking. "Hi," he said, and placed a hand on her shoulder. She slipped from his touch to reach her robe on the floor.

"I hear Iggy," she said. "You stay in bed."

At the breakfast table, Ignacio sat in his high chair, gnawing on buttered bread. Kavya stood at the counter, gazing into her teacup, and stayed put this time when Rishi placed a hand on her back.

"Why so glum?"

She looked up. "I miss my mom."

"Well, call her," Rishi said. He popped bread in the toaster, watched the coils turn orange.

"I've been calling her. You know that."

"Well, keep calling her. Call her three times a day if you have to. She'll have to talk eventually."

Kavya resented Rishi's solutions. She didn't want a practical solution. She wanted him to tell her that her mother was just so wrong, that Kavya had done the right thing, the best thing, that Rishi and Iggy were all Kavya needed and that they together would be the happiest of families.

Even Rishi's parents called with advice. Rishi's parents never called.

It was one of the things Kavya loved about them—that and the fact that they'd moved back to India, had given up their wide sidewalks, their supermarkets, and their sleek black Acura to return to a bungalow with a dirt driveway. (What she did not know, and chose not to imagine, was that now they had a driver to handle their Maruti Alto, that Rishi's mother spent her weekends at air-conditioned malls and at ladies' luncheons that meandered into teatimes and early-evening naps, that their bungalow in Hyderabad was three times the size of her bungalow in Berkeley, and that the dirt driveway leading to it gave way to a veranda of milk-white Kashmiri marble, swept three times daily by a bent-back servant who earned less than a Berkeley panhandler.) In any case, Rishi's parents had called when they'd heard about Ignacio, had cooed down the phone line to him, had congratulated them and asked questions. They spoke with the carefree bubble of parents who had given up and given in, who'd released their adult children to the world and returned to a life of self-fulfillment, who'd moved back to their homeland and remembered that, in returning home, they were giving up the need to prevail, to ward off the unstoppable wave of foreign influence, to stop and breathe and look around and renounce, at last, the great American fight.

Kavya's mother was still fighting. With Kavya, with America, and with the fact that no matter how she raged, her daughter refused to simply do as she was told. Uma Mahendra stuck to a few basic tenets. The first: Obey and be obeyed. The rule held that if one obeyed one's parents, unquestioningly, long-sufferingly, one would be rewarded, from the onset of parenthood to death, with several decades of sovereignty over one's own household. Her husband had conceded long ago to the rule. Kavya had not. What resulted was her mother's sense that she'd been cheated of a birthright. Her mother had been nursing this notion since Kavya was a disobedient child, and now that she was a disobedient adult, her sense of injustice had swollen to a sore and heaving tumor, large enough to show up on her silhouette, to change the way she walked. After decades of minor infractions, Kavya had gone and done something big. She had adopted a child. Or fostered one. The semantics made no difference to Uma. What had come before—the suspect boyfriends, the tattoo, the tax hiccup, the smoking——had been misdemeanors. This, however, this taking in of a child against her mother's wishes, was a very, very naughty thing to do. Uma would carry on in the face of her daughter's insolence, but not with an eye roll of exasperation. Disobedience, at the best of times, was met with a shrill telephonic tirade, with claims of poor health and imminent death, woven through with the conviction that if one did not obey one's parents, one's parents would surely die. Disobedience, at the worst of times, was met by silence. This was the worst of times. Uma fell silent, and from ninety miles away, Kavya felt it.

When Ignacio had been in the bungalow on Vine for five weeks, Uma still hadn't called. Kavya had called her, more times than she could count, and most often spoke to the answering machine. She spoke once or twice to her father.

"Hi, Dad."

"And how is your foster-care child?" he asked, his voice sleepy and distant.

"He's good. He likes his daycare."

"Very good." He snuffled into the phone, cleared his throat, and fell silent. Kavya's father was deeply comfortable with prolonged silence, even on the phone. Kavya knew it could stretch for minutes.

"Is Mom home?"

"Tuesday ladies' yoga."

She said goodbye. Her father was less gratifying than the answering machine. And she knew Uma was there, at home, listening. She knew that her disobedience had not, in fact, killed her mother.

In her immediate world, Iggy was adjusting, and Rishi was having an affair with the top secret Weebies project. She'd fallen into a pattern of quietly resenting her husband, of feeling overburdened with work and childcare, and then for feeling the shame of this burden, of not adoring seamlessly the motherhood she'd longed for. The fact that Rishi had virtually abandoned his new son to work night and day for Preeti's husband was an issue she'd decided to shunt to the sidelines. To take it in her hand and ponder it, to really feel every facet of that situation, was something for which she simply had no capacity. But on the surface, her daily life had fallen into a rhythm of functionality. Her pursuit of a family, which had started so simply and grown so complex, had flipped back to simplicity. Ignacio had begun stringing words together. Their days were flowing into their nights, sleep was being achieved, food was being eaten. Iggy no longer wept at the sight of the front door, no longer seemed to pine for a social worker. Now that she could relax with her son, she began to love him. She'd thought she'd loved him before, but this new sensation was something else. It was love that verged on physical desire, jagged and dense and alive inside her. If Ignacio were, one day, to go away, she doubted she'd survive.

It didn't worry Kavya, the boundless commitment of her soul. How else should she feel, after all? How else could one mother?

Iggy had been coughing since he'd arrived at the bungalow, a lingering remnant of some past bug. Every night, he'd finish his coughing and fall asleep, only to wake them in the morning with a full-throated "HEY!" And their house seemed to expand to fit this new life. But over the smooth mechanics of their days, Uma's silence hung heavy. The high whine of it kept her awake most nights, until pure exhaustion pushed her into sleep.

Later that week, Kavya left work early with a fever. In the heat and bustle of the sorority kitchen, she'd thought she was simply hot and tired. But as she creamed eggs and sugar in the mixer, watching the mechanical whisk dance loops around the twenty-cup mixing bowl, her vision began to swim. Her eyes seemed to cross. She blinked. Her vision crossed again, then swam. The room creaked and shifted like a cargo ship, and she found herself reaching for the countertop, gripping it with her fingers, losing her hold, and falling.

She landed hard on her elbow on the kitchen floor, and the room went dark and blotchy. A heavy shuffle, and Miguel was at her side.

"Hey, there," he called. He placed a hand on her cheek. "You with us? You alive?"

He came into focus. "Of course I'm alive." The room swarmed with stars.

"Who's the president?"

"Help me up."

He propped her up to sit.

"I'm all right," she said, and tried to stand. Halfway up, her head spun again. "Oh," she said. "No, no." And Miguel lowered her to the floor. Her chest was leaden, breathing painful. She closed her eyes and saw stars again, dozens of them, a meteor shower.

The next thing she knew, she'd risen from the floor in the sturdy harness of Miguel's arms. He was carrying her out of the kitchen.

"What are you *doing*?" she muttered.

"Don't worry, I won't drop you." They trundled clumsily, and she believed very strongly that he would drop her, but she couldn't protest. To keep off the nausea, she closed her eyes.

Growing closer was Martina McAfee's reedy trill. "Excuse me! Excuse me! What's going on?"

She stood at the kitchen entrance and Miguel pushed past her. She might have blacked out for a minute. When she came to, Miguel was opening the door of a car.

"What is this *car*?"

"It's my car," Miguel said. "It's my pretty little Pontiac."

The pretty little Pontiac was taxicab yellow, its hood streaked with black racing stripes. He buckled her in. "Let's get you home, Princessa. Where do you live?"

At home, Miguel deposited Kavya on her sofa, then sat beside her and placed the back of his hand on her forehead, on the side of her neck. "Your skin's hot," he said. "You want to call your man?"

"Rishi?" She considered it. Rishi would be at work. He would hem and haw about leaving. "No, thanks," she answered. Miguel got up and opened the fridge, guessed the right cupboard, and poured her a glass of juice. He found a box of Girl Scout Cookies and sat down beside her. He waited for her to take her first bite of a Samoa before he stood up.

"Okay," he said, and teetered in place, suddenly uncertain.

She looked up at him, chewed, said nothing. His passata-stained kitchen pants seemed not to belong in her Craftsman living room.

"I should get back, I guess. Back to the *wrath of McAfee.*" He made a monster face, arched his fingers into claws. "You got things taken care of here, right?" She nodded.

He stepped back, picked his keys up off the table, opened the door, and left.

"Thank you!" she called, but the door had already shut.

KAVYA HAD FALLEN ASLEEP, the last of a Samoa dissolving between her teeth, when the phone rang. Rishi: "Are you all right? Your work called. What happened?"

After a foggy debriefing, she was off the phone and asleep again. She listed in and out of dreams, half aware that she was sleeping, urging herself to wake, waking up in a dream state, moving about her day, only to realize that she hadn't yet woken. She found herself, in this dream, standing at the kitchen sink. She picked up a dream plate, crusted with egg yolk. And as she started to scrub it, it broke apart in her hands. She picked up a large shard of it, and this crumbled in her fingers, too. She picked up another plate, and it broke, and another, broken again.

The doorbell rang. Kavya sprang awake. Someone was banging. The phone was ringing.

She ignored it and lumbered to her feet. She opened the door to Uma, holding a cell phone at arm's length. She pressed a button and the house phone stopped ringing. Uma looked up, stricken. "What happened to you?"

"What?"

"Rishi called me! What happened? What happened to you?"

Kavya blinked at her mother. "It's just a virus or something," she said. The fact that they hadn't spoken in six weeks seemed not to matter now.

She pushed past Kavya and into the house, carrying a bag made of blue and white woven plastic, the same bag she'd toted around since Kavya was a child. She heaved it onto the counter and pulled out a stainless-steel tiffin carrier, Tupperware, her own serving spoons.

"I've brought you rasam," she said, watching Kavya from the corner of her eye. "And cabbage khichdi, and I made some rice, but I made it yesterday so maybe you want fresh rice, no? And some idli and some carrot halwa from temple, and some pickles, but I know you have pickles, and I know you have papadums, because last time I gave them. We can put them in the microwave, no need to fry. And I wanted to make you vada, but I thought I had no time—"

"Mom."

Uma began shoving dishes into the fridge, muttering about the shelf space and the mess. "You need to clean out some Tupperwares, Kavya. Too much mess means you can't even think. Every day I wipe the shelves, okay? Every day. I can't even think when I look in this fridge! It's making me crazy, Kavya."

"Mom?"

Uma turned to her, frowned.

"You drove here from Sacramento?"

"What else? You didn't answer the phone. Rishi told me you fainted, what was I to think?" Uma shut the fridge door and walked to Kavya. She placed her hand on her forehead, a hand on her neck. She grabbed her by the wrist and led her to the kitchen table. "Sit," she said.

Kavya sat. Uma sat beside her, wrapped broad, moist hands around Kavya's and beamed.

"And then?" Uma asked.

"What?"

"Any news?"

"Well. I have a foster child."

Uma's smile fell.

"That's why you are sick and fainting?"

Uma's meaning fluttered into the room, like a moth breaking from its cocoon. It flitted across Uma's face and drew out a conspiratorial smile.

She leaned in and whispered, "I think you're expecting."

Kavya snatched her hands away. "No!"

"Kavyaaah," her mother sang. "I think a baby is coming, Kavya."

"Mom, I'm not pregnant. I don't even want to be."

"Shuh," Uma hushed her. "Don't say such things. It is a blessing from God."

Kavya took one deep breath, then two.

"I have a baby, Amma. I have a baby already."

"I mean your own baby, Kavya. You will know what motherhood really is, kanna. This will be your very own, and you will be a mother."

"Okay—let's start over. I'm not pregnant, okay? Definitely not pregnant. And we have a child. Ignacio. You know about *Ignacio*, Mom. He's here."

Uma turned to look behind her, as if she expected the child to be lurking in a doorway.

"He's living with us and he's ours, okay? And you haven't even seen him yet! You haven't even—" She burst into sobs.

Uma's chair screeched back, and she stood, returned to the fridge, and pulled out a pot. She banged it on the stove, banged open a drawer, banged the stove on, banged a drawer shut. She turned on the stovetop fan. The kitchen fell silent but for the churning of the fan. Kavya wiped at her eyes and willed herself to stop crying. She crouched in her chair, and forced herself to stare at the ground, motionless. Uma crossed her arms and scowled at the rasam. Only the steam, rising from its pot, moved freely.

The room grew hot with it, hot with the anger of a mother and a daughter, and Kavya got up, at last. She went to her room and slammed the door, like a teenager, and like an angry teenager, she flopped onto her bed and cried into her pillow.

An hour passed. Kavya returned to the kitchen for a glass of water, her head heavy with the morning's vertigo. Her mother placed a plate of rice before her. It sat soaked in rasam, thin and tangy and peppery and soothing, just what Kavya had craved when she was pregnant.

"I'm going to my room," she said when she finished eating. In the face of being overlooked and disobeyed, Kavya didn't rage like her mother did. She receded. She turned past the question marks to a fresh blank page. She slept, her head still throbbing, for the rest of the morning and into the afternoon.

She woke to the sound of passing schoolchildren, in time to remember that she had a child of her own. That child was at daycare, and that daycare had rules. The clock read 5:45. Pickup was at six.

"Shit. Shit." She couldn't ask her mother. Her mother didn't even know what Iggy looked like. Her mother was frightened of the narrow Berkeley streets.

She dialed Rishi's work number.

Ninety minutes later, Ignacio entered, perched on Rishi's forearm, sucking on his own wrist. "I was late," Rishi said. "You couldn't have sent your mom?"

Kavya ignored this and took Iggy in her arms. "You must be hungry, little boy."

Rishi took one look at Uma, one look at Kavya, and disappeared to the bedroom. He did manage to greet his mother-in-law, but not the way he should have, not with any hint of filial respect or affection. Kavya pretended not to notice. Now, hitched to her hip as if he'd always lived there, was Ignacio. Sitting at the table, her eyes locked on the child, was Uma.

Iggy pointed to the window. "He likes the windows to be open," Kavya said. She walked him over, and they cranked the pane open together.

Then she turned to Uma. "Here he is." Iggy wriggled from her arms to the floor, where he grabbed hold of a chair to gain his balance. He cruised from chair to chair—something he'd started doing that week—stepping strongly, but holding on. Uma watched without speaking. Kavya half expected her to gather her things and leave. But Uma did not. She half expected her to melt at the sight of the child, undeniable now, and flawless. But Uma's reaction came from someplace that neither half of Kavya could have fathomed. Uma rose from her seat, returned to her paper bag, and pulled from it one last item, a tinfoil parcel, creased and scrunched enough to look like recycling. She unwrapped it with careful fingers, pressing out each metallic fold, until it lay open on her palm. At its center sat one round and golden *gulab jamun*, the size of a ping-pong ball. Its syrup pooled into the foil. It had been squashed on one end, and its pale insides peeked out from the amber crust. Gulab jamun: deep-fried and solid, bathed in syrup. Gulab jamuns spoke of spoiled, peachy-faced children, fat and soft in the arms of doting grand-

mothers. Uma lowered herself to kneel on the floor. Iggy stopped cruis-
ing when he reached her and squatted on the floor before her. The two
remained motionless, staring at each other. Neither smiled.

With maternal ease, Uma picked up the gulab jamun and popped it
into Iggy's mouth. Before he could turn away, before Kavya could say
No-wait-sugar-oils-trans-fats, Ignacio was chewing, the sweet as big as
his mouth, bulging against his cheek. Kavya could almost feel the crisp
dough breaking against her own molars, the warm nectar of it streaming down her throat, and for a moment she wanted the prize for herself.
She wished that it were hers.

And no, Uma and Ignacio were not fast friends from this point.
Ignacio scanned Uma with an appraising eye, gripped the seat of the
nearest chair, and hoisted himself to his feet. His hands moved from
chair to chair as he cruised back to Kavya.

"I will sleep here tonight," Uma announced. Kavya would wait to tell
her mother that the old guest bedroom had become the nursery, that her
mother would have to sleep on the sofa. A model Indian daughter would
have moved her husband and herself out to the living room and given
her mother the king-size bed. Iggy climbed back into Kavya's arms. He
clung to her neck, stroking with his fingers the slope of skin between
her ear and shoulder, the place where her fever resided, where Miguel
had placed his palm, and Uma. By now her skin had cooled, and Ignacio's hand was hot to the touch.

Uma leveled a long and quiet gaze on the boy. This is my child,
Kavya wanted to say. But something more than obstinance stopped her.
It was a long-buried superstition, unearthed in her mother's presence,
that one shouldn't name a thing before it existed on paper. Kavya was
Iggy's mother; this much she knew and had always known. But was
Iggy Kavya's child? He called her Mama. But surrounding this lone fact
were skulking apprehensions, stepping out now from the corners of her
happy Craftsman home and her healthy Berkeley life. She felt them in

the kitchen as surely as she felt the stormy heat of the rice cooker, its lumens of steam broken only by a breeze from the open window.

The next day was Saturday. Kavya wouldn't have to be back at work until Monday morning. This meant she'd have the weekend, hours and hours of it, to spend with Uma. Saturday morning, she woke with a start. Normally it was Iggy who woke her, shouting *Hey! Mama!* from his crib. But today she woke to silence. She leapt out of bed, her dizziness abated. Ignacio's crib was empty. Rishi's laptop bag was gone. In the kitchen, she heard the tinging of spoons on plates. On silent sock feet, she hovered just out of sight. Uma plucked grapes from their stems and placed them on Iggy's high-chair tray. She counted them out first in English, then Tamil. She counted them again in singsong, as he pushed each grape into his mouth. *Ondru, rendu, moondru, naalu.* The grapes filled his cheeks, like eggs in a sack, and juice squirted from his lips when he chewed. Kavya thought to stop it, to point out the choking hazard, to swoop in and cut the grapes in half, to cup her palm to Iggy's mouth and ask him to spit. But instead she watched. The food was chewed, the food went down. Iggy held up one finger, then two, then a third from his other hand. Uma laughed and clapped.

When Kavya entered, Uma sat up straight and sucked in her smile. She cleared her throat, raised her eyebrows, and rose from the table. "You are hungry?" she asked. "These days you eat breakfast, don't you? It's good for you to eat breakfast in the morning, Kavya. You need to keep up your energy."

"Good morning, Piggy." Kavya kissed the top of Iggy's head, then filled the teakettle and set it on the stove. "I'll just have tea," she said. She scanned the counter for Rishi's keys.

"He's gone out," Uma said. "He took his briefcase. Probably working, no?"

"Yes, he's probably working." Rishi seemed to have thrown himself completely into a company for children, seemingly to avoid the company of his own child. Sensing this chord of discontent, Uma reached out and plucked it.

"Does he always work like this?" she asked. "Weekends, too? Doesn't he help with the child?"

Kavya refused to reply. Rishi should have been home—he'd promised to do more. Her mother sensed this somehow. She was circling, waiting like a falcon to swoop.

"You are lucky, at least, isn't it?" Uma went on. "You didn't have to go through childbirth. Childbirth can make a husband very unhappy, isn't it, Kavya? You know your Appa was so angry after you were born? We had no sex for five months."

"Mom!"

"Five months, Kavya. I had stitches."

"Okay. That's enough."

Uma sat next to Iggy and ran her nails through his hair, from his crown down, from the nape of his neck up. She paused, rummaged through his curls, and squinted. "See this," she said, turning Iggy's head to expose a tightly wound dreadlock. Kavya waited, certain of a comment on racial mixing, the risks of shadowy genetics. Instead: "He's going to Kashi for pilgrimage, you see. He's thinking of his past life, when he was a holy man. And now he's planning to go back to the temple."

"Oh," Kavya said. "Okay."

"My hope is that you are keeping your husband happy, Kavya. He does not seem very happy to me."

She knew only that she missed him, that she wanted him home on a Saturday. It hadn't occurred to Kavya that Rishi could be unhappy. Stressed, yes. She was used to stress. His job came with a drip feed of stress so continuous that it eventually went unnoticed. But for him to be unhappy, and unhappy enough for her mother to notice, was something Kavya hadn't thought possible, especially now that she had what she wanted.

"He's not unhappy, Amma."

"Do you know this? You are sure?"

"I'm sure."

"But is he happy?"

Uma left later that afternoon. "Sacramento will be roasting," she said, fanning herself in anticipation. August in Berkeley was more muggy than warm. When she'd loaded the car with empty Tupperware, Uma picked Ignacio up. She took a slow, affectionate sniff of his cheek and put him down again.

"He's eating too much sugar," she said to Kavya. "Be careful with his health."

Kavya breathed deeply and smiled. She kissed her mother's cheek and picked up Iggy. Together, they watched the beige Lexus disappear, its windows glinting.

WHETHER RISHI WAS HAPPY or unhappy, whether such an abstraction could be captured and pinned to a life, like a slow-winged butterfly, was not something Rishi bothered to ask himself. He assumed that happiness was a constant, an immovable mesh, through which intermittent miseries passed and vanished.

At home, their domestic experiment seemed to be working. Iggy had accepted Kavya as his mother, or at least his mother for now, though he suspected that for a child Ignacio's age, there was no *for now*, only a series of forevers. Kavya was a natural mother. She moved fast and sharp around the kitchen in the mornings, bright with Ignacio, cheery and warm. She glinted with certainty. This was the Kavya he'd always known, but a sharper iteration of her.

They had names for each other; Kavya called Ignacio Iggy, Igs, and other more imaginative nicknames that Rishi couldn't have predicted. Iggy called Kavya Mama. Not a great creative leap, but better than what he'd called her before, which was nothing. As for Rishi himself, Iggy still called him nothing. In the face of Kavya's joy, her rabid embrace of motherhood, Rishi could only wonder if she'd ever felt such joy for her husband, or whether he himself had ever felt such joy about anyone, let alone Kavya, let alone the boy. Back in college, he'd fallen in love with Kavya because she didn't seem to need a boyfriend or hand-holder or assurances of impending marriage. She'd been wholly an individual, even as a half-awake college student, happy enough to follow her own meandering path. She wanted him, but didn't *need* him. She was Club Kavya, closed to membership, and Rishi her much-loved affiliate. Now her one-person club had taken a second member, and it wasn't Rishi. What was more—and this was the real shock—it turned out that she *did* need. But the person she needed was Iggy. She had woven herself inextricably with this two-foot-tall unexpected love, and while Rishi was fine and good and necessary for things like adult conversation, shared dinners, and sex, he felt increasingly like the dispensable member of the family.

It wasn't as if Rishi hadn't tried. In the weeks since his last earthquake day, he'd taken the boy to the playground, had swung him on the swing and sent him sailing on the seesaw. He'd taken the boy to a library story time. He'd fed the boy applesauce and made his breakfast three times, maybe four. He'd read him stories and held his shape-sorter while the boy tried to cram square blocks into triangular holes. Rishi had filled his end of the equation, had shuffled his variables, calculated and recalculated, but wasn't getting what he wanted, which was a sense of fatherhood. He didn't feel like a father, and Ignacio didn't feel like his son.

That morning, he had walked into the kitchen to find Uma slicing a banana. Without intending to, he backed into the living room, picked up his bag, opened the front door, and left.

Rishi got in his car and drove, planning to plant himself in a student café, where he could disappear for hours for the cost of a coffee. But instead he found himself leaving Berkeley, merging from 580 to 880, on a southward conveyor belt that would take him, without his express consent, to the Weebies parking lot. It occurred to him, pulling into the nearly empty expanse, that perhaps the father-son bond was an impossibility that no series of trials and recalculations could surmount. Ignacio was simply not his child, and while Rishi could provide for him the best of all resources, he wouldn't feel the pull of fatherhood that he'd always expected. Maybe, he thought, this was how all fathers secretly felt. Maybe only mothers needed children.

On a normal Saturday, he and Kavya would have lingered in bed, stood in line for brunch, wandered up the hills and back to bed for the rest of the languorous afternoon. Normal: When he and Kavya were enough for each other. Rishi's state of mind was shifting and cracked by multiple and conflicting forces. He was a father, and yet he was not. He was proud of his wife and frustrated. Beneath his awe for her devotion sat a destructive wedge of resentment at being left behind. He told himself he was working to ensure his future at the company so that the boy would have a guardian with a well-paid job, so that the boy could go to a private school if he needed to, where he would be treated like a child of privilege, not a minority. He remembered how the Latino kids at his own school in Ohio had been treated, largely ignored, unless being singled out for blame. He remembered the Latino kids in the detention room after school, their features muddled by the windowpane, their hands gripping the ends of their desks, hunched over, bored. This couldn't be Ignacio, Rishi thought. No child of his would spend his afternoons in detention. At a private school, Ignacio would be part of the inner circle. He wouldn't be Mexican. He wouldn't be adopted. He would simply be.

Hopping on a Weebike, Rishi maintained his passive state, letting his feet and the roads take him where they would. As he rode, the warm valley air made its way through him, untangling the knots of conflict that had begun to weigh on him so unrelentingly. By the time he arrived at Weebies HQ, he felt his shackles had fallen away. He looked up and saluted the baby atop the purple building. He flashed his badge to the guard and made his way up to Vikram Sen's office, expecting to find it empty. He wasn't sure what he meant to do with this visit; somehow it seemed perfectly natural that Rishi would pop in on a Saturday to say hello to the CFO of one of the western hemisphere's most successful corporations. He passed the programming center, where a group of programmers clustered in a far corner, hunched over their keyboards as if unaware that Friday had come and gone. He arrived at the marble foyer outside Sen's office, where Sally normally sat guard at her desk, managing the visitors who'd requested an audience with the Don. Today, the foyer and Sally's desk were empty but for the usual workday detritus—a coffee mug, a binder, a cell phone, and sunglasses. Peering down the hall, he saw that Sen's door stood ajar.

"Hello?" he called. He tried again, louder this time, then made his way down the hall, trying in vain to step heavily on the thick Persian rug that absorbed his every footfall. Reaching Sen's door, he raised a hand to knock and stopped. Through the six-inch crack in the door, he saw the Don, sprawled on his white leather sofa, eyes closed. Draped over Vikram Sen was Sally, her head on Sen's chest, fully clothed, her flaxen hair sprawling and covering her eyes. She lay on him like a child, and was in fact as small as a child, in comparison. Rishi had never noticed either her astonishing slightness or her boss's height. The two of them seemed to be sleeping, though Sen laced his fingers through Sally's hair. Together, they were in another world.

In Rishi's head, a bell clanged. His first thought: *Leave now.* His second: *What about Preeti Patel?* Preeti sat framed on Sen's desk, window-facing, oblivious. His third thought: *Get. Out. Now.* And he did, on mouse feet, soundless, thankfully, on the Persian rug.

"Rishi-bhai!"

Rishi stopped, considered making a run for it, but heard footsteps behind him. Sally, smoothing down her hair, gave him a pursed little smile as she passed, pulling down the sleeves of her sweater. Vikram Sen followed, holding his hand out to Rishi, his eyes fevered and glassy, his smile wide.

"Rishi-bhai! So good to see you! Come." Rishi's feet stayed planted on the rug. He felt sound vibrate against his lips but had no idea what he'd managed to say. Sen bustled him toward his office, a brotherly hand on his back. "Such industry!" he proclaimed. "At work on a Saturday? I see good things for you, yaar. Come in! Let's talk!"

In his office, "Have a seat, man. Sally! Two chai, please!"

Sen motioned for Rishi to sit. Rishi avoided the sofa, steered himself to the smaller desk chair, and Sen propped himself on his desk, his knees just inches from Rishi's nose. Rishi opened his mouth to speak, then closed it again.

"So," Sen said. "What brings you in on a beautiful Saturday afternoon?"

Rishi shrugged, said, "Work, I guess," and felt utterly lame. "And you?"

"I live here now."

Rishi smirked.

"No, actually, I live here now."

Just then Sally entered with two steaming teacups on a tray. She placed them on the desk with a sugar pot and teaspoons and left. "Thank you, Sally!" Sen called after her. When the door clicked shut, he got up, walked the expanse of rug, and lay down, flat on his back, sock feet flexed to the ceiling, and sighed.

"Shoes off, please, Rishi-bhai." He sighed harder, as if trying to expel some blockage of the spirit. He pressed his hands to his eyes. "What is this life, yaar?"

After a murky silence, Rishi rose. "I should go."

"Stay. Stay!"

Rishi sat. "Everything all right at home?" And then, "Maybe it's none of my business."

"No, it isn't. Any of your business. And no, it isn't all right at home." He opened his eyes. "What has Kavya told you?"

"Nothing."

"Really?" He turned to his side now, propped his head on his hand. "I thought ladies talked."

"Kavya's been busy. We have a kid now."

Sen seemed not to hear this, neither congratulated him nor asked for clarification. He lay back down. "Preeti was cheating on me."

Rishi fought off a fresh impulse to run.

"The illustrious, the beautiful, the breathtaking Dr. Preeti Patel," Sen continued, "was seeing another man. A married man. Before she met me. After she met me. And now? Who knows?"

Rishi's mouth went dry. "Oh."

"Oh, indeed."

"And—and so you're—"

"And now she says she isn't seeing him, not since the wedding. I think I believe her. Why would she lie? Why not go and be with this other man? Free country, yaar, you know?"

Rishi clung fiercely to the positive. "So she's not seeing him."

"We're getting better."

"But you live at the office."

"More or less. Not much different from when I lived at home."

"But—" Rishi cleared his throat. "Oh."

"Sally?" Sen cut in. "Sally is a girl I love. Sally is my survival, my right-hand woman. But she isn't my wife." He glanced over at Rishi. "You're a handsome fellow, Rishi-bhai. You must know what I mean. Girls you like, girls you love, girls you go to bed with. And then there's your wife. No one compares with the wife, right?"

The truth was, there had never been anyone after Kavya. He tried to imagine himself with another woman, with any of the women at Weebies who always had something to say to Rishi, whose eyes crinkled with pleasure at his arrival. He couldn't. He tried again: The redhead with the nose ring? The one with the long curly hair and the tattoo that crept up her neck? Surely all men harbored secret cravings for other women. Surely he too had dallied with such thoughts, but they skittered away, untraceable now. Sitting in Vik Sen's office, Rishi couldn't muster an ounce of desire for any other woman, theoretical or real. A sweet chai-making blonde in a soft gray sweater? Nothing. As he watched Sen rub at his eyelids, flex and point his toes, Rishi felt the morning's dissipated impulses gather like so many metal filings to a magnet, joining to form one clear and revelatory idea: Kavya was everything. He wanted nothing but her, frustrations and all. Regardless of whether she needed him, he needed her.

He needed to get home to Kavya, to the boy, as far as possible from this desert of parking lots and office space, back to the hectic and stifling Saturday sidewalks, the cool shadows of his home, his messy kitchen, a mug of tea.

"Stop," Sen said. "Before you leave. Why did you come here today, Rishi-bhai?"

Rishi shook his head. "I don't know. I needed to work. The VOC project—"

"Is causing you distress. I can tell. Is that why you came to see me?"

Rishi nodded.

"You're afraid I've given you an impossible task," Sen said. "You're afraid you'll fail."

Not only this, Rishi wanted to tell him, but when he failed, he'd lose this chance, his one chance, to do something real at Weebies, to be a part of something bigger than his beige office and his duct-simulation software.

"Don't be afraid of failing, Rishi-bhai," Sen said, reading his thoughts. "I led four different companies to the brink of destruction before they hired me at Weebies. Did you know that? It's not in my company bio. But it's why they hired me. Failure is knowledge. Nothing more. A little bad luck, some stupid decisions. Nothing more."

"Okay."

"You don't believe me."

Rishi shrugged.

"You've been to India?" Sen asked. "So you've seen those buses, right? The buses with the men hanging off the sides?"

"Sure."

"They hang off like this, no? Three, four, five of them across? And you wonder how the *bloody* hell they manage not to fall? What are they hanging on to? Who knows? But they hang on. Instead of saying *Too full, I'll get the next bus*, they run for their lives and jump onto these overcrowded things. And every time they do it, someone catches them, holds on to them, and they hold on too, until they get where they need to go. No?"

"Yeah," Rishi said. "You're right. They do."

"Imagine if they didn't take that chance? If they played the cool guy and stayed on the ground?"

"Yeah. I think I see."

"What would happen then?"

"They'd never get anywhere," Rishi answered. "They'd be stuck."

Sen raised one triumphant finger.

Feeling inexplicably uplifted, Rishi hopped to his feet and walked out.

"Run for the bus, Rishi-bhai!" Sen called. Rishi broke into a sprint down the hall, past Sally's desk, and into a waiting, miraculously open elevator.

Driving home again, he could see the full vista of the valley: the deserted parking lots, checkered with cars, the Caltrain tracks, the expanses of brown ground, mottled with water and green. And because today was a clear day, he could see the two silent towers of the Golden Gate, more red than gold. He'd read that the air force had originally wanted to paint the bridge yellow with black stripes. Some decisions were wrong from the start. As he got closer to home and saw the ocean and the Oz-like spires of San Francisco, something within him settled. The buildings he drove past grew smaller and closer, the sidewalks crowded, traffic stilted. He'd returned to the East Bay, where he needed to be. He'd made some wrong decisions and some right ones.

When Rishi got home and saw the kitchen light, he felt peace spread through him. He opened the front door. "I'm ho-ooome," he called. There was no reply. "Kavya?" he called again. He followed her faint voice to the living room. He could feel the drift of fever even before he reached the sofa where Kavya lay. Ignacio stood at her feet, thumping his forehead against her shins.

"Jesus," he said when he placed a hand on her neck.

Rishi carried her to bed, found the aspirin, and placed a wet towel on her forehead. She winced. "It's cold," she managed to say. "It's too cold."

He whipped the blanket off. "You need to cool off. Just for a while."

He could hear the knock of her knees as she shivered.

Ignacio scooted around the living room wearing nothing but a diaper, and the evening chill had raised a rash of goose bumps down his back. "C'mere, Ignacio. Let's put a shirt on." He scooped the boy into his arms. He felt the rattle in Ignacio's breath, the slight rasp in his chest. In the other room, Kavya lay in the dark, a wet towel over her eyes. Rishi had spent so much time outside of his home that he hadn't noticed the cloud of illness that permeated it. He had been neglectful. In the months since the Stratosphere project had begun, he'd retreated into himself, and now his family suffered. He went to the cupboard to search for the menthol rub, thinking he might clear up Iggy's chest. He lifted Ignacio and carried him into the kitchen. Against his own chest, through the boy's very skin, came a heated and harried thump, a small heart working fast. Ignacio's cheeks were hot, and his chest rose and fell more rapidly than it should have. From his throat, Rishi heard an alarming rattle. He picked up the phone and dialed.

The doctor was out of the office, his exchange said. The on-call physician would phone by dinnertime. Ignacio coughed again, this time wheezing violently. Rishi yanked open the kitchen drawer and riffled through it until he found a dog-eared black notebook, bent nearly in half, names and numbers and addresses rammed together in Kavya's frantic hand, a train wreck of information. From this, somehow, he picked the word *Preeti*, the numbers *415*. He hesitated for a moment, thinking of Vikram Sen, wary of encountering a teary and conflicted Preeti Patel. In the other room, Kavya moaned. Rishi dialed.

KAVYA PULLED HERSELF from a well of sleep and, surfacing, followed voices to the kitchen. Ignacio was holding himself up by Preeti Patel's knee but dropped to the ground when he saw Kavya.

Preeti beamed.

"What are you doing here?" Kavya asked.

Preeti's smile wavered. "Rishi called me. He couldn't get a hold of your doctor."

Kavya grew dizzy again and sat. Even in her fog, this sounded like judgement—of Rishi, of their doctor. "Can I have some 7Up?" she asked Rishi. She knew very well that they had no 7Up. She hadn't had 7Up for years and was unsure if it even existed anymore, but it was what her mother used to give her when she was sick.

Rishi sat next to her and took her hand. "I could get you some," he said. "I could get you some 7Up."

Preeti cleared her throat and produced an oblong case. She unlatched it and took out a stethoscope. "You say he's been coughing for how long?"

"Since we've known him," Rishi said. "For almost two months now. There's a thing in his chest, I think. A rattle . . . or something."

"And how are you feeling, Kavya?" Preeti asked. "Have you taken anything?"

"Just aspirin."

"Have you been drinking fluids?"

"Not really."

"How about some tea?" She turned to Rishi. "Can we get that 7Up, maybe?"

He nodded.

Kavya flopped back on the couch and closed her eyes and blew horsishly through her lips. She could feel Rishi and Preeti watching her, blinking. The sound of blinking in the room was deafening.

Preeti kneeled next to Ignacio, stethoscope in hand, and let him play with it. She showed him how to press the flat, round disc to his chest, to hers. And then, speaking in bright whispers, she placed the earbuds in her own ears and pressed the disc to his chest, his back. He squirmed.

"Hold still, sweetie." She listened again. She turned to Kavya. "Okay. He has a fever. That I can say for sure. It could be more."

"What does that mean?" Rishi asked.

"It's astonishing," Preeti said, "what small children can live with. They seem fine on the outside, and on the inside, they're barely holding on. But I'm not saying that! I'm not saying he's barely holding on. He might have a chest infection, that's all." She sat flat on the ground. "Sorry. I'm not great at this."

"So," Kavya said, sitting up now. "What exactly are you saying?"

"Come here." She took her stethoscope off and placed its buds in Rishi's ears. "Have a listen." When Rishi kneeled beside Ignacio, he sank into his arms. He let Preeti guide the disc along his chest, then his back.

"Around here," Preeti said. "Do you hear that? Sort of a hissing, staticky sound?"

What Rishi heard was a rush of wind, sprinting through trees, having its way with sun-dried leaves.

"So we'll call the doctor," Rishi said.

"Definitely," Preeti answered.

"He'll be fine," Rishi said to Kavya.

Kavya pulled herself back to the sofa and dug her face into a pillow.

"Ignacio?" Preeti said. "Is that your mama? And your papa?"

Ignacio fixed his gaze on Kavya.

"Papa?" Preeti said again. She pointed to Rishi. "Papa!" she said. Then she turned to Rishi. "Is that what he calls you?"

"Well," Rishi said. He and Kavya blinked at each other. "He doesn't—I'm not sure."

The room went silent.

Kavya lifted her head. "Rishi hasn't been around much. Iggy doesn't call him anything."

Preeti pursed her lips. "Papa? Dada?"

"Nana?" Rishi tried. "That's what I call my dad." He turned to Iggy. "Nana?" he asked.

Ignacio angled on Preeti a heavy-lidded gaze. A delicate bubble of saliva ballooned from his lips and burst. "Papa!" he said, and pointed to Rishi, the two syllables sharp enough to form a command.

Rishi, newly christened, took Ignacio for a walk to the store. Preeti and Kavya watched them leave, Preeti perched on the arm of the sofa, her gaze following the two out the door and, turning to the window, down the sidewalk.

Preeti leaned toward the window to watch them. "Do you think they'll be all right?"

"Is it that obvious he doesn't know what he's doing?"

She shrugged. "He probably knows more than I do."

Kavya covered her hands with her eyes, meshed her fingers against the room's stark ceiling light. It hurt to look at anything directly.

"He sounded pretty worried when he called," Preeti said. "And I was in the East Bay anyway, so . . ."

Kavya turned. "Worried about me?"

Preeti hesitated. "Yes. And Ignacio, of course." She paused. "He's wonderful, Kavya!"

"Iggy?"

"Yes, Iggy!"

Kavya smiled against her palms. "He is." She didn't tell Preeti of her deeper worries, the idea that her wonderful boy could be taken away. It wasn't a small possibility; she wasn't being a neurotic mother who feared her healthy child would stop breathing. She knew her only certainty was uncertainty. She knew that Iggy's real mother—she couldn't stop calling her that—could come back any day, and that Kavya's commitment wouldn't matter. Kavya had made a mansion of her love, but built it on shifting land.

"The fresh air'll be good for him," Preeti said, looking out the window at Vine Street. "What I heard was probably nothing."

"Probably."

"I think he really was worried about you, actually. Rishi, that is."

Preeti seemed to sense more than she should have, but this didn't surprise Kavya. Of course Preeti would know everything about her.

A quiet settled over the room.

"How are things with you?" Kavya asked.

Preeti shrugged. "Vik's taking me back. So that's good. I guess."

"Have you figured out the—situation?"

She considered this. "It depends what you mean. I guess the situation is managing itself. Huntley fucked with my head, and then I went to

Vikram for love and security. And that's where I am now. That's a situation, right?"

Kavya tried to smile.

TWENTY MINUTES LATER, Rishi turned onto Vine with a canvas bag of soy milk and 7Up, Ignacio perched on his shoulders. Preeti's white Prius was still parked at the curb. Through the living room window he could see the two women, both standing now. He wasn't ready to go in. He wasn't sure why. He turned and headed back to Shattuck.

In August, Berkeley went to sleep, its inhabitants trailing to the coast, the woods, the mountains. Those who didn't leave drew into themselves, their homes, their cocoons of quiet routine. They hid in the muggy mist of that month as college students returned, blocked up the crosswalks and the cafés. The people of Berkeley grumbled at the thought of giving their city back to twenty-year-olds. They groused about students who dripped across crosswalks in twos and threes, forcing drivers to idle endlessly. They resented the fact that their own college days were long behind them. They grumbled about the heat, and the cold. They grumbled about the unpredictability of this place that they loved, most essentially, for its unpredictability. And they tucked themselves into smaller versions of their lives, as the impatient night brought each day to a quicker close. They waited for a new beginning.

But today, Shattuck Avenue buzzed with life in the sun shower of early evening. Iggy spread his small palms over Rishi's ears, filtering the street noise. In a window's reflection, he noticed a leaf in the boy's hair, from an earlier brush with a birch tree.

"Papa?" Iggy asked, but said no more.

Rishi stopped at the corner and let the foot traffic wash over him. People carried bread under their arms, toddlers against their chests, pizza in promising brown boxes. A line had formed outside Green Pizza and trailed halfway down the block. People in Berkeley loved to stand in line for food; it meant they'd found something special, something worth waiting for. It spoke of their unflagging devotion to the best of the culinary best. People smiled at Rishi, at Iggy on the throne of his father's shoulders. People waved up at him, people pointed and grinned. People said hello. A man with a beard and a T-shirt that read *Live in a Yurt* gave Iggy a high five. Being a father made him a part of this place, Rishi realized. He was no longer just a scientist, a pizza eater, a line dweller, a street crosser. Ignacio rooted him to the hum of this sidewalk. Ignacio brought him to Earth.

They stood by the wall of open windows and listened to the dinner band, a jazz ensemble with a female singer. When Rishi looked up, he saw that Iggy was fixed on the double-bass player, who was plucking at the strings of the man-sized instrument, sending out a dignified thump. They stayed until intermission, Rishi swaying and Ignacio tapping a beat on his head.

When he walked back down Vine, the white Prius was gone.

He opened the door to a warm fog. He had nothing against Preeti, but he was happy she'd gone. He ducked into the doorway, careful of Iggy's head. From the kitchen came the scent of boiling pasta, empty and nutty and clean all at once. He heard a knife on a chopping board, Kavya sitting at the countertop, reclaiming her space. On his shoulders, Iggy sighed and wrapped his arms around Rishi's head. Rishi thought of their first meeting, the foster home, when he'd felt the undecided heartbeat, not in Iggy's chest, but in the house, in the air around them. The tripping pulse hadn't come from Rishi's heart, or Kavya's; nor was it a shared syncopation. What fed that odd little rhythm were three hearts, Rishi's and Kavya's and Iggy's, beating in quick succession. He'd expected to will himself into fatherhood, and had failed in many ways.

But now, in the orderly clamor of their kitchen, the alarm of illness quelled, the night fast approaching, and the boy's fat legs dangling down his shoulders, Rishi saw them as if for the first time—his wife, his child—and felt, at last, a sense of possibility.

SUNDAY MORNING, Rishi drove Kavya and Iggy to the emergency room. Iggy had been awake all night, barking deep wet coughs, and his fever had stayed stubbornly high. By morning, he could barely keep his eyes open, and his breath came in frantic gusts. The verdict: Kavya had the flu and Iggy had pneumonia. The boy's diagnosis filled Rishi's own lungs with nervous exhaust. He shook his head at the doctor. "That can't be possible," he said.

"It's pneumonia," the doctor said. He held a sweet rehydration drink to Ignacio's lips. "It happens. His pulse oxygen is lower than it should be—" He stopped short. "Are you okay? Do you need to sit down?"

"I'm fine," Rishi said, but sat down. From the examination table, Iggy reached out for him. The doctor placed the boy on Rishi's lap, then took Rishi's temperature.

Rishi looked down at his hand and saw that it was trembling, tapping side to side like a tabla player's.

"You're fine. Don't let this worry you, all right? We'll start him on an antibiotic. He'll be fine."

Rishi nodded. "Modern medicine," he said, hoping to comfort himself. Ignacio took Rishi by the ears and brought his face close, so close that Rishi could feel the puff of each quick breath from his nostrils. Iggy pressed his forehead to Rishi's, squeezed Rishi's cheeks between his palms, leveled his eyes—wider now, more alert—to his father's, and poured into them a wave of calm.

That night, Kavya rolled herself in the duvet and slept diagonally across the bed, and it was Rishi who slept on the floor by Iggy's crib. If

Ignacio knew about past lives, in the way young children sometimes did, he didn't let on. The blanket across his chest, the hiss of breath through his nostrils, seemed to be all Iggy knew. His dreams, the picture shows that coursed behind his flickering lids—these would constitute the depth and width of living, until his eyes opened and the show leaked away and he returned to this world, to this father who watched him sleep. He slipped a finger through the crib rail, and instinctively, Iggy wrapped his own fist around it. Rishi measured his own breath to Iggy's, and listened to the rattle in his chest. He lay awake, anticipating the boy's next cry. He worried that they'd broken him.

Most parents worry. Most parents worry from day one that their child will stop breathing, that their child will fall out of bed, be crushed in the night by a falling light fixture or sat on by a cat. Most parents experience the worry and push their way through it, so that by the time they're parents of two-year-olds or three-year-olds, individuals who really are capable of destroying themselves, they've learned not to worry. Even when they should. Rishi, however, was a newly born parent, and fearful. Maybe this was a good thing. Maybe it was fear that turned him, that early August morning, into a father.

36.

AND ONE DAY, IGGY BEGAN TO WALK. HE WAS EIGHTEEN months old. It happened in the evening, when both Kavya and Rishi were home. He'd been pulling himself around the dining table, as usual, while Kavya chopped an apple-jicama-cabbage slaw. She picked up an apple wedge and bit into it. At the sound of the wet crunch, Iggy swung around and took a step away from the chairs, and another, until he found himself with nothing to hold on to, teetering forward, backward, in midair. Kavya stopped chewing, and watched. Iggy looked up at her, but didn't thump down on his behind, like most children did. Instead, he tottered in place until he'd struck a balance. And then, very carefully, as if a miscalibrated angle would bring him crashing down, he raised his arm and pointed to the apple, crimson and cream, in Kavya's hand.

She knelt down and coaxed him forward, holding out the apple slice. "Apple?" she said. "Apple?" She felt like she was spying on the universe's inner mechanics—the crack of a bird's egg, a vulture feasting on carrion, a squirrel-chase through the branches of an oak. Iggy's first steps were part of a greater unstoppable force, more animal than human. He took one more courageous step and fell forward at last, smacking his palms to the floor. "Bravo!" Kavya whispered. "Bravo!" And how human it was, after all, this feat, the swell of pride when it happened. How human, to stand for an apple, to step strong for its cardinal promise.

In the weeks that followed, Iggy got used to falling. In the weeks that followed those, he began to run. Rishi started getting up with him in the mornings to play chasing games in the living room. Ignacio nearly stopped walking altogether, and ran from room to room, stopping only to get down on his knees for the three steps between the kitchen and the living room.

Kavya was aware, of course, that there was a mother out there who had missed these first steps. But the thought of this woman, angel or devil, whoever she was, sent a chill through her. She grew hollow and painfully cold at the thought of another woman wanting what she'd come to think of as hers. And, she reminded herself, this woman, this mother-woman, had been there for Ignacio's first months. Kavya found herself mourning Ignacio's infancy. She found herself staring at the almost-two-year-old, thinking about the aching fragility of a newborn, the absolute dependence that could carve both terror and bottomless wells of awe into new mothers. Kavya had known none of this. She could close her eyes and imagine Iggy's infant legs, bowed around the girth of a diaper, folds of fat around his knees. She wondered how thick the pads of his feet were then, if they were as soft and pillowy as his palms still were. Then she reminded herself that she had Iggy now. He was hers.

Now and then, Kavya caught a feature she hadn't noticed before, the square spread of his feet, the astonishing musculature of his calves. He leapt and landed like a leopard. He moved with a physical grace that had no match in Kavya's family or Rishi's. Another man and another woman had created this boy, and he was flowering in foreign soil. As Iggy learned to walk, then run, then leap, the butter of infancy melted off. He gained the stridency of a child—elbows, shoulder blades, teeth like moonlit pebbles. And words. Apple. Hot. Woof. Papa. Hi. From his mealy mutterings, actual sentences emerged. And from these sentences sprang meaning, intention, and a beastly will.

. . .

HER MOTHER was on the other end, asking about Ignacio. The very fact of this buoyed Kavya to such heights that she hardly cared that Uma called him *Yignacio*. Maybe now, Kavya told herself, her mother would call her every two days, as she'd always done. Kavya would share stories with her about the things Ignacio had said, questions about low-grade fevers and opinions on doctors and schoolteachers. Her mother would give advice that wasn't asked for; her mother would lament the state of modern-day parenting. Her mother would be her mother again. As the pace of their talk slowed and the phone call wound down to its natural end, as Kavya opened her mouth to say *Okay . . . well*, her mother said, "One more thing."

"What?"

"Preeti is having a baby. Preeti is pregnant."

Of course Preeti was pregnant. Of course, of course, of course. Six months earlier this news would have sunk Kavya. But now, she said goodbye, picked up the phone again, and dialed.

"Congratulations!" She tried to lean lightly on the exclamation point, but her voice felt shrill.

"Thanks," Preeti said.

"How do you feel?"

"Not bad."

Kavya waited. "Vikram's?"

A long pause. "I saw Huntley once. Just once." She started to speak, but stopped herself. "It's so over. I'm sure it's Vik's. I can feel it, you know?"

Kavya didn't know what to say to this.

"I didn't plan this. I so didn't plan this."

"Yeah, well. You are married."

"Yeah. And everything else."

"Yeah."

"I guess my body wanted to get pregnant, you know? I went off the pill when Vikram took me back, but I didn't think it would happen this soon."

"Uh-huh." How easy for Preeti, of course. How easy.

"I thought it would take a year or so for things to kick in. Or longer. I'm no spring chicken."

"But you seem to work."

"Yes, I seem to work. I seem to have a cervix with a tourist information center." A pause. "How's Iggy?"

"Good."

"I can tell. I can hear you smiling."

"I think you're going to be a great mom," Kavya managed. "No matter what happens."

HER LIFE WAS A BERKELEY BUNGALOW: small and sturdy, plain on the outside, but surrounded by expensive plants. What warmed this stucco block was Ignacio. And Kavya was learning to be a mother. Not an eat-sleep-poop mother, but a singing, storytelling inventor of a universe. The sort of mother she'd fantasized about being. She found that she could make Ignacio laugh just by blowing air onto his cheek, and doing it again. And again. She found that he laughed every time she did it, no matter how many times, each burst of pleasure its own singular surprise. She found that she could tell stories. Old fairy tales that she half knew, she could give new endings. New stories, she could spin from nothing, welding new facts to old tropes to come out with tidy tales of vengeance, salvation, discovery. As Iggy learned new words she became a mix master of storytelling. Car! Dinosaur! Buzz Lightyear! He'd call the words and she'd come out with a story about Buzz Lightyear and his car, his dinosaur, his redemption.

Ignacio was speaking, his English crisp and clamoring with momentum. He learned at a supernatural rate. And when he said something new and astonishing, she picked him up, swung him through the air—and yes, she'd read the manuals about not overpraising, about conditioning excellence—she swung him through the air and kissed his face, the skin fragrant with spit and dewy heat. She took every opportunity to press her lips to the sweet plum of his skin, and before long, it would not have occurred to her that his skin was not her skin, that she had not borne him from some humid cave of her own desire.

She rushed from work each evening with the urgency of a nursing mother. Her breasts lay slack and empty, but her chest swelled with need, and with the belief that he was waiting for her. When she arrived at his daycare, unlatched the safety gate in the foyer, he ran to her, strong arms around her neck. His faith was effortless, his need steadfast.

37.

THE GAS MASK ARRIVED. A DAY EARLIER, ANOTHER HEAR-
ing had been held in Ignacio's name. This one determined that the foster parents of Ignacio Castro Valdez were doing an adequate job. Joyce
Jones had phoned that morning to inform Rishi that he and Kavya were
proving adequate. Rishi was glad that he'd answered and not his wife,
who would have taken this stamp of adequacy as an outright accusation.

"Come on, Iggy," Rishi said. "Come with me. Let's test this thing
out." He helped Ignacio down the steps to the garden, over to the earthquake kit.

"This is our emergency earthquake kit," Rishi said. He unlatched the
plastic crate and took from it his own gas mask. "See this, Iggy? This is
my gas mask. This is if the air gets bad. It'll help me breathe."

He put the gas mask on and Ignacio's eyes grew wide, his face flushed
crimson. He opened his mouth and screamed. He screamed again,
called, "Mama, Ma, Ma!" He called, "Papa!" He turned from Rishi and
curled into a protective ball. Rishi whipped the mask off.

"It's me, Iggy. See? It's me."

Iggy calmed down, pulled his lips back together, huffed through his
nose, a thread of snot flaring and receding from his nostril.

"Hey, come here," said Rishi. He sat cross-legged on the ground.

Ignacio climbed into his lap and examined his face. It was a relief to be in a child's world, where kindness was the standard operating mode, where clarity was the order of the day, and adult posturing kept its distance.

Hearings had been happening, quietly, for months. Rishi and Kavya had little say in what went on, and Joyce had told them to stay home. "It's a checkup we do," she said. "We think about next steps, and we don't need to hear from you. Do you understand?"

Rishi picked up Iggy's mask. "This," he said, "I got for you. And when you get bigger, you'll get a bigger one." He hesitated, and then, "Do you want to try it on?"

Iggy picked up the mask and dropped it. Rishi helped him lift it. He pointed out the eye screens, the filter that looked like an alien snout. "This is what keeps the air clean, see?"

Face-to-face with the mask, Iggy pressed his nose to the metallic snout, his eyes against the eye screens. He made a sound.

"On? Should we put it on?"

Ignacio nodded. Slowly, waiting for the boy to squirm away or run, Rishi lowered it over his head.

"Can you breathe?" Rishi asked, and pantomimed puffing and whooshing breaths.

Ignacio whipped his head around, looking for something. He was hearing his own breath, Rishi knew, isolated in the mask and amplified.

"I wished I had a gas mask when I was a kid. I wanted to be a soldier. Did you know that? I was gangly, way too skinny, and my mom told me I was too skinny to be a soldier, which I now think was her way of getting me to eat."

Ignacio's face was pointed straight at Rishi's. He couldn't see the boy's eyes, but there was no peripheral vision in a gas mask. Iggy could only be looking at him.

"And then I thought I'd be a doctor, and I went to this science camp when I was eleven."

Iggy pulled at the snout.

"Can you breathe?" Rishi went to remove the mask, but Iggy pulled away. "You're all right in there, I guess. Maybe you'll go to science camp when you're bigger. Right? Would you like that?"

Iggy blocked a hand over one eye screen, then the other.

Rishi had told Kavya about an earlier hearing. She'd reacted so badly that he'd kept the second a secret. The matter was out of their hands, and this enraged his wife.

"I don't know why I thought of being a soldier," Rishi said. "It seemed like the next best thing to being a superhero. Maybe I thought I could save people, you know? Maybe that's what I wanted to do. I guess I'm doing that now. Sort of. Saving them from bad air." He took Iggy's elbow between two fingers and gave it a gentle shake.

A plane buzzed overhead. An outdoor band was playing somewhere in town, and the rhythmic snare and bass trailed into the yard. Still wearing his mask, Iggy dropped to his knees and began building a pile of wood chips. He had to point his snout straight at the ground to see. Rishi watched him build one stack, then another, until he'd made a small campus of wood-chip towers. Soon the distant music stopped and Iggy's breath, whooshing through the mask, was the loudest sound in the yard.

"A gas mask," Rishi said. Iggy looked up. "A *gas* mask for the Stratosphere. If we could wrap a gas mask around the entire programming center, Iggy—we could line the walls in filters!" Rishi peered in the hollows of his eyeholes. He thought of the highways that snaked around their little town, the refinery by the water. Maybe it was bad air that had made Iggy sick. Even a place like Berkeley could fill a small pair of lungs with generations of industrial sin. If he could purify the universe for this boy, his boy, he would. That's what WeBreathe would do. WeBreathe wasn't for other babies. WeBreathe was for Iggy.

Iggy stared quietly at Rishi, nodded, and resumed his building. He

squatted over his project, picking up and placing each chip with astonishing care. Any other kid, Rishi guessed, would have pulled the mask
off by then, or would have fought it off in the first place. Ignacio trusted.
Rishi ran a finger over the little arm, the skin so soft that Rishi grew
vertiginous, as if fingering the edge of a towering cliff. Ignacio had put
the mask on because Rishi had asked him to. He trusted Rishi to make
the right choices. "Ignacio," he whispered, and the boy turned to him.

It was wrong. Wrong to put a gas mask on a boy, wrong that children
had to know about gas masks and bad air and the violent earth. It was
wrong what they'd done to their world. Iggy would build his towers
of wood, and Rishi would protect him. He was wrung dry by a desire to
wrap the boy in his arms, to swallow him into the warm envelope of his
own body.

38.

So the guard came for Soli.

The hope of freedom did flutter past, but vanished as soon as she was handcuffed again. She didn't know what she'd expected, having grown accustomed to a system in which her expectations meant nothing. She wanted only to know where she was going, and why, and where her lawyer was, and whether he'd know how to find her. "Where's my lawyer?" she asked a guard, who grinned at her, then took her possessions and handed them to another guard.

"Hands" was all he said, and cuffed her wrists together. She got on an airplane, her hands shackled to a chain around her waist, that chain chained to the woman before her, and her chain chained to another, a whole chain of chains, dragging down the runway, climbing the steps to the plane, sitting in their seats, metal digging into their behinds, their backs, their wrists.

As the engines revved from a whine to a full-throated chorus, Soli forgot about the metal. She couldn't breathe in all the way, couldn't breathe out. The thrum of the runway sent a thrill up her spine as she watched the ground speed past. She was back on the train, the wind in her eyes. But as the plane's nose tilted up and away from the earth, she gasped and twisted away from the window. She squeezed her eyes shut, expecting the worst. A plummet. A scree of destruction. But the plane rose, the ground grew light, and Soli, at last, permitted herself to look. Outside her window, the sky was luminous. Below, California shrank away and spread its quilt of soil and field.

Maybe we're going back to Berkeley, she thought. Maybe this is working. Two hours later, Soli felt that California was gone. "Where are we going?" she asked the woman next to her.

"Stop talking," said a guard from farther down the aisle.

"Where are we going?" she called back.

"No talking" was all he said.

"Are they taking us to Mexico?" she asked.

"Cho! No way I'm going to Mexico," said the woman next to her, her skin black against the sun-blinded window.

They landed in the deepening dusk. She didn't know where she was, only that she was cold. It was November everywhere, and November here meant that the cold brought sound, a cavernous shudder. It hummed down their spines, gripped their ankles, and froze them to the worn and weary tips of their toes.

She was put in a cell with two other women who looked at her when she walked in and then looked away and kept talking. She turned to the guard as he pushed her through the cell door.

"I have a little boy. He needs me. I have a lawyer!"

"So do I," said the guard. He smiled and shook his head. "Now get some rest."

Outside the prison walls, the world continued its drunken surge, teetering, as ever, on the brink of ruination. Arabs revolted, and Americans. Drones like alien saucers flew overhead, manned with cameras. Americans still raged against Muslims, until they grew tired of raging against Muslims and switched to Mexicans or anyone resembling a Mexican, including Muslims. Hurricanes disappeared entire islands, palm trees bent in the raging winds. Villages vanished under mudslides. On land, grown women were dying their hair purple, and hipsters walked the streets of San Francisco, wearing sleeves of embedded ink up their arms. Iran enriched uranium and pundits worried, and China had more money than God, and the iPhone was making everything better and everything worse, and birds were angry and pigs thieving. Superheroes were back, all over the place, in every theater, because they were needed. The free people outside the prison walls needed supermen and wonder women to wrench them from the ditch they'd dug, arms flailing, bodies sinking into the squelching soil.

BUT INSIDE HER PRISON, all Soli knew were four walls, a cot, a freezing yard. She didn't know the names of the guards or the other inmates. She didn't know what color her new uniform was or what species of food was spread across her plate three times a day or how it tasted or whether it made her thirsty or sleepy. She didn't know if the table where she spent most days was round or rectangular, if the yard had grass, if the men kicked a soccer ball or if the women gathered in clusters.

She knew this: They'd taken her away. From Ignacio, from Adrian Alvarez, from the last thread that had sewn her to her life. There in prison, in this faceless and nameless prison, the sun neither rose nor set.

Only the wind blew, a rough and dirty wind, a monstrous and foreign wind. It whistled through the yard and up Soli's shirt, ran its old-man fingers around her nipples and down her back. She told herself stories of the wind—that it had come from Ignacio, blown from California by his small body in a playground swing, his legs thrust forward, his head back, laughter spouting from his throat.

Her fourth day there, she managed to call Adrian Alvarez. She'd memorized his number almost instantly from the business card he'd pressed against the window their first day together. She waited for three hours to use the prison's single phone and got to it that day before free time was over, before lockdown, before head count and dinner. It cost five dollars a minute to call him collect from prison, and the guard manning the phone informed her that no one would take her call, not for that price.

"Adrian Alvarez," Adrian Alvarez said. He accepted the call. "Soli? Hello?"

"Hello."

"Where are you?"

She let out a single sob, then swallowed the rest down. "I don't know," she said.

"What?"

"I don't know. They took me away."

"What happened? Did you sign something? I told you not to—"

"I signed nothing. I signed nothing. They tried to make me but I wouldn't."

"We had things going, Soli. We were getting you a hearing."

"The lady said I'd be stuck there for months."

"What lady?"

What lady. It was a good question. A lady in a uniform. A lady with a red mouth and fuzzy face. A lady with the small print written right between her lips.

A guard slammed his club against the wall.

"I don't even know where they've—" A beep sounded in her ear.

"Wait! December twelfth. December twelfth is your hearing. You'll need to call in, do you understand? I'll get the number to you."

"I don't have a pen."

"You don't have a pen." His sigh this time was desperate. "I'll get the number to you."

"Okay."

"Call me every day, Soli," he said. "I don't know what's going to happen from here. I just don't know."

"What does that mean?"

"Let's just hope they don't deport you. I'll see what I can do from here."

"Wait— Where am I?" The line hit a wall of static. "Adrian?" The guard yanked the phone from her and slammed it down.

Wherever she was, Soli knew Adrian wouldn't be able to help her. She'd learned the lesson that all women learn, sooner or later: If there was something to be done, she'd have to do it herself.

Maybe Santa Clara was watching all this from her sickbed, a sad movie on her wall. But there were so many sad movies to watch in that place—why Soli's? Soli had learned from Adrian, weeks earlier, that Silvia was in a detention center in the north of the country. Daniel and Aldo were with their father. Salma had most likely been sent back to Mexico without her children. Her children were with a relative. They would be fine, Adrian said. They're young enough to forget. Maybe he thought this would make Soli feel better.

Life in a detention center was an exercise in waiting, and every second she sat on her ass with nothing to do, every moment she spent wandering the yard like a cow put out to pasture, her grip on Ignacio was slipping. Every second was another second for him to forget her, for the world to close up around the mother who'd left him, until all that remained was a pebbled scab of memory. And when the scab fell away, which of course it would, only new skin would remain, pink and soft, a soft pink world without Soli.

On the day that would change her life again, she was walking through the center of the yard, the sun gazing carelessly, when she noticed a guard notice her. She stopped, planted her feet, and looked back. She thought he would turn away then, but he didn't. She thought he might be looking past her, surveying the prisoners, doing his job. But no. She looked at him, then lowered her head and looked at him hard, and he looked back with eyes sharp enough to shear her skin away.

Let's be clear: This was no romance.

Two nights later, he opened the door of her cell. "Let's go," he said. The two other women in the cell looked at each other and she felt their eyes on her back as she left.

Did she know where this was going? She had an idea.

The guard walked fast, his feet striking hard on the green tile. The ceiling lights bounced off his scalp with each step. He headed for the door and she followed. *He's letting you out*, she told herelf. *He's sending you away.* She whispered the rosary. She had never been outside at night.

The cold in that place was like a shove in the chest. That night was the coldest she'd ever known, but the guard seemed not to notice. He hadn't stopped to put on a coat, and she didn't have one, either.

"This way," he said again, and led her along the side of the building, around a corner, to the side of another building. When they reached the back of a stone cube, they stopped. On one side was wall, on the other, a chain-link fence. He was breathing hard now, puffing clouds of hot air that hung in the night.

"What are you doing?" she asked.

"Take your top off." He backed her up against the stone wall. His fingers slipped under her shirt and she cried out.

"Shut up," he said. "They'll hear you."

39.

Kavya was on the highway, Ignacio asleep in his car seat. She barely registered the route signs and drove by pure avian instinct toward Sacramento, toward safety.

The phone had rung that evening as she walked through the door with Ignacio. Immediately she recognized the static of the Department of Social Services, a very specific tick that made it impossible to fully register what was being said. Joyce's voice rustled through the line.

"Could you repeat that?"

"The mother," Joyce said, "will be pursuing reunification with her son."

"The mother," Kavya said aloud, "will be pursuing reunification with her son."

"That is correct."

But how? Where is she? she wanted to ask. She didn't.

"What does that mean?" she asked instead.

It didn't matter what it meant. Kavya knew what it meant. It meant that someone was coming for Iggy. She asked Joyce for an explanation only because she hoped that somewhere inside it she'd find a loophole to thread herself into. It's just a technicality, Joyce might have said. But she didn't.

"The mother has a lawyer," she heard Joyce say.

As far as Kavya knew, she was Iggy's mother. When and how she'd arrived at this state of certainty, she couldn't say. But there she would stay.

"I need to go," she said, and hung up.

Kavya didn't get a lawyer. Instead, she got her keys. What she'd meant, what Joyce wouldn't have guessed, was that she needed to *go*. Berkeley was suddenly rife with peril. It was a Friday, and Rishi had cycled to the Weebus. Iggy followed her through the house as she gathered diapers and stuffed clothing in a canvas bag. Onesies dripped to the hardwood floor as she went. He trailed behind her and gathered them.

As she drove, she thought about lawyers. If the other mother had one, she would need one. After an hour, she'd reached the brown-and-green plateau that spread before Sacramento, and beyond this, the spray of high-rises that made up its skyline. At its center, a single tower, covered in windows, caught a last gasp of light from the setting sun.

From the end of the driveway, Kavya could see the astonished outline of her mother's head, cocked at the kitchen window and pulsing with attention. She cut the engine as Uma half ran down the drive. She ignored Kavya and headed straight for the backseat, where Iggy sat sleeping.

"Is he all right? What happened? Why you are here?"

Kavya could only stand at her door, shivering, staring across the car at her mother.

She opened her mouth to speak and a cloud of vapor puffed from her lips and startled her into silence. She tried again.

"The mother," she said. "She wants Iggy back."

Beyond the drive, the neighborhood was caught in a soundless winter haze. Christmas lights twinkled on a house across the street, but everything else was still.

"Come inside. It's getting cold."

Uma's kitchen was a laboratory of bubbling pots. A vat of dal spat steam from its lid. She was boiling tea in a saucepan with sugar and milk and cardamom.

"It's not a good idea, Kavya-ma, taking him out on these cold days. At this age, you don't want him to get sick. It's not necessary." Uma carried on as if the news of Iggy's birth mother had stayed on the driveway and bore no relevance to her indoor world. "You know, Kavya, that I am allergic to the cold? It makes me cough like anything, just being in the cold. Definitely it's some kind of allergy."

Kavya hadn't mentioned the pneumonia to her mother, and now she never would. "You can't be allergic to the cold, Amma. That doesn't exist."

"I see. Now you're an expert on existence, is it?"

The two women watched Ignacio run to the far corner and pull from Kavya's bag a plastic shape sorter. He sat with it, pushing square blocks through square holes, round blocks through round holes.

"This one," Uma said, nodding at Ignacio. "See how he's putting the correct shape in the hole? With you, it was always the triangle in the round hole, the square in the triangle hole. Always making things impossible."

Kavya, for a few moments, was letting the thought of the birth mother walk through the room and out the door. What she wanted, there and then, was a cup of tea. Uma stirred the saucepan, her eyes on Ignacio, who'd opened a cupboard and started pulling out Tupperware.

"Kavya, I'm going to say something. Don't get mad."

"Here we go."

"In India, we have a saying." And Uma launched into a series of sentences that Kavya half understood.

Uma translated: "When you make dal for another woman's child, keep it a little bit raw."

And she fell into silence and stirred the tea, coaxing upward its plumes of steam.

"And?"

"Anyway," Uma said. "That's what they say."

Neither spoke for several seconds. Uma was waiting this out, Kavya knew. This was her cue to ask for an explanation. Kavya would not indulge her.

From the stove came a hiss as a fountain of milky tea bubbled over the edge of the saucepan and spilled down its sides, pooling across the stove and sending through the kitchen the smell of lost milk, burnt sugar.

Rishi called at dinnertime. "Where are you?" he asked.

"Hi."

"Are you okay?" A heavy pause. "Are you leaving me?"

She had to smile. "I'm not leaving you."

"Are you sure? What happened to the house?"

Kavya had left a rumpus of half-opened drawers and scattered clothes.

"Rishi?"

"I'm here."

"Joyce called. The mother wants him back."

"What do you mean? You mean the birth mother?"

Kavya didn't answer.

"Can she do that?"

"She's being deported. She wants to take him back with her."

"She can't just decide to do that," he said. "No. No, we'll look into this. I'm sure there's something."

Kavya wanted to believe him. Here was the hope she'd been waiting for. But when Rishi offered it, she couldn't latch on.

"Listen, babe. Where are you?"

"Sacramento."

"Sacramento?"

"It was the only place."

"You packed up with him and went to Sacramento? I don't think you can do that."

"What do you mean?"

"If they find out you picked up Ignacio and ran off with him—"

"Are you going to tell them?" she asked.

"No."

"I'm not on parole. I can take him where I want."

"Are you coming home?"

"I'm staying here for now," she said. "I just need to. I'll be back tomorrow."

RISHI ARRIVED BY TRAIN that night, after Ignacio had gone to bed in a Pack'N Play lined with blankets. They sat at the kitchen counter, Kavya spooning leftover rice and fish onto Rishi's plate. Her parents were in the family room and Tamil soap operas blared from the television.

"You didn't have to come."

"I wouldn't have slept tonight."

"And now you'll sleep?"

"No." He reached across the counter for her hand. "I probably won't."

From the family room came the overamplified slapping sounds of a fight scene. A trumpet flare.

"What happens now?"

"Well," Rishi said, "we get a lawyer. We fight our case." He paused. "We do have a case, you know."

"We do."

He heard himself say the words that a few months ago would have felt untenable. "Iggy's best interests lie with us. Being with us would be the best thing for him." Now he believed it.

"Really?"

"Do you not think so? We could give him back. If that's what you want—" Saying the words sent a trill of fear through him. "If that's what you want, Kavya, that's what we could do."

"No. I'm not going to *give him back.*"

"Good," Rishi said.

"But what about the real mother?"

"The real mother." Rishi ran his fingers over hers, smoothing out the wrinkles around each knuckle. "You taught him to walk. You stayed up with him all those nights. You're a real mother, too."

"I know."

"What we have to do now, Kavya, is we have to engage. If we're going to fight for Ignacio, we've got to run for this bus. Do you get that? We've got to stop thinking about their side, and fight ours. Run for the bus."

Kavya thought about this. "Run for the bus," she said. "We owe him this."

Rishi tensed, nodded. It sounded right coming from her. When she said it, his doubt evaporated. "Yes."

That night, they both lay awake for hours. On her bed with the canopy of yellow flowers, a Boris Becker poster staring down at them, they lay awake and listened to the mutters and chirps that Ignacio made in his sleep. We may never hear them again, Kavya said to herself. This may be one of the last times. Don't be so dramatic. It was Rishi's voice in her head.

Why did people love children who were born to other people? For the same reason they lived in Berkeley, knowing the Big One was coming: because it was a beautiful place to be, and because there was no way to fathom the length or quality of life left to anyone, and because there was no point running from earthquakes into tornadoes, blizzards, terrorist attacks. Because destruction waited around every corner, and turning one corner would only lead to another. So it made sense to stay put, if put was a place like Berkeley, with its throb of lifeblood, of sun and breeze and heart and anger and misplaced enthusiasm. She'd built her love on a fault line, and the first tremors had begun.

The next morning, she woke to the glare of the sun. Rishi was already awake, staring up at the ceiling. He turned to Kavya.

"We'll be fine," he said.

"I believe you."

Kavya had never had a problem speaking up for herself—she'd been an impetuous child, according to her mother, and by college her fighting voice had fully ripened and become her own. Its volume her own. Its California monotone her own. This fight felt right but scared her still.

"There'll be a hearing," Rishi said. "I'm pretty sure we won't be a part of it. It'll be a county thing."

Scarier than the fight was the idea that she wouldn't be allowed to fight. She would be a bystander to her fate. She knew little of what to expect in the coming weeks. She knew only that she couldn't think of losing Iggy. The thought of losing him was blinding. But in her blindness she found certainty, if not clarity.

They set off for Berkeley the next morning. Rishi drove. The outlet malls fell away and they drove past fields and signs for farm-fresh produce. Kavya sat up and pointed at a large, block-printed panel at the side of a field. *Harjeet Bhupinder Orchards.*

"You don't see that every day," Rishi said. "We should take Iggy there one day."

Open weekends, the sign read. Apple picking, pumpkin patch, Christmas trees. Not much surprised Kavya after twenty years in Berkeley, but the name on that sign caught her eye. Not that Indians didn't own land; Indians had a hand in most industries, farming included. It's just that they rarely announced it on a sign. Immigrants were supposed to own things quietly. Proclaiming themselves invited the wrong kind of attention, from the evil eye to more immediate retribution. The surest sign of an immigrant business was an American flag on the door. But perhaps this Harjeet Bhupinder felt secure enough not to worry about that. Maybe with this announced identity came the belief—the very American belief—that success and happiness weren't always temptations of fate.

WHEN SHE GOT TO the sorority Monday afternoon, she found Martina McAfee waiting for her at the kitchen door.

"You're here."

Kavya stopped and placed her bag on the ground. She'd missed work that morning, claiming she had a doctor's appointment. Really, they'd been to a lawyer.

Kavya crossed her arms. "Do you want to discuss something?"

"I do, Kavya. I do need to discuss something. But we don't have the time right now. You've missed two and a half days of work in the last two weeks. Plus your three weeks of family leave. Think about that."

Martina McAfee was wearing a patriotic sweater and red starfish earrings. Her lips cut a thin line across her face.

Kavya nodded. "I'll take that on board."

"Miguel is waiting."

"Thanks." And she pushed past Martina, into the humid well of her kitchen.

"She kick your butt?" Miguel asked.

"Not yet."

"You all right?" Miguel watched her as he chopped a bunch of parsley.

"Eyes on the knife," Kavya said.

They worked in silence until dinner prep was done.

That morning, Rishi and Kavya had walked three blocks, with Ignacio in his stroller, to the office of Eva Cabral. "Here we go," Kavya said. They climbed a set of wooden stairs and knocked on a door.

"Come in," they heard.

At the far end of the room had stood a woman leaning over a desk, rifling through a stack of papers. She wore a red kaftan that swung down to her knees. She'd blinked at them, as if they were no more than three ghosts known to wander the Gourmet Ghetto.

"Is this Eva Cabral's office?"

"I'm Eva Cabral. Yes." She didn't welcome them in. "Are you in the right place?"

"I think so," Kavya said. "We're the Reddys. We called—"

"Oh, *God*," the woman said, and smacked her forehead. "Yes. I'm so sorry. Of course. Come *in*. I was sure we'd planned to meet tomorrow. My assistant's away. Right? Wasn't it tomorrow? Well come in, anyway, have a seat. Let's go back to my office, actually."

Rishi turned to stare at Kavya. She ignored him.

"It may have been tomorrow," she'd said. "I was pretty sure it was today, though."

Rishi took her by the hand and led her through the room.

"So," Eva Cabral said, landing heavily in her armchair. "What seems to be the problem?"

"We're foster parents," Rishi began. "We have a little boy? He's almost two?" He'd said this as if Eva Cabral might have heard of this particular little boy, the almost-two-year-old who lived in North Berkeley.

"You're a foster parent?"

"Yes, I am."

She smiled, at last. "I find that so admirable. You've come to the right place." She frowned. "On the wrong day." She grinned. "Just kidding."

"The thing is, we've run into a problem," Kavya piped in.

"Can you smell that apple pie?" Eva Cabral stood and cranked open her window. "They drive me crazy with that apple pie!" She had the spangle-toothed smile of a PTA president. She beamed at Ignacio, then walked over and took him from Kavya, hitching him onto her hip. Ignacio grunted and wriggled to the floor.

She pulled out a play table and scattered some blocks across it.

"Have a seat," she called to Ignacio loudly, as if speaking to a foreigner. "Toys for you! See the toys?" She sat down herself, set her elbows on the desk and interlaced her fingers.

"So what's up?"

Rishi sighed. Kavya feared he would get up and leave. She had, for some reason, a good feeling about Eva Cabral, so she clutched Rishi's arm and laid out their story, the facts of the hearing and the danger of losing Ignacio for good.

After sitting still and listening, Eva Cabral had agreed that, yes, what they had going for them was the best-interests angle.

She rapped on her desk with long, buffed fingernails. "You're the best parents for him. No question. Not in my mind."

Rishi began to nod.

"But." Eva held up her hand. "But. You two are not actually actors in this decision. I'd be happy to represent you, but we'll be witnesses to that hearing on the twelfth. We'll be spectators. The people talking? They'll be the state, the mother's lawyer, the case worker. We can't sue anyone or file any motions ourselves."

When Kavya looked over, Rishi was still nodding.

"BUT. That doesn't mean we can't be there," Eva Cabral said. "We'll be in that courtroom, the three of us, guns loaded—figuratively speaking, of course—and we'll be *present*.

"This is what we focus on," she continued. She reached out and covered Kavya's hand and Rishi's with each of her own. "Being there. We'll give this our best shot," she said. "And it's a good one."

Rishi leaned in. He and Eva nodded at each other. It may have been a play of the room's fluorescent lights or the fast passage of a wind-blown cloud, but Kavya could feel, from the very heat of his arm, that Rishi had a goal in sight.

IGGY HAD SPENT THE WALK HOME leaning out of his stroller, twist-ing around to watch Kavya.

"Where is it?" he asked.

"Where is what, Iggy?"

"Where is it?"

"What? Where is what?"

"Where *is* it, Mama?" he squealed, his face crumpling with frustra-tion.

Kavya shook her head. "I don't know, Iggy. I don't know where it is. It's all right. Okay?" She turned to Rishi. "He knows something's wrong."

They walked in silence.

"You heard her, didn't you? You heard her say we wouldn't have a say in this."

"But we'll be there, Kavya."

Kavya said nothing.

Home again, Iggy pointed to the window. She let him crank the lever to open it. He pointed to the sky. "Sky," he said.

"Sky!" Kavya repeated. He'd never said the word before. "Sky! *¡Cielo!*" She said it once in Spanish, then stopped herself. "Sky," she re-peated. "Blue sky."

He pointed to the eucalyptus tree that hung from above and yelped with pleasure. "Tree," Kavya said. "Eucalyptus. It smells good, Iggy. It smells like lemons."

Now Miguel leaned against the worktable. "You've been stirring that batter for fifteen minutes." Kavya came to. She'd been watching the mixer spin and lost herself in the airy dance of blades around the bowl. If only she could move so lightly.

"So this is where the handsome sous-chef gives his boss a good talking to," he said. "What's the matter with you, woman?"

"I haven't slept," Kavya said. "For days. Two days. Can I ask you something?"

"Ask me anything." He moved the mixing bowl over a giant cake pan, letting the batter cascade in smooth, even sheets.

"Are you legal?"

He said nothing for a good while, holding the bowl over the pan, staring as the batter ran down to a few desultory glops. He let the bowl drop to the counter, walked back to his work station, put on his gloves, and started hacking a chicken to pieces.

"Oh," Kavya said.

"Not a good thing to ask. Okay?" He hacked away at the chicken. "Am I legal," he muttered. "Are *you* legal? Do I have the legal right to exist? Yes I do."

"That's not what I mean."

"I know what you mean. And I'm telling you. That's just not something you ask."

"Oh."

They worked in silence for a long time, until Miguel said, "It just so happens that I am documented."

She turned to him. "Thanks. Thanks for telling me." She paused. "Do you have a green card?"

"I came over when I was nine," he said. "They gave us asylum."

"Well, good. For you."

He snorted, shook his head.

"Asylum from what?"

"From some fucked-up shit back home, is what." He slammed his knife into a joint, and a chicken leg leapt across the counter. "Why'd you want to know?"

She didn't answer. She'd overstepped another boundary, asking him to justify himself that way.

"I answered your question," he said. "Now answer mine."

"Just wondering," she lied. "I was reading about it. About immigration."

This seemed to satisfy, and they worked side by side as the afternoon wore on, through dinner prep and service, until the kitchen had been cleaned and put to rest, and they parted with a quiet goodbye.

40.

RISHI WAS SUPPOSED TO BE BUILDING AN AIR-FLOW MODEL of the retrofitted programming center. He'd told himself that working from home that morning would allow him to focus. Instead, he found himself drafting a letter. The letter constituted his show of support for his wife, he told himself. He was drafting a letter to the birth mother of Ignacio Castro Valdez, stating their desire to adopt her child. It was a humanizing letter, and Eva Cabral had told him to write it. It would show the birth mother that Kavya and Rishi weren't monsters, that they had Iggy's best interests in mind, that they would give the boy a mother and father's love. "And I'll check it over when you're done," Eva had said.

Hammering faintly, the thought returned that they were being cavalier, assuming their right to Ignacio when his birth mother was very much alive. This was not something that politically sensitive, culturally attuned Berkeleyites did. But in the previous months, Rishi's feelings about Iggy had ballooned in a way that had thrilled and frightened him. He couldn't let go. The thought of losing his boy stirred nausea and terror he hadn't felt since his days volunteering in a hospital. It was making him physically sick.

"You should take the lead, Rishi," Kavya had said. "I can't do this alone."

"What does that mean?"

"You should be leading the fight here. You were almost a lawyer."

"We have Eva."

"Eva's not us. No one cares about this more than us."

Her conviction fed his. It kept him upright in this fight. And yet, there were times when Kavya withdrew from the moment, the house, the world, staring at her hands, blinking rapidly, as if she'd forgotten who and where she was. At times like this, her doubt floated through the room like odorless gas. It filled his head, but he couldn't see it. He couldn't smell or taste or touch it, and therefore couldn't stop it from slipping its fingers beneath him, and tilting his moral ground until Rishi went sliding, dizzy and bracing for a fall. His conscience wagged a finger in those moments, insisting that Rishi had no right to this battle.

He sat staring at his computer screen, unable to conjure a word, even the wrong word. The cursor, a silent metronome, counted down the wasted morning. Some part of him wondered exactly who his wife was, whether she was becoming a person he'd be less likely to love.

And that was it—he couldn't write because he couldn't decide who he was, who his wife was. The Kavya he knew wouldn't take another mother's child. Even if that mother left the child shirtless and cold, barking for attention. But the Kavya he knew couldn't live without Ignacio, either. Losing Iggy would mean losing Kavya, and that was not something he could tolerate. She hadn't been sleeping. She'd barely been eating or speaking. Kavya felt something for the boy that he couldn't see and she couldn't voice.

This much was clear: no matter the contradictions, Rishi would fight through the moral fog. Kavya was blinded. He was not. It would fall to him to parse the darkness. And from this thought, he drew strength.

He tapped one key and then another.

I am writing on behalf of myself and my wife.

The house fell into silence. Footsteps on the sidewalk drifted off. Through the slats of the kitchen window, the sun edged behind a cloud and the room darkened. Even his breathing grew dim.

We are the foster parents of Ignacio Castro Valdez.

41.

The phone rang. Mahendra, Uma. Kavya ignored it. No good could come of her mother at 6:45 on a Saturday morning. Ignacio was awake already, and lay with his knees bent, as long now as the changing table. Kavya slung a wipe between his butt cheeks, folded it expertly, and took another swipe. In the bathroom, washing her hands, her eyes were bruised with exhaustion. The dark circles were badges from a thousand small battles.

At 8 a.m., as she slipped Ignacio into a jacket for a morning walk, the phone rang again. Patel, Preeti. The timing brought with it a sense of urgency.

"Hello?"

"Were you sleeping?"

"I have a toddler. What is it? Are you okay?"

"Have you looked at the newspaper?"

"We don't get one."

"Oh. So your mom called me."

"Sorry," she said, but was beginning to understand that something was wrong.

"It's in the papers. You're in the papers."

"What?"

Preeti paused. "The adoption," she said. *"You."*

Kavya was in the news. She opened her laptop and found the article online. Kavya and Rishi were on the Local page of the *San Francisco Chronicle*, a picture of them from their Mexico trip, the sleek white plains of a boat behind them, wineglasses in hand, toothy and sunsplashed. It was a Facebook photo. *Berkeley couple seeks custody of undocumented immigrant's child.*

The article was hardly a paragraph long. When she tried to read it, the lines slid from her grasp. She hung up the phone.

Rishi lay in bed, his eyes open. She thrust the laptop at him.

"What the . . ." he said. She watched his eyes slip across the lines of text, as befuddled as she was.

"How'd they even know about us?"

"Her lawyer." His eyes flipped to Kavya's. "Or ours. I'll call her now."

Still on his back, he reached for the telephone and dialed. Kavya had a sudden overwhelming urge to absent herself from the phone call that was about to happen, and returned to the living room to find Ignacio waiting patiently, quietly. He smiled at her, and let a single quarter drop from his mouth.

"Jesus Christ," was all she could say. From the bedroom, she heard Rishi's voice rise and drop, and then cease altogether. The biological mother's lawyer had leaked the news.

Later: Uma Mahendra.

"What is the meaning of this, Kavya? Why you put this in the paper?" Apparently, Uma Mahendra kept abreast of her daughter's life by subscribing to her daughter's local paper.

"I didn't, Mom. *I* didn't."

"Who, then? That Rishi? Put him on the phone."

"It wasn't Rishi. It was the other mother's lawyer."

Uma made a spitting sound. "Lawyers," she said. Kavya could only agree. That evening, when the article's existence had settled into her, she looked at it again. It was too short to be either damning or sympathetic. *A Berkeley couple is hoping to be granted custody of their foster son. The toddler is the son of an undocumented immigrant from Mexico, who is currently incarcerated in a detention facility and awaiting deportation. The child is a U.S. citizen.* It went on briefly.

"It's neutral in tone, at least. We should be thankful for that," Eva said over the phone the next day. It was a Sunday, but she'd answered her cell when Kavya called.

For a few days, the story grew quiet and seemed to have vanished. In an election year, in a world at war, her saga was a mere crumb of circumstance. She and Rishi assured each other of this, lying in bed at night and watching the dark together, locking gazes over the breakfast table as Ignacio banged his spoon and fork, staring at each other in the bathroom mirror as toothpaste frothed from their lips. But the calm that settled over their lives was not to last. It seems the big things—war, famine, the economy—get left to work themselves out. It's the crumbs that are picked up and examined, that delineate the path of a struggle.

EVA CALLED WEDNESDAY MORNING. "Kavya," she said, "stay away from campus if you can. And tell Rishi, too. It's nothing to worry about, but there's a student group that got wind of Saturday's article. They contacted me yesterday to let me know what they'd be doing today. Just a demonstration. A peaceful one."

"And what exactly will they be protesting, Eva?" Kavya knew the answer already.

Eva sighed. "There are people out there, Kavya, who think that a birth mother's rights take precedence over all other circumstances. No matter what."

And of course, Kavya went to campus. Thoughts of Martina followed her there, but going to work was not an option. Protests started at noon on Sproul Plaza, she remembered from her student days. As the clock tower played its twelve o'clock carillon, students began to gather. She only counted three at first, and then a fourth. They stood uncertainly around the Free Speech plaque embedded in the plaza floor, and it both pained and pleased Kavya to see that she'd stirred so little rage. And then she heard a distant chant. She turned. From Telegraph Avenue, a crowd advanced, headed by a television cameraman, stumbling backward to stay ahead of the group. At its head was a girl no older than twenty, short and slight. But her voice was big. She didn't need the megaphone she held. When she called out, the mass behind her responded. But like most real protests, this was a scattered affair. They weren't on a film set, so the group moved in weak clusters, not as a cohesive mass. And though they chanted back at the leader, their shouts bounced off trees and faded in the rumble of traffic. But as they neared, two lines, tossed out and sent back, emerged strident and clear above the surrounding noise.

"Blood!"

"Blood!"

"Is thicker than money!"

And as they drew closer, the gaps filled and the crowd grew, body by body, until it was a solid entity with a united voice. Kavya lost her breath to their physical mass. There must have been fifty, sixty of them. She struggled to inhale as they drew in close, barely taking notice of her. Nobody recognized Kavya. She resolved to stand her ground as they pooled around her, and for five seconds—six—she did. And then, to her private dismay, she turned and scampered behind a tree. From behind its trunk, she watched.

The girl in charge began speaking. The megaphone hung at her side, her voice loud enough to carry across the plaza. "Solimar Castro Valdez," she shouted, "is a mother who loves her child. She's also undocumented, so they locked her up in immigrant jail."

The crowd fell silent.

"The Reddys are a couple in Berkeley. They decide they want to adopt. They decide they want Ignacio. Solimar's child. The child of a woman who is *alive* and wants her son *back*. Guess what?"

"What?" someone answered.

"You don't need *a green card* to love your *child*. Only some folks think a *Mastercard* can get them whatever they want!"

Shouts from the crowd.

She raised her index finger to punch out each word. "You can't go around taking what you want just because you've got money and a nice house! Am I right?"

The crowd roared yes.

"Am I right? ¿Sí o no?"

"¡SÍ!"

They don't know how nice my house is, Kavya thought. They don't know if I have money. But there was no one to listen to Kavya. No one on the plaza would be taking her side, and who could expect them to? She was on a side of her own, cowering behind the wide trunk of a redwood, thankfully invisible. She scanned the faces—beautiful and young, strong with the certainty of their beliefs. She'd been one of them once, cushioned at student demonstrations by friends and the ferocity of their beliefs. But those friends had trailed off to other coasts and other lives, their collective steel softened. Now she was the enemy.

If she could have stayed objective, she would have found this funny, astonishing, maybe a tad flattering. They were taking time out of their day to protest *her*. They were young. They were children. And they seemed unshakably sure of themselves. They didn't have to see the gray, these children. They could rest comfortably in the black and white.

Her phone rang.

"Where are you?" Rishi asked.

"At work. Why?"

"Liar."

"What do you mean?"

"Look at the back of the crowd."

"What?"

"Just look."

She peered into the line of bodies, and one of them stepped away from the group, waved, shrugged. Rishi. He motioned for her to join him, to which she shook her head, vigorously, no.

"Come on," he mouthed. She wouldn't.

"Come on!" he shouted. Several people turned to look. Most of them turned away again, but a few continued to stare. Kavya considered running. If she sprinted from her redwood to the grove of oaks nearby, she could vanish onto Telegraph Avenue and reach her car without anyone seeing her.

But this possibility ended a second later, when Rishi, her husband, her chosen partner and target of the afternoon's gathered rage, jogged from the back of the crowd to the front of it, waving down the speaker.

"Rishi!" she shouted. "Get back here!" Her maternal instincts must have kicked in then, because she bounded toward the crowd and found herself, panting, at Rishi's side. "You don't know what you're doing," she said to him. "These are angry people." She pulled but couldn't move him.

"It's them!" she heard someone say. Murmurs grew to shouts and the next Kavya knew, a wall of young, strong, beautiful faces stood shouting, spitting their anger, at her.

"Hold up!" the girl in charge yelled. She raised her megaphone. "Shut up! Silencio!"

The girl took two large, exaggerated steps, and stood hip to hip with Rishi. She looked him up and down, once and then twice, to hoots and laughter from the crowd.

"Now *this* guy," she shouted, "has some *fucking huevos!*" From the bubbling din, a thin wave of laughter, a few more shouts.

"To show up here? To show up *here?*"

She ripped through a Spanish scree that Kavya couldn't understand. Whatever she'd said got the crowd going, and soon the students had joined voices to shout, in perfect unison, *"Baby stealers, go home! Baby stealers, go home!"*

Kavya grabbed Rishi's hand, pulled him away from the crowd. Rishi resisted. "We're going," she growled.

"Go back to your pretty little house, baby stealers!" the girl shouted, her face contorted now with the snarl of a small and vicious bulldog. Her voice rang clear across the plaza, and chased them out the campus gate, onto Telegraph, and back to Kavya's car.

"That's right, Mama, you'd better run for the hills! Get in your beemer and *drive* your asses home!"

42.

His skin was as dark as Soli's. His eyes were two black tunnels. His name tag said D'Cruz. Something was missing from those eyes, a flame extinguished. She wanted to ask him what he'd lost. She wanted to know what cold syrup slid through his veins. He began coming for her at night, when the others had gone to sleep, and soon she found herself waiting for him. Not because she looked forward to it.

The pain of it, the stench and chill and barbed rip of it—these followed her from the cold nights to the sleepy days. She asked herself why she'd locked eyes with the guard. It was a bold and stupid thing to do. She'd done it, she finally decided, because it had seemed, for a mere second, that D'Cruz saw the person in her. And even if she hated and feared him now, she'd grown so accustomed to being nothing, that to be something, even a slave, felt like a key to a secret room. Sometimes she imagined telling Señora Cassidy about this, about what this man was doing to her. "But, Soli!" she would have said, "Soli, honey, you're being *raped*." She would have whispered the last word, circled her long fingers around Soli's arm, looked into her with tea-saucer eyes.

Soli was building up her defenses, getting used to the hands of men traveling where they would. Any man would descend to this, given the right set of circumstances. This place, this country, was no different than back home. Opportunity here was a multi-willed creature. Its tentacles spread in all directions. Some days, she would spot D'Cruz across the yard, watching her. When she looked back at him, he'd turn away.

And then it was December. Outside, the cold could have flung her to the ground. The air was sandpaper against her cheeks, and still, they were forced to roam the yard each day, for thirty minutes after breakfast, after lunch, after dinner. One morning, they were given sweatshirts to wear. And when she zipped hers up, she could hear the winter laughing.

The hearing was approaching. It was ten days away, then seven. The air crackled with cold, waiting for snow. Soli had managed another call. "Call the cell," Adrian said. "It's more reliable than calling the court. We'll figure out a speaker connection."

One night, she was out with the guard. He lay on top of her, the bare tops of his thighs still weighing her down. Her head was on the ground, where the frozen concrete had numbed away the pain. Usually, he got up right away, zipped himself, and walked her back to her cell. That night he didn't move. In the well of her neck, a puddle grew. It was too cold for sweat. Tears or blood. They weren't hers. She twisted her head to look.

No tears, no blood. An icicle had formed on the guard's nose, and was dripping onto her shoulder.

He looked her in the eyes. He wasn't about to move.

"Where are we?" she asked.

"Behind the kitchen," he said.

"But where are we?"

His gaze sharpened. "Washington. Outside Seattle." He got up, she got up. They went inside.

THE NEXT NIGHT: "Is it near California? This place?"

"Is Washington near California?" He frowned. "Some would say yes."

"How can I get back to California?"

"You won't."

. . .

THE NEXT MORNING, there was no line for the phone.

"Shut down," a woman told her. "The phone's shut down."

She turned to a guard. "I need the telephone."

"Shut down," he said. "No telephone today."

December the twelfth was three days away.

The phone line was down the next day, too. Nobody said why.

THE NEXT NIGHT: "I need to get in touch with my lawyer."

D'Cruz sighed. His eyes hardened. She feared she'd said the wrong thing. If she began to bother him, if she pestered him and transformed this arrangement of theirs into something that didn't suit him, he would end it. Her tie to the inside would be gone.

December the twelfth was two days away.

THE NEXT NIGHT: "I need to use the phone," she said to him, and slid her hand up his thigh. "I need to use the phone," she said.

His voice shivered with desire. "I'll see what I can do. Not now." And he said no more.

The next day she did something she'd never dared, and walked up to him in the yard.

"I need something. Remember?"

He dropped a sideways gaze and said nothing.

"I need to contact my lawyer," she said louder, Nacho's small arms around her shoulders urging her on. "I have a hearing tomorrow, re-member? My son?"

"Shut up," he said. "Stop talking to me."

She walked across the yard to the other guard, her own voice echoing in her head. Since the day of the buggy soup, she'd barely heard her own voice; it had withered to a faltering flame, but the thought of Nacho stoked it back to life. A large white man with no hair watched her approach. It seemed that the entire yard had grown silent and turned to watch.

"I need to use the phone," she said.

"Get in line."

"The line has thirty-seven people. I counted."

He smiled down at her. "So you'll be thirty-eight."

The noise of the yard rose and hid her shame. "I have a hearing tomorrow and I need the telephone," she said. "I need to call or I'll lose my son."

This made him smile. He chucked his chin at D'Cruz. "Why don't you ask your buddy over there?"

She turned to look at D'Cruz, and even from that distance she could see his jaw clench.

Turning back to the second guard, she said, "I need your help."

The man leaned down until his breath stung her eyes. "Mexicans," he said. "Always on the lookout for a fuckin' handout." Soli went hard inside. What she saw in that moment—what she would remember always—was the gray, uneven stubble on his poorly shaven chin.

In one corner of the yard, a group of men were juggling with their feet, sending a single rock leaping from their knees to their ankles. In another corner, a row of women sat and talked, rolling pebbles between their fingers. The lunch hour was running down, and then lockdown would begin. She left to wait in line.

One phone, thirty-eight people. The line barely moved, and before long they were sent back to their pods for lockdown. She sat and stared at her two cellmates and they stared back at her. Two hours later, a stampede passed her room. Free time had begun. She waited twenty minutes for someone to unlock her door. And when she was out, the line was bigger than it had been before. She didn't get on the phone that day.

That night, D'Cruz didn't come for her. She lay awake and waited—not for him, but for a sign that something would happen, that the next day would not come and go in silence, that she wouldn't lose her child to a telephone line.

43.

THE BEDROOM DOOR SHUDDERED OPEN, CATCHING ITSELF on the hardwood floor. It was December, and every morning started with a blast of heat through the floor vents that caused the house to bloat and rise against itself. The floor was too high for the door, the door too wide for its frame. Running feet stopped at her bedside, and as she swam up from her dream, she sensed a cloud of heat just inches from her face.

Kavya opened her eyes. Ignacio, his face level with hers. He touched his sleep-warmed forehead to hers. "Iggy," she said, "you're out of bed."

She jolted upright. "How did you get out of your crib? Ignacio?"

Rishi lay beside her, eyes closed.

"How'd you get out, Iggy?"

"He jumped," Rishi mumbled.

"What?"

"He jumped out of his crib. He's been doing it for weeks."

It was Tuesday, the day before the hearing. Kavya had wanted to take the day off, but after she'd missed lunch service on the day of the protest, Martina McAfee warned her another absence would get her fired. She'd asked for Wednesday off, and had explained why. Martina McAfee had asked no questions about the reason for her court date, had only crossed her arms and waited for several seconds. "Okay. But it comes off your paycheck."

She dropped Iggy off at daycare and lingered at the safety gate. Inside the playroom, he sat with a pile of blocks, his back to her, slim and sturdy, his hair flicking the tops of his shoulders. This might have been their last day together. "Iggy!" she called. But Ignacio didn't hear. Already, he'd abandoned his blocks and stood at a train table, pushing a single black locomotive over a wooden hill, past some wooden trees and across a bright red drawbridge.

At Gamma Gamma Pi, the specter of the coming day threw the kitchen into shadow. Kavya kept her coat on for most of the morning. Even the steam from the pasta pot was cold.

"I'll be there with you," Eva Cabral had said. "We'll be a presence in that room, and they'll consider your position because they won't be able to ignore it, with us sitting there."

"Will the mother be there?"

"The birth mother? No. Probably not. But, Kavya, you'll need to keep in mind what your position is."

"I know my position."

She knew she didn't have one.

A fault line. A landslide. A pit. She'd built her love on a deep dark pit, a void in the earth, an abscess of unsanctioned need. The state of California stood by, shovels in hand, waiting to fill it in. But with what? With everything she'd ever wanted? With a lifetime of Ignacio? On Wednesday, that pit would fill with promise, or with the debris of what might have been.

"Hey," she heard. *"Hey."*

She looked over.

"Pot's boiling over."

She grabbed the lid of the vast pasta pot and shrieked at the scalding metal.

Miguel rushed over and lifted the lid with an oven mitt. "Cheap-ass pots, man."

She watched his fingers wrap a wet cloth around her hand.

"What's the matter with you today?"

"Everything." She sighed and said nothing more.

Miguel set to work chopping carrots for his salad. The thud of a blade on wood filled the room. She strained the pasta and shook it into a chafing dish.

And then: "It's my boy. His mother wants him back."

Miguel's knife fell silent. "I know. I heard about it."

"She's being deported. To Mexico."

"And she wants her son back."

"Yes."

When Miguel said it in six blunt words, it sounded simple. The mother wanted her son back. The mother. Her son. Mother, son. Of course she wanted him back.

"So what's happening?"

"There's a hearing tomorrow."

"Oh," he said. "Oh. So. Well."

"What?"

"So if it's her kid, and she's being deported, he goes with her, right?" He put his knife down and turned to face her.

"If you don't think about the fact that he was born here. That he has a *right* to stay here, as an American citizen."

"A right to stay with you, you mean."

"Is there something wrong with that?"

"What about his mother?" He crossed and recrossed his arms. "I mean, it seems simple to me. She wants her kid back, she gets her kid back."

"Yes, Miguel," she snapped. "It's very simple. It's really very simple when you don't think about how this affects me." She looked up at him. "Or Ignacio. Ignacio knows me now. He calls me Mama. This is about what Ignacio wants, too."

"What does Ignacio want?"

Miguel stared at her. From above, she heard the footsteps of descending sisters, summoned to the dining room by the twelve o'clock chimes. Kavya started to answer, but couldn't. She felt what Ignacio wanted; she understood his need fully and precisely, but she couldn't strap words to it. She had no answer for Miguel. She put on her oven gloves, picked up the serving dish, and headed for the kitchen door.

That afternoon, she rushed through dinner prep. As the evening fog began to roll across the kitchen window, she decided she'd had enough. "Cover me," she said to Miguel, untying her apron.

"Cover you?"

"Please, Miguel. *Please.*" She stood before him, apron in hand, and watched him consider. "I'll pay you extra. Twenty. For every hour tonight."

"I don't want your money," he said. He nodded at the door. "Go ahead." She left without another word. At the daycare, she stepped over the safety gate and wrapped Ignacio in her arms. He dug his nose into the curve of her neck and stayed there, as if he knew. And then he wriggled from her grasp and ran back to the train table.

She packed him into the car and drove him to a shopping center in Emeryville. She needed shoes for the hearing the next day; all she had were sneakers, clogs, and stilettos.

"No one'll be looking at your feet," Rishi had said.

"I'll be looking at my feet."

On the way to the shoe store, Kavya paused outside a children's store. In the window display, the faceless plasticine models wore sweaters appliquéd with polar bears and penguins, ice-skating, sledding, striped scarves around their necks.

"These are cute, Iggy. Don't you think?"

Ignacio sat curled over his stroller, sucking voraciously on its nylon-covered T-bar.

"Let's try some on. Come on."

Kavya hadn't been a mother long enough to realize that most mothers didn't take their kids shopping for kids' clothes. Ignacio fussed in the store, wriggled and wheezed, allergic to the very air. When she held a sweater to his chest, he grabbed it and threw it to the ground. He strained against his safety belt. When she released him, he climbed out and slipped under display racks to hide, ducking from rack to rack in a game of cat-and-mouse that left Kavya stranded at the front of the store, childless and calling his name. She finally treaded slowly around the store, quietly enough to escape his ears, and found two brown shoes poking out from under a rack.

"Iggy!" she cried, and fell upon the shoes, wrestling his small body to the ground and tickling him until he screamed with laughter. She didn't care that she was sprawled across the shop floor. She didn't care that other mothers and the store clerks were staring.

She bought Ignacio four sweaters that weren't on sale. They were more expensive than anything she'd bought herself that year.

Leaving the store, she thought about the summer. Summer was six months away and she had nothing for him to wear. She drove him to a large children's store at the edge of town. There, she filled her cart with clothes for that year, the year after that, and the year after that. She cleared the clearance rack. She emptied the shoe rack. She bought Ignacio a pair of sneakers that squeaked when he walked, and another that lit up. She bought him shoes for every year that she might not be with him. She bought him rain boots in three sizes and raincoats in four. She bought him one umbrella, child-sized.

She stockpiled diapers and training diapers, underwear and socks. Footed pajamas and summer pajamas, undershirts and T-shirts and swimming trunks and floaties and an inflatable pool toy shaped like a snail. Diaper rash cream, baby lotion, bath gel. Bath salts that would turn the water every color of the rainbow. A pack of race cars, a box set of Winnie-the-Pooh books, a Spider-Man backpack. A teddy bear, a plush duck, a set of bendable action figures from a movie she'd seen advertised. She bought him a tricycle and cases of crayons, of washable markers, of watercolor paint. A pencil case, binder paper, pencils, and a sharpener. She bought him pads of paper bigger than he was, and coloring books. These she put back, remembering that coloring books stifled creativity. She bought a parenting book on fostering a child's creativity, and a kitchen set complete with a miniature rolling pin and colander. She filled three shopping carts, rolled one to the checkout and ran back for the other two. Two clerks helped her wheel her carts out to the Prius.

They arrived home long after dark, Ignacio wailing with hunger. Rishi raised his eyebrows at her.

"What?" she said. "We were shopping. There's stuff in the car."

He sighed, went out the car, and from the kitchen, shredding cheese for Iggy's quesadilla, she heard her husband's roaring obscenities.

"We needed that stuff," she said, stepping away from him when he stalked into the kitchen. "Iggy needs that stuff."

"Iggy needs this stuff? He'll need some of it when he's twelve! What's gotten into you?"

She shrugged. Her world, after the shopping frenzy, had grown very still.

"Did you get your shoes?"

"I'll wear my clogs."

44.

THE MORNING OF THE HEARING ARRIVED WITH THE SHRIEK of a guard's whistle. Her wake-up call. Soli was at the door before the whistle stopped blowing. She leapt for the corridor.

"Not so fast, Conchita." The guard grabbed the back of her sweatshirt. "You stand here and wait to be counted," he said.

She stood. She waited She was counted. She ran for the phone. Running was prohibited. Let them shoot me, she thought. I won't be walking when they do. She reached the corridor where the phone was kept. No one was waiting!

Only a guard.

"Shut down," she said.

"What?"

"Shut. Down," she said.

"No. No, I need the phone. It's not possible."

"NO PHONE. *Compren-day?*"

But there was a phone. Soli could see the phone. The phone existed.

Soli tried a different tack. "Señora, they are taking my son away from me. I need to call the court. I will lose him. The phone in the office? The office phone?"

Her jaw clenched. "Get back to your cell."

"I need the phone."

Silence.

"I need the phone."

"I'm calling backup." She looked slightly frightened.

"I need the phone!" Soli growled. She shoved the guard to the side and ran for the phone, but the guard was faster and stronger. She tackled Soli to the ground, caught Soli's flying fist, and pinned her arm to her back. She clawed at the guard's face. The woman rolled Soli onto her front, and another guard cuffed her wrists. All she could do was yowl and curse, a cat in a one-sided fight.

"I need the phone," she wept, her body heaving and shuddering.

Arms like a rogue current dragged her down the hall. It took two men to take Soli away, kicking at the walls, her heels scraping along the corridor. One set of hands she recognized. One set of hands had been places on her body she'd never seen with her own eyes. She knew where she was going. She screamed and spat at them. She cursed their mothers and their babies. She pleaded.

"Don't put me there. Please. Don't put me there. Please."

A door opened to a cushioned, sunlit closet. The hands threw her in, and she bounced off a wall and landed hard on the padding.

The door shut.

From a skylight, the sun glared down.

HOURS CAME AND HOURS WENT. Somewhere in Berkeley, people were walking into a room, saying things about Soli and her son. A decision would be made. She didn't move from the floor, but curled into herself, her knees to her belly, her breath steaming down her breasts. The sky above was gray like the cushioned walls. Darker gray, and then black. The night passed. She didn't move.

The only place she could be was no place. The only safe place for her was this soundless void.

December twelfth came and went. Soli stayed in the room for two cycles of white sky and black night. Many hours in, when the hunger in her stomach had spiked and finally numbed, Soli had a vision, flickering on her wall, the hearing in the Berkeley courtroom. Nacho! She could see him in a wooden chair, his fat legs hovering a good foot above the ground. She saw Adrian Alvarez, stalking about the courtroom, speaking in crisp and authoritative English. She could see the judge with kind eyes. The judge would ask for her and see that she was absent. The judge would take stock of this and write it down. Words would stream through that courtroom, weaving and circling and then floating to rest. The judge would finish it all with a decision, a judgment. And this would end it.

She prayed to Santa Clara, she said her rosary, parsing out invisible beads, and she fell asleep, at last. When she awoke, it was daytime. The sun through the skylight had filled her with warmth and she knew— she *knew,* all at once, that Ignacio would return to her. A boy belonged with his mother. It was a biological imperative that every human understood. Adrian Alvarez would have to say nothing. Soli wouldn't have to call. It was a law of all kingdoms—human, animal, heavenly. Children stayed with their mothers.

For two days, she lay on her back and watched the sky change. When the weight of it threatened to crush her, she huddled in the corner and watched food come and go. Her body was a solid block of will—no room for food, none for doubt.

And then they let her out, walked her back to her pod.

"I need the phone," she said to the guard. He shut the door and left.

45.

THE MORNING OF THE HEARING, KAVYA WOKE UP, SHOWERED, dressed, and vomited. It happened so suddenly that she had no time to lunge for a trash can. One second, she was fastening her top button and the next, she found herself covered in a yellow sheet of bile. The white fabric of her blouse clung to her breasts, and she took it off, all of it, her pants, even her underwear, to start again.

When she got to the kitchen, her mother was waiting. She'd asked her to babysit that day, had explained to her the reason for the hearing, the possible outcomes. She could have taken him to daycare, of course, but something in her wanted her mother there, in case things went very badly, in case she needed to come home, quit her job, and crawl into bed for days.

"He had his Cheerios," Uma said, by way of greeting. "This is what you're wearing?"

Rishi looked up from his laptop. "That's what you're wearing?"

She'd found a long black skirt and a black turtleneck sweater to re-place what she'd vomited on. Everything else she had was too casual or too flirty or too something. Her ultimate goal was to clothe herself, to make it to the courthouse and through the hearing.

Iggy sat in his booster chair, his chest and shoulders rising higher over the tabletop than she remembered. "You grew!" Kavya said, unstrapping and lifting him from the chair. He pointed to the living room window. "Should we go see? What's out there?"

She walked him to the window, and like a good parent, she narrated what she saw. She narrated the passersby, the students with backpacks, the homeless woman with her crate, heading to her corner for the day, the comers and goers carrying bags with baguettes shooting from their depths. All the while, she watched Iggy's reflection. She memorized his smell, the firm clutch of his arm around her shoulders. She tried to imagine how it would feel to have him torn from her grasp, to see him recede to nothing, a shadow, and then a memory. The thought made her nauseated. Tears sprang forth and she couldn't stop them. She cried without wiping away her tears. Ignacio was watching her now, searching her eyes, thrusting out his own lower lip and huffing. He swept his palm over one of her cheeks, then the other.

"Kavya," Rishi said. He took the boy from her and she let him. "Let's go. Hey." He paused. "Hey, he'll be fine. Okay? I've got some toast for you."

He handed Iggy to Uma. Uma cooed and sang to him, picked up her bag to search for whatever indulgence she'd smuggled into the home. And before Kavya could say goodbye to Iggy, Rishi pulled her out the door.

Eva Cabral met them outside the courthouse and walked them, hand in hand in hand, to the hearing.

"Familiar faces," Rishi mumbled, and pointed to a group outside the courthouse—the RAZA kids, twenty or so of them, the bulldog leading the charge.

"*Buena suerte, Mama-Papa Mastercard!*" she yelled. Rishi cleared his throat, wrapped an arm around Kavya's shoulders, and led her into the building.

The courtroom was the size of a small classroom, with a slightly raised desk at the front, where the judge sat. She was a young Asian woman, surprisingly young, with short hair dyed blond, and glasses that cut straight across her face. Joyce Jones was there, and two lawyers—one for the child welfare department, one for the birth mother. "No birth mother," Rishi said. Five people Kavya had never seen before sat in the benches behind them.

"They're here for other hearings," Eva explained. "After ours." It hadn't occurred to Kavya that their hearing was just one in a series. They sat down in the front row to watch.

Later that day, that night, the next day and night, lying in bed, eating cereal, soaping her arms in the shower, Kavya would try to piece that hearing together, to reassemble its parts, believing that an hour so crucial couldn't simply slip from her memory, a wasted by-product of the legal system.

First, the birth mother's lawyer spoke. She could remember the sharkskin gray of his suit, the curly brown hair that reminded her of Ignacio's, but she couldn't remember his name. She did remember the way he twirled his pen over his fingers like a propeller, sitting at his table, waiting to speak. "Soli Valdez has proven herself a proficient and loving mother, Your Honor. Her only legal trespass has been to cross the border without immigration documents. Her right to her child cannot be morally questioned, and should not be terminated by the faceless mechanics of the state." He said the things that Miguel had said, and more, packaged with oratorial sheen.

"And where is your client today, Mr. Alvarez?"

"She's being held at the Belle Plain detention facility in Washington State, Your Honor. She was scheduled to phone in, but is most likely being prevented from doing so."

"By whom?"

The lawyer cleared his throat and looked down. "I don't know" was all he could say.

She remembered how surprising it was that the judge spoke during the trial, and asked questions, counterposed arguments, participated in the scrimmage of reason and rhetoric. The judges on television were stern onlookers that barked at interruptions and threatened to find people in contempt. She remembered this judge asking the question she dreaded: "And why shouldn't Ignacio Valdez go back to Mexico if that's where his mother ends up?"

"Your Honor," the county lawyer said, "Ignacio Valdez is a dependent of the state of California now. It's our job to make some tough decisions on his behalf." Kavya had never seen this lawyer before.

The judge asked Joyce to describe the circumstances that Ignacio would find himself in, if he were to be sent back to Mexico.

"The birth mother," Joyce began, "comes from a place called Santa Clara, oh, gosh. Po, po—" Joyce stuttered over a syllable, and then gave up. "Santa Clara is in the Oaxaca region of Mexico."

"And do we know anything about it?" the judge asked.

"Your Honor, it isn't on a map. Not even the regional maps. What we do know is that they've shut the school there, that the village is economically depressed, and that most young adults, like the birth mother, have left it to seek work elsewhere. Many of them have also migrated illegally."

"Is that relevant, Mrs. Jones?" the judge asked.

"Not extensively, Your Honor," Mr. Alvarez cut in.

"Let Mrs. Jones continue, please."

"What we have found is that Ignacio would have a significant lack of male role models in his mother's hometown, Your Honor, aside from the birth mother's aging father. The region itself has had significant problems lately with drug-trafficking gangs and local mafias, which would make this a dangerous environment for a child."

"Has the mother applied for asylum?"

"No, Your Honor."

"Does anyone know why?"

The courtroom looked to the birth mother's lawyer.

He cleared his throat. "It wasn't thought to be—to be a likely outlet, Your Honor."

"So Miss Valdez never mentioned gang violence or drug trafficking."

"No, Your Honor, but that doesn't—"

"Thank you."

"Your Honor." The lawyer stood, placed his pen on the table before him. And then he spoke rhapsodically of his client's devotion, of the truths of motherhood that he couldn't possibly know, that Kavya herself was just discovering. He said things that made perfect sense. He said things that made Kavya's hope sink into a mulchy pit. And for a good long while, the judge let him. Beside her, Rishi shook his head.

"Thank you, counsel. Now would you please let us continue?"

The lawyer sat.

"Mrs. Jones?"

Joyce Jones continued. "We'd be sending him to a virtual war zone, Your Honor. If the violence hasn't reached—" She paused to look down at her notebook. "If it hasn't reached Santa Clara yet, then it's only a matter of time."

The mother's lawyer cut in again. "We'd be wrong to send him back there, Your Honor, after his mother gave up everything to get herself here. To give her child the opportunities he wouldn't have in Mexico."

"Are you recommending that the mother stay, too?"

This worried Kavya. The judge seemed to be advocating for the birth mother. For Miss Valdez.

"Of course it would be better if the mother stayed," the state lawyer said. Kavya squeezed Rishi's hand and he squeezed back, nearly crushing her. "In an ideal world, Your Honor, the mother would stay, the child would stay, we'd have housing support for everyone. But we're not going to turn immigration policy on its head here, are we? This is a dependency court."

"I'm aware of what sort of court this is." The judge fell quiet for several moments, running a pen across her stack of paper.

"Can you speak to the quality of the foster parents, Mrs. Jones?"

"The foster parents are present, Your Honor." Kavya could barely breathe.

"And?"

"They are gainfully employed, and own their own home. They've issued a written statement of their commitment to the child. They are married and financially stable, and live in a part of Berkeley with very good schools and cultural opportunities."

"And where are the foster parents?"

The lawyers and Joyce turned to look at Kavya and Rishi. Rishi nodded. Kavya started to stand, but Rishi held her down. The judge blinked rapidly, her eyelids fluttering over them. The eyes at the front of the courtroom rested on them for an interminable stretch of time, and just when Kavya thought her nausea would spill over, they turned away again.

"Thank you."

What Kavya remembered next was the judge sitting back and sighing.

"My job," she said, "in cases like this, is to uphold the existing policies of California child welfare, and to allow the child welfare system to operate within the framework of existing law. The state will treat Ignacio Valdez as it treats all dependents, regardless of his mother's status. My understanding is that the birth mother of Ignacio Valdez has not pursued any of the requirements of her reunification plan. I must also take into account that Miss Valdez is not present, either in person or via telephone. It's unfortunately not my place to consider why Miss Valdez has not attended the stipulated courses, or pursued recommended counseling. The simple fact is that she has not. It is not my place, either, to consider where Miss Valdez is now, or why she hasn't been able to participate in today's hearing."

The judge paused here. She tapped her pen on her desk, watched it pendulate from side to side, and seemed to lose herself for a few moments in the rhythm of this.

"My finding is that Ignacio Castro Valdez shall, at this time, remain with his foster parents"—here, the judge looked down at her sheet— "Kavya and Rishi Reddy." Their names rang through the courtroom, and Kavya felt her chest flush itself of breath. She'd been holding it in since the judge started talking.

The judge went on: "A follow-up hearing will be scheduled for six months from now, to reassess the case and decide whether termination of the birth mother's parental rights would be appropriate. For now, the court grants custody of Ignacio Castro Valdez to his foster parents." She banged her gavel.

46.

Two days later.

"Adrian. What happened?"

"Soli. What happened? Why didn't you call?"

"They wouldn't let me use the phone. Why didn't you call here?"

"I tried. They wouldn't let me speak to you."

"So." She squeezed her eyes shut. "What happened?"

A pause. "The foster parents were granted continued custody, Soli. They'll be pursuing adoption."

She collapsed into the wall. Only the phone cord held her up, but she wouldn't let go. "What does that mean?"

"It means you need to stay in the country. As long as you don't get deported, we have a chance."

"And if I do get deported?"

"If your removal proceedings go through, then you'll be sent to Mexico. And you'll have to fight this case from there. Is that a possibility for you? Would you be able to do that?"

The impossibility of this nearly sank her. "What next?"

"Just hold on, Soli. Stay where you are, and we'll figure this out."

She put the phone down before Adrian could say more.

That night, D'Cruz came for her. They were outside, arms crossed against the cold. "Where am I going from here?" she asked him.

"Back to your country."

"When? When are they sending me?"

"Any day now," he said, and ran a finger down Soli's cheek.

"I have a son," she said.

"So do I."

"If they're sending me back, I need to be with him. I need him with me."

"Where's he now?" he asked.

"With some people. I don't know them."

For a moment, he looked sad for her, and then he wiped this away and lay down on his back. "Take off your pants," he said. "Let's finish."

She let D'Cruz take her that night and the next night because it was all she could do; she told herself that if she served a purpose, then perhaps she'd get to stay in this jail, this country, for another week, another month, long enough to fight.

Sometimes Soli didn't know whether to be thankful, or whether to tell this country, her country, theirs, to go to hell. All she knew was that, one night, things worked out. Santa Clara was looking out for her hometown girl.

D'Cruz came to get her, as always. As always, they stopped outside the kitchen.

"Are you cold?"

What a question to ask, she thought, in the middle of this place, in December.

He slipped a key from his pocket and opened the door of the building behind them. Inside, the air smelled like steam and the floor was wet. A long steel table split the room in two, and at one end stood a gleaming metal door.

"Solimar," he said. She turned to look at him. He'd never said her name before.

"What are we doing here?" she asked.

He answered by grabbing her around the chest and hoisting her to the countertop. "The floor's wet," he said. He climbed on top of her and they lay flat on the metal table.

As he yanked down his pants and jabbed himself into her, she let her eyes roam. Above were skylights that let in the moon. A wispy night cloud passed overhead. Just to her right was a window. And beyond it, a gift.

What must Santa Clara have thought that miraculous morning, lying sick in bed, as the mass first flickered on her wall? She must have thought she was dying, or that the Lord had seen her at last, that she'd been blessed beyond her deserving. What Soli saw beyond the kitchen window, naked from the waist down and leaning painfully on her elbows, were trees. Trees for miles, and nothing else. No fences, no watchtowers. They must have thought an inmate would never make it as far as the kitchen. In the far distance were the gray spires of a factory, a plume of smoke. But before this, only forest. As the guard howled and gushed out his insides and whispered, *Thank you, thank you,* Solimar built a plan.

He leaned heavily on her, panting, swallowing hard. She was waiting quietly, as she'd learned to do, when a flash caught her eye. Stuck to a metal bar, glinting, whistling with reflected light, was a row of knives. From meat cleavers to serrated saws to long thin blades. She would need just one. Just one small knife. Something to cut an apple with. Something someone would take on a picnic. But her pants were pocketless. They'd taken away her bra.

They were dressing again, hopping into their underwear and pulling up their pants. The cold through her toes was furious. When the guard bent down to tie his shoes, Soli held her breath and swiped for the wall. A few minutes later, they headed back, the guard walking slow and cool. Soli followed, her heart hammering. Stuck into the bushel of her ponytail was a knife, the smallest of the bunch, the kind you'd take on a woodland stroll.

SHE SPENT THE REST OF THE NIGHT AWAKE, listening to the ants pass in and out of the crumbling brick corners of her cell. She bit into her wrist until she left teeth marks, hoping to chew through her mistakes, to chew a tunnel back in time to the day she'd lost Saoirse at the playground.

She spent the morning on her knees, praying that she wouldn't be sent away that day. She listened for the heavy tread of a guard, the clack of keys in her door. None came. Praying for the first time in such a long time was like trying to remember the words to a childhood song. The world crept in, and the Devil, pulling her thoughts to pieces. She had trouble focusing on anything but the knife beneath her mattress.

They know, she had told herself. They know about the knife. How could they not? They would have looked for it in the morning and seen it wasn't there. They would have suspected a prisoner, of course. And they'd have cameras in that kitchen. Of course they'd have cameras. This was a prison. At last, she was turning into the criminal they'd said she was. You did a bad thing, the Devil said. He knows, your guard. He know's what you've been up to. Stealing. Lying. They'll take you away, the Devil said. You'll never see Ignacio again.

That day in the yard, Soli tried to catch her guard's eye. She wanted him to smile at her. Even a look would have made her feel better. But he gave her nothing.

I'm over, she told herself. I'm doomed. At dinner, her stomach ached terribly.

And then came the night. She waited at her door. There was no clock in that room, but she tapped the seconds off with her toe. She tapped out one hour. Three thousand, six hundred taps of a toe. Two hours passed. The knife sat tucked into the waistband of her panties. With every movement, the tip of its blade twitched against the cleave of her behind. She tapped her toe 21,693 times. At the base of her neck, in the heavy hang of her cheeks, she felt the morning. The tears were too tired to come, but the sorrow arrived, silent and dry.

And then she heard a key at the end of the corridor. Footsteps. His footsteps. She knew them from the way his hips moved. He walked, always, like he was going to a dance club. Hope flickered at the base of her spine. Footsteps at her door. A key in the lock. An open door. D'Cruz.

She tried to smile.

He didn't smile back. She reached for his hand but he flicked it away. You're trying too hard, she warned herself. He marched her out to the kitchen, pushed her to the countertop, and before she could draw a breath he crammed his lips to hers.

He whispered in her ear: "I know what you're doing."

At the dip between her buttocks, the blade of the knife slipped into her skin. She gasped.

"I know you're trying to trap me," he said. "I won't fall in love with you, puta," he said. "You're just my whore, you got that? You won't get out through me."

Her guard broke away from her. He sulked like a little boy, leaning against the counter, his arms across his chest.

Through the window in the ceiling, the moon shone down. She stepped into its square of light. She tried to speak, but her breath caught in her throat.

He sniffed. "They're taking you tomorrow."

She stopped herself from crying out.

"Take your pants off."

She had practiced what to say, and now the words, thankfully, found their own way out. "Wait. Let me do this."

She reached for his belt buckle, fingers fumbling. *Dios te salve Maria.* She prayed to steady her breath. *Madre*—*dulzura y esperanza.* Leather slipped from metal and the belt came loose. In that moonlit kitchen the only sound was the steamed breathing of D'Cruz. Beneath this, she could barely hear the soft scratch of the knife against her back, the slip of blood between her buttocks as the blade, with every movement, angled into her skin.

She undid his button. She brought down the zipper. Tooth by tooth. *A ti clamamos . . .*

"You're praying?" he asked.

She squeezed her eyes shut.

Y después de este destierro . . .

Just then, she felt a shift in D'Cruz, a pulling away. He was looking at her. He was seeing her at last. Through a heady cloud of fear, she sensed the foment of knowledge. The air in the room was icy clear. He knew. Danger sliced through her, an immaculate blade. She slid the knife from her pants—*Dios me salve!*—and slammed it into the inner flank of his thigh.

The cry rose to a scream. It echoed through the kitchen. The scream of the beast. Soli knew it well. It rose to the moon. It flooded the room. She climbed to the counter. Cranked open the window. She jumped. She was gone.

47.

Dawn leaked like a rumor through the sky. Threads of daylight sweetened the dark, no streetlights, only the moon. The sky here spread free from the business of buildings and fences and crossing power lines. It had been a long time since she'd seen daybreak.

She started off running. Winter in Washington was not a kind place. Not for a girl in a sweatshirt and nowhere to go. She ran for minutes, for hours or years. She ran until the dogs in her head stopped barking. And then she stopped and turned and found that she was alone. For the first time since she'd arrived in this country, she was beautifully alone. There was nobody. And if there were, they wouldn't know who she was, or care.

On that road, the ground was all rock, broken highway that no one cared for. These were the charcoal cousins of the rocks in Popocalco, no problem for her feet. Rocky ground, she could navigate. It was the smooth that made her stumble.

Nobody has heard of Solimar Castro Valdez, the woman who escaped from immigrant detention. If you ask the authorities, she doesn't exist. Detention centers don't lose inmates. If you ask for her record, they'll shut the door on you. If you ask the Cassidys, they'll tell you, truthfully, that they know nothing. She walked until she saw, on the horizon, a glorious golden *M*. It glowed in the distance like the holy manger. As she drew closer, the rush of highway traffic grew louder. And when she reached its doorway, her hunger wrenched to life. She stood in the clean, sacred light of a streetlamp.

A woman in a duffel coat stood at the door, blowing into a steaming paper cup. Her hair was pulled into a tight brown ponytail, her face pillowy and windblown. "Just opened," she said, gazing into her cup. "Breakfast time, huh?" She looked up at Soli as she said this. And that's when she saw her. What the woman saw: her plain gray sweatsuit, a wolfish glint in her eyes, the shadow of hunger, and the smudge of blood across her cheek. She looked at Soli's hands and saw them shaking.

She'd forgotten how it felt to be seen. It scared the love of God from Soli. She turned and ran.

"Wait!" the woman called. "Stop!" She ran after her, her footsteps heavy and off rhythm. Soli turned to see her bent over her spilled cup, shaking coffee from her fingers. She raised an arm in a wide wave. "It's all right," she called. "I'm all right."

Soli stopped. If the woman pulled out a phone, she would run again.

"You can't be out here," she panted, approaching. "We need to get you inside."

Soli kept going. It was safer outside than in.

The woman caught up with her and took her by the sleeve. "You cannot be out here dressed like that, my girl."

She pulled her by the sleeve to her car. "Get in," she said. "We'll get you some food."

If you asked the Cassidys, they would tell you she was loved.

The woman came back out with a paper bag that warmed the car. "Egg muffin 'n' fries and a coffee," she said.

Soli hadn't eaten since the day before and she tore at the food before she could question who this woman was and why she was feeding her, or what would become of her now that she was in this car. The woman watched Soli eat. "Wild as a wolf," she said, and started the engine.

This much she'd learned: Strangers could astonish with their kindness. Strangers could be savage. But no matter what, strangers never disappointed, because she expected nothing from them. It was the people she knew, who liked and even loved her, who could let her down most cruelly. And she could let them down, too.

The woman didn't ask for Soli's name or offer hers.

The woman with the windblown face drove down the highway, surrounded by woods, until she came to the concrete edge of a city, with skyscrapers in the distance. She parked before a squat yellow building with a sprawling, fenced-in yard at the back. A chicken scooted across it, bobbing her chin.

"Is this the police?" Soli asked, ready to run.

"Honey. No."

A man came out who stood almost taller than the doorway. He wore jeans and a green shirt, and over this, a soft gray bathrobe.

"Hang on," he said, and disappeared into the house. He came back wearing glasses. "Can she pluck a chicken?"

"She sure can," answered the woman.

He nodded at Soli. "What's your name?"

"Clara."

"Clara, go down to the kitchen door and tell them you're on prep. Tell them I sent you."

And when he stopped talking, he seemed to focus in a new way. He looked her up and down, he saw what she was wearing. "We'll get you some better clothes," he said. "To start you off." He nodded and closed the door. His footsteps faded away.

His name was Elmer, and he was good.

Elmer owned the Pick-a-Chicken, the only one in America and possibly the world. It was a place both top secret and wildly popular. The idea was that customers walked into a yard to find the chicken they were going to eat. They didn't kill it themselves, but they did see their food alive before they ate it.

"It's honest eating," Elmer told her. "It's conscious carnivorism, you know what I mean?"

She nodded, and was only half lying. In Berkeley, there were plenty of people who cared about animals but still ate them. Brett Cassidy would have stood in line for a chicken he could talk to. Still, even if a customer picked up his chicken and stared into its narrow little face and said, *Chicken, I'm going to eat you now,* the fact didn't change that an animal was being slaughtered so that someone from Seattle could eat it.

And this place, this Pick-a-Chicken, was never empty. Customers, sometimes famous ones, waited in a line out the door. When a famous one came in, he got seated right away and the waiters started whispering and grinning like idiots. And that's when they yelled at the workers in back, for taking too long or underseasoning a chicken or leaving a drip of sauce on the rim of a plate. You'd think that no one would want to pick a chicken. You would be wrong.

There were too many people in that kitchen; Elmer just kept taking them in, as long as there was work to do and customers out the door. Iselda was another plucker, and Meera ran the rotisserie. Alejo was a fryer in the kitchen and Alfred a dishwasher. Bobby and Romeo were on slaughter. Mostly they were covered in blood and kept to themselves.

Soli made just enough to buy food and build slowly the stash of money that would take her back to Nacho. She spoke to Mama and Papi the day she arrived. "I'm okay," she'd said. "They've let me out." There was far too much to say, so she left it at that.

Then she dialed Adrian Alvarez's number from the rickety pay phone outside the restaurant.

"Where's my child?"

"He's with his foster family, Soli. The Reddys."

"The Readys?"

"The Reddys."

Adrian spelled for her their full names. They lived in Berkeley.

"How did you get out?"

She told him, and it thrilled and frightened her to speak aloud of what she'd done.

He whispered a string of curses, and then, "Really? You're telling the truth?"

"Please," she said. "I need to find him now."

"Soli, I'd strongly advise you not to contact the Reddys. That could make things very complicated for you, even if you don't officially exist."

"But you know," she said. "I never officially existed here. Did I?"

"They're good people, Soli. I know that probably doesn't help you now, but they're doing their best for Ignacio. Not all foster families do, you know? The mother speaks Spanish with him—"

"I am the mother."

"You're right." He paused. "Are you safe, Soli? Where are you?"

"I'm Clara now. Not Soli."

"Clara. Okay. What's your new last name?"

"That's a good question, Adrian Alvarez."

Elmer gave his workers apartments above the restaurant and they lived two or three to a room. There were seven others in Soli's apartment. It was crowded, but the alternative was to live silent and alone on that forgotten edge of Seattle. They worked until late, but the mornings were theirs, and they could go where they wanted, as long as they were back in the kitchen by noon.

"If there's a knock on the door," Iselda told Soli, "never answer it. None of us knock on the door, okay? So if anyone does, it's La Migra. And you climb out the window. You hide on the roof if you have to."

One evening, as they mopped the kitchen floor, Soli told Iselda about Ignacio, about all she'd lost, about what she'd done to the guard. She'd grown to like Iselda and her quiet ways. As she spoke, Soli felt a few brave petals open within her, the first to feel the sun again. Iselda had leaned her mop against the wall and stared.

"Please," Soli had said. "Keep it to yourself."

Iselda shook her head.

"Please, Iselda. Tell no one."

Iselda walked over to Soli. "We've all been through things," she said. She took Soli's mop from her. "Go get some rest."

The next morning, as Soli sat up in bed, still registering the day, Iselda stepped into the room with a cup of coffee. She lay a gentle hand on her shoulder. "New day, m'ija. Sí?"

48.

IGNACIO TURNED TWO IN MARCH. KAVYA THREW A PARTY
for him and invited his daycare friends, children she'd only seen in passing, from the safety gate, and parents she'd never spoken to. A hearing
was scheduled for June. They would travel to the same courthouse, this
time with Ignacio. A judge—maybe the same one—would ask fewer
questions. She would terminate the rights of Ignacio's birth mother.
Rishi and Kavya would start their adoption proceedings. Ignacio would
be theirs.

Sometimes Kavya caught herself watching her husband and her son
as if they were a film, a fleeting series of rapidly flipping stills that one
day would flip into silence and darkness. She tried to catch these moments before they flipped away. *Remember this*, she'd tell herself, when
she and Rishi and Iggy lay in bed together on a weekday morning, all of
them a little too warm, a little too lazy to get up and start their day.
Remember this, she'd think, when Iggy tasted his first anchovy-stuffed
olive, smacking his lips with surprise. *Remember this*, when Iggy climbed
into her lap and held her around the chest, let her bury her nose in his
hair. Someday, he would be too old.

There were times when she thought about the greater balance of
things, when her karmic calculator reared its meddlesome head. She
wondered if she'd suffered enough. She knew there were others, others

very close, who had suffered unspeakably so that she could carry on with her happy and healthy days. Sometimes she imagined her world jolting and reeling, toppling down a hillside. She imagined the Big One—if not *the* Big One, then *a* Big One—ramming into the gentle percussion of her days, demolishing what was hers. There were times, when she found a cluster of fruit flies on a banana or when a chill wind blew under the door and through the house, that she wondered if things had worked out too well, whether a reckoning was on its way, when it would arrive, and how.

49.

THERE WERE DAYS WHEN SOLI'S ONLY GOAL WAS TO PLUCK each chicken to its naked base and reveal the pure, pimpled flesh beneath. Every bird, stripped of its workaday jacket, was a bird set free. Hers was a small life, but noble in its simplicity. The customers, they came, they ate their chickens, and they went home. They were happy to have eaten, and Soli and the others were glad enough to have worked, to have been able to clean up, lock up, and go home. And if, one day, the rap at the door found them, the flash of a badge, they would scatter to the wind like dandelion seeds, and push their roots down elsewhere. They would start new lives, and new lives again.

Those first days, Soli had wanted out. She had felt fearful and wild, an animal that ruptured its chains, a mother rabid for her child. But as she settled into the routines of freedom and work, she realized that getting back to Ignacio wouldn't be easy. She couldn't show up penniless and planless. The Pick-a-Chicken would be a place to recuperate and make money, to remember the human ways.

Elmer used to watch her when he thought she couldn't see. He had money, yes. One day, he asked her if she'd like to go to another restaurant with him. To eat with him, not to work. He said it just like that, gruff and nervous. To eat. Not to work.

She told him no. And thank you. She watched the rapid flutter of his lashes, and she wanted to change her mind to save him from this embarrassment. "Watch out," Iselda said when Soli told her. "Men don't like the word no. If he asks you again, say yes. Or he'll find a way to make life hard for you."

Elmer never asked Soli again, and her life stayed more or less the same.

She showed up in Elmer's office one afternoon. The money from a few weeks' work had roused in her the first peeps of confidence. He offered her a seat.

"I need to find a telephone number," she said. "Can you help me?"

He scooted his chair into his desk. "Sure thing." She showed him the names she'd etched into her palm. And within seconds, a few clicks, an answer. He wrote it down and slid it her way.

"Thank you."

He gave her a thumbs-up.

As she stepped out the door, he said, "Clara."

"Yes?"

"Stay out of trouble."

It took her three days to find the courage to dial the numbers. The area code was comforting. Soli could see the woman before she heard her voice: ski jacket and jeans, flat shoes, fresh skin, and bright eyes. Her phone rang three times.

"Hello."

Her throat collapsed and the words slipped away.

"Hello-o," the woman repeated. *"Hello?"*

Soli hung up, then dialed again. When the woman answered, she disconnected again. She didn't have her words. Not in English.

"Hello? Who is this?"

And she forced out the sentence. "This is the mother of Ignacio Castro Valdez," she said, descending immediately into tears.

The phone clicked, and the woman was gone.

"You can't hang up on me," she said. The dial tone hummed in response. "You can't hang up on me!" She said it again and again, hoping the repetition would make it so, until she was shouting it. She felt the foghorn of her voice rise from her throat. And when the dial tone clicked into silence, she was hardly there to hear it.

Soli was a spider dangling from its own weak thread. She was crying now through bared teeth, kicking uselessly at the walls of the phone booth. Two arms pulled her from the booth and held her until she stopped shaking. When she realized where she was, she saw that her palms were wrapped around her elbows, held in place by two large hands. Elmer had found Soli, her web torn. His shirt sleeves were soaked. They stood, unmoving, for many minutes, until the rise and fall of his chest brought her back again.

"I need to get back."

"I know."

LATER, IN ELMER'S OFFICE.

"I need the money, señor. To get back to my son."

He sighed, scratched at something on the surface of his desk. "Clara, you all need money. All of you. If I gave you money? Then what? How'll I say no to the others? What makes you different from them?"

She stared into her lap. He was right. She'd had the chance to set herself apart from the others, and she hadn't taken it.

"And how do you figure to get back to California?"

"I'll fly. I'll drive. I'll walk."

He smiled. "And? You arrive. And what do you do?"

"I take my son back."

"How? Will they give him back? Will you kidnap him?"

"When he sees me, he will know me."

"Will he?"

She let this question take its place in the room.

"And if he does? Where'll you live, Clara? What'll you do?"

For this, she definitely had no answer.

A new thought came to her. "Can I see them?"

"See them. Their picture?"

She nodded.

"Easy," Elmer said. He clicked and tapped. And there they were, the people who were keeping him, their cheeks pressed close, two wineglasses held between them, their sky awash in gold.

"But they're not even American."

Soli and Elmer sat in silence.

"Save your money, Clara." He tapped on his keyboard, and turned the screen to her. "See that? Seattle to San Francisco. Bus fare. This is all you need."

Soli sat up straight. One hundred and forty-five dollars. "I can make that," she said. She had one hundred and seven rolled into a Band-Aid box in her room.

"And then you'll need some more to live—to eat." He smiled. "You'll have a little mouth to feed."

SHE DIDN'T CALL HER PARENTS OFTEN, but when she did, she'd say, "Times are hard, Mama."

And they'd say, "What's happening?"

She'd been through an opera of small hells and made it out the other side, but all she said was "I'm fine. Everything's fine. I'm working in a new place now, and I'll send something soon." They knew only that Soli had been locked up, then let out, and that now Silvia was in a bona fide American jail. It was the new family shame, and no one discussed it.

"Don't worry about us," they'd say. And she yearned for them when

they said that. "You've done so much for us. Think about coming home."
What she couldn't tell them was that she couldn't come home without
her child.

ONE MORNING twelve weeks after she'd arrived, she entered Elmer's
office. "I have the money," she said. "I'm going."

Elmer sat back. "Well," he said, and nothing more. He let his eyes
rest on her face, her hair.

"I see you cross yourself every morning." He opened a drawer in his
desk and from it drew a string of beads. "I don't use these anymore, but
I've held on to them. Can't very well throw out a rosary, can you?" He
held up the polished spheres of honey-colored wood, anchored by a cross.

"It's yours." He poured the beads into a small heap on the table.

"Thank you," she said, and wrapped them around her palm.

"Your name means 'clear and bright,' Clara."

She nodded.

"It's the name of a saint," she added. "She watches over my town. She
is the saint of television."

A grin, a gap between his front teeth. And then he stopped smiling,
leaned forward, and said, "Who's going to watch over you, Clara?"

She fingered the beads, rubbed smooth now by someone else's circu-
lar prayers. "Thank you for this." And she broke out into the day, clear
and bright. The winter was weakening and the sun sparked through the
branches of the trees, stoked by the fuzz of nascent leaves. A solemn
wind blew the hair off her shoulders. It was a wind that didn't chill, that
simply made its way north. It was a Popocalco wind.

Already, the buds of sanguinaria were emerging. Their tight ivory
petals still cowered from the cold, waiting for a warmer day to open. In
America, they called it blood root. This sounded to her like raw birth,

the crimson shreds that followed in the wake of new life. To her, this had nothing to do with the actual flower, simple and white with a yellow stamen, as unmarked as a new soul. Soon, the spring would ram its hard little head into the world. And she'd be back where she started.

Inside, Ignacio's old cells pattered through her. They ran and leapt. They played escondido. They were hers to keep, his gift.

50.

WASHINGTON MORNINGS WERE THE STILLEST SHE'D KNOWN.
She woke most days to a thick gel of silence, no trains or early joggers.
But on her final morning: a sudden crunch of leaves. A hiss at the window: Alejo. "It's time." Iselda rose from her bed and ran a towel under
the tap in their room. She swiped it across Soli's forehead, over her
cheeks and chin, dabbed softly at her eyes, a gentle communion. In Iselda's eyes, dark specks marred the white, one shaped like a bird, another as brown and square as a piece of toast. Soli would remember
these. Iselda knelt with Soli as she closed the suitcase she'd bought from
the local Goodwill, and helped her yank the zipper around a stubborn
corner. When she started to rise, Iselda grabbed her by the forearms.

"Not yet," she said. "We should pray." They took out their rosaries
and said the *Padre Nuestro* one time, and once again. Another hiss from
the window, Alejo growing impatient. "It really is time," Iselda said.
She kissed Soli's cross and folded the rosary into her hand. She held her
close and whispered a final blessing, then pushed her out the door. In
the minutes before dawn, the sky was bitter blue, the leaves shivered
black on their branches. Alejo waited with his engine running.

Just weeks before, this trip had felt impossible, but now she saw that
impossibility was only ignorance shrouded by poverty. Over ten hours,
a somersault of day and night, she would travel down the haunch of this

country, back to California, Berkeley, Ignacio. Still, seated on the Greyhound bus, a firm clasp on her ticket, she expected something to happen. The yank of the leash. The brusque American *Hey!* It could have come from anyone. The bus driver? Or one of the passengers—surely one of these people would sense that she was a false woman, a runner, a stabber, a chicken stripper.

Her incredulity shrank with every passing hour. She cataloged all she'd been through—prison and escape and the weeks and weeks of dollars stashed away—to make it seem real. She thought back to the day she'd given birth, the victory of it. Her ribs ached with desire. At the twelfth hour, she saw in the distance the glassy bay, the graceful swoop of the Golden Gate, and she knew she was home. The road rumbled beneath her, forward propulsion that grounded her to her mission. She would arrive.

At sunset, Soli was back in Berkeley. The city that day was covered in clouds, but nothing about it had changed. The first thing she did was find the house. Elmer had tracked down the address. It stood three streets from the Cassidys'. All this time, these people had been three streets away, waiting.

She had arrived, yes, but wouldn't truly be home until she glimpsed her son, if even for just a moment. That first night, she lingered on the corner of their street, breathless with the thought of seeing him again. He never came out. He would have been sleeping by that evening hour, her well-kept boy, trained to a healthy routine. She left her suitcase against the outer wall of the old familiar bakery, just around the corner. She found a bin of buns and pastries—almost new, a little stale.

Make no mistake. She had a plan. Every step of it balanced on a crumbling precipice of good fortune, but she decided that she'd had enough bad fortune. Her good luck must have gathered like the dollars in her Band-Aid box. But then, she thought, gazing at the house door and willing it to open, perhaps she'd been lucky all along—to escape the prison, to find Elmer, to save her money and spend it, to find herself back here, just feet from her boy, in a neighborhood that was practically hers.

"I think a shelter must have closed," Rishi said, drawing the blinds. "I've been seeing more homeless people around. New ones."

"Huh. Hopefully it's a shelter and not a mental hospital."

"I'll talk to the police when I get a chance. They shouldn't be on our street. They're supposed to stay on Shattuck, right?"

Kavya shrugged. "Is that the rule?"

Rishi parted the blinds again with his fingers, but the woman who'd been lingering on the corner, young, with long hair, clean-looking, maybe newly homeless, was gone.

Soli waited for the night to deepen, for the hour when the main street was quiet and the windows dark. An occasional car passed. In the distance, a siren rose and wound itself back down. Living her quiet non-life in Washington, plucking chickens and waiting, she'd been doing more than she realized. She'd spent those days remembering how to climb a moving train, gathering her propensity for action over wisdom.

A small part of her, the well-mannered girl her parents had raised, was horrified. But the rest of Soli wanted only to see her son and was willing to violate the most basic rules of human dignity to do so. She approached the house on cat feet. The day's warmth had gathered in the adobe walls and radiated now to her touch. The kitchen faced the street, as did the living room with its large window. Around the side of the house, she saw a gate. Prayers sprang to her lips, steadied the pound of her heart. One window looked in on a bathroom, another on a large bedroom. Through the dark, she could make out the topography of the bed, two long bodies stretched beneath covers. She followed the wall until she came to the next window. White-and-red draperies hung half open. A light cast a bluish glow.

And there he lay, in a very small bed against the opposite wall. Ignacio in the moonlight. Her knees faltered, her vision swam, and she had to kneel. She might have fallen there, defeated at last by the sight of her son. They might have found her vanquished in a tangle of ivy. But she held herself up by the forearms and rested her head against the window. His eyes were closed. His eyebrows arched and sank, arched and sank. His lips made suckling motions, his cheeks working rhythmically.

"Nacho." The word tumbled from her lips, the only offering she had.

And then she saw it: her first chance. A gap between the base of the window and the white stucco wall. A gap she could push her fingers into. When she planted her feet and bore down with all her strength and *pulled*, the window didn't budge. When she crammed her palms against the upper edge of the window and *pushed*, the frame stayed stuck. It was splintered and old, this window, but it was locked.

When she looked back in the room, the small body sat upright in its bed. A blanket swirled around his knees. He blinked in the dim light, rubbed at his eyes. And then she watched his vision focus, his lids pop wide. He saw her. To be seen, by Ignacio, at last, was almost too much. *"Nacho,"* she whispered. *"Nacho, it's me! It's me! Open the window, m'ijo. Open it, Nacho!"* Blinded by tears, she couldn't see him anymore. He faded into the moonlit blur of the room. She sank to the ground, pressed her head to the spiny stucco wall, and wept.

She looked up again to meet a face. He hovered above her, nose smudged against the glass, hair spilling into his eyes, blinking down. He raised his hand and pressed his palm to the window.

"Nacho," she cried, this time louder than she should have. "Nacho!"

He called through the glass. "Mama. Mama!"

From deep within the house, a light switched on. A voice. Thudding footsteps. The door swung open and she saw a head and wild hair, shoulders and the curve of breasts. His room flooded with light.

Soli was gone. She crept on her belly to the nearest bush, hid beneath its foliage, and made her way back through the gate, down the sidewalk, running now through the dense night, down Shattuck, turning one corner, and another, until she was sure she had vanished.

THE NEXT MORNING, she woke chilled to the bone. The sun hadn't risen, but the garbage trucks rumbled nearby. Voices and pans clattered behind the bakery door. She had slept an hour, maybe, but she could stand. Her legs would hold her.

Would she present herself to the Cassidys? She couldn't bring herself to. The prospect of them looking at her in *that* way, or of not looking at her at all, of turning her away, of turning her *in*, made street life preferable. You are homeless, Soli, she told herself. You're like the woman with the milk crate, but you don't have a milk crate, only this suitcase, heavy and filled with possessions that grow more useless with each passing hour.

Her night on the street had left its mark. Mud streaked her shirt and the seams of her underwear dug into her groin, moist and bladed with sweat. In her suitcase, clean clothes waited. She made her way to the Cassidys' house. She wouldn't ring their bell, but had an idea of when they'd be home, and when they wouldn't. She needed to get warm. They kept a key by their kitchen door, tucked under a wormy rock, behind a hydrangea bush.

The door opened. "Hello?" she called, just in case. It was midmorning, the house empty. No one was home, not even a housekeeper. But the place was clean. Clearly, they'd found another Soli, someone to polish their ceramics and hold at bay the incessant tide of their belongings. She went first to their bathroom, where at one time she'd been afraid to take a shit. She was still afraid, the prospect of someone coming in from a morning jog nearly paralyzing, but her body ached with cold. Just a trickle of water, she thought, some hot water on my feet and my face. She ran the faucet in the tub. She let the sumptuous heat of it run through her fingers, then took her sock off and stuck her foot in. A moment later, her clothes were off, and before she could stop herself, she stood in the shower, the water turned up to scalding, and let it pelt against her breasts until her abdomen tightened with breathless pleasure. She picked up a bar of soap that smelled of roses and swept it between her breasts, under her arms, along the shaft of each thigh. She dried herself with a towel that hung on the door, the panic swelling again, and dressed as quickly as she could, checking twice, then three times, that she'd left nothing behind.

The door to the señor's office was open, the lamp on. She bit her lip, peered into the room. It was empty, and something—the habit of turning off the lights in this house—carried her to the desk. On it sat a pair of wire-rimmed glasses. She picked them up and before she could stop it, her thumb smudged the lens. There it was, her fingerprint, clear and small. She rubbed it off with her shirt, dropped the glasses to the table, and got out of there. Outside their back door was Saoirse's old stroller, gathering cobwebs. Soli took it.

A faded diaper bag, mostly empty, sat in the undercarriage of the stroller. It gave her an idea. She brushed it off and hung it on the handlebars. Inside it was a blanket, which she draped over the hood of the stroller, keeping her imaginary child out of the sun.

This much she knew: The so-called American mother had put her Nacho in a car that morning. She couldn't follow her fast enough, and lost her a few blocks down Shattuck, when she turned east and up into the hills. Soli would have to wait. So she waited, making her way through the Gourmet Ghetto, moving often enough to not raise suspicion. She wasn't hungry, either—her system, it seemed, had purged itself of physical need. Intention, distilled, was her fuel. With the stroller and clean clothes, her clean hair, she was just another nanny.

51.

"IGGY," KAVYA BEGAN, WATCHING HIM LIFT CHEERIOS TO his mouth on a wavering spoon. She tried to lighten her voice. She practically sang the question: "Why did you go to the window last night? Did you have a dream?"

Iggy crossed his eyes over the spoon. "I see," he said.

Kavya met Rishi's eyes. "What's that, Iggy? You see?"

"I see this!" With one small finger he pointed to something, to nothing, to a patch of ceiling.

"He saw something."

"I'm calling the police," Rishi said. "We can't have homeless people creeping around our house at night."

The homeless, Kavya thought. Of course.

Leaving Iggy's daycare after pickup that afternoon, she shared the story with another woman, a friendly mother named Alison. "It could be night terrors," Alison said. "This is the age when their dreams get vivid. I took Milton to craniosacral therapy when his began. He said he was seeing ghosts. I'd say it helped. The ghosts went away, at least."

Skulking itinerants. Nightmares. Ghosts. The explanations were plentiful, but neither Rishi nor Alison had mentioned what sprang first to Kavya's mind: the mother.

. . .

APRIL WAS BERKELEY'S WARMEST MONTH, the secret subseason before the summer fog descended, when the East Bay opened to a bath of light and sky. Soli sat at a café table. She'd spent a dollar on a day-old muffin. When she spotted Nacho's red car turning onto his street, she got to her feet and followed, careful to maintain a distance. She'd returned to their house that afternoon, and tried more windows. It had taken her far longer than it should have, as every slam of a car door sent her skittering into hiding, her ears hammering with fear. The windows had been locked, every one of them. Soli was no thief. She knew nothing of breaking glass or loosening locks. From half a block away, she watched Ignacio's woman take him from his car seat. Instead of heading straight into the house, she picked Nacho up and plopped him in a stroller. They turned back to Shattuck and headed down that busy street. Soli knew exactly where they were going.

THIS CLOSE TO THE DINNER HOUR, the playground still buzzed with nannies and parents, a rampage of children tearing through their after-nap energy spikes. The woman released Ignacio from his belt and he was off, stumbling across the sandpit to the low slide. Soli gasped at the sight of these, his first steps. The first she'd seen in daylight. He was a boy.

She pushed her empty stroller to the spot on the playground farthest from the woman, and sat on a bench. On the outside, she looked like a nanny. She knew this playground well. She scanned the periphery for anyone who might recognize her—park regulars or sitters from Saoirse's preschool. Nobody.

Turning back to her boy, she couldn't stop watching his strong little legs, train-jumping legs, Checo built into every step.

Ignacio climbed up a small ladder, turned, and called to the woman. How different she looked, without the plastered smile from the computer screen. This unsmiling version squinted across the swing set, settled on Soli, and focused. Soli's breath caught. The woman's eyes settled on the covered stroller, and then she looked back at Soli and stretched her lips into a noncommittal smile, the smile parents gave to nannies. Ignacio had begun scrambling up the wide slide and careening down it. How many sunset adventures had she missed with her boy? How many days of watching him sail on swings, kicking his legs, raising his arms to the sky? Soli permitted herself a lingering look at the woman, her brown skin, her nest of wavy black hair. In her gaze, even from this distance, Soli could see a mist of love. She couldn't deny this, and it shrank her inside, the love. It shamed her, and made her feel for a moment that she was a creeping specter, come to haunt this tranquil play. How sure the woman seemed that she belonged there, that she belonged to Ignacio. The setting sun raised a glow on her cheek.

And then, Ignacio: "Mama!" He was looking straight at Soli. "Mama, look!" He turned then to the woman, and called again, "Mama, look!" He slid down the slide on his stomach, stopping himself with his palms and inchworming off. He fell to a squat in the sand.

"Great job, Iggy!" The woman clapped her hands. "Do it again!"

"Bravo, mi amor," Soli whispered. Iggy. His American name.

THE SUN WANED, and children and parents trickled away. Soli felt her chances slipping, though she couldn't specify what those chances were. Her only hope for that day had been to see Ignacio, to be near him again. Across the playground, the woman looked at her watch and rose from her seat. Soli began to tremble. She watched the woman walk to

Ignacio, pick him up by the waist, and swing him in a circle. She kissed him on one plump cheek, then the other. Soli nearly cried out then. But instead, she rose and pushed her stroller to the exit. And then: *"Soli!"* A voice shot across the playground. A flash of auburn hair, longer and lighter now, flying from a swing. *"Soli!"*

52.

THE WEEBUS PULLED UP AND RISHI GOT ON, HEADING HOME. Like the other riders, he popped his earbuds in as soon as he sat down and would spend the ride leaning into his laptop, wholly oblivious to time or traffic or the shimmering marvel of sunset on the bay. He was modeling the programming center, and was eager to show it to Iggy—he'd inspired it, after all. Iggy would understand none of it, but would still, Rishi knew, listen with rapt attention, his eyes following the bounce of his father's lips. After an hour, the slap of a tomato on his window brought him back to the world. Protesters gathered on their usual patch of the Oakland stop. The bus moved on to Berkeley, and his cell rang.

"Hello?"

"Rishi-bhai. How's it going?"

He was in the process of designing his room-sized gas mask. That morning, he'd taken a swatch of an activated carbon bed filtration system to Weebies HQ. Vik had fingered the rubber fibers, whistled appreciatively. Rishi had explained how the fibers could be installed throughout a room to filter out pollutants. He'd felt, at last, the coagulation of disparate plans. The stomach-curdling anxiety that had gripped him all these weeks was slowly dissipating.

That week, they'd be finalizing the details of the WeBreathe package, Rishi and Vikram Sen. Really, this meant that Rishi did the leg-work, gathered and prepared the data, and presented it in digestible condition to Vik, who then asked CFO-like questions, most of which sent Rishi back to the drawing board, often for good reason. Vikram Sen was a smart man with an uncanny ability to make others feel good about working very hard on his behalf.

Rishi had yet to achieve a zero-VOC reading. He was getting close—closer with every new indoor filter, with every air-flow recalibration, and now with his gas mask idea, he'd be closer than ever. But still, the Stratosphere was less than pure.

"How's it going on your end?" Rishi asked.

"Listen, Rishi-bhai. After last week's meeting? I had a talk with TED."

"Who's Ted?"

"TED. As in TED Talks. You know about TED Talks?"

"Everyone knows about TED Talks."

"They liked the WeBreathe idea. No. They *loved* the WeBreathe idea."

Rishi's heart began to trot. TED Talks were watched online by mil-lions of people, all over the world. In all his pre-career fantasy play, he'd never imagined himself giving a TED Talk. This step would take him, his career, his prospects, to an entirely new level.

"July," Sen said.

"July. That's in a little over two months, Vik. I don't know if I could prepare a TED Talk by July." By July, they'd know if Iggy would be theirs.

"Sure you could!"

"But I'd have to rehearse it. Memorize it!"

Rishi heard nothing. "Hello?" He wiggled the wire on his headset. "Vik?"

"Yes," Vikram said, still barely audible. It sounded at first like Sen was whispering, then whimpering. And then, creeping like bile from his gut, settling and sloshing between his ears, was the understanding that Vikram Sen was laughing.

"Vikram."

Sen could hide it no longer. "Rishi-bhai!" he guffawed. "What a wonderful TED Talk you would give!"

"Okay."

His laugh was a braying, throaty shout. It was the sort of laugh that Rishi, under other circumstances, would have found infectious.

"Okay, Vikram."

Sen choked on a final spew of mirth, and finally calmed. "It's just that they look for names, Rishi. When they can get them. Big names get clicks. Right?"

"Right." Rishi fixed on the tomato seeds stuck to the Weebus window. He picked at one, knowing full well that it was on the wrong side of the glass.

"You've been absolutely invaluable to this project, yaar. I couldn't have got this together without you."

"I know."

"So I'll need a PowerPoint. Just basic ideas. Preliminary. EOD tomorrow. I can have Sally working with it by Monday. Twelve slides, right?"

"Sure."

"You're right about the memorizing, yaar. Won't be easy."

"Okay. No problem, Vikram." He hung up, sank into his seat, and pulled his earbuds out with limp arms. Nothing's changed, he told himself. You just misunderstood. Poor consolation for a Friday evening. The air in the Weebus was thick with the body odor of thirty people who needed to sleep, to eat, to shower. It buzzed with the radiation of their laptops and plugged Rishi's nostrils with lingering dismay. They were hypocrites, all of them, for breathing this shitty air. Hypocrites for tap-tapping on their laptops when they could have been out on a Friday evening, watching a sunset, feeling the spank of wind on their skin. He'd play in the yard with Iggy when he got home. He'd feel better after that.

WHEN HE GOT OFF THE WEEBUS in Berkeley, he hoped the cycle home would awaken him. He was going to a safe place, he told himself. In the bungalow on Vine, he knew that Kavya would greet him in the kitchen, that Iggy would be posted in his high chair, that Rishi would sit beside him and help him spear his pasta shapes. Rishi would help Iggy brush his nine teeth, and Kavya would bathe him. Then Rishi would kiss the boy good night, and he'd vanish into the bedroom for his nightly story.

When he did arrive, Kavya was banging pots in the kitchen. A mishap at the fish shop—Iggy grabbing at clams, Iggy screaming—had left her razor-tense. A salmon fillet sat burning and sticking on an overheated pan. Rishi grabbed it, shook the fish free, and slid it, dry now, ruined, onto a plate. Kavya stood before the open fridge. She was staring at the milk.

"Okay," he said. "You're going out."

"Out where?"

"Out of the house—out to a bar or something. Out for the night."

Kavya sighed. "It's a little late for a sitter."

"Forget the sitter. Call up one of your girlfriends and leave me with Iggy. Seriously."

Kavya closed the fridge, considered him for a few moments. "You think you could do it? Dinner and bath and bed?"

Rishi had no idea if he could do it, since he never had. He was fairly sure he'd manage to feed their son to some capacity, and most likely put him to bed with some semblance of a cleaning beforehand. It couldn't be harder than living out the evening with this version of his wife.

"We'll be fine. Call someone."

"Maybe," she said. "I'll think about it."

The truth was, she had no girlfriends. Rishi was girlfriend and boyfriend to her. As if he knew this, he said, "Try Preeti. She could probably use a night out."

"Preeti has a two-month-old," Kavya said. "She's probably exhausted. Going out is probably not what she needs right now."

"Yes!" Preeti said. "Yes, yes, yes. I'll come out to you. Should I come out to Berkeley? Could we try that Mexican place with the beer garden? Comal? Oh, wait. No, it's fine, I can pump. I'll pump. The nanny's staying in tonight, anyway."

So Kavya planned a girls' night out. She would meet Preeti downtown for drinks, and they'd follow their whims from there.

53.

"You! New girl! What's your name again?"

"Clara," she answered. "How many times do you plan to ask?"

The man at the burrito counter grinned. "Looking good, Claracita. Looking good!"

She pinched at the rice kernels her washcloth had missed. She straightened the chairs, then got on her hands and knees to pick a fork up off the floor. A whistle flew from the burrito counter and Soli ignored it. She'd been working there as a nonemployee for the past two days—it was how she stayed off the streets.

And guess what? Give a Mexican woman a dish towel in a Mexican restaurant, and everyone assumes she belongs there. Including the kitchen staff, including the burrito rollers behind the long counters and the customers who filed from the order line to the cash register. This was how Soli ate for two days, camouflaging herself among the tables that spread twenty deep, wiping away rice and bean detritus and wadding up tinfoil. She tried, at first, to balance plates on her forearms, until she noticed a bus boy who carried everything in a brown plastic tub. She found her own tub, and focused instead on her belonging-face, her don't-question-me face. For two days, she joked with the burrito men, smiled when she felt their eyes on her. She learned to grab order tags for hot dishes from the kitchen and search out table numbers.

If the restaurant had an owner, he never showed up. If it had a man-
ager, she managed to stay off his radar. It was a big enough place that
she could vanish out the door a few times a day with a foil-wrapped
burrito, and no one questioned her.

In the evenings, she watched Ignacio's house, never daring to sit
down. Homeless people sat. Housekeepers and nannies stood and
waited for their rides, their buses, their legitimizing companions.

It had been Saoirse who'd spotted her at the playground that day,
Saoirse who'd cried out the old name. An initial tug had pulled Soli to
this crackle in the atmosphere—she'd nearly let herself turn to see the
little girl, to measure the growth of her face, her curls, her sprouting
height. Instead, she fled. She flew through the gate with her empty
stroller. But when she ran, she felt heads turn and eyes follow this sudden leap in the evening's pace, and so she slowed. She was breathless.
Her vision blurred until she couldn't see and had to sit on the nearest
bench, her head in her hands, ignoring the bus that stopped and opened
its doors for her.

In the morning, she would go to the barbershop she'd passed a thousand times before. Hacking away at her own hair would leave it tufted
and lunatic. This place charged fourteen dollars for a haircut. She had
the money. She would spend it. She would cut her hair short and even.
She would look respectable.

Earlier that evening, returning from the restaurant, she'd had to sit
down, her shins aching from the day's work and the nights of bad sleep.
She found a nook across from Ignacio's house, between a rhododendron
bush and a giant agave, where the ground was soft with red-brown
mulch. The air here was righteous with the smell of wood chips. Her
belly was full of shrimp burrito, her head heavy with the weight of it.
She would wait for dusk as she always did.

She must have dozed off. The slam of a door had brought her back.
The sun had fallen but its light remained. Ignacio's woman emerged

from the house. Her hair was down now and sprang over her shoulders, framing the brown face, the storybook eyes. She got into the red car and pulled off the curb, ticking quietly down the street, around the corner, away. A single sideways glance, and she would have spotted Soli, still tucked between rhododendrons and agave.

The taste of digested shrimp sat thick and acrid on Soli's tongue. She thought about toothpaste and wondered where her next real shower would come from, if she'd ever have one again. She wouldn't return to the Cassidys'. She'd been too bold.

And then the house's door had opened. The man ambled out, as brown as the woman, the man from the picture with the wineglasses. He stretched his hands to the sky, rose to the tips of his toes, and swung his arms in wide circles. He called to someone in the house. Ignacio emerged and jumped into the man's arms, then clambered onto his shoulders. They picked up a ball from the porch and headed to the side of the house, disappearing to the back. Soli squatted and watched. She could hear the flare and dip of their voices. The squeal of a baby laugh, a clench in her throat. She stood.

The evening was cooling. Clouds canopied the town and summoned the wind. Leaves rustled at her feet and whipped around her ankles. She watched the leaves leap and swoop and fall again. She watched the wind gather, billowing the hem of her skirt, climbing her legs, gathering velocity. The wind doubled over itself, tripled and gathered speed, gathered voice. Wishhhhh, it said. The wind rose and filled her lungs, filled her heart. It took hold of the trees above and sent branches flapping. And with a sudden gale the wind blew south and drove itself into the house. A click, and the front door opened. She peered across the street. Yes, the door was open.

Soli looked left down the street, then right. She looked behind her and took one step onto the sidewalk. This was her chance—for what, exactly? She couldn't know yet. But the street was silent and empty.

The mother was gone. The father. No. She was mother and father. She bolted across the street and through the open door. The television rattled from another room and a clock ticked noisily from somewhere in the kitchen. She was a wolf again, searching for shelter, ears piqued for predatory footfalls. A cartoon on the television played to an empty room. What am I doing here? she asked herself. She searched for a keyhole of opportunity, for a way to wrap herself around this blessing, this break in the family fortress.

54.

WHEN KAVYA ARRIVED AT THE RESTAURANT, SHE SPOTTED Preeti next to a heat lamp, her shoulders bared to the last dregs of evening sun. She sat with her eyes closed, her back arched, as if she were completely alone. Her middle sagged as it never had before, and she looked, frankly, exhausted. But when she saw Kavya, she leapt from her seat and threw her arms around her friend. They ordered cocktails laced with mezcal, and chips with guacamole. Preeti grew giddy with her first drink and hot rosettes bloomed on her cheeks. Heat radiated off her arms and Kavya began to perspire just from sitting beside her, but it was the heat of joy, not drunkenness, and it was infectious. Preeti was overjoyed to be out, to be sitting in the night air, to be among adults and the sour bouquet of alcohol and food, beneath an umbrella of dark descending.

She dug an elbow into Kavya's ribs. "Don't look! That bartender's checking you out."

Kavya, unpracticed, turned around immediately to see Miguel behind the bar, frozen mid-pour, staring at her. They'd seen each other only a few hours earlier, but in this new context, she felt she hadn't seen him in months. Since the custody hearing, they'd barely spoken, daunted by the task of addressing the obvious. Ignacio was all Kavya could think about in those early days; she'd find herself smiling for no reason during lunch and dinner prep. Miguel, she knew, didn't approve of her form of motherhood. And if she asked him to, he wouldn't hesitate to say so. From behind the bar, he nodded, waved, and she waved back. He returned to pouring.

"I work with him," Kavya explained. "He's my assistant chef."

"He's beautiful," Preeti said, her eyes lingering, then clouding. "Does it ever bother you?"

"What, Miguel?"

"No, no. Just this idea that you're a mom now, and getting older. We're almost forty, and we're someone's mom. Though maybe it was different for you. You had to really struggle for this. So maybe it's different . . ."

Kavya listened to the words trail away.

"But remember?" Preeti went on. "When we'd go to bars and see guys there, and there would be this sense of—of possibility? And they would see us, you know? Like really notice us."

This rang a bell, though Preeti figured nowhere in Kavya's memories. "I remember that. But this is what we wanted, right? To be married? To have kids? That's why we went to those bars."

Preeti looked doubtful. "But even before that. Like in high school. Remember climbing out of windows to meet boys, and—"

"Excuse me?"

Preeti licked chili salt from the rim of her glass. "Remember that feeling, though? Like you'd do anything just to see some boy you liked?"

"You climbed out of windows? You? Climbed out of windows?"

Preeti shrugged. "Maybe I used the door. You get my point. Didn't you ever sneak out?"

"You were a very bad girl, Preeti Patel."

"Like you weren't."

"But you were such a Goody Two-shoes!"

"Goody Two-shoes," she said, shaking her head. "Who says that?"

Kavya set her drink down, genuinely flummoxed. "How did you do it all? With the grades and the colleges? And the spelling bee?"

Preeti rolled her eyes. "The fucking spelling bee. I was a trained monkey."

"Well, well," Kavya said. "Sex and drugs and rock and roll. Did your parents know?"

"Well, they caught me once, going out the front door when I thought they'd gone to sleep. I drove them nuts. I think I genuinely made them crazy for a while. No drugs, though."

"And there I was, thinking you were such a good girl."

"The comparisons to you were endless."

"Please."

Preeti donned a thick accent. "Look at this Kavya, such a sweet girl, so respectful to her mother, see how she likes to cook, Preeti, every night she helps to make the dinner, why you cannot be like that? Such a loving child!"

"No. I don't believe a word of it. You're a compulsive liar."

"I was for a while, actually."

Across the table, the two friends grinned. Kavya felt a cloud lift. The courtyard around them had grown boisterous with groups gathered around the fire pit, clustered around picnic tables, swarming around the bar.

"Let's not be like that," Kavya said. "With our kids. Let's not compare them to each other. Let's not make them feel like they'll never be good enough."

Preeti sat back and sipped on her drink. "Good idea."

KAVYA WALKED HOME AFTER MIDNIGHT and went straight to Iggy's room. He lay in a shaft of moonlight. She sank to the ground beside his bed and rested her cheek on his pillow. He was two years old and changing with astonishing speed. His nose was growing longer, sharper, the angles of his face more pronounced. But his cheek still smashed and spread against his pillow, as a baby's would. His lips, open and pink, were still petal-smooth. She blew drunkenly at his face, fluttering the fringe of his lashes. She smiled at herself and closed her eyes and felt mildly ridiculous, a foolish, fawning mother.

As sleep began to weigh her down, she went to her own room, plucked the contacts from her eyes, and fell straight into bed. In his sleep, Rishi took her hand, grounded her to the bed as the room spun. She was glad for him, glad for the deep oblivion of sleep. She sank into it, watching the spirals of imagined light that swirled behind her eyelids. In the morning, she predicted, she would regret this.

The next morning, she woke to a cool room. When she sat up, expecting a thunderclap of a headache, none came. High-quality mezcal. From the clarity of a full night's sleep sprang the discovery that she'd had an excellent time. Turning to her left, she let herself watch Rishi, his profile taut and handsome, even in unguarded sleep. She couldn't remember the last time they'd woken up on their own like this.

Rishi's eyes opened. He gazed at her, then squinted at the window. "What time is it?"

55.

WHAT RISHI NOTICED FIRST WAS THE BILLOWING CURTAIN. The drapes in their bedroom had never moved this way before, filling with air and flattening, not even on warm days when they slept with their windows open. That morning, the white fabric rippled with an unfamiliar wind.

The next thing he noticed was the time. "Nine forty-three."

"Where's Iggy?"

Ignacio should have come in long before this, wedging between them with his cold feet. They should have been up on this Saturday morning, eating breakfast, heading for the park, the café, the grocery store. Rishi began to understand why he felt so awake.

"Ignacio?" Kavya called, her voice hoarse. No answer came.

"Ignacio!" he bellowed. His voice carried better than hers. "Iggy!"

He waited for the thrum of Iggy's footsteps, always at a run. He tried again. No answer came and no little boy appeared in their doorway or jumped on their bed, knocking into them with hard head and elbows.

"Maybe he's sick," Kavya said.

"I'll go see."

The hallway was cold. "Iggy," he whispered. A tunnel of cold air rushed through the house, sucking shut their bedroom door. Rishi rubbed at his arms to warm them. Even in the hallway, he sensed a shift. "Ignacio?" But the name stuck in his throat, and when he reached Iggy's door, he knew why. The bedroom window was open. The sheets were pulled back. Ignacio was gone.

He marched through the house. "Ignacio! Iggy!" From room to room. The kitchen was empty, the television dark. His toys lay stacked in the corner of the living room. Outside the window, the leaves of a Japanese maple shuddered. All else was still.

Back in the hallway, he nearly crashed into Kavya.

"Where is he?" she asked. "Where is he? Iggy!" He heard her scurry to the bathroom. "Iggy?" She followed him to Iggy's bedroom. Rishi leaned out the window, looking for something—he didn't know what.

"Iggy?" he called out the window, as if the boy might have appeared from behind a bush. Kavya tried calling his name. She opened the closet. She pulled the bed covers clear off and threw them to the floor.

She streaked past Rishi in the hallway. "The mother," she gasped.

Rishi grabbed her by the arm. "Kavya—"

"It was the mother!" she shrieked, and yanked herself away, pushing past him and running down the hall. He heard the front door open. He heard his wife's voice, broken now and frantic. She called out to the street, to the bakery-goers and dog-walkers on a Saturday morning. "Ignacio!" she cried. "Ignacio!"

56.

IT WAS THREE IN THE MORNING. THE LAST HOUSE LIGHT
had long been extinguished and the streets were silent. Earlier that evening, she'd snuck into the house and unlatched the bedroom window
before slipping out again. Returning at the darkest hour, she crammed
her hands into the gap and pulled. The window had gasped open. She
stuck her head in and heard the bedroom door judder, the breeze from
the window shaking it in its frame. When hard work fails, luck, the
lesser brother, steps in.

Her first foot knocked a toy over, and Ignacio stirred. The second
she placed more carefully. And then she was in his room. He lay in a
bed that was just the right size for him, with wooden rails that ran along
the wall. She ran her fingers through her newly short hair, fingered the
tips, suddenly self-conscious. In his bed, Nacho clutched a soft toy and
sucked at the night. This small, dark world of his, it was made just for
him, a loving nest. Soli's American boy. Could she have left him there?

At his bedside, she knelt down and whispered their old song. *"Nacho,
Nacho-o-o."* She lifted him—how sturdy he had grown! His legs were
solid, his arms sure. He wrapped himself around her and tucked his
head into her neck, as he always had, and she was nearly knocked down
by the smell of him, the scent of her boy. She'd never known it existed
so specifically, or that she'd been living without it. She could have stood

in that room all night, breathing him in. They would have caught her in the morning, her nose buried in his hair. *"Time to go, Ignacio,"* she sang. He chirped like a bird in his sleep.

They climbed back through the window, landing softly in the ground cover. She lowered him into the stroller and crouched beside him. "It's you and me, *amorcito.*" He didn't wake. She buckled him in and set off.

The night was blushing away. Soli felt safe still, in the purple half-light, and the hour between night and day was so cold it sent her flying over sidewalks and through alleyways. She crossed the streets without waiting for the lights to turn. She listened for the ghost-whistle of the BART train, and heard it soon enough.

She had questions for Ignacio. One day, she would ask them. *Was I making a mistake?* She'd never have her own little Gourmet bungalow or a car that clicked its way through town like a stealthy beetle. Would these things have made a better life for him?

The tunneled din of the BART station must have woken him. He opened his eyes and saw Soli—clearly this time, with a flint of recognition. She was certain she saw it. Days later, she would cling to that spark. He'd known her once. And again?

Did you know me that morning when you came to, Ignacio, blinking against those green-gray lights?

He woke up to see Soli, then swiveled to look behind, and saw nothing but a lonely ticket booth. He shrieked. He shook his head so hard she feared he would damage himself, and so she squeezed her palms to his face to stop him. "Mama," he cried. "Mama! Where is it?"

She knelt and took him by the elbows. "Nacho. I'm here. This is Mama." She wrapped her arms around him, though he was almost too small to hug, but he walloped her with the side of his head and her vision went swimming.

And those people. Would they have loved you more than I did? Will you wish someday that I had left you with them? She had many hours to think that day, and a lifetime to revisit her deed, and here's what she would discover: This story, this fight for a boy—it wasn't about the boy. It was about his mothers. It was about a law that grew from the deepest roots of their being.

A bus pulled up in front of the station, and it was full, even at four on a Saturday morning. The people boarding were neither shoppers nor tourists, no one heading to work in a sky-high office. Around her sat fluorescent vests and beige uniforms, heading to the city to clean floors and raise buildings. Soli and Nacho would take the bus as far as the port, and then they'd be gone, heading down and down, to the farthest edge of Nacho's country. They'd find a school for him, a job for her. They'd find a life. And there they would stay. And if one day, they were forced over a border, they would go, the two of them, to where the sky meets the land and the earth turns a corner. They'd step into whatever awaited them, in his country or hers.

NACHO SPENT THE BUS JOURNEY with eyes glued to the window, to the telephone lines in the distance. Soli feared there was something wrong with him. She feared that they had broken him.

They arrived in San Diego around lunchtime and went straight to a restaurant in a busy shopping district, where she had a contact, Iselda's niece. The girl met Soli at the back door, leaned against the door frame, long and slim in black jeans.

"Do you have service experience?" she asked in English. "Front of house or back?"

"Front, back. I've been all over the house."

This made her laugh, and she let Soli in the kitchen.

That first evening, she took Nacho to the seaside, a small harbor with a boardwalk. Around them, people milled in familial clusters, held hands, and walked out onto the short docks to watch the bobbing boats and the horizon beyond. Soli hoped the boats and the fresh salt air might inspire Nacho to forgive her. He'd been on a bus with her for eight hours, and then in the dark of a dirty motel. She thought the sun and wind and seagull cries would help him feel at home again. It was dinnertime when they reached the harbor, and the air was dense with the smell of fried fish. The sun was angry that day. Even as it dimmed and sank, it burned orange at the ocean's edge. The fire in the sky threw the rest of the world into shadow. They were ghosts in its wake.

"Nachito," she said. "How about something sweet?" Around them were pretzel stands, an ice-cream shop, a man in a pink cowboy hat selling pink wispy clouds of sugar. Ignacio didn't answer, but his gaze lingered on the man.

"Okay, then." She stepped over to the stand and paid the man. He offered her three spools for the price of two, and she spent a good twenty, thirty seconds convincing him that she did not want three spools of the fluffy pink stuff.

When she turned back, Ignacio was gone. The stroller stood in place, its chest buckle still fastened. He'd slipped out and lost himself in the crowd. He was nowhere. "Nacho!" she cried. "Ignacio! Come back!" People turned. A few stopped.

"You lose your kid, lady?" a man asked.

"Nacho! Where are you? Stop this now!" She raised a cotton candy wand, held it like a torch to summon him back. "Nacho!"

"That him over there?"

And there he stood, on the far side of the dock, steady as a lighthouse amid a current of legs. In the fierce sunset, he was nothing more than a black shadow, boy-shaped.

"Ignacio," she called. "Come back to me!"

He stood and watched her, knowing somehow that he was in control. He turned away and stared out at the water. Soli drew near, carefully, the way one might approach a captured animal. She held her hands out and walked slowly, until they stood a few feet apart. When she kneeled and offered him the spool of pink, he looked at it, looked up at her, and took her hand. But he would not take the cotton candy. He was led back to his stroller and buckled in, but still he refused the candy, and she was left to chew at it herself, as if she were the child in need of consolation and he the tolerant guardian. It was crystalline and wooly and clung to her lips.

That night, in their cheap motel, she turned on the news. *A state-wide search*, it said. *From his bedroom. His biological mother. Illegal immigrant. Any information.* And there, on the screen, a picture of Ignacio and one of Soli, taken at the county jail. Following this, to her utter amazement, was grainy video footage of Soli pushing her child, slumped in his stroller, down an empty Berkeley sidewalk. She could have been anyone—any housekeeper, any waitress. A little brown, a little round. But he shimmered on the screen like a mirage. He was a luminous little boy. There would be eyes everywhere, looking for him. They had to go.

57.

Kavya heard the doorbell ring. It had been eight days
since Iggy was taken, and the droves of reporters outside their door had
petered to a trickle. And the trickle, searching for a new angle, had
begun asking questions that made Kavya uncomfortable. To her door
and over the phone came feeble lines of questioning, suggesting dark
possibilities. Mrs. Reddy, do you have contacts in India? Mrs. Reddy,
when did you last see your child? Was he well behaved? Was he a burden? Kavya and Rishi had stopped answering the phone. They ignored
doorbells and Eva Cabral scolded them for it. Keep the press interested,
she said. The more coverage you get, the more likely they'll find him!
But Kavya was barely functioning. She couldn't face the questions
hurled at her front door like raw eggs. They were planning a press conference in two days. They would answer questions then.

Uma showed up four days after Iggy vanished. The same day, Kavya
got a call from Miguel. "They offered me your job."

"Take it," Kavya said.

"I thought about it. I was going to take it. But I didn't."

"Take it."

"I negotiated a raise and health insurance and an extra week of vacation."

She sighed. "I hope it was a big raise."

"It was." He paused. "You're coming back."

Kavya didn't answer this. She tried to summon a memory of the evening at the restaurant, the last of her happy, healthy life.

"You there? Kavya?"

"Yes."

"You'll be back."

"Okay."

"Why don't you tell that man to mind his business?" Uma asked when Kavya hung up. "You want me to tell him?"

"You mind your own business, Mom."

Uma wrapped her arm around Kavya's waist. "Enough of that." She led her daughter back to the kitchen table.

From where she sat, she could see the mound of toys in the corner of the living room, a half-built tower of blocks that she couldn't bring herself to dismantle. She couldn't face another day and night of this house, these walls, not knowing. She couldn't wait any longer for other people to find her son. She sat down and picked up the phone again. Rishi was at work, because there was nowhere else to be.

"Hello?" His voice was hollow. It sucked from Kavya the few drops of conviction she'd gathered.

"How are you?"

"Fine."

"Look. Rishi." She felt suddenly foolish, but she let the words out. "We need to do something."

He sighed. "I know."

"We need to find him ourselves." Kavya didn't know specifically what this meant, and neither, she guessed, did Rishi. From the stove, Uma watched her daughter carefully. She tipped a cup of milk into a saucepan of tea and waited for it to boil.

58.

WHAT RISHI FOUND IN OAXACA WAS A VERSION OF HIS OWN family's past. The airport taxi took him through streets lined with shops open late into the night, low adobe huts fronted by garage doors and painted bright blue, yellow, pink, like the cramped and sooty storefronts of small-town India. Solitary bulbs hung from wires, sending a fluorescent shank of light through each archway—harsh, but not unwelcoming. These were Indian streets, minus the hillocks of garbage and inexplicable rubble, minus the stray dogs that sifted through them, minus the cattle that loped through traffic.

Rishi had left Kavya in bed. She had spent four days in bed when he decided to leave. Ignacio was officially missing. The police had pored over their home, interviewed their neighbors, asked them questions that felt at times like barely veiled accusations. The day Ignacio went missing, he and Kavya had moved about the house like shadows—weak and flat with disbelief, pinned to the ground only by their feet. And then they went through a busy phase—filing reports, traveling to the police station, organizing search parties through the surrounding neighborhoods. They'd done interviews on television, fielded reporters at their door, and soon—sooner than expected—there was nothing left to do. Kavya took to her bed and stared at the drapes. "I saw her," she'd say to

Rishi, every time he crossed her path. She said it each time with a sense of awe, in a state of perpetual discovery. "I saw her at the playground, Rishi."

He knew she'd want to come with him, so he left without telling her, with only a note to assure her that he'd return. You need to keep the search going, he'd written, I'll do everything I can to bring Ignacio back. He'd called Uma and asked her to come back to the house and watch Kavya, to make sure she ate and washed herself. "Will she want me to be there?" Uma had asked, a question that had surprised Rishi. Uma had never asked, never seemed to consider, whether her daughter wanted her anywhere. Uma was a woman who assumed her authority without a second thought, and her question brought to light the instability of their world post-Ignacio.

Rishi was giving himself four days to find his son.

After dropping his bags off in his room, he approached the hotel's concierge, a woman with a face he'd seen on Disney princesses, all eyes and smile.

"I need a taxi to Santa Clara," he said. "And maybe a guide? Who speaks English?"

"Señor? Where would you like to go, sir?"

"Santa Clara?" He showed her the page in his notebook with the name of the birth mother's town. "And a place to stay there. A hotel. Please."

If Soli had been there, standing next to Rishi in that terra-cotta lobby, she would have broke down laughing. A hotel in Popocalco!

The concierge smiled and said, "I'll see what I can find."

What she found was a driver named Helio, scheduled to arrive at four the next afternoon, hours later than Rishi had hoped to leave. He paced his hotel room all morning, tried and failed to work on the Weebies PowerPoint. At 5:30, Helio appeared in a green Toyota Camry. By 5:35, they were off.

. . .

THEY ARRIVED IN POPOCALCO at dinnertime. It was a low and dry
place, bordered by vast tracts of land. "Those used to be farms," Helio
said. "All of this, farmland. No more."

The town was less of a town than a stretch of dusty road peppered
with some widely spaced homes, three shops, and a bar. Outside the bar
a village square spread luxuriantly, hemmed in by stone archways. Vast
white bricks covered the ground, bleached clean by the sun.

Riding along a dirt road, Rishi kept his eyes glued to his window. He
peered into shop fronts, into the dark doorways of adobe huts and tidy
brick houses. He searched for Ignacio wherever it seemed people might
be. He searched the streets for children, but saw none. A few old men
strolled by the roadside. Others sat outside their houses, shut their eyes
to the low evening sun. He searched for Ignacio in these faces. An adult
who looked like Iggy might have been a family member. The thing was,
they all looked like Iggy, but they all lacked the essential spark.

"We're here," Helio said. What he'd called a hotel was really just a
house with an extra room, owned by a woman named Dolores. He
walked through its doorway and into a plume of familiar smoke. Incense
burned in a corner beneath a framed portrait of a young man.

Helio nodded gravely to the woman. She had streaks of gray in her
hair, an unlined face. She softened when she looked at Rishi, but she
didn't smile.

"Dolores had a son," Helio said. "You're staying in his room." He
pointed at Rishi. "Americano," he said.

"Americano?" Dolores asked, then shook her head. "No, no es americano."

"She says you're not American."

"I got that."

Dolores took Rishi by the arm and led him to his room. She watched him roll his suitcase to the wall, and then she pointed to the bed. "Mi hijo," she said.

"Sí."

And she left him to himself for the night.

Two thousand miles away and two hours behind, beneath the covers of a rumpled bed, his wife lay in shreds. Rishi would have three days in Popocalco. In the morning, he would find the Castro Valdez home, where Soli and Ignacio were sure to be living. He'd memorized her face and her name, its parade of syllables. The next day, he would find out where she lived. He would find her.

In the meantime, he had no hope of sleeping. He was closer to Ignacio than he had been in two weeks. He'd felt him the moment he'd stepped off the plane in Oaxaca and into the muggy afternoon, and the feeling had grown stronger as he neared Popocalco. Ignacio steamed across this land, rested on its pillows of stagnant air. Ignacio was everywhere.

Helio met him at the breakfast table the next morning. He sat down across from Rishi, nodded when Dolores offered him a coffee, and waited for Rishi to speak. Rishi had spent most of the night looking out his bedroom window until he woke, still sitting upright, his arms weak with exhaustion. They passed a silent minute, sipping. "What's the plan today?"

"I need to find a Mister Valdez. Or Castro Valdez? Do you know him?"

Helio grinned. "I know many men named Valdez. But Castro Valdez—you're speaking of Solimar's father."

"Yes! Yes." Rishi tried to sound calm. "Do you know her?"

"Of course I know her. I've known her since she was born. She went to the North. Is she back?"

"I think so. I think she is. I'd like—I'd like to visit her."

"You know her, then. From California?"

Rishi nodded.

The Castro Valdez home stood away from the main road, among patches of fallen corn. Dried white husks bowed low to the ground and lay in stacks. If this had been a different time, a different story, the sight of these husks would have thrown Rishi into a frenzy of invention. He would have seen in them materials for building, insulation, creation—renewable and untapped. Now they looked like an ancient massacre. Rishi stepped out of the car before it stopped moving. He ran up the drive. A fist, his fist, was knocking on the door.

A woman opened it. She stood as tall as his elbow, her hair dark and cropped close to her head. Her eyes were brown and bottomless. She squinted up at him, as if he were too bright to view directly. He knew this look. He knew the eyes. These were Iggy's eyes.

"Buenos dias," Rishi said. He needed Helio. But Helio lagged behind, peeking up at the sun through the filter of his fingers.

"Helio!" he called. "Get over here." Helio looked over, surprised.

"Can I help you?"

Rishi turned. A man stood in the doorway now, nearly as small as the woman, his mustache straight, his skin buttery brown. The smallest smile fluttered across his lips and then vanished.

"Mister Valdez?" Rishi began. "Señor Valdez? Are you the father of Solimar Castro Valdez?"

"What happened?" The man took a step forward. "Where is she? What happened to her?" The woman, Soli's mother, pulled a cross from her pocket and began fingering its beads. Rishi took a step back. He'd had no real idea of what to say.

"I'm looking for your daughter. For Solimar. Is she here?"

He smiled, bemused. "Soli? She lives in the States now." His English was clear and clipped. He looked down at Rishi's shoes. "Who are you? How do you know her?"

The true answer was too complicated. Not even Helio, who stood now just behind Rishi, could translate the true answer. Rishi pushed on. "And Ignacio?"

That's when the man noticed Helio, and stepped forward to take his hand in both of his. Helio spoke gently to the man, nodding toward Rishi, explaining, it seemed, the how and why of this foreigner's arrival. The woman broke in, speaking almost inaudibly.

"I'm looking for Ignacio," Rishi repeated. He turned to Helio. "Tell him I'm looking for Ignacio. For Solimar's son."

"Soli has no son," her father said. He laughed, shook his head. "Soli has no son! Who are you?" The father looked past Rishi for an explanation.

Helio cleared his throat. "Mister Rishi? Do you have the right information? There is no child here."

"Your daughter has a son," Rishi said. Pinpricks of sweat sprang to his forehead and trickled past his hairline. "She has a child named Ignacio. He was our son—"

Helio spat out a rapid stream of Spanish, and the father answered him. As they spoke, the volume rose. The mother joined in, her voice a whispery undercurrent. The father's face twisted with anguish. Helio sounded insistent, was repeating the same phrase over and over. Whatever he was saying did not please the father, who stepped forward and shoved Rishi in the chest. He was shouting then, pointing a sharp finger into Rishi's face, backing him down the drive.

"Okay!" Helio cried. "Okay! No problem!" He grabbed Rishi's arm. "Señor, let's go. No problem!"

Rishi jerked his arm from Helio's grip, but the father was yelling now. His voice, his anger, had formed a wall around the house. Rishi would not penetrate it. The father stopped shouting, at last, and capped his tirade by spitting at the ground. Rishi didn't budge, and watched him as he walked back into his house, slammed the door, and sent up a cloud of dust.

In the car, the two men sat in silence. Helio revved the engine. "Okay, señor. We'll go to Teotitlan now. Your wife like rugs?"

"What happened there?"

"¿Señor?"

"Why was he so angry?"

"Oh. Well."

Rishi waited.

"You said the boy was your son?"

"Yes."

"Mister Rishi. You said the boy was your son. You said that Soli was the mother. You understand what you said?"

It was clear now. He'd said that he and Solimar had had a son. As far as the father knew, Rishi had knocked up his daughter and left her. He sank his head into his hands. Something like a laugh leaked out of him. "Turn the car around, Helio. He got it completely wrong."

Helio slowed to a stop, spent a good long while looking at Rishi, and then sighed. He turned the car around. When they reached the house, the father stood at his door, his arms hanging at his sides.

"Translate for me, Helio. Please."

The two men stood before Soli's father. He glanced down at them, but seemed barely to register their return.

"Señor," Rishi began. And Helio translated. "I don't know your daughter. I have never met your daughter. But I know her child, Ignacio. I am looking for him. Is he here with you? Do you know where he is?"

The father spoke past Rishi, to the hills behind him. "You have the wrong house, whoever you are. My daughter has no son. No child. No husband."

His eyes rested on Rishi now. "If you know of a son, you know more than I do. All I know is that she's in America now. And if she will be back, and when she will be back, only the valley knows."

"You got it now, señor?" Helio asked. "She isn't here." And with that, he turned and headed for the car, leaving Rishi and the father standing face-to-face with nothing left to say. When he started the engine, Rishi considered letting him go. But he would need Helio.

Back in the car, Helio patted him on the shoulder: "Let's get lunch." In Dolores's kitchen, Rishi ate voraciously, filling the void of his morning with rice and beans and freshly made tortillas. He crammed entire tortillas into his mouth, spooned beans down his throat without chewing them. He ate without speaking. He ate too much, too quickly. An hour later, the tortillas and beans and rice formed a thick coating in his stomach, his throat, made his legs heavy and his mind dull. He longed for a salad, for the crunch of watery leaves on his tongue. He longed for a bracing wind. He longed to run.

"Where you going?" Helio asked as Rishi passed him on the patio.

"Running."

"Running?" Helio crossed his arms. "Running from who?"

"I need to get my blood moving."

"No, no. Bad idea, señor. No es posible."

But it was possible. The wet heat of the valley seeped into his joints and loosened them. The sun ran its hands over his neck and his ears. He ran past a new brick house, surrounded by construction vehicles. Perfect round nests balanced on the power lines above. He ran past cacti flattened by the roadside, probably obliterated by a passing dump truck, a builder's Jeep. His feet slushed over the sandy road, roughening the silence.

He had one full day left, one day in which to accept defeat or find a new path of investigation. He would go to the nearest city. If the woman were looking for work and a way to support her son—his son— she would surely end up in a city. He would ask Helio about this. The next day, he would search the city.

For several minutes, Rishi made his way through fields of old corn. They reached out with dry hands, combing over the stranger in their midst. He ran faster, ducked away from the meddlesome stalks, but still they found him. He spent several minutes running in one direction, until all he could see was corn. It felt like he'd run a mile, but it was hard to tell in the unfamiliar weight of this air. When he turned back around, the sparse scatter of buildings was gone. He was lost. He ran on, until the back of his head throbbed and his throat ached. Swallowing didn't help. Hot cramps shot up his legs and yanked him to a halt. He moved one foot, then the other. He fell to the ground.

Above, the sky spun. A tickle at his knee brought him to attention. Looking down, he saw a squad of fat red ants coursing up his legs, navigating the forest of his leg hair. He jumped to his feet and smacked at his shins. He shook his leg in the air like a frenzied dog. "Shit!" he shouted. "Shit!" He slapped at his legs and pinched the ants from his skin, but he couldn't get all of them. Some had gone up his shorts and disappeared. The thought of them making their home in the crevices of his body made him writhe and curse, scratch at his skin until it bled, until tears of frustration and disgust took him over. He squatted in the sea of dead corn. It had been so long since he'd last shed tears that it took him a few moments to realize what was happening. He was crying. He lay on his back, half numbed by the sun, and let it overtake him.

In the thirteen days since Ignacio disappeared, Rishi had been holding down his panic as one held down a wave of nausea. But like nausea, it forever threatened to rise up his throat, against his weakened tongue. Traveling to Popocalco had slowed its climb. The journey had given him a concrete mission and kept him from sinking, as Kavya had. For a few days, he'd had a plan. It was essential to have a plan, simple though his was.

And what of this plan? He'd based it mostly on the expectation of finding Soli here, in her parents' home. And now he envisioned himself in Oaxaca City, scanning faces. Knocking on doors. Holding up a photo of Iggy, a mug shot of Soli. To whom? Store owners? Housewives? Not even her parents knew where she was. His plan was wearing thin, and it was getting harder to push down the panic that threatened to climb from his mouth and cascade into despair. The difference between panic and despair was hope. Despair saturated the afternoon heat, infused every drop of sweat with the reeling loss of Ignacio. Despair swarmed. He rolled onto his side and cried. He had lost all control, was ugly now, crying though bared teeth. He was shamed and helpless. He had unraveled, had been unraveling for days, and now he was finished, stretched across the valley floor, his limbs sifting through the sandy soil. Who would gather him up, wind him back around himself, and carry him home?

He lay in the well of the dry and surrendered basin, until the sun grew dim, diffused, and dipped low. He'd finished crying a while earlier, his ducts tapped dry. He needed water, badly. If only it would rain, he thought. If only he could sit up, look around, find the village, mercy in a glass of water. He found relief, at least, in the shadow of a cactus. It was a grandfather cactus, older perhaps than the redwood. It was a stereotype of a cactus. It looked like a spiny green man waving hello; it might have appeared, wearing a sombrero, in an ad for a Mexican restaurant.

He tried to get up, but rolled onto his back instead. He couldn't stop himself from staring into the sun, and amid the globules of blinding light, he saw this: Kavya in a red dress, her eyes two deadened chips of wood. Ignacio, squatting in the garden, stacking wood chips into patient towers. Ignacio, leaping from the porch steps and into Rishi's arms. Ignacio ascending, saddled in a baby swing, his head thrown back and gulping against his own laughter. Ignacio, perched on his shoulders, the backs of his knees, two perfect wells for Rishi's thumbs.

His vision had gone ragged, but slowly now, his eyes began to focus. They homed in on a single needle. He blinked, squinted, rubbed at his eyes. From the needle, miraculously, hung a single drop of water. He reached up, coaxed it onto his finger, and dabbed the moisture to his lip. Where had it come from?

If this cactus could create water from dry land and arid sky, substance from absence, then surely there was no such thing as nothing. Zero, much as Vikram Sen would hate to hear it, was a myth. He could quarter something, halve it, grind it to invisibility, but it would never be gone.

He struggled to his feet. His head throbbed. The ants had either left his body or found some numbed and hidden grotto of it, for Rishi saw no sign of them. He headed back the way he'd come, first at a slow walk, and then working up to a jog. His body rallied against chains of thirst as he gained speed, ploughing into the heat and the headache. In the burnt-out caverns of his lungs, he'd found air. In his overboiled muscles, strength. There was no nothing. There was always water, always time, always hope. Even in the soundless void of his Berkeley bungalow, there was hope. There was Kavya. There was home.

They spent the evening going door-to-door around Popocalco. It required Helio's complete cooperation, and at first, Helio was not being cooperative. Rishi had the cash to convince him. They went to every inhabited building in the village, even those technically without doors. It cost Rishi 1,500 pesos, but it was a thing to do. It was a thing someone in America would do, if they were looking for a child. The faces at these doors flickered with recognition at the mention of Soli, but no one knew where she was. No one had heard of Ignacio. It was almost a comfort to return to Dolores's house, its walls stained and bare, the dirt drive immaculately swept. It lacked the adornments—agaves, colored tiles, bells on the door—that he'd seen on the other houses. It was plain and still, a house that had lost its son.

The next morning, Rishi's final full day in Mexico, they stopped at a cash machine in the center of Oaxaca and he took out another three thousand pesos. He gave a thousand to Helio, and saved the rest for the consulate. He imagined a meeting with an official behind a large wooden desk, a passage of currency from one palm to another, a promise made, a problem solved.

What Rishi found was a long line, a take-a-number system, and a bored woman behind a double-layered wall of glass.

What he came away with, four hours later, was a promise. The consulate had met with him personally and laid out a plan—a surprisingly lucid one—of dispersing information to regional police departments and the Mexican press. He would contact the American embassy, and Rishi would be hearing from the FBI. Rishi wasn't sure what to make of these promises. If they were real, if they happened, they would surely lead somewhere. But something—prejudice, perhaps, or fatigue, or just plain despair, told him that these steps would never be taken. They were shadow-promises—bold in the light of day, but soon enough forgotten.

ON THE DRIVE BACK to Popocalco, he realized he'd forgotten to bribe the consulate. The pesos lay in a fat rolled stack in the pocket of his jeans. He kept his eyes fixed firmly out his window.

"It's a terrible story," Helio said. "Your story. The boy. It's terrible."

"Yes."

"This boy was yours?"

"We were adopting him. He was almost ours." Rishi paused. "He was ours."

As they turned off the highway and entered Popocalco, a text message buzzed. Kavya: *Anything today?*

Rishi: *I spoke to the consulate. Plan in place.*

Kavya: *So you didn't find him?*

Rishi wanted to laugh at her. He wanted her to hear him laughing at this, the simplicity of her hope.

He texted: *Nothing.*

He added: *Yet.*

Kavya: *Come home, Rishi.*

Tomorrow.

I need you here. Come home.

I need you. Come home. She was summoning him, as she had in the old days, at the start of all this. Kavya, at home, her grief and her deadened will forming a gutter in their mattress. Rishi would find her and pull her out.

LATER, RISHI PACKED HIS SUITCASE and prepared for a sleepless and sweaty night. He'd come here, he realized, expecting to find the woman, to find his boy, to take him home. He'd come looking for answers, and what he found was an answer of sorts. The hills had an answer. Go home, they told him. We have nothing for you.

A light tap at the door. Helio. He held up a flask. "Cactus," he said. "Made here." Rishi followed him onto the front porch, where Helio took the first swig. The flask held homemade mezcal, Rishi managed to learn, extracted and fermented in a copper tub. "For a long time, he's been making it," Helio said. "Memo Romero. Donkey man. Same tub. Never washes it. This is the secret." They drank until Rishi couldn't sit upright anymore. He lay back on the porch. The moon blurred. Even the dark blurred.

"You'll be all right in the morning," Helio said, and helped him up. "See you then." He shook Rishi's hand.

When Rishi closed his eyes again, what he saw was the father of Soli—the small smile that had flit across his lips. Rishi fell asleep out there, for how long he didn't know. He sat up. In his drunken exhaustion, he could see that smile more clearly than ever. There was something to it. The man had been hiding something. He'd been mocking Rishi with that smile, his show of indignance. What occurred to Rishi then, what punched him with its obvious truth, was that he'd never been inside the house. That old couple had kept him on their porch. And for what? To keep him out. To keep him from seeing what there was to see: Solimar, and with her, Solimar's child. Rishi's child.

He stood up and ran to the end of the drive. He knew where the village center was, and began walking toward it. His phone told him it was four in the morning, a few hours before dawn. The boy would be asleep now, and so would the mother. The forces of inevitability were closing around Rishi, propelling him forward. The events of the past three days were lining up like obedient boxcars, linking together a train of logic, there on the valley floor.

He had one more step to take.

Guided by a vague memory of the village layout, Rishi found a familiar strip of houses. A few windows were lit, but there were no streetlamps and the path ahead was solidly black. He'd never made his way through such dense darkness. Halfway down the main road, he came to a low wall he recognized. This was the house. He slipped through the gate.

At the door, he raised a fist, instinctively, to knock. He stopped himself. A light push, and the door opened. He found himself in a sitting room with a low sofa, a straw cot pushed against the wall, and a televi-

sion. The ceiling hung just inches above his head. A cloud of moonlight passed through the window. The air here was almost too thick to
breathe. Beyond this room, he found a kitchen, and branching off of it,
a third room. A bedroom.

They would be in the bedroom, asleep. Rishi listened for the tick-
tick of Iggy's sleep-suckling. Instead, he heard crickets, a faraway bark.
He stood alone in the sitting room and listened to the whistle of breath
through his own nostrils. If Ignacio was here, what would Rishi do?
What would happen if he stepped into the bedroom to find his boy
asleep on a bed? If Ignacio was here—he couldn't finish the sentence.
The room grew lighter. Somewhere, the sun was rising.

He stepped over the threshold into a bedroom. And in a bed, sleeping on its side, its face turned to the wall, a small body.

"Iggy?" he whispered.

From where he stood, the boy looked comically small, no longer than
half the length of the mattress. He snored softly, then shuddered at
something in a dream. Rishi took one step and another. He would take
the boy in the night. He would win him as he'd lost him.

"Iggy," he said, bending over the boy. "It's me." He nudged his hand
under an arm, his fingers sinking into the flesh of a soft shoulder.

He heard a snuffle, a murmur. The body in his hands stiffened and
turned to face Rishi.

Rishi reared back. This was not Ignacio. This was an old woman. A
small woman. This was Solimar's mother. The woman stared out from
her sleep, as if trying to decide if Rishi were more than a vaporous
dream. He watched, unable to move, as she pushed through to the waking world.

He should have run.

She screamed. The shock of sound sent Rishi reeling, backpedaling
for the door. She screamed again, squeezed her eyes shut, clasped her
palms together, and sobbed. From another room came a bang, heavy

footsteps. "Majo," a man shouted. "Majo! Querida!" And in the doorway stood Soli's father. He held a sickle in one hand, dark with age, freckled with rust. Rishi couldn't take his eyes off it. He'd never seen an actual sickle before.

For a few long moments, the man stood in the doorway, waiting for Rishi's next move. And then, all at once, Rishi was falling to the hard stone floor. The old man was astonishingly strong, and had pinned Rishi's arms to his back. He leaned over him, his face just inches from Rishi's.

Rishi struggled, kicked out, and brought the old man crashing down. The mother shrieked and tumbled off the bed, ran to her husband and crouched down beside him. The man lay panting, his breath rasping from his throat. He cradled his knee, rocked back and forth, his face twisted with pain.

Rishi cursed quietly. From where he lay, he tried to speak, but couldn't. The room now was beginning to fill with light, and when he turned to the doorway, he noticed another man, and behind him, more heads, more people drawn by the commotion. The sitting room filled as man after man filed in. The old lady rocked beside her husband, speaking quietly. When Rishi got up, she whimpered and scooted away. He watched her cross herself once, and again.

"I'm sorry," he said to her. "I didn't mean this." At some point that night—or was it days before, months before?—he'd crossed a border between right and wrong. Six men stood around him now, and more waited beyond the doorway. The father teetered to his feet and limped to join them.

From the porch came the shuffle of feet, an angry shout. The old man hissed, and the house fell quiet. Rishi watched closely the rise and fall of the man's narrow chest, the gleam of sunlight on his forehead. He noticed that his own arms had risen and hovered now around his head. Some part of him had surrendered.

The father took two steps toward Rishi. He raised his sickle and spoke clearly, slowly, in English. "What do you want from us?"

Rishi looked around at the waiting faces. He cleared his throat. "I want my boy."

The old man's mustache twitched. He lowered the sickle and shook his head. "We have no boy for you," he said. "We have nothing for you here."

Rishi waited.

"Go home," the old man said, as if he understood what home was to Rishi, the depth and swell of what awaited him there.

It was clear that he had lost. The faces in the room waited for him to go, or to speak, but he had no final words. He thought only of Kavya's message: *I need you. Come home.*

The onlookers parted as Rishi passed through them. When he reached the door and looked up again, he met a collective unwavering gaze. He'd never meant to anger these people. They were old, most of them, as craggy and solid as the hills that had borne them. He had come for his boy, and that was all. He hadn't wanted to hurt them. He hadn't meant them any harm.

59.

KAVYA COULDN'T SAY WHAT DAY OR DATE IT WAS. SHE LIVED now in a twilight of sedatives and sleep. One nameless, numberless morning, she woke to a sudden dip in her mattress. She saw first a waist, a belt, familiar brown slacks.

"Kavya? Wake up, please?" A gentle hand on her shoulder.

"Dad?" She looked around. "Where's Rishi?"

"Time to rise, Kavya-ma. I have brought you some tea." A china cup steamed primly on her bedside table.

She tried to piece together memory and information, but nothing clicked. "What are you doing here?"

Her father didn't answer, only drew the cup and saucer from the table. "Sit up. Drink this."

She obeyed, more out of surprise than desire. They sat together for a long and silent minute.

"It is very bad, Kavya," her father said. "This thing that has happened to you. To our family." He shook his head, as if only just realizing. "A very bad thing, indeed."

It felt good to hear this simple acknowledgment of what was true, free of questions or indictments or speculation. "I know," she said, and the tears trailed fresh. Her father reached out and wiped them with his fingers.

"How did you get here, Dad?"

"We have a new-fangled contraption, kanna-ma. An automobile, it's called."

She felt a smile inside. "Where's Mom?"

"Tuesday ladies' yoga."

"You drove here alone?"

Her father raised an eyebrow and cleared his throat. "I am a simple man, Kavya. But I can drive a car."

They sat together for a while longer, until Kavya's father took her by the arms and helped her stand. She stumbled into the shower, and when she emerged, she found him at the sink, gingerly holding a plate and patting it with a sponge. She settled onto a chair and watched him. Wet sponges and dirty plates were foreign to her father, but he swiped at each smudge of food with a determination to obliterate it.

Ten minutes later, he'd collected a stack of four clean plates and deposited them in a cupboard, ignoring the dishwasher altogether.

"Kavya-ma. Sometimes the things that happen can be changed. Sometimes they cannot. Which time is this?"

There it was, the question she'd been hiding from. Could what happen be changed? Should it? Did Kavya's pain delineate the rules of right and wrong? It was too much to answer. Kavya shook her head and stared at the counter. Then her father stood beside her and wrapped an arm around her shoulders. He was clumsy, thin, calm. When she leaned into his chest, something inside her snapped, the same ligament of control that had snapped many times over the preceding days, releasing each time a flood of rage. It didn't scare her father. He stayed still even as she screamed, even against the monster wails that overtook her. He didn't try to stop her, but waited for her to let out what was left, her last throaty cries.

Kavya emptied herself. Her father made her tea and two pieces of toast. She watched him learn to use a butter knife. "Well," he said an hour later, "your Amma will be wondering." He gathered his keys and jacket and made his way to the door. Kavya walked him to the porch, where the early afternoon was fresh. He laid a hand on the crown of her head. "Bless you, Kavya," he said. "Life will get better."

KAVYA WOKE FROM A NAP that had woven the afternoon to the evening. She was sure she'd heard the doorbell. Reporters, she thought, though Preeti had dropped by the day before with a roasted chicken from a nearby deli. She'd sat next to Kavya in bed, bereft of words. They spent the afternoon not speaking, but staring at their knees, once the scuffed and bony knees of children, now strong and round.

The doorbell rang again. Kavya shuffled out of bed. "Who is it?" she called weakly, not expecting an answer. She opened the door. Rishi stood breathless on the porch. He was unshaven, older than when he'd left. The dusk erased his outline. He was a smudge of himself. He dropped his bag and nearly fell into her, wrapped his arms around her and clung to her.

They stood this way for a long time. "Come inside," she said. She pulled him into the house, picked up his bag, and followed him into the bedroom. Together, they gazed at the bed where she'd sought refuge for so many days. All those days, she hadn't been hiding from her troubles. She'd been accepting loss. She watched him stare at the bed as he slowly realized this. Kavya hadn't been waiting. Kavya had been grieving.

Over the past two weeks, a kind of surface tension had held Rishi together. It had kept him whole through the press conferences, the police interviews, the op-eds, the local news coverage, the phone calls from his parents and Kavya's, the e-mails from old friends and cousins, his trip to Popocalco, even his run through the cornfields. Nobody could have known how feebly he was held together. Only Kavya knew. Only Rishi. He sank to the bed, not from fatigue, but from an emotion he couldn't name, except to call it a gravity of the soul, the same that had pulled Kavya to this bed and held her there for days. As his head sank into his pillow, his surface broke, at last. He spilled over. He spread shapeless. This was sorrow, the deepest he'd ever known.

Kavya wrapped herself around him. His whole body was coated in a cold sweat, and he shivered. "I need you with me, Rishi."

They had wanted to love. They had gone too far. They had taken a woman's child. She could see that now, though the truth didn't fill their empty bungalow or bring back the light and sound of Iggy, the warm and lustrous body they'd come to consider theirs. She stayed in bed with Rishi, rubbing his back, at once essential and useless. Grief was a solitary practice, though they would cling to each other that day and in the days to come.

That evening, Kavya got out of bed to make Rishi a cup of tea and a tuna sandwich. A week later, she would return to the kitchen of Gamma Gamma Pi, pulling her livelihood from the brink of extinction. She would cook up vats of chili and risotto and chicken soup with dumplings, the scale of production a comfort. Now and then, the memory of Iggy would pull her from the busy present and leave her engulfed in tears, Miguel standing by with a strong hand on her shoulder, a dish towel at the ready.

Eventually, Rishi would break away from Weebies and take his first brave steps onto the market. He'd develop his own product, the purest air possible for American homes. For homes around the world. For office buildings, schools, gyms, hospitals. He, Rishi Reddy, would make the world a better place. It had come upon him that day, as he lay beneath the cactus: the realization that everyone around him was taking risks. Vikram Sen had done it and won big. Preeti Patel was still doing it, risking the facade of perfection she'd so assiduously constructed; she might end up winning, whatever that meant for her. Kavya risked her heart and was fighting her way out of a tar pit of loss. Solimar Castro

Valdez, whoever the woman was, had risked country, life, and limb. Rishi, for once, would be the one to take a risk, even if it meant fail-ure, foreclosure, moving himself to a smaller life before emerging anew. Kavya would stand by him. He would belong to himself. Rishi Reddy. Rishi Ready.

But until then: What was there to do but carry on? Slowly, they would gather themselves up again. Every evening, he and Kavya would come home to each other. Dinner, tea, books, sofa. That's all they would muster, until the hurt, day by day, slackened its grip. It would always hurt. They both knew this. They would seek refuge in a quiet under-standing.

60.

IN THE BEGINNING, THERE WERE SEVEN DAYS. ON THE FIRST, she stole him from his bed.

On the second, they left their new home for Mexico. It was easy getting back in. No questions.

On the third day, Nacho refused to look at Soli. They were making their way south through Mazatlán, on a bus full of strangers, and she was his only friend. Still, he wouldn't turn his face to hers—not when she asked him questions or told him stories or sang him songs. He jutted his chin to the open window and stayed like that. He stuck his nose into the wind of the new country, sniffed at it, like it smelled familiar, squinted into it, like he was cataloging its contents.

On the fourth day, he refused to eat. He refused even when Soli told him a story of a little mouse who'd found a talking piece of cheese. They reached Mexico City that night, Dey-Effe. And even through the smog of his silence, Soli could tell he was ill. She found a motel run by a tall Chinese man, and she found some food. Ignacio refused it. She cried to him then, for the first time. She begged him to eat, but he wouldn't. That night, he had an accident in the hotel bed. With a thunderous eruption that woke her from her sleep, he wet his pants and left a frothy stream of shit on the sheets. She peeled the covers from the bed, ran them under water in the tub. And when they left that morning, she said to the man, "I'm sorry. I'm very sorry." He blinked at her and said nothing, because at the time, he didn't know.

On the fifth day, they found a place to live. Nacho ate three crackers and drank some water that Soli had boiled. His bowels held together.

And on the sixth, she found work in a restaurant, washing dishes in an outdoor kitchen. For six days, she was Ignacio's enemy.

On the seventh day, she woke to the sun's glare. He lay next to her, his eyes wide open.

"Ignacio?" she said. "¿Estás bien, amor?"

He climbed into her arms. He dug his face into the curve of her neck, and soon she felt the tickle of warm tears.

"Nachito," she said. "What's wrong?"

"Scary."

It was the first thing he'd said in seven days.

She thinks about that morning still, and wonders what brought the change. She wonders if a final slat of knowledge clicked into place on that seventh day, bringing to Nacho's short memory the memory of *her*. Perhaps he remembered Soli, truly and completely, the mother, the body, the milk, and the smell of her. Or maybe he'd simply given in to what had happened.

Eventually, he would forget it all: the house in Berkeley, his child-sized bed, the early-morning escape, the bus, the predawn harbor. He would grow, become a man, and know her as his mother. She wouldn't be the woman at his window. She would be Mama.

61.

In the days that become their new life, Nacho begins to speak to her, asking the questions you'd expect from a child, about the world around him, the whys and hows of daily living, questions at once minute and profound. Not once does he mention his old home, his bed, his playground, the others who loved him. Soli learns to give him space, to wait for him to come to her, to take her hand or burrow into her arms. She is like a shamed and grateful lover.

When Soli works, a lady named Rosa picks Nacho up from preschool. She has a lazy foot. Soli doesn't know what else to call it; her right foot drags behind her when she walks. She lives a floor above them, and at night they hear the slush-slush of her foot as it slides across their ceiling. This frightens Nacho at first, but he soon stops noticing.

One day, she calls Mama and Papi. "I live in D.F., Mama. I have a son."

Her announcement is met with heavy silence, and then, "What have you done, Solimar?"

"I'll tell you when we come. Don't worry." She will take him home to Popocalco, where it all began. Mama will know him, and Papi. He'll see the dollar houses, the bleached facades and adobe walls. She'll show him the new television in his mamita's house, the roof Soli paid for, the tiled floor. But for now, she's building them their own life and filling it with the things a boy needs: school and friends and space to run.

. . .

It's a Saturday in late October. They go to the Colonia Jamaica, and Nacho pulls her to the flower market. The first of November is a few days away, and the market is jammed with shoppers, ladies placing their orders for the big day, filling their sacks with daisies and carnations to prepare for the holiday. In the flower market, the air is heavy, the smell of calendula thick enough to feel mildly toxic. Soli and Nacho walk down aisles of gladiolas and sunflowers, pure-white lilies and birds-of-paradise with sharp and flawless petals. The marigold stand, the busiest of all, is presided over by the fattest man Soli has seen outside the States. He sits on his stool and frowns down on his customers, like they're so many bees buzzing around his otherwise restful day. When Nacho grabs her hand to pull her down the swarming aisle, she lets him lead her. Together, they braid themselves into the crowd, and they're gone.

Nacho stops moving when they see the fruit man. Soli buys him a bowl of mango slices, doused in lime and chili. She indulges him more than she should. Often, she thinks of his other parents, and it frightens her to imagine that someone might come for him. The police, the government, the man and woman themselves. But this is a big city, an ocean of buildings and roads and surging tides. Nacho and Soli are two small drops in it, undetectable, unlikely to be seen, unlikely to be missed.

But that Saturday, in the scrum of the fruit market, someone does recognize her, impossibly, inevitably.

"Soli!" She walks through the marketplace and hears her old name. It gets lost at first in the bustle of the crowd, but she hears it again. "Soli!"

She stops and turns and what she sees sucks the breath from her. Nutsack. An apparition, her train-top English tutor, older now and somehow taller. She half expects him to dissolve into the crowd. She can't remember his real name, so when he reaches her, at last, she says, "Nutsack. How did you find me?"

"What are you doing here?" Nutsack asks, out of breath himself. "I thought you would make it over."

"I did."

"You made it? To California?" His smile expands and vanishes. "Why did you leave?"

Soli can only shake her head. A tug at her hand, and she looks down to find Nacho.

"Checo," Soli says. "What happened to Checo?"

Nutsack stares down at Nacho, then looks at Soli with a new understanding. And then his face falls, and Soli knows. Nutsack crosses his arms, shuffles his feet, and says, "He didn't make it."

"He's back in Mexico?"

He shakes his head. "No. He didn't make it."

"Oh."

"I'm sorry."

She sees fear in Nutsack's eyes. "The men? With the guns?"

"They shot Checo. But he got away."

"And?"

"We all got away," he says. "They robbed us all, but then they let us go. We tried to get Checo to turn back and go home—he was wounded in the leg and arm. But he wouldn't. He said, I've come this far already."

"I see."

"So we crossed the desert, a pack of us together. Only Mario and I made it to the end."

"Checo didn't make it."

Nutsack stares at the ground.

"Was he buried?"

When Nutsack doesn't answer, Soli lets him go.

That night, after she's put Nacho to bed and finds herself alone, she sits at her window and watches the alley below. She opens the window to a sweet evening gale, redolent of gasoline and autumn leaves. He *was* buried, she assures herself, out there in the desert, properly and decently, with a short and parch-throated Mass. The coyotes sang in his honor, the cacti bent their spiny heads, and for a moment, the desert fell into shade. His last thoughts were of her, of Soli charging down the street with a jug of wine for a belly, lying on the trackside in the early morning chill, hidden and scared in the back of a truck. Soli, of all the young travelers, had the best chance of making it. She'd carried a piece of Checo inside, driving her forward, relentless as La Bestia, even before she knew it existed.

Soli would make an altar for Checo. He would come to see them, a breeze in the room, imperceptible to all but her. He would dance with the skeletons on a crisp October night. She'd put out a jug of wine, some rice and beans, a stolen bottle of water. She wouldn't have a picture of him, only a living, breathing memento, rebel-haired and three feet tall.

Together, Soli and Nacho swim through the hazy basin of the city. She works. He plays. He goes to school. Some nights, when Soli returns, always past midnight, he wakes up and comes to her. Not at a run, but with the tumbling step of a sleepwalker. She picks him up and covers him in kisses. Rosa with the lazy foot looks on.

If this is a story, it's one with no right ending. If this is a dream, it is a dream made solid, a dream grown to a little boy with a waist and shoulders, calves that wrap around his mother's hips.

They live in a one-room apartment with water-stained walls and carpet that's been burnt in places. This is their dollar house, for now. The boy has filled it with light and sound. He's run too fast and scuffed its walls, as little boys must do. She's brought him to a life on the border of safety and fear, rectitude and abandon. She's brought him to a life that's a constant question, of where he belongs and to whom. Of who the criminal is, and whether Soli did wrong. But she tries to shelter him from these darker spools of thought. He is a boy. His life will be simple.

And what of America? Thirty-two months. A dream. She still parses through the fibers of those days. Eventually, Soli will tell Ignacio about the place called Berkeley. He'll be grown then—a man, maybe, grown beyond belief. That's when he'll stop simply feeling her and start to see her again. And what will he see but his own skin, wrapped around a woman he once hardly knew, whose eyes and cheeks dig beneath his own. And when he sees her, will the grasses bend and the winds recede? Will the sun hide its brazen face and leave them be? And will the sky, the mothering sky, kneel down around them?

She will tell him his story. This is the story, Ignacio, of a girl with a secret. This is the story of a lion-car, a devil-beard, a voice like a mountain flute. This is the story of a house covered in vines, of little boys with warrior legs and princely hair. This is the story of oceanic air, of evenings wrapped in sun. This is the story of the wind, rushing through the trees, alongside a train, across the valley floor, billowing the drapes of a bungalow home. This is the story of the sun and the wind and the child they bore. This is the story of the sun and the wind, dragged aground by the meddlesome earth.

acknowledgments

I must first acknowledge the brave people whose real struggles inspired this story: immigrants, both documented and undocumented, immigrant rights advocates, foster parents, adoptive parents, and those who have undergone fertility treatments. In particular, I'd like to thank the following individuals who answered countless questions and helped me to locate resources:

Angélica Salceda, Anne Less, Annika Hacin Sridharan, Christina Mansfield and Christina Fialho of End Isolation/CIVIC; Jazmin Segura of SIREN; and Seth Freed Wessler.

U.S. immigration policy is in a continual state of flux. This novel refers mostly to policies that existed in 2012–2013. As of this reading, immigration law has largely remained unchanged, and more than five million children in the United States have at least one undocumented parent. I am grateful for the time and generosity of Aarti Kohli, of the Asian Law Caucus, who helped me understand how undocumented immigrants experience the criminal justice system; César Cuauhtémoc García Hernández, who spoke to me about his research into immigrant detention centers; and Omar Riojas, who shared his knowledge of undocumented migrants battling for custody of their children. The story of his client, Encarnación Bail Romero, was the first I came across in my research.

I am grateful to Eric Ballon, who let me shadow him in a sorority kitchen for a day; Nirupa Sekaran, who answered many questions about fertility treatments; and Manohar and Anand Sekaran, who answered various slightly worrying questions about legal procedures and medical ailments, respectively. Social workers at the Department of Social Services in Oakland, California, let me sit in on a foster care information session. Carolyn Gregory, Sandy Swing, Esme Howard, and other Bay Area parents spoke to me by phone, welcomed me into their homes, and shared their very personal stories of adoption and foster care. When cafés got too loud and libraries got bedbugs, I was grateful for the San Francisco Writers' Grotto, where I could always find focus, good conversation, and an empty desk.

The following publications were instrumental to my research: *Underground America: Narratives of Undocumented Lives*, edited by Peter Orner; *Toddler Adoption: The Weaver's Craft* by Mary Hopkins-Best; *Shattered Families: The Perilous Intersection of Immigration Enforcement and the Child Welfare System* by Seth Freed Wessler; and *Due Process and Immigrant Detainee Prison Transfers: Moving LPRS to Isolated Prisons Violates Their Right to Counsel* by César Cuauhtémoc García Hernández.

Writing this book would have been a very different experience without the grace and hospitality of Michael Sledge and Raul Cabra, who hosted me at Oax-i-fornia in San Jerónimo Tlacochahuaya, Mexico; and Pablo, who drove me through the beautiful small towns of Oaxaca and shared his own immigration story. My time in Oaxaca was made possible by a faculty research grant from California College of the Arts.

When a novel enters the world, only one name goes on the cover, but so many others make it possible. A few good friends and excellent editors slogged through my early drafts: Anita Amirrezvani, Jessica Arevalo, Caitlin Myer, and Meghan Ward. Thanks also go to Stacey Lewis, Alvaro Garduno, and Wylie O'Sullivan, for their advice and insights later in the writing process. When this project began to feel like an impossibility, members of the San Francisco Writers' Grotto reached out with advice, empathy, and encouragement, proving once again that San Francisco is the best literary city anywhere.

My agent, Lindsay Edgecombe, championed this book from its first sentences. My tireless editor, Tara Singh Carlson, read through this book more times than I ever could. Her patience, energy, and literary laser-vision astound me. Thanks also go to Helen Richard, who helped this novel over the finish line; to Karen Fink, Alexis Welby, and the publicity team at Putnam; to Kristi Leunig and Matt Rappaport, who gave me a quiet place to write; and to Robert Humphreys, Robert Waller, Daniel Grisales, and Blake Whittington for their photographic work.

To my parents, I owe gratitude for their patience, encouragement, many hours of babysitting, and for making their own courageous journey into a new American life. I couldn't have begun this book without Spencer Dutton, my fiercest supporter and first reader, or without my sons, who make me feel lucky every day.